A DARK PLACE

A DCI DANNY FLINT BOOK

TREVOR NEGUS

INKUBATOR
BOOKS

Published by Inkubator Books
www.inkubatorbooks.com

ISBN (eBook): 978-1-83756-441-5
ISBN (Paperback): 978-1-83756-442-2

PROLOGUE

3.00 a.m., 13 July 1991
Sheffield City Centre, South Yorkshire

The rain had been falling relentlessly all night.. The windscreen wipers on the small van were now struggling to cope with the volume of water. The big man driving slowed the vehicle down and brought it to a stop.

In one way, the inclement weather had assisted his task, as there had been very few people wandering the streets – including patrolling police officers.

The problem caused by the incessant, torrential rain was that his search to locate an ideal candidate for his much-needed final test had so far proved in vain.

And so he decided to leave the city centre and patrol the industrial areas on the edge of the city. He had previously seen congregations of homeless people in those locations.

The flotsam and jetsam of society. These were the people who were down on their luck, the bankrupts, the victims of acrimonious divorces, or addicts of all kinds. People who nobody would ever miss, people he saw as a disposable asset, waiting to be harvested.

After another fifteen minutes of driving, the rain finally stopped, and he found it easier to see through the van's windows.

In the doorway of an industrial unit, which during the daytime sold laminate flooring, he could see what at first appeared to be a pile of rags and cardboard. It was only the movement of a small terrier-type dog that made him look again.

He stopped the van opposite the doorway and took a closer look, winding the driver's-side window down. At the very back of the doorway, he could see the vagrant huddled as near to the door as he could get without activating the alarm. He had pulled an old quilt and sheets of dry cardboard over the top of his ragged clothes in an attempt to shield himself from the worst of the elements. All that was now visible was the man's head. Wild eyes peered out from a grime-stained face. His hair was long and matted, and he had a bushy, unkempt beard.

The driver of the van quickly looked around. There were no other down-and-outs in any of the other doorways on the road. He had finally found his perfect subject; it would be down to him now to capitalise on this opportunity.

He grabbed the thermos flask and the plastic lunchbox, which contained a dozen or so corned beef sandwiches, and got out of the van.

As he approached the homeless man, he saw him draw

his knees up to his chest, and he heard the small dog standing in front of him growl a warning.

He held up the flask and sandwich box and said, 'I'm not here to hurt you. I'm part of an organisation that helps the homeless. On nights like this when the weather is so bad, we patrol the streets to see if we can help in any way.'

There was no response from the vagrant beneath the cardboard.

He persisted. 'If you don't need any help, will you at least have a hot drink and something to eat? I've got corned beef sandwiches, if you or your dog want a bite to eat?'

Whether it was the offer of a hot drink, or food for him and his dog, it stirred something in the homeless man, and he said, 'Why would someone like you want to help me?'

'The organisation I'm with will help anyone who's had bad luck or fallen on hard times. Nobody's here to judge you.'

'I wouldn't mind a hot drink.'

'Do you want a sandwich as well?'

'Can Snapper have one?'

The man grinned. 'Of course he can, especially if it stops him growling at me.'

'Don't worry about Snapper, he's harmless. He's my best mate.'

The homeless man dragged himself from beneath the quilt and the cardboard and stood up. He appeared quite unsteady on his feet and placed a hand against the wall to catch his balance.

'Are you okay?'

'I'm okay. I just haven't moved in ages. Moving around can make you colder, and I'm already fucking freezing.'

The man handed over a couple of the sandwiches and

said, 'Why don't you give these to Snapper and sit in the van for five minutes. I can put the heater on full blast, you can have a hot drink, something to eat and get warmed up.'

'I'm stinking, mate, don't you mind?'

'I told you I want to help. I can see how cold you are. Five minutes in the van will get you warmed up properly.'

Without saying another word, the homeless man took the two sandwiches and placed them down in front of his small dog before shuffling towards the small white van.

The driver unlocked the van and got in. The homeless man turned and said, 'I won't be long, Snapper. Get them sarnies down you, lad.'

As soon as both men were sat inside the van, the driver turned the ignition on and ramped the heater up to maximum. Hot air blasted out of the vents. The homeless man was right, he reeked, and the hot air hitting his damp, soiled clothing filled the van with a disgusting smell.

Now that he was in the van, the driver could see the homeless man was only in his early to mid-twenties. When he spoke, his accent was local to South Yorkshire. He was thin, almost skeletal, and had the gaunt, jaundiced appearance of a drug addict with deep-set eyes surrounded by dark shadows.

The driver said, 'I've got some hot sweet tea. Do you want a drink?'

The homeless man was already devouring one of the sandwiches and nodded. 'A hot drink would be great, my friend.'

He grabbed the offered full beaker with both hands.

The driver cautioned him, saying, 'Be careful, it's hot.' Then watched as the man wolfed down the scalding hot liquid.

Draining the mug, the addict held it back out and asked, 'Could I have another?'

The man smiled and poured out another full beaker. As he handed it to the homeless man, he said, 'Take your time. I don't want you to burn yourself.'

Once again, the man swallowed the hot drink in one go, gulping it down, spilling some of the sweet liquid, which then trickled from the sides of his mouth into his wild, bushy beard.

He finished the drink and let out a loud belch.

He sat quietly for thirty seconds in the stifling air of the van and then said, 'I don't feel too good.'

'You probably drank the tea too quickly. Take a minute, and you'll be fine.'

Slurring his words slightly, he said, 'I don't know about that. I feel pissed. Was there any booze in that tea?'

'Just a small tot of whisky to help warm you through. Hope that's okay?'

The homeless man didn't answer.

His head had lolled forward, and his beard was now resting on his chest.

The driver grabbed the man's hair and pulled his head back. The whites of his eyes were showing.

He was unconscious.

He got out of the van and walked round to the passenger door. He yanked the door open and dragged the man out of the passenger seat and round to the back. He propped him against one of the back wheels and opened the two doors.

He was about to lift him into the back of the van when he heard a growl behind him. He turned to see the small dog baring its teeth and snarling. The man grabbed the box containing the sandwiches. He walked towards the doorway, moving the dog out of the way with his boot before tipping the remaining sandwiches onto the floor.

The dog instantly followed its nose and started eating the discarded sandwiches off the floor of the doorway.

The man then lifted the unconscious addict into the back of the van, climbed in and secured his wrists and ankles with plastic cable ties before wrapping gaffer tape around his head to silence him, should he wake. He left the man's nostrils clear so he could still breathe.

He closed and locked the two rear doors and got into the driver's seat. He lowered both windows at the front of the van, to let in the fresh, cold air, which would help eradicate the stench.

He poured the remnants of the drugged tea from the flask onto the road and slowly drove off.

Snapper finished the last of the corned beef, then looked around at the deserted street. He crawled back onto the familiar pile of rags and cardboard and settled down out of the rain, which was once again falling steadily.

1

1.00 p.m., 20 July 1991
Worksop Golf Club, Windmill Lane, Worksop,
Nottinghamshire

DCI Danny Flint parked his car next to all the other police vehicles, in the far corner of the car park at Worksop golf course.

As he got out of the car, he was met by DI Rob Buxton, who was already wearing a full forensic suit and gloves.

Danny asked, 'Where's the body?'

'Just in front of the first green. This is a weird one, boss. The body has been elaborately staged. Rather than me try to describe it, you can see for yourself. I've never seen anything like it.'

As the two detectives made their way along the fairway of the first hole, Danny could see the tent that had been erected a few hundred yards away. He could see scenes of crime personnel moving in and out of the temporary structure.

He said, 'Any identification on the body?'

'Nothing. Body is that of a white male, approximately mid-twenties, very thin. Looks to me like an addict, who's probably been sleeping rough somewhere.'

'Killed here?'

'I don't think so. My money's on this being a deposition site. When you see the staging, you'll understand my thinking.'

'What time was he found?'

'The head greenkeeper arrived at six o'clock to do his course inspection. Rest of the greenkeeping staff arrived at seven o'clock, expecting to prepare the course for today's golfers. They've not touched this green but have been working on the other greens around the course. The first members started arriving at seven thirty. By that time the head greenkeeper had found the body and had contacted the club captain.'

'Is the club captain here now?'

'He's here. He's spent the morning in his office on the telephone, cancelling members who had booked an early tee, trying to prevent them having a wasted journey. He's not happy and keeps wanting to know when he can open the course.'

'He's not happy? Maybe if he had called this in as soon as he heard what had happened, we would have been gone by now. I know that the first call to the police was logged at nine thirty. I don't understand why the captain took so long to make that first call.'

'The club captain, Henry Travis, lives the other side of Retford. It took him a while to get here. He insisted on seeing the body for himself before he made the call to the police.'

Danny tutted as they reached the forensic tent. He quickly donned the forensic suit and gloves that Tim Donnelly handed him. Just before he entered the tent, the scenes of crime supervisor handed him a mask and said, 'You need to put this on before you go inside, sir.'

Danny slipped on the mask and stepped inside. The sight that met him was indeed a strange one, and he instantly understood Rob's thinking.

The body had been staged using a wooden pole. The man was in a sitting position, and the pole had been placed down the back of his scruffy clothing before being driven into the soft ground. This meant the man had remained propped up in a sitting position, facing back down the fairway towards the first tee. The man's hands had been tied with green twine, then positioned around his own throat, so he appeared to be throttling himself.

Danny stepped forward to have a closer look at the injury to the top of the man's head. He had long, matted hair and an unkempt bushy beard – all unwashed – but the hair on the top of his head had completely disappeared. A large gaping hole covered the top of his scalp. The hair, flesh and bone in that area had been eaten away. Inside the open skull, the brain tissue had been transformed into a congealed, brown, jelly-like substance.

Danny turned to face Tim. 'Acid?'

'I'm no expert, sir. But it's got to be something extremely corrosive to do that. The stench in here is awful. I've told all my staff only to come in with masks on, and to strictly limit the time they're in here.'

Danny and Tim stepped back outside the tent.

Danny removed his mask and said, 'I want you to take the tent down, Tim. It's dry, and I don't want those fumes bottling up in there. God knows what they are.'

Then he turned to Rob and said, 'Is there any way the public could see the body if we take it down?'

Rob pointed to the hedgerow that ran along the side of the first hole. 'Windmill Lane runs along the side of this fairway. It's a narrow country lane, but the public do have access. There are plenty of gaps in the hedge where people could view what we're doing here.'

Danny nodded. 'Okay. And that's probably the way the killer brought the body here. He would have needed a vehicle. Is the lane still open?'

'Yes, sir.'

'Right,' Danny instructed. 'I need Windmill Lane closed to the public immediately. I need the Special Operations Unit calling out to undertake a detailed search of that hedgerow. We need to try to identify where the killer parked up to bring the body here. I want this tent down for safety reasons, so blocking the lane will also prevent members of the public or the press getting too close. Get uniform staff at each end of the lane: they are to stop the public gaining access. I don't want Tim and his staff breathing in that crap, mask or no mask, until we know exactly what we're dealing with. It's quite breezy out here, so hopefully that will help to clear any fumes.'

'I'm on it, boss.'

As Rob turned to walk away to organise the roadblock and the Special Operations Unit staff to carry out the search, Danny shouted after him, 'What time will the pathologist be here?'

Rob shrugged. 'He should be here by now, boss. Seamus

was notified just after I got here at ten thirty. I'll chase him up.'

'Good. Because we need this body moved as soon as possible.'

As Tim and his staff got to work dismantling the protective tent, Danny was left alone with his thoughts. Questions filled his head.

Who was the dead man?

Why had he been targeted for such a grisly death?

If this was a deposition site, where had he been killed?

How had he been killed?

Why the elaborate staging?

He was snatched away from the multitude of disturbing thoughts by the loud voice of Seamus Carter ...

'I'm so sorry it's taken me so long to get here. My bloody car gave up the ghost just outside of Mansfield. There was no way to contact anybody at the roadside, and by the time I'd found a phone box and called a taxi to get me up here, it wasn't worth ringing the control room. Then, to make matters worse, when the taxi dropped me off, I realised I didn't have enough cash on me to cover the fare. Luckily, Rob saved the day and paid the taxi driver what he was owed before he turned nasty. Anyway, enough of my woes, I'm here now. What have we got?'

Danny said, 'Your day isn't going to get any better, my friend. I've never seen anything like this. The tent will be down in a minute or two, and you can see for yourself.'

'Any reason you're taking the tent down?'

'Whatever agent or chemical has been used to kill this unfortunate soul, it's still giving off foul-smelling, acrid fumes. I didn't want to risk anybody breathing it in. For all I know, it could still be toxic.'

'The message I got from the control room was that acid had been used. Some acids when exposed to the air can give off toxic fumes. So a wise precaution, Danny. The breeze will help clear any fumes, but I'd still advise wearing a mask when moving around the body.'

As Seamus donned an oversize forensic suit, the tent was finally removed – and he was able to inspect the body.

After fifteen minutes he beckoned Danny to step forward again. 'It's almost certainly an acid that's been used, but I've no idea at this time what type or strength it is. Contrary to popular belief, not all acids can eat through flesh and bone to this extent. My best guess would be some sort of hydrofluoric acid, but until samples are taken from in and around the wound site, we won't know for definite.'

'How long would it take to do this amount of damage?'

'Again, it depends exactly what's been used. I would estimate at the least twenty-four hours, at the most seventy-two hours. But these are just best guesses, Danny.'

The big pathologist paused and then said, 'What I can tell you is that this was done over a long period of time. You can see the different degrees of burn. I think this poor fellow has been immobilised in some way, and the corrosive substance was then systematically dripped onto the top of his head over several hours.'

'Bloody hell. That's horrific.'

'It gets worse. He was undoubtably alive for a long time while this was happening. Once the acid reached the brain tissue, mercifully death would have come quite quickly.'

'Why do you think he was alive?' Danny asked, appalled.

'If you look closely at his forehead, or what's left of it, you can see a linear bruise just above his eyebrows, where his head had been securely fastened. The bruising would have occurred as he struggled to move his head away from the acid. There are also linear bruises to his wrists and ankles. He'll have been strapped down somewhere, probably in a similar sitting position to the one he's in now.'

'The pain must have been horrendous.'

'Certainly, at the beginning. But acid attacks the nerve endings first, so once they had been burned away and rendered useless, the pain ironically would have lessened. He would still have experienced terrible pain from any splashes of acid on new flesh. It would have been an awful, prolonged, agonising death, Danny.'

'Anything else you can tell us from the scene or the staging?'

'This has taken the killer considerable time. The killing and staging of the corpse will have taken hours, if not days. He would have needed privacy. I can't see any evidence yet of a gag being used, so the killer obviously wasn't bothered about noise from his victim. That tends to suggest a remote location. Anything else will have to wait for the post-mortem.'

'Thanks, Seamus. What time will you be ready to do the post-mortem?'

'To be on the safe side, shall we say four thirty this afternoon?'

'Where?'

'Bassetlaw Hospital mortuary is the nearest, and the facilities there are good. I'll need you to contact the control room so they can book a slot for that time.'

'How soon before we can move the body?'

Seamus turned, spoke briefly to Tim Donnelly and then replied, 'We should be good to move him within the hour.

The only delay could be getting a specialist undertaker here.'

'Why a specialist?'

'Mainly because of the fumes issue, but there's also an issue of preservation of evidence. We could lose the contents of the skull if we tip or move the body from its current position. Tim says he knows which firm to call, so we should be good to go in an hour or so.'

'Okay. I'll contact the control room about the mortuary and see you there at four thirty. Any unexpected delays, contact the MCIU office and let me know.'

Seamus nodded. 'Will do, Danny. Can you arrange for a car to get me to the hospital, please?'

'Of course. Consider it done.'

Danny took off the forensic suit and gloves, placed them in the black bin liner and made his way back down the fairway to the clubhouse, where he found Rob talking to a group of gathered MCIU detectives.

Danny asked, 'What have you organised so far, Rob?'

'I've got acting DS Bailey starting the little bit of house-to-house there is to do. There are about fifty houses on Windmill Lane, and they all have a view of the lane. It's a good bet that a vehicle was used to deposit the body sometime last night, so Helen and her team are trying to find a witness.'

'Any joy so far?'

'The few people they've spoken to have all said that it's not unusual to see vehicles up and down the lane all night. It's frequented by courting couples, so nobody pays cars coming and going much attention.'

'Do we know what time the last people left the golf course?'

'According to Henry Travis, the last golfers left the clubhouse at eleven thirty last night,' Rob told him. 'The lights were all turned off and the staff had left by midnight. That's relevant because the lights from the clubhouse illuminate the first fairway.'

'Which means the body was brought here sometime between midnight and six o'clock in the morning. Hopefully, that will help narrow down any questions for the house-to-house teams. Do we have any statements yet?'

'Simon Paine is getting the witness statement from the head greenkeeper, and I've got Ray Holden lined up to take the statement from Henry Travis.'

'We're going to need a list of all the members who were in the clubhouse last night,' Danny said. 'They'll all have to be seen and spoken to. This body has been left here for a reason. That reason could be linked to the golf course and its members somehow.'

'Do you think so?'

'It's one possibility. On the other hand, it could be that the body was deposited here simply because it's remote and the killer knew the body would be discovered early. Seems to me this is someone who wants the world to see what he's done, what he's capable of doing.'

'That's a chilling thought.' Rob rubbed his arms, as if literally cold. 'That somebody could be so disturbed they kill in such an unimaginable way.'

Danny nodded; he couldn't help but share Rob's sense of horror. 'I can see CCTV cameras on the side of the clubhouse,' he observed. 'I take it you've checked the footage?'

'Andy looked at it when we first got here. There's nothing of any value on the tape. The cameras cover the car park, but when they were installed, the council insisted that they didn't pick up any passing vehicles on Windmill Lane.'

'Typical.'

'Talking of Andy, he got a message to go straight to headquarters from here this morning, to see the chief constable. I hope he's not in any bother.'

'It's the opposite. Andy's seeing Jack Renshaw to get promoted today.'

'That's brilliant.' Rob smiled broadly, genuinely pleased. 'I did hear a rumour that Tina was leaving us; is Andy going to take her slot here on the unit?'

Danny shook his head. 'I asked the same question, as he would have been a perfect fit, but the chief's thinking about posting him to Special Branch, to fill the vacancy there.'

'Andy will love that. That's right up his street.' Rob paused. 'Hang on a minute, if you asked the same question, that means Tina is leaving.'

Laughing, Danny said, 'Do you know something, Rob. You've missed your true vocation. You should have been a detective.'

'Yeah, yeah, very droll. If Tina's going, who's taking her place?'

'Do you remember Sara Lacey?'

'Detective sergeant from Worksop, who worked on attachment with us on the Joanne Preston inquiry.'

'Yep, that's her.' Danny nodded. 'Well, when she finished her attachment with us, she was promoted to detective inspector. She starts here permanently next week.'

'Good. She's an excellent detective.'

Echoing what Mark Slater had said to him earlier, Danny said, 'Glad you approve, mate. Now I need to speak to Henry Travis; where is he?'

'He's waiting in his office at the clubhouse. This way, boss.'

2

4.30 p.m., 20 July 1991
Bassetlaw Hospital Mortuary, Worksop, Nottinghamshire

Danny looked across the mortuary at the body of the unknown male found at Worksop Golf Club. With all his ragged clothes now removed, the man looked painfully thin. His ribs were showing through his emaciated body. The brown jelly-like substance that was once the dead man's brain now rested on the stainless-steel bench where it had oozed from what was left of his cranium.

The atmosphere in the sterile environment of the mortuary felt even more oppressive than normal. As well as the bright white lights, there was a constant hum from a high-powered extraction fan that was battling to remove the fumes still being given off by the corrosive substance that had killed the man.

Everyone in the room was wearing full protective clothing, including masks.

Seamus Carter looked at Danny and said, 'I'm going to make a start. The sooner I can get the head and brain contained, the sooner the fumes will lessen.'

Danny nodded and watched carefully as the skilled pathologist set to work obtaining samples in and around the skull. He carefully collected the congealed brain matter and placed it all into a Teflon container that would resist the acid's corrosive properties.

Once that had been done, he started on the rest of the examination, directing the exhibits officer, DC Jeff Williams, as to what other samples he would need to bag up as exhibits. The two scenes of crime staff present took photographs and made a video recording of the entire examination.

After almost two hours, Seamus stepped away from the cadaver and motioned to the two senior detectives to follow him.

Danny and Rob followed the pathologist outside.

Seamus said, 'There's no doubt about this one, gents. Cause of death is massive damage to the brain caused by an as yet unknown corrosive substance. My advice would be to submit the entire brain, such as it is, to the Forensic Science Service for them to do a full analysis to pinpoint exactly what type of acid has been used.'

'Is it safe to transport?'

'If you leave it in that Teflon container, it will be fine. Over time the fumes being given off will start to lessen and become less toxic. The accompanying paperwork will need to inform the scientists what you suspect it is, and what safety steps you have been taking. They should know it contains some sort of acid when they see the Teflon container, but better safe than sorry.'

'Anything else we need to know from your examination?'

'Rob's instincts were right. There is evidence that the dead man was an intravenous drug user. There are needle and track marks at various locations on the body, and his general emaciated and undernourished state would tend to suggest he was a rough sleeper.'

'Any other significant injuries?'

'The linear bruising I pointed out at the scene around the forehead, wrists and ankles, I can now confirm are ligature marks. He was strapped down and immobilised for a long period of time.'

Rob said, 'Anything to help us identify him?'

'I've seen no previous operation scars or tattoos. I'll obtain a full set of fingerprints and get X-rays of his few remaining teeth done. If he is a rough sleeper, the fingerprints will be your best bet. Not many homeless people have access to a dentist, and looking at the state of his teeth, he hasn't seen a dentist in years.'

Danny said, 'Anything else we should know?'

'The only other thing I'd say is this, over the years I've seen a lot of deaths caused by acid and other corrosive substances. In all that time I've never seen anyone killed so deliberately and painstakingly using acid as this. For me, this seems all about sending a message. I've no evidence to back that up, but because the manner of the death is so bizarre, that's my take on it.'

'Thanks, Seamus. When can you let me have your report?'

'I'll get it to you within the next couple of days.'

3

9.00 p.m., 20 July 1991
MCIU Offices, Mansfield, Nottinghamshire

As Danny and Rob walked into the main briefing room, the gathered detectives fell silent.

'I'm going to keep this short,' Danny said. 'It's been a tiring day, and I expect a similarly long day tomorrow. I just want to go over the progress made today and outline what needs doing tomorrow. Helen, I'll start with you. How are you getting on with the house-to-house enquiries on Windmill Lane?'

Helen Bailey stood. 'We've made good progress this afternoon and evening,' she said. 'We're easily halfway through and should finish it over the next couple of days.'

'Do you have enough staff?'

'I've had three pairs working on it today. If I have the

same numbers tomorrow, we should be able to complete the job.'

'Good. Have you turned anything up yet?'

She shook her head. 'Not yet. What we're finding is that people don't take much notice of cars using the lane. It's a cut-through, and the residents are used to courting couples using the lane.'

'Okay. Keep at it and don't lose anything for the sake of speed. Make sure everyone's seen.'

'Will do, sir.'

Danny looked for Tim Donnelly. 'Tim, anything forensically?'

'Not much at all. The SOU search team found a multitude of tyre tracks in the soil at the side of the lane adjacent to where the body was found. I've had the marks photographed, but it would have been impossible to take any meaningful casts.'

'That's a pity. Did the search yield anything else that may have been dropped by the offender?'

'No.'

'How soon do you think we'll have a definitive answer about the type of corrosive used?'

'All the samples have been submitted to the Forensic Science Service for a full analysis. Turnaround time is currently running at between seven and ten days.'

'Did you stress the urgency?'

'I always do, boss. And I will chase them to see if we can get an answer quicker.'

'I take it the fingerprints taken after the post-mortem have been submitted?'

'All done. I'm hoping to have an answer on identification

over the next couple of days. Always assuming the man has a criminal record, of course.'

'Thank you.' Danny nodded. 'I take it none of your staff are suffering any ill effects from being exposed to the fumes earlier?'

'Everyone's fine.'

'Good. Keep me informed of any results, please.'

'Will do, sir. Photographs from the scene and subsequent post-mortem will be available for viewing tomorrow.'

Danny turned to Rob and said, 'Talking of the post-mortem, can you give everyone an update about the findings.'

'Of course,' Rob said. 'Cause of death was brain injury caused by the unknown corrosive agent. The post-mortem revealed that this substance was administered slowly over a long period of time in such a way that the victim was made to suffer a prolonged and agonising death. You all need to bear this in mind. The person who committed this murder has a cruel, vicious streak. He's not satisfied with simply killing his victim.'

He paused to let that message sink in and then said, 'The other things of note are that the victim was a drug user, who injected drugs, and was almost certainly a rough sleeper.'

'Thanks, Rob. Any updates from possible witnesses at the golf club?'

'Statements have been obtained from the head green-keeper, the club captain and the club professional. We took one from the club pro because he was also on scene early doors to open the shop.'

'Anything of interest?'

'Nothing. Obviously, the body was discovered by the

head greenkeeper, but he saw nothing of any evidential value.'

'Okay. How about the list of club members who'd used the bar the night before?'

'We've now obtained the full list of names and addresses, so we can start working through them tomorrow. Until we find out who our victim is, there's not much else we can do. As you know, the cameras at the club covering the car park didn't yield anything either.'

Danny addressed the room. 'Okay, everyone, complete anything that needs doing urgently, then get off home. I want you all back on duty at seven o'clock tomorrow morning. Thank you for all your hard work today.'

He scanned the room before saying, 'Rob, Helen, Jag, I need to see you in my office before you leave.'

Ten minutes later, the three detectives walked into Danny's office.

'Grab a seat. I won't keep you long.'

Once they were seated, Danny said, 'Helen, good work today. It's never an easy task keeping on top of a house-to-house enquiry, and I'm pleased with the progress you and your team have made. Same again tomorrow, please.'

Blushing slightly, Helen said, 'Thank you, sir.'

'I won't keep you. I just wanted to acknowledge your hard work. I'll see you in the morning.'

Smiling widely now, Helen stood and left the office.

Danny then turned to Jag and said, 'I asked to see you because I've some good news. The chief constable is going to promote you to sergeant within the week. You impressed so much during your recent promotion board that he's decided to promote you in post. You're going to be the next detective sergeant on the MCIU and will replace DS Wills, who's also been promoted.' He paused and held Jag's eye. 'Are you happy to stay in post?'

Jag's face took on a shocked expression. 'Of course I'm happy to be staying here. I'm just feeling a little shocked, that's all. When Helen was asked to take the role of acting sergeant to cover Rachel's absence, I naturally thought it wasn't my time yet.'

'I see.' Danny smiled in recognition of Jag's thought process. 'But first of all, congratulations; you thoroughly deserve this promotion. You were always the next candidate for a permanent promotion, Helen hasn't sat a promotion board yet, so this is no reflection on her skills – it's just come too early for her. I also know how difficult it can be to be promoted in post and find that you need to start dishing out orders to people you've worked alongside for years.'

'That might be true on other departments, sir. But here everyone works as a team. I don't see it as giving orders, more like guiding talented people onto their next task.'

Danny looked at Rob. 'I think he's got this supervision lark cracked already, don't you?'

Rob said, 'Definitely,' then stood and shook hands with Jag, saying, 'Congratulations. As the boss says, it's very well deserved. And it goes without saying, if you ever need any advice, you can always talk to me.'

Danny then shook hands with Jag too. 'I'll see you in the morning,' he said. 'And until you've seen the chief and had it made official, I want you to start as acting DS from tomorrow.'

'Thank you, sir.'

As Jag reached the door, Danny added, 'One last thing. This is just between us three until it's made official. And for

God's sake, look surprised when the chief constable asks you if you'd like to be promoted in post, okay?'

Jag laughed out loud. 'Of course. Thank you, sir.'

As Jag left the office, Rob said, 'I'm sorry to see Andy leaving. He was one of the four originals from the Jimmy Wade inquiry, but Jag will do a great job. He's a bloody good detective and already has the respect of everyone on the MCIU.'

'I'll echo every one of those sentiments, my friend, but that's the police force. Friends and colleagues are always moving on; it's the nature of the job.'

'Too right,' Rob agreed. 'I'll see you in the morning, Danny.'

'Bright and early. I've had a thought about another possible line of enquiry, but we can talk about it properly tomorrow.'

'Sounds intriguing?'

'It occurred to me earlier that the consensus is our victim was homeless and a drug addict. Tomorrow morning, I want you to start researching people who are known to sleep rough in the local area. There can't be that many homeless people in and around Worksop. The drug squad and local CID might be able to give you a heads-up with local addicts.'

'It's possible, always assuming our victim's local. It won't hurt to have a look, in case we can't get a definitive answer from fingerprints. Hopefully, he'll have had a criminal record, and then we can find out who our dead man was in life.'

4

9.30 a.m., 21 July 1991
Woodland near Welbeck, Nottinghamshire

The big man didn't need to stoop as he entered the tunnel, the roof was at least a foot above his head, but it had become a habit, and he loped along in a slovenly manner. The head torch he wore illuminated his way as he got deeper inside and the light from the entrance disappeared.

In the distance he could see the wire cages that were bolted to the tunnel's intricate arched brickwork. There were six cages in all, spaced about a yard apart. It was his intention to fill these cages with those people who needed to pay their debt.

Having checked that the cages were all securely fastened, he moved further along the dark tunnel until he came to a single wooden door on the right-hand side.

He unlocked the padlock that secured the door and pushed it wide open, wrinkling his nose at the acrid stench issuing from within, as it affronted his sense of smell.

This chamber was his killing room.

Taking several deep breaths, he entered the small room and inspected the heavy wooden chair that was bolted to the stone floor. The chair was coated with a thin sheet of Teflon, which would help to prevent his chosen instrument of death damaging the wood.

The room smelled of urine and faeces and an overarching acrid smell that was indescribably bad. It was here that he had carried out the essential final experiment on the homeless man. An experiment that was needed before he could start his planned killing spree.

As a man of science, everything he did had to be carefully thought out and tested beforehand. The death of the down-and-out, abducted from Sheffield, had literally been the acid test. It had been a partial success, but had also highlighted a major flaw in his plans.

He was happy the specialist equipment he had manufactured to administer the steady drip of acid over several hours had worked perfectly; it had achieved the desired result. The issue it had raised was time. The whole process had taken way too long. It had taken almost seventy-two hours for the hydrofluoric acid to break down the calcium in the bone of the skull and finally reach the victim's brain. He had pondered long and hard over the problem and had come up with a solution. It wasn't perfect, but he knew if he mixed sulphuric acid with the hydrofluoric acid, the calcium would be broken down and the bone eaten through more quickly. The one drawback with the idea was that the already acrid fumes given off as the acid did its grisly work could turn dangerously toxic: the mixture of acids might produce a chemical reaction.

He had already purchased an old Second World War gasmask from an army surplus store in the city, which he would need to wear when inside the killing room. All he needed to source now was enough sulphuric acid to kill his intended victims.

He checked the drip-feed mechanism of his specialist machine, and once he was satisfied that all was in good working order, he replaced the padlock on the door and started to make his way back out of the tunnels.

He still had a lot of work to do; he now had to establish where he could get his hands on the large quantity of sulphuric acid he would need.

It wasn't the sort of commodity you could buy in bulk without people asking far too many questions.

As he emerged from the darkness of the tunnels back out into the peaceful woodland, he felt energised and excited. His mission was drawing closer to success. It was only a matter of time before he could take action to gain the revenge he so desperately craved.

5

10.30 a.m., 21 July 1991
Force Headquarters, Nottinghamshire

Danny had spent half an hour painstakingly going through the circumstances of the man's death at Worksop, listing the priority enquiries he had instigated at the scene, as well as the follow-up enquiries that still needed to be started.

Mark Slater had listened carefully to the grisly details of the man's death and winced on a couple of occasions as Danny described the theories put forward by the pathologist, Seamus Carter.

When Danny finished speaking, Slater leaned back in his chair and said, 'What kind of twisted brain thinks up a death like that, never mind carries it out?'

'That's just one of many unanswered questions I still have. The main problem for me is there's zero forensic evidence at the scene, very few remaining house-to-house enquiries to complete in that area, and no apparent witnesses.'

'You still have a lot of work to do, speaking to the golf club members.'

'That's true, but I don't see this investigation taking off properly until we can establish exactly who the dead man is.'

'Are you hopeful of a quick identification?'

'Dental records are a non-starter, as it appears the dead man hasn't seen a dentist in years. I don't want to generalise, but it's not very often that people sleeping rough, especially drug addicts, haven't encountered the police at some stage.'

'You're thinking a fingerprint match?'

'It's got to be our best bet.' Danny raised his eyebrows, hopefully. 'We'll need a positive result from the fingerprint identification bureau sooner rather than later.'

'Are there any other enquiries pending?'

'The Forensic Science Service have been sent all the samples taken from the body, so we'll be able to establish exactly what type of corrosive agent was used to kill this man. That could generate a lot more enquiries as we trace businesses that sell such substances to the public.'

'Sounds like you've got everything covered, Danny. Is there anything you need from me?'

'I was wondering if there's any way DI Lacey could join the department sooner. A lot can happen in a week, and it would be good to have her here at the beginning of this investigation rather than trying to play catch-up when she arrives.'

'That's a good point. I'll make some calls and see what her availability is. Hopefully, I can get her in post sooner rather than later.'

'Thanks. The only other thing is the press appeal. I'm going to see the press liaison officer when I leave here. It's my intention to give out the usual generic information: a body has been found, time and place, that we are treating the death as suspicious, that we have launched a murder investigation. It will be a general appeal for any possible witnesses to come forward. I don't want to make any mention of the cause of death yet. The killer's use of acid could easily cause panic among the public. Any thoughts on that?'

'It's your call to make, Danny. Personally, I think it's the right move. The public don't need to be told the horrific details of the man's death at this time, and you're not going to lose anything by not making the specifics public.'

As Danny reached the door, Slater said, 'I'll be in touch when I've an update on DI Lacey's situation.'

6

8.00 p.m., 21 July 1991
Thorpe Lane, Shireoaks, Nottinghamshire

After using false details to make countless telephone enquiries, the killer had managed to find a source for the sulphuric acid he would need before he could start his mission.

Addison's Fertiliser and Pesticide Ltd was the only premises locally that carried stocks of the ten-gallon drums of acid he required. The drum weighed approximately eighty pounds, a weight he could lift easily, and it wasn't too bulky to carry physically. He had calculated that he would need at least six of the drums to fulfil his purpose.

He parked his van on the lane that led to the remote industrial estate on the edge of the village of Shireoaks and looked at the vast single-storey warehouse that made up Addison's factory. He knew the plant manufactured all types of fertilisers and pesticides, which were then sold in bulk to the many farms spread across the county and beyond. It was a large company, and the fleet of delivery lorries parked to the side of the factory was testament to just what a thriving business it was.

He allowed himself a small smile of satisfaction as he observed the remoteness of the site. The process of manufacturing fertilisers and pesticides required using some of the deadliest chemicals, and no doubt strict planning regulations had stipulated that the factory was built well away from any housing or general population centres.

He got out of his van and walked slowly around the factory's perimeter fence. He gripped the fencing and found it was made of plastic-coated metal chain link and would be easily breached with the set of heavy bolt cutters that lay in the rear of his van.

He had no intention of forcing entry until the small hours of tomorrow morning, but he needed to use the last light of the day to reconnoitre the factory properly. He still needed to determine the type of alarm system he would encounter, and any other security measures that might be in place.

He was pleased that there didn't appear to be any on-site security personnel. The gatehouse at the front of the factory, which monitored all visitors and deliveries during business hours, was now in total darkness.

As a precaution, he had brought one of the two twelve-bore shotguns he owned with him. He hoped he would be able to get what he came for without any unwanted interruptions, and the weapon could remain loaded but unused in the van.

He stealthily scaled the fence at a remote part of the

factory, slipped between the rows of parked lorries and crept towards the main warehouse. He had two final checks to make. The first was to establish the locations of any security cameras and spotlights; the second was to make a close inspection of the intruder alarm system he would need to bypass.

Once those checks were completed, he could leave the area and return tomorrow morning before first light.

7

Danny and Rob were in the office discussing the lack of progress on the task Danny had set Rob, which was to speak to as many homeless or rough-sleeping people in the Worksop area as he could find.

Rob said, 'It's like smashing my head against a brick wall, boss. As soon as I identify myself as a police officer, nobody wants to engage or speak to me. The level of distrust is staggering.'

'Understandable,' Danny acknowledged. 'But did you get any leads at all?'

'Nobody I spoke to could recognise the description of our dead man, and no one has noticed anybody else missing. If I'm being honest, it's a bit of a thankless task.'

'How many people do you think you've spoken to today?'

'I started at the local nick and asked where the rough sleepers congregate, then went out searching with Sam Blake. I reckon I spoke to at least twenty, and Sam must have talked to a similar number. They're all very reluctant to give any personal details, so we couldn't even make a record of who we'd seen.'

There was a knock on the door, and Jag walked in. He handed Danny a document and said, 'Sorry to interrupt, but you're going to want to see this, sir.'

After a quick scan of the document, Danny exclaimed, 'Yes!' He passed it to Rob and said, 'Fingerprints have an exact match. Our victim has been identified as Terrence McAvoy.'

Jag said, 'I did a nominal check on the database as soon as I received his details. His date of birth is sixth March 1966, making him twenty-five years old. He's known to the police in Sheffield city centre and has previous convictions for shop theft, burglary and possession of Class A drugs. He's served one custodial sentence of six months for burglary. That was two years ago. There's also a warning marker on the Police National Computer showing he's an intravenous drug abuser and has hepatitis C. 'I've completed all the checks I can think of at this time of night, but so far I've drawn a blank on any next of kin.'

Danny was thoughtful and then said, 'First thing tomorrow morning, Jag, I want you and Sam Blake to travel up to Sheffield and find out everything you can from the local police. Once you've done that, I want you to talk to as many homeless people as you can find in that area. Someone must have noticed that he hasn't been around. If you do find any family for him, I'll want you to speak to them as well. It's important we try to establish exactly when and where he was abducted.'

'I'll give Sam a quick call now,' Jag said, 'so we can make an early start tomorrow.'

As Jag left the office, Danny said, 'We needed this break, Rob. It's important we establish whatever we can about the background and associates of our man McAvoy.'

'I'll make sure Jag knows the importance of his task, boss.'

Danny rubbed his hands together as he added, 'Let's hope this positive ID will move the inquiry forward.'

'Absolutely,' Rob said. 'So, are you ready for the pub now?'

Danny suddenly remembered that Andy had arranged a drink at the Railway to celebrate his promotion. He said, 'You go on, and I'll meet you there. I just need to finish this report first.'

'I'll have a quick chat with Jag before I leave. Don't be too long, boss.'

Rob left, leaving Danny alone in his office.

He felt a surge of optimism at the identification of the dead man but knew there was still a hell of a lot of work to be done before any real progress was made.

Suddenly, the strident ringing of the telephone on his desk disrupted his thoughts. He snatched the receiver up and said sharply, 'DCI Flint.'

'Danny,' Mark Slater said, 'I thought I might find you still at work. Just wanted to let you know, I've spoken with Sara Lacey this evening, and she's happy to start work on the MCIU tomorrow morning. She'd intended using up her remaining annual leave before she transferred, but once I'd agreed to hold her leave days over to next year so she wouldn't lose them, she was more than happy to start tomorrow.'

'That's great news. I look forward to welcoming her onto the department. I've an update for you too, Mark. We've just had a positive fingerprint identification for our acid victim. He was Terrence McAvoy, a twenty-five-year-old drug user from Sheffield. I'm sending Jag Singh and Sam Blake up there first thing tomorrow morning; I need them to uncover as much background information as they can.'

'That's positive. Let's hope it can move things forward, Danny. Goodnight.'

Danny replaced the receiver and then glanced at the report in front of him. Thinking better of it, he grabbed his jacket and walked wearily out the door.

8

8.30 p.m., 21 July 1991
The Railway, Mansfield, Nottinghamshire

Danny walked into the lounge bar and was surprised to see just Rob and Rachel sitting with Andy in the corner.

Andy waved and walked over. 'What are you drinking, Danny?'

'A pint of Guinness for me, cheers.'

He looked around the empty bar and continued, 'Where is everybody?'

'This is it.' Andy smiled. 'I didn't want a big do; I just wanted the three people I've worked with the longest. The original four from the Jimmy Wade, coal killer inquiry.'

Danny raised his glass and said, 'Here's to the memory of those dark days, Andy.'

Andy raised his own glass. 'Dark days but a great team.'

The two detectives joined their colleagues, and Danny said, 'How's the maternity leave going, Rachel?'

She lifted her glass of fresh orange juice and said, 'Oh, it's just marvellous. I can't even have a proper drink to celebrate Andy's brilliant news.' She took a sip and then continued, 'Seriously, it's great, but I'm starting to feel a little bored already.'

Rob laughed. 'Make the most of this boredom because when that little one arrives, you'll be craving a bit of downtime.'

Danny looked at Andy and asked, 'So, when do you start on Special Branch?'

'I don't. The chief has asked me to head up a brand-new squad. It's going to be called the Covert Surveillance Unit and will be a team designated solely to providing the force with their own twenty-four-hour surveillance capability, including any covert rural observations, as well as foot and vehicle surveillance.'

'You sound excited by it. I thought you would have wanted the Branch?'

'I'm excited that this is something I can build and mould myself,' Andy said, taking a long drink of his pint. 'Going in at the beginning, overseeing such a dedicated unit – I think will be both a massive challenge and an amazing opportunity.'

'It certainly sounds interesting. Where will you be drawing your staff from?'

'Mainly from the regional crime squad and the Special Operations Unit. There will also be an opportunity for other officers who show a real aptitude for the work.'

'The Mr and Mrs Greys of the force,' Rachel said with a grin.

'Exactly. The chief has already ordered me to lose my smart, clean-cut appearance. I've got to admit, never in my wildest dreams did I ever expect to hear a senior officer give me that order.'

Danny smiled at Rob and said, 'I reckon you could pull that one off quite easily, mate.'

Rob grinned. 'Yeah, very funny. I've got three teenagers at home; I can't afford bespoke suits and gold cufflinks. I'm strictly a Burton's bargain basement man.'

'Nothing wrong with that,' Danny said as he raised his glass. 'I propose a toast to Detective Inspector Andy Wills, head of the new Covert Surveillance Unit. Cheers.'

The gathered detectives all touched glasses and offered their colleague their individual congratulations.

Danny finished his drink. 'I'm not going to make it a late night, Andy, but I really do want to wish you all the very best. It's been a pleasure working alongside you, and I'm sure that once your new unit is operational, the MCIU will be putting plenty of work your way.'

'I look forward to that, boss,' Andy said as the two men shook hands warmly. 'Cheers.'

9

2.30 a.m., 22 July 1991
Thorpe Lane, Shireoaks, Nottinghamshire

Gary Stringer slipped his Barbour waxed jacket on and looked down at the expectant, excited face of his golden retriever. The dog had seen him pick the lead off the small table in the hallway and knew it was time for a walk.

Gary had just finished his latest evening shift, getting home just after two twenty. His usual routine when he was on this shift was to walk the dog before he went to bed so he could then sleep through until ten when the dog would need walking again.

Following his recent – and acrimonious – divorce from his wife of ten years, he now lived alone. He had remained in the marital home and paid his ex-wife a lump-sum settlement to move out. It meant he now had very little disposable income, and walking his dog was one of the few pleasures he had left.

After spending eight long hours sitting behind the wheel of the police patrol car, he was always pleased to stretch his legs and get some fresh air before bed.

Gary had been a traffic department sergeant for seven years, and he loved his job. However, the job had been a major cause of friction between him and his wife. That and the fact he wanted a family, and she didn't. The rows had gradually become more and more spiteful until after one particularly vicious argument, they had both decided it would be in both their best interests to give up on the marriage and agree to a divorce.

The acrimony had come over the amount of money his ex-wife wanted from him in order to move out of the marital home. It had been Gary's home before they were married, and he vehemently disputed the amount she was now claiming she was owed. It had eventually been settled in court, and although he was now very poor, Gary was a much happier man.

Slipping the lead onto his dog's collar, he whispered, 'Come on then, Bruno.'

His semi-detached house sat at the junction of Thorpe Lane and Shireoaks Road, directly opposite St Luke's church. Gary stepped onto the block-paved driveway and carefully closed and locked the front door.

He and Bruno followed their usual route, straight across the junction to the church gate, then a left turn on to the narrow footpath that ran along the side of the River Ryton. Once on the footpath, next to the narrow river, he let Bruno off the lead so the dog could have a run up and down the path and carry out his toilet business.

After four hundred yards, man and dog turned away from the riverbank.

Gary shouted, 'Bruno! Come here, boy.'

Obediently, the dog came quickly to heel, and Gary clipped the lead back on before they walked back on the road.

They then turned towards home and began walking along Thorpe Lane, through the small industrial estate.

As they approached the Addison's factory, Gary could see a small white van parked adjacent to the fence that bordered the lorry park of the fertiliser factory. He could see the van doors were open, and there was a big man loading something into the back of the van.

He checked Bruno, who had also seen the man and was now straining at his lead, and whispered, 'Be still, Bruno.'

As he walked nearer, he saw the man load the last of what appeared to be a number of heavy barrels into the rear of the van and close the doors.

'What's going on? What are you doing?'

The man spun around, and Gary saw his expression change from one of shock to something more neutral as he quickly regained his composure. The big man smiled and said, 'Everything's fine. I've just had to mess around for almost an hour changing the tyre. I realised I'd got a flat as soon as I left work, so I had to stop and change it.'

Yeah, right, Gary thought, *pull the other one, mate.* To the man he simply said, 'Do you work around here, then?'

'I'm on the late shift at Addison's.'

The off-duty police officer knew that Addison's didn't

employ a night shift, which meant this man was indeed lying to him. Glancing to his right, towards the factory, Gary saw that a neat hole had been cut out of the factory's perimeter fence.

He took his warrant card from his pocket, held it out towards the man and said, 'My name's Sergeant Stringer. I'm a police officer, and I want to see what you've got in the back of the van.'

The man smiled. 'No problem, officer. It's just the flat tyre and some tools.'

He turned and opened the rear doors.

Gary immediately saw the barrels stacked in the back of the van and said, 'Don't move.'

The man swiftly turned to face him, and to his horror Gary saw he was now looking at the wrong end of a double-barrelled shotgun.

The man pointed the weapon at Gary's midriff and grunted, 'Back off.'

Gary stemmed the panic starting to flood his body, held out his warrant card again and said firmly, 'I've just told you I'm a police officer. You need to put the gun down and give this madness up. You won't get away with it.'

He saw the flash from the barrel and heard the crack as the man pulled the trigger. The force of the shotgun blast at such close range lifted him off his feet and sent him hurling backwards. All the air was knocked from his body as he smashed into the hard tarmac, and he let out a terrible groan as pain raked through his chest.

Gary felt the dog lead slip through his unmoving fingers. He then heard a second shotgun blast and a single yelp from Bruno.

Then doors slammed, the van engine started up, and the vehicle was driven away.

As he lay on his back gasping for breath while trying to draw air into his shredded lungs, Gary stared at the streetlight directly above him as it slowly faded into blackness.

10

4.30 a.m., 22 July 1991
Thorpe Lane, Shireoaks, Nottinghamshire

Danny was pleased he had called time early on Andy's celebratory drink the night before.

When he received the phone call from the control room informing him of another suspicious death, just over an hour earlier, the last thing he would have wanted was a thick head from too much alcohol.

He was now standing with DI Sara Lacey near to the pool of congealing blood on Thorpe Lane. Two scenes of crime personnel were retrieving samples from the blood. A yard or so away from the bloodstain was the covered body of a dead golden retriever.

Danny, who had just arrived at the scene, asked Sara, 'Who alerted the police?'

'Police were called by Gary Stringer's next-door neighbour, who reported hearing two loud bangs that sounded like gunshots.'

'Where does Gary live?'

Sara pointed back along Thorpe Lane towards the small village of Shireoaks and said, 'His is the first house you come to when you enter the village. It's the corner house directly opposite the church.'

'What did the police patrol find when they got here?'

'It took them five minutes to arrive, and they spoke to the neighbour first. She told them the gunshot noise sounded like it had come from down Thorpe Lane. The two cops went looking and found Sergeant Stringer in the road outside the Addison's factory. He was barely clinging to life.'

'What's his condition now?'

'It doesn't sound good, sir. The two uniform lads did everything they could to stem the bleeding, and an ambulance was on scene within ten minutes. The problem is that the blast from the shotgun hit him square in the chest, and he was having severe difficulty breathing. Rob's at Bassetlaw Hospital monitoring the situation. The last update I had from him was that Stringer had been rushed into emergency surgery to try to repair the damage to his lungs and help him breathe.'

Danny remained stern faced as he surveyed the scene. He could see Tim Donnelly standing near to the large hole in the perimeter fence, which was now illuminated by a bright white spotlight being powered by a nearby portable generator.

He walked over and raised his voice to be heard above the din of the generator. 'What have you found so far, Tim?'

'The killer wasn't bothered about leaving the shotgun cartridges. We've recovered both from the roadside.' He paused and then continued, 'That could mean a couple of things. Either he's a clean skin with no previous convictions or any dealings with the police and isn't worried about leaving prints, or he's not very savvy forensically.'

'Let's hope it's the latter and you find his prints on the cartridge cases. Anything else?'

'We've also recovered the black leather wallet containing Sergeant Stringer's warrant card.'

'Where was that?'

'Right next to the pool of blood.'

'Do you think it fell from his pocket?'

'I doubt it. It looks like he was identifying himself to the killer.'

'Bloody hell. Anything else?'

'From the cut marks on the fence, it looks like heavy bolt croppers were used to cut the hole in it. Everything's been photographed, but judging from the size of the hole, I'd say he either miscalculated how much he needed to cut, or he's a big sod.'

Danny nodded. 'Have you got all the samples and photographs you need from the blood on the road and from the dead dog?'

Tim nodded, his face sombre.

'In that case,' Danny said, 'as soon as you can, I want that blood washed away. I don't want people standing here gawping later.'

'Understood, boss. A local vet has been called out, and she's on her way to take the dead dog away.'

'Thanks, Tim. It looks like it could be a burglar who's been disturbed in the act. Have you made a start on identifying and examining any point of entry in the factory yet?'

Sara interjected, 'As soon as the ambulance had taken

Stringer to the hospital, the uniform cops who first attended searched the parts of the factory they could access from the outside. They couldn't find any point of entry. I've had the control room calling out the factory keyholders since I arrived. It took ages for any of them to answer, but one has been contacted now and should be here within the next five or ten minutes.'

Danny looked at his new detective inspector and said, 'Not quite the first day you imagined, Sara?'

'You could say that, sir. I didn't expect my first call-out to be on my old patch at three thirty in the morning. And I certainly didn't expect it would involve the shooting of a colleague, a man I know well.'

'That's tough, I know,' said Danny as kindly as he could. 'Tell me about Sergeant Gary Stringer?'

'He's a good cop. A perfect fit for his role on the traffic department. The blokes who work for him all speak extremely highly of him.'

'Do you know him personally?'

'I never socialised with him,' Sara said. 'You know how it is – CID detectives and traffic officers don't tend to mix that much. Whenever I've seen him at work, he always seems very good-natured: he likes a laugh. I do know he recently went through a very messy divorce.'

'How recent and how messy?'

'It would have been around six months ago. I don't think there were any third parties involved when he and his wife separated. It just got messy over money. From what I heard, and this is only a rumour, his ex-wife really took him to the cleaners financially.'

'Okay.' Danny nodded thoughtfully as he changed his focus. 'Strange that the uniform lads couldn't find a break-in at the factory. Do you think this could be a set-up and has nothing to do with the factory?'

'Anything's possible,' Sara agreed. 'I like to keep an open mind on these things. If you're asking me if his divorce was bad enough to cause his ex-wife to be involved in something like this, I'd say probably not.'

'What about people he might have upset on duty?'

'That will be one line of enquiry, sir. But traffic officers generally don't encounter the same number of big-time criminals as some detectives do.'

'True.' Danny nodded his agreement. 'But, as you say, we'll need to thoroughly look at that angle. Who knows, he may have breathalysed the wrong person or arrested a serious criminal for a traffic offence.'

Their conversation was interrupted by DC Jane Pope. 'DI Lacey, the keyholder's finally arrived and is about to unlock the factory.'

Danny said, 'We'll talk more later, Sara. I'm going to leave you to supervise this scene along with Tim Donnelly while I go to the hospital. I'll need to know exactly what condition Sergeant Stringer's in when I brief the chief constable later. Have you enough staff here?'

'There's me, Helen Bailey acting sergeant and five other DCs. We should be fine.'

'Okay. Let me know if you find a point of entry and, if so, what's been stolen that was worth shooting an off-duty cop for. Keep in constant liaison with Tim and his staff. Any other potential scenes you find, I want them examined and photographed immediately.'

'Understood, sir.'

Danny walked back to his car. His thoughts had already turned to his shot colleague. He had seen more than enough gunshot deaths during his career as a detective, and he knew that being hit in the chest by a shotgun fired from close range very seldom ended well.

Danny sighed, his heart heavy. He fully expected to be briefing the chief constable later about the murder of an off-duty police sergeant.

11

Danny could see Rob sitting at the end of the long corridor. He was leaning forward, holding his head in both hands. He cut a desolate and forlorn figure.

He must have heard Danny's footsteps echoing along the corridor, because he looked up to see who was approaching. Danny waved a hand in greeting and said, 'Any news?'

Rob shook his head. 'Gary Stringer's been in surgery since just after three o'clock. It was a case of needs must. Without the operation to try to repair the damage to his lungs, he would have died. The doctor told me it was a matter of when not if.'

'Bloody hell, mate.' Danny drew in his breath sharply,

shocked at the starkness of the situation. 'Who's keeping you updated on what's happening?'

'The operating theatre's at the end of this corridor. I've been sat here on my own since they took him in. It's a waiting game, boss.'

Danny sat next to his colleague. 'I understand Gary's divorced; do we know who his next of kin is?'

'I've asked the control room that same question, but they haven't come back to me yet.'

'Have you had any sort of break since you got here?'

'I'm okay,' Rob said, though he looked anything but. 'There's a drinks machine along the corridor. I've had a few of their awful coffees. And thank goodness I left the Railway just after you last night.'

The operating theatre door opened, and the noise of it made both detectives turn their heads. Danny watched as a stern-faced surgeon approached them. He was still wearing his green scrubs and head covering.

Danny said, 'I'm Detective Chief Inspector Flint. How's my colleague?'

'I'm so sorry, Chief Inspector,' the surgeon said, his voice sombre. 'We did everything we could, but unfortunately the damage to his lungs was irreparable. That combined with the amount of blood loss he'd already suffered at the scene meant the operation was always risky. But it was a risk we had to take, as the operation was his only chance of survival. His heart gave out while we were working on the lungs, I'm afraid, and we couldn't get him back.'

Danny cursed under his breath and then said to the surgeon, 'I want to thank you and your team for everything you've done and tried to do. It's much appreciated by all of us. I'm just sorry the outcome wasn't better.'

'As we all are, Detective. I understand your people will need access to the operating theatre to gather evidence.'

'We will need some time, but I'm conscious the room will be required by medical staff as soon as possible. This is Detective Inspector Buxton; he will remain here and supervise the evidence gathering from the theatre and will arrange for a Home Office pathologist to get here as soon as possible. We don't want to inconvenience your surgical teams any more than necessary, so he will ensure we act with expediency.'

'Please take as long as you need, Detective. We all understand you have a job to do. The operating theatre will be vacated by our staff shortly; they have all been instructed to leave everything in situ.'

Danny extended his hand and shook hands with the surgeon. 'Thanks again for all your efforts.'

As the surgeon returned to the operating theatre, Danny said to Rob, 'I'll get hold of Tim Donnelly and make sure he's travelling here as soon as possible. He has other staff at the scene who can examine anything found at the factory. I want everything here done right. This man was one of our own, and I don't want to miss anything. I'll contact the control room and get the pathologist travelling here, as a matter of urgency.'

Rob's whole face and manner were totally crestfallen. 'I really thought that once the ambulance got him here alive, he would just have the op and be able to make a full recovery,' he said, his voice subdued and shaky. 'I don't believe this.'

Danny had always feared the worst when the injuries that Sergeant Stringer had sustained were described to him.

He had seen first-hand the devastation caused by a twelve-bore shotgun at close range.

He put a hand gently on Rob's shoulder and said, 'I know you're distressed by this, and I understand that; it's terrible.' He paused quietly for a moment. 'But, Rob, you still have an important job to do here. We owe it to Gary to make sure we don't miss any evidence that might help us catch the bastard who did this.'

Rob nodded. 'I'll be fine, boss. It was the look on that surgeon's face as he walked towards us. I just know that's an image that's going to stay with me for a long time.'

'Me too, Rob.' Danny sighed. 'What I need to know is: what was so bloody important at that factory that it was worth the life of a police officer?'

12

Danny had been surprised to see Detective Chief Superintendent Slater waiting for him in his office when he arrived back at the MCIU.

He hadn't been surprised to see every other member of the MCIU waiting to be briefed on the death of their colleague. Bad news travelled fast.

He briefed the remaining staff, who had not been called out by the control room, on the urgent enquiries that needed starting as soon as possible. Once that was done, he returned to his office to speak privately with Mark Slater and give him an update on the priority actions he had taken thus far.

'This is a bad business, Danny,' Mark Slater said. The chief has contacted me to tell you that anything you need, you will get. He's already spoken to Chief Inspector Chambers at home this morning, and he's arranged for two sections of the SOU to be ready and at your disposal.'

'Thank you, that will be a massive help, sir. We've a mammoth task ahead of us. Although it's a small village, size-wise, there are a lot of residential properties in Shireoaks, so the house-to-house enquiries will be a large undertaking. Then there are over seventy staff working at the Addison's factory, who will all need interviewing, and possible statements taken.'

'That's one reason I'm here,' Slater said crisply. 'I wanted to save you time trekking out to headquarters to brief me when you've already got your hands more than full. I've come out to you so you can brief me on what you've got organised so far, and I can then relay that to the chief constable on your behalf.'

Danny felt a real sense of relief that Mark Slater was so completely different to his predecessor, Adrian Potter. Potter would never have dreamed of taking such a decisive and helpful action; in fact, he always seemed more intent on hindering an investigation than helping.

He said, 'Thank you, sir. That's much appreciated.'

Slater nodded. 'The chief has asked me to tell you that he does want you at the press conference, which is booked for three o'clock this afternoon, though.'

'I understand. I'll make sure I'm at headquarters for two thirty so there's plenty of time to brief the press liaison officer with any updates.'

'Good. Now what have you organised so far?'

'At the main scene, Addison's factory at Shireoaks, I have DI Lacey, DS Bailey and five detectives, as well as scenes of crime personnel. The actual shooting occurred outside the factory on Thorpe Lane. That scene has been completely worked. Samples and photographs taken. Also recovered on Thorpe Lane was Sergeant Stringer's warrant card, so we're working on the theory that he produced his identification to the offender, who we think he may have disturbed committing a burglary at the factory.'

'Okay.'

'The warrant card is significant because it rules out the offender being familiar with Gary Stringer. If they had known each other, there would have been no need for him to identify himself.'

'It also means the killer was totally indifferent about shooting a police officer.'

'My thoughts exactly. We're looking at someone prepared to do anything to get away. The team at Addison's are now searching the factory, working alongside scenes of crime personnel; they've confirmed the point of entry and are looking for any other scenes they find inside. They are also trying to determine exactly what, if anything, has been stolen.'

'Any progress made on that?'

'I'm expecting another update at nine o'clock from DI Lacey, but as I say, they've now established the point of entry into the factory. One of the up-and-over metal doors at the loading bay, the ones used by the delivery trucks, had been forced using a trolley jack. Strangely, they haven't yet found any evidence of a damaged padlock in the area. All the loading bays should be secured with a padlock overnight.'

'I take it you'll be having a close look at the loading staff today, then.' Mark leaned back in his chair, thoughtful. 'Is there a chance this could be an inside job?'

'It could be, I'm certainly not ruling anything out. We'll be interviewing all the loading bay and security staff who were at work yesterday. The other strange thing we've found is that nobody at the factory can tell us what, if anything, has been stolen. The offices at the factory weren't touched, and the warehouse where goods are stored seems to be the only part of the factory entered by the thief or thieves.'

'Surely, it won't take long for the office staff to determine what stock they are missing, if any?'

'I thought that, but apparently a full stock take is due to happen later this week, and the last one was carried out over three months ago.'

'Do you think that's another pointer towards this being an inside job?'

'Yes, but as always, I'll keep an open mind. We'll fully interview all staff and security personnel as soon as we can. If this was set up by an employee, I'm confident we'll determine that.'

'Anything forensically from the factory?'

'Nothing startling yet, but it's still early days.'

'I take it the factory has an alarm system in place?'

'It does,' Danny confirmed, 'and it was bypassed at the loading bay. Scenes of crime are trying to determine exactly how that was done, and DI Lacey has organised for an engineer from the alarm company to attend to assist us with that.'

'That's good work. Quite a baptism of fire for your new DI.'

'True, but I've no concerns about DI Lacey's ability. She's an experienced, competent detective and supervisor. I'm confident she'll be managing that scene very well.'

'Anything else from the factory?'

'That's it. I'll update you throughout the day if anything major is discovered.'

'Okay. Who have you got at the hospital?'

'DI Buxton, DC Singleton and Tim Donnelly, the scenes of crime supervisor, have completed everything at the hospital and have already returned the operating theatre to the medical staff. They've exhibited everything used during the emergency operation and arranged for statements to be obtained from the lead surgeon and the anaesthetist.'

'I take it there's now a Home Office pathologist involved?'

'Seamus Carter has been on scene at the hospital throughout that process and will be carrying out a full post-mortem examination later this afternoon.'

'What time?'

'It's scheduled to start at five o'clock today,' Danny said. 'I'll be in attendance along with DI Buxton and DC Singleton.'

'I'll want an update as soon as that's completed, Danny. Have you got all your staff working on this investigation now?'

'DC Singh and DC Blake had already arranged to visit Sheffield today and set off just before six o'clock this morning. They are there to trace any associates of Terrence McAvoy. I thought it best to leave them to carry on with that, as they had made such an early start. I can summon them back if needs be.'

'That's your call,' Mark said, 'and let me know how they get on with that enquiry. Tell me what else has been organised for this morning's shooting.'

'Will do. As a priority another enquiry I've instigated is Sergeant Stringer's victimology. I've tasked DC Lorimar and DC Holden with that. They'll be looking at Gary Stringer's personal and private life. Everything will be fully examined. Relationships, finance, all the usual, including his recent divorce.'

Mark raised his eyebrows and sighed. 'I know it can be an unsavoury task for fellow officers to go delving into a colleague's private life, but no stone must be left unturned, Danny. This could be nothing to do with a burglary gone wrong, and everything to do with Gary Stringer the person.'

'Agreed,' Danny said with a nod. 'I've also got DC Jefferies making enquiries into Stringer's work life and career to date. She'll be examining all arrests made and any reported interactions with the public over the last twelve months. This will include input from the Complaints and Discipline department to establish if he's been the subject of any internal or external complaints over that same twelve-month period.'

'You mentioned he's recently divorced. Is his ex-wife still his next of kin?'

'Personnel have his next of kin listed as his parents. They live in a village near Newcastle and have been notified by Northumbria Police. Officers from that force are conveying them to Nottingham later today. Northumbria's chief constable insisted on arranging transport for them.'

'Good,' Slater said. 'Jack Renshaw had let me know that Northumbria Police were involved with this. What have you arranged for them when they arrive?'

'I've tasked DC Lisa Bettridge to meet them and take care of them until I can speak with them personally. I'm hoping to do that before I attend the post-mortem at five o'clock. The force has already arranged for accommodation at a guest house in Mansfield.'

'I want to be kept updated on the parents as well, please,

Danny. I'm sure the chief constable will want to meet them and offer his condolences.' And then Mark Slater stood to leave. 'Good work, Danny,' he said. 'I'll let you crack on. Don't forget to keep me updated and to be at the press conference later.'

Danny smiled. 'No problem.'

13

12.30 p.m., 22 July 1991
Addison's Fertiliser and Pesticide Ltd, Shireoaks,
Nottinghamshire

Sara Lacey was becoming more and more frustrated as she spoke with Vanessa Symonds, the company secretary.

She fought to keep her voice and mood level as she spoke. 'I can't stress the importance of that information. We need to know exactly what has been stolen during this burglary.'

The other woman said, 'I totally understand, and I'm not being deliberately obstructive in any way. The problem is over the last week we've received several deliveries that have been unloaded and then partially used, so we can't determine the exact numbers just yet.'

'Is that normal to partially use an unloaded delivery?'

'It shouldn't happen,' Vanessa admitted, 'but unfortunately it does. What can sometimes occur is that the plant has been so short of a certain product or chemical that it leads to a backlog in the manufacturing process.' She paused before continuing, 'This means that there's the odd occasion when the delivery has been unloaded into the warehouse on pallets before the stock is properly entered into the company's records, the pallets get opened, and product is removed to clear that backlog. The pallets are then counted for the stock take.'

Sara looked away in frustration. 'How soon can you let me know if anything is missing?'

'It will be a few days before I can speak to all the heads of manufacturing and establish if anything was taken from the pallets in the way I've just described.'

'It really needs to be quicker than that, Ms Symonds,' Sara insisted. 'This is a murder investigation, and the information I'm asking for could be crucial to finding the person responsible for that murder.'

'I understand, and I'll chase it all day today. Hopefully, I'll get that information to you faster. From everything we've checked so far, there doesn't appear to be anything missing, but we'll keep looking.'

'I would really appreciate that.' Sara took a deep breath to steady her rising sense of annoyance. 'In the meantime, I'll need a list of all the chemicals and other products that have been delivered that aren't properly accounted for. That will at least give us some idea of what could be missing.'

'It will be quite a long list,' Vanessa said levelly. 'We manufacture many different types of fertilisers and pesticides. The processes involved use various chemicals, some of which are highly toxic and dangerous to handle.'

Sara nodded. 'How soon can you let me have the list?'

'I'll make sure you have it by the end of the day, Detective.'

'Thank you. Who do I speak to in personnel to obtain details of all your employees?'

'That will be Janice Carruthers. I'll introduce you and make sure you get her full co-operation. As a company, we're deeply saddened about what happened to your colleague, and we want to do everything we can to assist you with your enquiries.'

'Thank you,' Sara said as graciously as she could. 'That's very much appreciated.'

As they began to walk from the warehouse back towards the company offices, they were met by Helen Bailey, who said, 'I've been trying to find you, boss. I think we may have had a small breakthrough.'

'Step to one side,' Sara said in a low voice, guiding her colleague out of Vanessa's earshot. 'Now tell me.'

'Yes, boss.' Helen's tone matched Sara's as the two women stood close together. 'I've been viewing the CCTV footage in the gatehouse, with the head of security. The camera that's trained on the delivery vehicle car park shows a partial view of Thorpe Lane, as it runs alongside the perimeter fence. In between the parked lorries, you get a glimpse of a small white van being driven along Thorpe Lane, away from the factory.'

'Any identifying features on the vehicle?'

'Unfortunately, it's a side view only, and there doesn't appear to be any significant markings. It's definitely a plain white Ford Escort van, though.'

'Is there a timer on the camera?'

'Yes, the van is sighted being driven away from the factory at two thirty-five this morning.'

'Around the same time the witness heard the two gunshots.'

Helen nodded and added, 'I've gone back through the tape to see if I could spot the vehicle earlier, and I found it being driven on Thorpe Lane in the opposite direction just before two o'clock.'

'How far's the hole in the fence from where you can see the vehicle?'

'About forty yards. I've been outside to have a look. The camera view couldn't pick up the hole in the fence, as it's just out of shot.'

'Deliberately so, no doubt. The person or persons who did this are meticulous in their planning, that's for sure. Have you seized the tape?'

'Yes. The head of security has also given me a list of employees who have been sacked or recently disciplined. Plus, he's provided me with the names of any current employees he has concerns over regarding petty pilfering from the factory. He's a retired cop and is keen to help us.'

'Good to have him onside.' Sara nodded. 'Did he say if they've had any other recent burglaries at the site?'

'The last one was six months ago. The thieves broke into the offices and stole computers and broke into the drinks machine to steal the coins.'

'We need to check if anyone was arrested and charged with that offence.'

'I will check it, but I think it's doubtful. He's never been contacted by the police with an update, so it seems unlikely that anybody was ever charged.'

'You're probably right, but cops have been known to

forget to contact the victims on occasion. Check it anyway.' Sara smiled at her colleague. 'This is good work, Helen.'

Then she turned and walked the few paces back to face Vanessa Symonds and said, 'Let's speak with Mrs Carruthers, shall we?'

'Follow me, Detective.'

14

DC Lisa Bettridge knocked once on Danny's door and waited. She was new to the MCIU and still unsure of the team's protocol.

Danny shouted, 'Come in.'

As Lisa walked in, Danny said kindly, 'I've always run an open-door policy here, Lisa. If the door's shut, it means I'm in a meeting, but I still want you to knock and come in. If it's open, like it is now, just knock once and walk in. Okay?'

'Yes, sir. I'll know for next time. I wanted to let you know I have Mr and Mrs Stringer in the main office. I'm later than planned because the first thing they wanted to do was go to Worksop to see their son.'

'That's understandable. I take it you did the formal identification at the same time?'

'Yes, sir. I took them to their accommodation and let them settle in there for a while, then brought them here to meet you, as ordered. I've also been told to make sure they're at headquarters for four o'clock, to see the chief constable.'

'Good job,' Danny said. 'Tell me, what are their first names?'

'Mrs Stringer is Pam, and her husband is Frank.'

'Okay. Would you show them in, please.'

Lisa left the office, returning moments later with Sergeant Gary Stringer's grieving parents.

Danny stood up to meet them and extended his hand to Mr Stringer. He said, 'I'm Detective Chief Inspector Danny Flint. I'll be leading the investigation to find the person or persons responsible for your son's death.'

As he shook hands with Frank Stringer, he felt the power still in the elderly man's grip and noticed the myriad of blue-black scars on the back of the man's hand. Danny knew that strong grip and those scars were testament to a life of hard coal-mining work underground.

As soon as Lisa told Danny that Gary's father's name was Frank, it stirred memories of his own deceased father. Now, as he shook hands with the retired collier, those memories of his own father grew even stronger.

He asked them both to take a seat and said, 'I'm so sorry for your loss. I want you to know we will not rest until we catch whoever is responsible for this awful crime, and that you can call me anytime, day or night. Do you have any questions for me now?'

Pam Stringer shook her head and dabbed tears away from her eyes with the crumpled tissue she held tightly in her hand.

Frank Stringer made eye contact with Danny and said quietly, 'How did this happen, Detective?'

'We believe Gary interrupted a burglar breaking into a factory and tried to detain him. He was off duty, but still he bravely tried to intervene. That was the measure of the man.'

'He always was a good lad.' The ex-miner blinked hard before adding, 'He was determined not to follow his old man down the pit, because he thought it was too dangerous and liked to see the sky above his head. When he told me he was joining the force, I was overjoyed. No pitman ever wants their son to work underground.'

'My father was a collier,' Danny said gently, 'and I remember having a similar conversation with him when I told him I was joining the police. Gary was an excellent police officer and was destined for even higher rank than he had achieved already. He was very well respected by us all.'

'That's good to hear, Chief Inspector, and I thank you for that. Promise me you'll get whoever it was who did this to my boy.'

'What I can promise you is that none of us will stop working until we make that happen, Frank. You have my word.'

'Thank you.'

For the first time since she had walked into the office, Pam Stringer spoke. Her voice cracked with a suppressed rage and deep, troubled emotion as she virtually spat out her words. 'You need to concentrate on that grasping cow he married. I wouldn't be surprised if she was behind all this.'

The remark was filled with real venom, and Danny remained silent as Frank turned to his wife and said, 'Hush, Pam. You don't know that.'

With true anger in her voice she said, 'I know she only

married him for what she could get. And when she didn't get the house, she swore to make him pay. What else do I need to know, Frank?'

Danny stood and said, 'This has been a long, deeply traumatic day for both of you. I think you should have some time alone, to rest a little. Please be assured we will explore all angles.'

Frank helped his wife to her feet and said, 'I think you're right, Detective. My wife is tired and emotional. We are both in shock. We'll talk to you again soon. And thank you for seeing us. I feel happier now I've met you in person and looked into your eyes. You look like an honest and determined man to me, so I'm trusting you to catch this murderer and give us – and Gary – justice.'

15

5.00 p.m., 22 July 1991
Bassetlaw Hospital, Worksop, Nottinghamshire

Danny stood alongside Rob Buxton as Seamus Carter started his post-mortem examination of Sergeant Stringer.

He had dashed from the press conference at headquarters to the hospital, to ensure he was present at the post-mortem of his colleague. He now watched, stern faced, as the pathologist worked methodically tracking the path of each individual lead shot through the man's chest. The surgeon had already removed two of the shot from his left lung before Gary Stringer died on the operating table.

The pathologist traced each lead shot and removed it, and Danny felt a chill run through him as the small ball of lead clattered into the stainless-steel bowl. A record was made of the track each shot had taken and the subsequent damage caused to the vital internal organs.

Both lungs had been drastically damaged, but the final piece of shot was found near the spine. The pathologist carefully tracked this lead shot and found that it had passed through the left atrium of the heart, at the same time as causing a minute tear in the pulmonary aorta.

Seamus said, 'You need to see this, Danny.'

Danny reluctantly stepped forward to get a closer look as the pathologist said, 'The damage to the lungs was substantial but could possibly have been repaired by a skilled surgeon.' He then pointed to the heart and said, 'The cause of death was this pellet that has passed through the heart. Unfortunately, the tear in the pulmonary aorta, just here, was the fatal factor. Even though it's minuscule, that tear would have been irreparable and was the major factor causing Gary's heart to give out. He would have lost blood at a steady rate until his body could no longer function. I'm sorry, Danny, but that's what killed your colleague.'

Danny nodded and stepped back as Seamus continued his work. The full post-mortem examination was methodically completed in total silence as a sombre mood filled the room and Danny reflected on what had been a long, emotionally testing day.

Trying to come to terms with the violent death of a colleague was always traumatic for every officer involved, but after meeting with Gary Stringer's parents earlier, Danny now felt the strong emotional impact on himself.

He was aware of it and knew it was something he would need to suppress if he was to make the correct decisions during the investigation and not the ones driven by an overriding desire to make the person responsible pay for what they had done.

Seamus's voice brought him back to the present. 'I'll let you have my report first thing tomorrow morning. Do you have any questions?'

'Thank you,' Danny managed to say. 'Have you taken samples for a full toxicology examination?'

'All standard tests and samples have been taken and exhibited. My report will show the cause of death as a gunshot wound to the chest, causing damage to both lungs and the heart.'

'What about the lead shot you removed. Can you tell me anything about that?'

DC Singleton, who was acting as the exhibits officer, spoke up. 'I've measured the lead shot as I exhibited it, sir. It's 00 buckshot, 0.33 inches in diameter. I'm a shotgun licence holder myself, and it's similar ammunition to what I use for pheasant shooting. The number of shot matches up as well. Typically, each cartridge will contain eight lead shot of that size.'

Danny looked at his detective and said, 'Thanks, that's useful. Is that type of ammunition hard to get hold of?'

'Unfortunately not, sir. Most people use something similar. Any farmer who holds a shotgun licence will probably have a quantity of that type of cartridge. It's general purpose.'

Danny nodded in acknowledgement. 'I want you to follow that up, as you obviously have a good knowledge of the subject. Make sure it ties in with the cartridge cases recovered at the scene. You may be able to trace where those cartridges were purchased.'

'Will do, sir. This type of shotgun cartridge is extremely common, though.'

It was then that Danny turned to Rob and said quietly, 'Let's get out of here. I need some fresh air.'

16

It wasn't very often Danny was asked to drive to headquarters to meet alone with Chief Constable Jack Renshaw. He knew exactly what the meeting would be about. The chief would want to hear for himself exactly what Danny had organised for the investigation into the cold-blooded murder of Sergeant Stringer.

As Danny walked along the corridor towards the chief's office, his secretary said, 'He's asked that you go straight in, Chief Inspector. He has another meeting scheduled for ten thirty, which he won't want to delay.'

Danny nodded as he walked past her desk, knocked once on the door and waited to be invited inside.

Jack Renshaw was sat behind his desk; he was wearing a dark blue business suit instead of a uniform. He said,

'Thanks for being so prompt, Danny. I've got the police authority here soon to talk to me about budgets.'

Danny sat down and waited for the inevitable question.

Renshaw steepled his fingers and said, 'A terrible business. I had a long meeting with Sergeant Stringer's parents yesterday. They told me you had spoken to them earlier in the day. His father seemed very impressed by you. Thank you; that's appreciated.'

'I wanted them to be able to put a face to my name, if they needed to contact me, sir.'

'Indeed. Good idea. Where are we at with the investigation?'

Danny took his time and carefully outlined each of the individual strands of enquiry that would make up his investigation strategy.

After he had finished speaking, the chief said, 'Pam Stringer seemed very adamant that her former daughter-in-law, Rhea, would be behind all this – and motivated by money. What's your opinion?'

'As I've just outlined, all associates and family will be looked at in detail. Mrs Stringer expressed a similar opinion to me yesterday when we met. I'll make sure that Gary's ex-wife will be the subject of a full inquiry.'

'That's good to hear, Danny. We ignore family dynamics at our peril.'

'I have to keep an open mind to every possibility, sir.'

Renshaw then waved his hand in a dismissive manner and said, 'I know that's what you think I want to hear, but what are your gut instincts telling you?'

Danny was thoughtful for a moment. 'If I were a betting man, which I'm not, my money would be on this being a burglary that Gary unwittingly stumbled upon. A simple –

and tragic – case of being in the wrong place at the wrong time.'

The chief nodded. 'I tend to agree, although what the hell is there at a pesticide factory that's so valuable this person decided he needed the insurance of a shotgun to steal it – well, that beggars belief.'

'We're working with the factory management to ascertain exactly what's been stolen. There's a hold-up, unfortunately, because of their slapdash method of stock keeping.'

Jack Renshaw glanced at his watch and saw that his other meeting would need to start in a few minutes' time. He said, 'It sounds like you've got everything covered, Danny. I want you to keep me apprised of all developments. If you can't get hold of Mark Slater, I want you to feel free to contact me direct. Understood?'

'Yes, sir.'

'Anything to report on your other current murder investigation – of the homeless man?'

'Ongoing, sir, and although we've all been focused on what happened yesterday, I'll ensure that both inquiries are investigated equally, sir.'

'I know the temptation would be to drop everything else and concentrate on your colleague's death, Danny, but we can't be seen to do that. I want progress on both investigations. Keep me informed.'

Danny knew that signalled the meeting was over, so he stood and said, 'Yes, sir.' But just as Danny reached the door, Renshaw added, 'Before you go.' Danny paused and turned to face the chief, who continued, 'I spoke with the parents yesterday about having a full police honours funeral for their son. Neither of them wanted that and have asked they be allowed to have a quiet service, just for close family, at St

Paul the Apostle church, in their home village of Choppington.'

The chief paused for a moment before adding, 'Obviously, I told them that we would respect whatever they wanted to do. They asked me how long it would be before the coroner would release their son's body. Can you speak to the coroner on my behalf and let the parents know as to when that's likely to be, please, Danny?'

'No problem, sir. It might not be for quite a while. But I'll keep Mr and Mrs Stringer informed.'

Renshaw said, 'Thank you. One last thing, I'm seeing DC Jagvir Singh tomorrow to inform him of his promotion to detective sergeant. Tell him to be here, suited and booted, at eleven o'clock.'

And with that, Danny really was dismissed.

17

8.00 p.m., 23 July 1991
MCIU Offices, Mansfield, Nottinghamshire

It had been another long day. The second full day of the inquiry into the murder of Sergeant Stringer and Danny wanted to hear first-hand from his two supervisors about what progress had been made.

He leaned back in his chair and said, 'As from tomorrow I'm going to split the teams. Rob, I want you to concentrate on the Terrence McAvoy investigation. I know you probably want to concentrate on Gary's murder, but we need to progress both, and I'm aware that Sara has been directly involved with all the enquiries at Addison's so far. Are you okay with that?'

Rob was thoughtful for a second and then said, 'You're right, I would prefer to work solely on finding Gary's killer, but I also appreciate we do have another ongoing investigation. I'll do whatever you ask me to do.'

'Thank you. As soon as you've established what enquiries have already been done and what still needs completing, we'll talk about manpower. I've been looking at it myself this afternoon, and I think the outstanding enquiries could be managed by a DS and four DCs. If you feel you need more than that, we'll have a conversation.'

Rob said, 'The house-to-house enquiries have now been completed, and there are no significant follow-ups. What will take time are the interviews with the golf club members and whatever Jag and Sam turned up from speaking with the homeless people in Sheffield city centre.'

Danny rested his elbows on the table. 'Speaking of Jag, he's seeing the chief tomorrow morning and will be promoted to sergeant. I want him to be the new DS on your team, Rob. I'll put Jeff Williams, Sam Blake, Simon Paine and Jane Pope with you to start with.'

'Okay, boss.'

Now Danny turned to Sara and said, 'The remaining staff will be working with you, Sara. I know that Tim and his team haven't found anything of forensic significance inside the factory, so there are no follow-up enquiries to be done there, but I'm conscious there are still a lot of people to be seen at the factory and to complete the house-to-house enquiries at Shireoaks. Please use the two sections of SOU at your disposal to get a grip of those. They are very experienced, and their sergeants know exactly what is required.'

'Will do, sir.'

'That will free up your staff to concentrate on speaking to the factory employees. Any progress on what was stolen yet?'

'Vanessa Symonds has given me a list of eleven different

chemicals that have been delivered and partially used. I'm hoping that, by tomorrow morning, she'll be able to tell me exactly what's missing.'

'Chase her first thing tomorrow,' Danny said firmly. 'We need that information. What sort of chemicals are we talking about?'

She glanced at her notepad. 'It ranges from glyphosate, acephate, metaldehyde and various types of acid. I've never heard of most of them.'

'Right,' said Danny. 'And how are Glen and Ray getting on with the ex-wife?'

'Rhea Stringer has a cast-iron alibi for the night of the murder. She has a new boyfriend who confirmed she spent the night with him at a hotel in Buxton, Derbyshire. The hotel CCTV has been checked, and the two of them are seen booking in at six o'clock the evening before, and she doesn't leave the hotel until ten o'clock the following morning.'

'Why a hotel?'

'The boyfriend is married but separated. He told Glen Lorimar that it's a precaution because he doesn't want to risk messing up the divorce process by being accused of adultery at this late stage.'

Danny let out an exasperated sigh. 'Are they checking her known associates to see if it's possible she arranged everything and conveniently used the hotel stay for an alibi?'

'They're doing just that, boss. I know they were thinking along similar lines. It's still a work in progress. It's a similar situation with Fran. She's researching Sergeant Stringer's previous arrest history, trying to ascertain if he made any significant enemies during work hours. She hasn't found anything of note so far, but after liaising with our complaints department, we can scratch that line of enquiry. The sergeant hasn't had a complaint from a member of the public for over five years.'

'One last thought, Sara. I'm conscious that different officers are involved in different investigations, and these should be linked so they can cross-check results. You've got Fran looking at Sergeant Stringer's work history and people he may have crossed paths with. Part of her brief was to cross-check any names that come up against shotgun licensing. Nigel is looking at the type of shotgun ammunition and anything he can reveal about the type of shotgun used. Part of his brief was to check on any recent burglaries where shotguns have been stolen. I'm not sure who you've allocated to check on the recently sacked staff at Addison's, or the list their security provided of employees they have petty-pilfering concerns over. That list of names should also be cross-checked with shotgun licensing. You need to keep a grip of those three lines of enquiry and ensure they're all tied together in a cohesive way. We don't want anyone slipping through the cracks because one detective thought that person had already been cleared by another detective. Does that make sense?'

'Absolutely, sir,' Sara said smartly. 'I'll get a grip of that. I'll make Nigel the point of reference for all shotgun-licensing enquiries. That will ensure continuity.'

'Okay, good. I want you to both brief your teams as to who's going to be involved with what. I want everybody back on duty at six o'clock tomorrow morning. Rob, before you leave for home, have a quiet word with Jag about his appointment with the chief constable tomorrow morning. Tell him, from me, to wear his best suit and for God's sake not to be late.' Danny smiled. 'Oh, and pass on my congratulations.'

18

8.45 p.m., 23 July 1991
Oakmere Park Golf Club, Oaks Lane, Oxton,
Nottinghamshire

He had waited patiently in his van for over an hour. Watching golfers walk from the clubhouse back to their cars. Most were in good spirits as they discussed the merits, or otherwise, of their golf.

None of them paid any attention to the hulking figure sitting alone in his van.

He had chosen this location carefully. Although there were private members at Oakmere Park, the driving range was open to the public, and the car park was accessible to non-members. On the many visits he had made to recce the location, he had never seen any security personnel, and he knew the lighting was well below standard.

He also knew that his target regularly visited the driving

range after work, just so he could spend thirty minutes smashing white golf balls aimlessly down the range before driving to his home in the nearby village of Halam.

He had watched Sir Anthony Pemberton's grey Jaguar XJ40 sweep into the car park thirty minutes ago. He'd smiled as he saw the silver-haired businessman get out of his luxury saloon and retrieve his golf clubs from the boot.

Dusk was already closing in, so he knew Sir Anthony wasn't there to play a full round. He kept watching and saw his target make his way onto the driving range.

As the car park emptied, he manoeuvred his white van until it was parked directly beside the Jaguar.

By the time he saw Sir Anthony making his way back to his car, there were only five vehicles left in the car park. Twilight was turning to night, and the few substandard lights that illuminated the car park had come on automatically.

Both the Jaguar and his white van were parked in one of the many deep shadows of the car park. He silently eased open the driver's door of his van and slipped out of the vehicle. As soon as he heard the boot of the Jaguar close, he stepped out from behind the van and stood immediately behind the ageing businessman.

He could see the man fumbling with the car keys. Just as his target placed the key in the driver's door lock, he made his move, stepping forward a final pace and smashing the heavy wrench into the back of the man's head.

The blow wasn't enough to kill, but it did render his victim instantly unconscious. Having incapacitated the old man, he scanned the car park and was relieved to see it was still empty.

He opened the back doors of the van, lifted Sir Anthony

off the floor and threw him in. Climbing in after him, he deftly secured the old man's wrists with cable ties. He picked up a length of oily rag from the van floor and tied it around the man's face so it covered his mouth. This would effectively drown out any screams, if he regained consciousness before they arrived at the place where he was to be held.

But as he climbed back out of the van and locked the back doors, he could already hear low moans and groans coming from the stricken man.

He smiled when he saw the keys for the Jaguar were still in the driver's door.

Leaving the keys where they were, he started the engine of his van and drove it slowly out of the car park.

His planned abduction of Sir Anthony Pemberton, the CEO of the global Future Visions Pharmaceuticals, had gone like clockwork, and it was now time to start his mission in earnest.

Very soon the entire world would be made aware of and understand the dreadful wrong that this man, and others, had allowed to happen.

19

5.30 a.m., 24 July 1991
Woodland near Welbeck, Nottinghamshire

Sir Anthony Pemberton carefully touched the back of his head and winced as a bolt of pain shot through his entire body. There was huge swelling there and a deep cut that had started to scab over.

Whoever had hit him had meant business. The last thing he could remember was slipping his car keys into the driver's door.

Now, as he sat quietly in the darkness, he tried to take in his surroundings.

He could just make out the faintest showing of light coming from one direction, but it looked a long way away. As his eyes became accustomed to the dim light, he realised he was in some kind of tunnel. The floor was made of grey flag-stones, and the arched walls had been constructed with red brick. These were not small tunnels. The width looked to be around eight feet and the height possibly as high as nine. It was hard to estimate given his sitting position and the dim light. His hands were still bound with a plastic cable tie, but at least they were in front of him, so it wasn't too uncomfortable.

'Help,' he shouted. 'Help! Can anybody hear me?'

His shouts reverberated down the long tunnel, and then there was silence. The effort of shouting had caused the pain in his head to increase and pulse through his brain, so he didn't shout again.

Instead, he sat quietly and listened. The only sounds he could hear were the constant dripping of water and a scurrying noise that emanated from the darkest end of the tunnel. He tried not to imagine what horror was causing that sound.

It was obvious to him that wherever this tunnel was, it had long been abandoned.

He reached out with his bound hands and could feel that he had been left sitting in a small wire cage, which had been somehow bolted into the brick wall of the tunnel. The cage was just high enough for him to sit up straight, and wide enough for him to have his legs out in front of him, although he had to slightly bend them, drawing his knees up towards his chest to fit. It wasn't an uncomfortable position to remain in, but the cold from the stone floor was starting to seep through his suit trousers, and he could feel himself starting to shiver.

Using the tips of his fingers, he felt around the cage until he found the door. Running his fingers around the edge of the cage door, he located a heavy padlock that was being used to secure the bolt.

Suddenly, he heard footsteps approaching from the end of the tunnel that offered the meagre light in the distance.

He could see torchlight flashing across the arched walls and the roof of the tunnel.

Ignoring the pain he knew it would cause, he bellowed at the top of his voice, 'Help me!'

The bright white light that had been bouncing off the walls was now shining directly in his face, blinding him. He heard something metallic being placed on the floor beside the cage, and he squinted to see what it was.

As his vision calmed down again and became accustomed to the light, he could see the object was in fact a metal storm lantern, which now illuminated the immediate area, showing the extent of the tunnel, which disappeared into the distance in both directions. The harsh torchlight was then switched off, and Anthony looked up through the cage's wire mesh to get a first glimpse of his captor.

What he saw was nothing short of terrifying.

A huge man wearing what looked like hooded blue overalls, heavy boots and a gas mask, which looked like it had last seen service in the Second World War, stood in stony silence in front of the cage. He could hear the man's heavy breaths as he drew air in through the mask's filter.

Recovering slightly from his shock at seeing such a horrific figure, Sir Anthony said, 'What the hell are you doing? Why have you brought me here?'

The big man said nothing and unlocked the padlock on the cage door. Fearing more violence, Sir Anthony shuffled backwards deeper into the cage to try to put any distance he could between himself and his captor.

He watched as the man placed a packet of digestive

biscuits and a plastic bottle of water inside the cage before closing the door and replacing the padlock.

The man slipped two thumbs under his mask and lifted it slightly off his face so he could speak.

He squatted down until he was at eye level with his captive and growled, 'Eat and drink something. I'm not going to keep you here long.'

'Who are you?' Sir Anthony said. 'What's this all about? Is it money you want?'

The man stood up and said, 'I don't want anything from you. You'll know everything there is to know before you leave here. Make the water last; you won't be getting any more.'

Sir Anthony watched as the man picked up the storm lantern. As the lantern was raised, he caught a glimpse of five or six identical cages, lined up next to his own, before the light was extinguished.

As his captor switched on the blinding white light of the other torch and started to walk away, Sir Anthony shouted after him, 'You can't do this to me! Let me go this instant!'

The man turned and walked back a few paces, then growled through the gas mask, 'You can shout all you want. Nobody's going to hear you down here.'

20

10.00 a.m., 24 July 1991
Force Headquarters, Nottinghamshire

D
anny cut a worried figure as he said, 'I know the chief's pushing for a quick result, and it's still early days, but I'm worried sick at the lack of progress we're making on both murder inquiries.'

Mark Slater steepled his fingers below his chin and said, 'Haven't you got anything I can take to the chief?'

'I think you need to tell him how it is,' Danny said. 'After hours of hard work, we've almost exhausted the house-to-house enquiries at Shireoaks and the interviews with staff at the factory.'

'Didn't the press appeal turn up anything?'

Danny shook his head. 'We're getting nothing coming in at all from that. I think one of the problems is that Shireoaks is such a small, out-of-the-way place. Nobody really has any reason to pass through it. Unless you live there, there isn't much reason to visit. I've put a team on researching previous industrial burglary offences in that area, to see if we can link anything to the Addison's burglary. I've already extended that enquiry across the border into South Yorkshire, and we still haven't uncovered anything useful.'

'What about this vehicle sighted on the factory CCTV? I know you had high hopes for that.'

'Unfortunately, although we can identify the make and model, there's nothing on the images we have that make the vehicle identifiable. You wouldn't believe the number of white Ford Escort vans registered in this county alone; it's staggering. Unless we can narrow the search down considerably, it just isn't cost effective to even start on that avenue.'

'Okay.' Mark sighed. 'Do we know what was stolen in the burglary at Addison's yet?'

'DI Lacey received a telephone call late last night. It was from Vanessa Symonds, the Addison's company secretary. The only stock she can find that's unaccounted for is a substantial amount of sulphuric acid.'

Mark Slater raised his eyebrows. 'That sounds pretty significant. Exactly how much is substantial?'

'They are still working to confirm that it's actually missing and, if it is, exactly how much has been stolen.'

Now Mark really did look puzzled. 'That sounds strange. Who steals sulphuric acid?'

'Sara Lacey has already stressed that point to Ms Symonds and asked her to establish the exact amount that's missing as quickly as she can. Apparently there's several possibilities. That the acid has been stored in the wrong location, or it could have been delivered to the wrong warehouse. It's a bit of a logistical nightmare, to be honest, but DI Lacey has got the matter under control. Which means we should have a definitive answer very soon.'

'Good,' said Mark. 'And have you instigated enquiries about this type of acid?'

'We have. I don't understand why anyone would want that amount of sulphuric acid. There's certainly no resale market for chemicals in general, let alone something as dangerous as acid.'

'And have you made any progress on the McAvoy investigation?'

Again, Danny shook his head. 'We're rapidly running out of leads. All the members at the golf club have now been interviewed. Nobody has seen or heard anything of interest. The few houses on Windmill Lane, the road that leads to the golf course, have all been visited and the residents spoken to. Again, nothing of note. The enquiries we carried out earlier with South Yorkshire police have confirmed that Terrence McAvoy was a rough sleeper who frequented various locations in Sheffield city centre. We've now obtained a witness statement from another rough sleeper, who last saw McAvoy on the night of thirteenth July.'

'Was that in Sheffield?'

'Yes, sir. McAvoy was seen walking towards an industrial estate on the edge of the city, at about ten o'clock that night. McAvoy even spoke to our witness, saying he was moving out of the city centre because he'd had some trouble with young lads, who kept having a go at him.'

'Well, that does sound promising. Did this witness say anything else?'

'Only that McAvoy seemed okay and that he was pushing his usual shopping trolley and had his small dog with him.

They didn't talk for long because the weather was rotten that night, and neither of them wanted to get wet through.'

'That's something I can tell the chief, at least. I take it you're following that lead up?'

'DS Singh and DC Blake are returning to Sheffield today and will be visiting premises on the industrial estate to try to establish if anyone remembers evidence of a rough sleeper being in that area. It's a long shot, but right now we haven't got much else to go on.'

'Okay, Danny. I know everyone's working flat out. The chief has asked me to tell you that he's arranged another press appeal for the Sergeant Stringer investigation this afternoon.'

'That soon?'

'Apparently, the press has been bombarding the switchboard with calls for an update. It's always a pain once the national media get involved. We must give them something, or they start making their own crap up.'

Danny couldn't help but let out a sigh. 'What time do you want me back here?'

Mark Slater picked up on Danny's frustration. 'No need for you to be here in person, Danny. Send me over a brief report highlighting what you want to tell them, and I'll do the appeal with the press liaison officer. I know you've already got your hands full trying to drive the two investigations forward. I just hope we can get a breakthrough on one or both of them soon.'

Danny was thoughtful and then said, 'Thanks for taking that load off my shoulders. I'll prepare something for the press appeal and get it to your office before two o'clock.' He paused before adding, 'I just pray that breakthrough you want doesn't arrive because we find another poor soul like

McAvoy. I have a nasty feeling we haven't heard the last of the person responsible for that man's murder.'

Slater's face showed that he shared Danny's concern. 'I bloody well hope not. I can just imagine what the press would make of that. It doesn't bear thinking about.'

21

10.00 a.m., 24 July 1991
Southwell Police Station, Nottinghamshire

Sergeant Louise Causer was checking the last of the crime files submitted by her shift. She had used the quiet early morning shift to catch up on all the onerous paperwork generated by the hard-working officers of her new section.

As a newly promoted sergeant she understood the importance of keeping on top of her shift's paperwork, as it helped to keep them motivated and enabled them to progress with their work.

She had just placed her pen on the desk when she heard a woman's voice shout, 'Hello.' It was coming from the front counter area. Aware that she was the only officer still in the small police station, she walked from her office to the main entrance to see who was there.

Standing on the other side of the glass hatch was a slim, smart woman who looked to be in her late sixties, early seventies. She was wearing what appeared to be a mink fur coat, over a powder blue Chanel two-piece suit.

Sergeant Causer slid back the glass and said, 'Can I help you, madam?'

The woman said in a soft, well-spoken voice, 'I do hope so, Sergeant. My husband didn't arrive home from work last night, and I fear something awful may have happened to him.'

'Has he ever stayed out all night before?'

'Not when he isn't away on business. He spent all day at his office yesterday, so I was expecting him home.'

'Okay.' Louise smiled in a way she hoped was reassuring. 'There could be any number of reasons why he didn't arrive home as expected, and most of them aren't going to be bad news, so try not to worry. What's your husband's name?'

'Sir Anthony Pemberton. We live at Greystone Lodge on Church Lane at Halam.'

'Thank you. And how old is Sir Anthony?'

'He'll be seventy-one this year.'

'And you said he didn't come home from work. Where does he work?'

'He's the chief executive for Future Visions Pharmaceutical Company. He's been running their UK operation for the last twenty-one years. He's planning on retiring later this year, so he's been spending a lot of extra hours at work, trying to ensure a smooth handover to his successor.'

'I'm sorry I haven't heard of Future Visions,' Louise said. 'Where are they based?'

'The head offices and main laboratories are in Beeston. My husband commutes every day.'

'Does he drive himself?'

'Yes. He drives a grey Jaguar. The registration number is 481 AWP. You see, his middle name is William; it's a personalised plate, which I bought for him years ago.'

'Have you called his office today?'

'I phoned first thing this morning and spoke with his secretary, Moira. She told me that Anthony was still in a meeting with Jurgen Hauptmann when she left at six o'clock last night. Worryingly, she also told me that his car wasn't there when she arrived this morning.'

'Who's Jurgen Hauptmann?'

'He's currently head of Research but is going to be Anthony's successor as CEO.'

Sergeant Causer tried to phrase her next question as tactfully as possible. 'Does your husband ever go anywhere else after work before coming home?'

Lady Pemberton was thoughtful for a moment, then said, 'The only place he's likely to go is his golf club.'

'Which club is that?'

'Oh.' The woman paused. 'The name of it escapes me, but I know it's near Oxton village. You see, I can't abide the wretched game.'

Louise nodded in sympathy. 'Let me have your contact details, and I'll start making some general enquiries. Have you called any of your husband's friends or business acquaintances yet?'

She shook her head gently and said, 'I wasn't sure what to do for the best. Obviously, I'm extremely worried. That's why I've come to you people for help, but the last thing I want is to embarrass Anthony in front of his friends or business associates. As you said earlier, there could be any number of reasons why he didn't come home last night.'

Sergeant Causer wanted to reassure the woman; she was obviously worried. 'First of all,' she said, 'I'll make all the usual enquiries with hospitals and with our traffic department, just to make sure he hasn't been involved in a car accident. I'll also put out an observations request that will go to all officers on patrol to look out for his Jaguar. Then I'll drive out to the golf course at Oxton myself, to see if he called in there last night.'

'Thank you. That's very kind. Is there anything you want me to do in the meantime?'

'I think you should go home and wait by the telephone. By the time you get home, he might already be there and wondering where you are. If he is, just call the police station and let me know he's back safe and sound. My name's Sergeant Louise Causer.'

'Thank you, Sergeant Causer. Do you really think he's okay?'

'I'm sure he's fine. You wait and see, there'll be a perfectly good reason behind this, so try not to worry. I'll be in touch as soon as I know anything.'

Despite the confidence of her words, as she watched Lady Pemberton leave the police station and walk slowly towards her black Mercedes saloon, Louise Causer was deeply worried.

Something didn't sound right at all. A seventy-year-old, highly successful and respected knight of the realm didn't disappear into thin air.

However, as a newly promoted sergeant, the last thing she needed was to earn herself a reputation as a panic merchant, so she determined to make the phone calls, put the observations out and visit the golf course herself – before she even thought about involving CID.

22

11.30 a.m., 24 July 1991
Oakmere Park Golf Club, Oaks Lane, Oxton,
Nottinghamshire

The first thing Sergeant Louise Causer saw as she drove into the car park at Oakmere was the Jaguar. She read the registration plate with mounting horror: 481 AWP.

She parked next to the sleek grey car and got out. She tried the doors and the boot and found the car was secure.

With her concerns growing closer to dread by the second, she walked to the pro shop.

'My name's Sergeant Causer, from Southwell police station. I'm looking for the club professional?'

The tall, athletic man behind the counter stood up and said, 'That's me, Graeme Checkley. What can I help you with?

'There's a Jaguar parked in the car park. Do you know who owns it?'

'If it's the grey XJ40, that belongs to Sir Anthony Pemberton. He's a member here.'

'Is he out on the course?'

'No. I haven't seen him today. He was here last night. He came in and got a token to get a basket of balls for the driving range. He wasn't here that long. I saw him leave the range at around nine o'clock. I remember because he was one of the last people here.' He paused before saying in a conspiratorial whisper, 'You know what it's like. I start work every morning at seven thirty, so by the time it gets round to nine o'clock at night I just want everyone to sod off so I can go home.'

'Long days for you,' Louise agreed. 'Was Sir Anthony with anybody else last night?'

'No, I don't think so. I didn't see him with anyone. I was a bit surprised when the car was still here when I left.'

'Didn't you think that was strange?'

'To be honest, I just thought he'd seen somebody he knew and gone for a quick drink in the clubhouse bar. That's what tends to happen, and when the car was still here when I arrived this morning, I thought he probably had one too many drinks and either got a lift or a taxi home.'

There was a long pause, and Louise looked hard at him. 'Go on,' she said.

'When I saw the car keys still in the door this morning,' he told her, 'I did think to myself the old fellow must have been very tipsy.'

Sergeant Causer echoed his words. 'The car keys were still in the driver's door?'

'Yeah. The car was locked, but the silly sod had left the keys in the lock.'

'Where are they now?'

'I've given them to the club captain this morning, for safe keeping. That's an expensive car.'

'Is the captain still around?'

'He's out on the course. He had a four-ball booked for a ten o'clock tee time this morning. He won't get back here until two or three o'clock this afternoon.'

'Are there any security cameras that cover the car park?'

'We only have one security camera, and I'm responsible for it. The monitor's in the office. It's recording now; you can have a look at what it shows.'

'Thanks. Does your system record images?'

'Only for twenty-four hours, then it records over the top.'

'What time does it start to record over the top of yesterday's images?'

'Three o'clock, every afternoon.'

'So last night's recording will still be on the tape?'

Graeme nodded. 'It should be; the system changes automatically unless I stop it manually.'

Sergeant Causer followed him into the office and saw the small monitor. The images were of very low quality, but she could still make out the front and the passenger side of the Jaguar.

'Can we view the recording on this monitor?'

'Yeah. No problem. What do you want to look at?'

'You said Sir Anthony left the range around nine o'clock, so let's see if we can see him walking back to his car. Even if he went for a drink, he surely would have put his golf clubs back in the car first.'

As Graeme rewound the tape, he said, 'He may have

taken the clubs back; sometimes the members just leave them outside the clubhouse.'

It took almost five minutes to rewind to the relevant time. As they both stared intently at the grainy images of the car park, Graeme suddenly said, 'That's Sir Anthony. He's taking his clubs back to his car by the look of it. Looks like you were right; he's going to put his clubs away first.'

The ghostly black-and-white image showed the old man raise the boot and replace the golf clubs before walking around to the far side of the car. A large dark shape appeared behind him, poised as if apparently watching over him.

Sergeant Causer exclaimed, 'Whoa! Did you see that?'

'Good grief.' Graeme nodded. 'That bloke just cracked him over the head.'

As they watched, they could just make out the lower half of a white van leaving the car park almost immediately after the assault.

'Do you recognise that van, Graeme?'

The pro shook his head. 'Can't say I do. I don't think it's one of our regulars. The driving range is open to the public, so we do get all sorts here.'

'And when you left shortly after this,' Louise said, 'there was no sign of Sir Anthony in the car park?'

'No.' Graeme had a worried, horrified expression on his face. 'Where do you think he went after he was clobbered like that?'

'I don't know, but I'm going to need to seize this tape. Does that cause you any problems?'

'Not at all. We keep a couple of spare tapes in case they're needed. I can just swap them over. Can I ask, what the hell's going on?'

'Let's just say I'm more than a little worried about Sir Anthony. Is there anybody working in the clubhouse yet?'

'Yeah. Natalie's just opening the bar.'

'Would she have been working last night?'

'She was on duty until closing time, around eleven o'clock.'

'Okay. I'll need to have a chat with her.'

'Follow me,' Graeme said. 'I'll introduce you.'

23

12.30 p.m., 24 July 1991
Crown Industrial Estate, Sheffield, South Yorkshire

Jag Singh and Sam Blake walked into the reception area of yet another small business on the huge industrial estate less than a mile from Sheffield city centre.

This was the industrial estate where a witness had seen the murder victim Terrence McAvoy shortly before he died.

Jag tapped on the glass partition that separated the public from the lone secretary in the reception area.

The young woman stopped typing, walked to the counter, slid the glass partition back and said, 'Can I help you?'

Jag showed his identification and said, 'I'm Detective Sergeant Singh, and this is DC Blake; we're from Nottinghamshire CID.' He paused very briefly. After seeing the chief constable at ten o'clock that morning to get promoted, before driving to Sheffield to resume enquiries, it still felt strange to Jag to introduce himself in that way. 'We're visiting every unit on the industrial estate,' he went on, 'to see if anyone remembers seeing a homeless man sleeping in or near the premises.'

The woman instantly became quite animated. 'We had one of the scruffy gits sleeping here not so long ago.'

'How long ago?'

'I don't know. About ten or twelve days ago, I reckon. Dave in packing will know for sure, because he had to get rid of all the shit – I mean rubbish – the dirty sod left behind.'

'You didn't see the person yourself, then?'

'No. There was no one here that morning, but he'd left all his crap in the doorway. It reeked of something unmentionable, if you know what I mean.'

'Has this happened before?'

'Not here. I've seen homeless people on the estate before but never down this part.'

Sam said, 'What had been left in the doorway?'

'Old blankets, a filthy duvet and cardboard on the floor. A load of tat in a shopping trolley.' The young woman started to laugh. 'I remember Dave getting the fright of his life when he tried to shift the blankets, because there was a little dog underneath, all curled up. Dave thought it was a big rat and nearly crapped himself.'

Jag tried to keep his face neutral. 'Is Dave around this afternoon?' he said. 'Can we talk to him?'

'Yeah, he's about, and I don't suppose he's rushed off his feet. Things are a bit quiet right now. Just a sec.'

The woman disappeared through a door at the rear of reception, returning a short time later with a lad who looked to be around eighteen. He appeared nervous at the prospect of talking to two detectives and constantly picked at the acne on his face.

'Hello, Dave,' Jag said. 'Can you tell me about this stuff you had to move from the doorway?'

A puzzled expression descended over Dave's spotty face, and the secretary said abruptly, 'What the tramp left behind, you dope. I told you that's what they want to ask you about.'

Dave responded slowly. 'Oh, that stuff,' he said, eventually catching on. 'Yeah, I had to shift it all. I dumped it in the skip round the back.'

'Is the skip still there?'

'Yeah. It only gets emptied once a month. There's still not much in it yet.'

'And this young lady tells me you had a bit of a fright when you were shifting it?'

A broad grin appeared on Dave's face, and he coloured up a little. 'Yeah. There was a bloody dog under the blankets.' He laughed at the memory. 'I thought it was a massive rat.'

'Obviously you didn't put the dog in the skip, Dave. What did you do with it?'

Before Dave could speak, the secretary interrupted. 'I called the council dog warden. He came and took it away. I bet the poor little thing's been put down by now. They only keep them for seven days, and I bet the scruffy git who left it here won't have gone to pick it up. I feel quite sad about that poor little dog.'

Jag looked at her in surprise. He found it odd that she appeared to show far more compassion towards the small dog than she did for the unfortunate homeless person who had been forced to take shelter in the doorway.

Ignoring those negative feelings, he asked her, 'Do you have any CCTV covering the unit? Maybe as a deterrent to any would-be burglars.'

'There's nothing as fancy as that. We have an old burglar alarm, but we only manufacture plastic screw tops for water bottles. Nobody's interested in stealing stuff like that. The only thing of any value in this place is the computer I use in the office.'

Jag nodded, and then Sam spoke directly to Dave. 'Can you show me the stuff you chucked in the skip?'

'Yeah, of course.'

As the two detectives were following Dave to the back yard, Jag turned to the secretary and said, 'Can you let me have the telephone number for the council dog warden you called?'

'Of course, no problem.'

The two detectives surveyed the rubbish in the bottom of the industrial-size skip; the stench from the duvet in the corner was overpowering.

Jag turned to Sam and said, 'I'm not pulling rank, mate, but I've got my best suit on today. Can you fish that out?'

Sam grimaced, but before he could answer, Dave clambered into the skip and retrieved the old duvet, asking eagerly, 'Where do you want it, Detective?'

Jag replied, 'Just spread it out on the car park so we can see it all, thanks.'

As Dave willingly did as he was asked, Sam whispered, 'Are we really going to take this as an exhibit?'

Jag nodded. 'Get one of the big paper sacks from the boot. Too right we're taking it.'

24

1.00 p.m., 24 July 1991
Southwell Police Station, Nottinghamshire

Sergeant Louise Causer was deeply concerned about the assault she had witnessed on the blurry video recording. She now feared that Sir Anthony Pemberton wasn't just a missing person. There was a real possibility that he had been assaulted and abducted.

Her conversation with Natalie in the clubhouse bar had revealed that Sir Anthony hadn't been in for a drink the night before, which meant he had never made it to the clubhouse after the assault. Which meant it was a mystery: it appeared he had simply vanished after being struck by the big, shadowy man in the car park.

The other thing that really concerned her was the brief sighting of the small white van leaving the car park immediately after the assault. She had read all the latest bulletins on the unsolved murder of her off-duty colleague at Shireoaks, and like every other officer on the force, she understood a small white van was believed to have been involved in that offence.

She now had a decision to make: she had to inform the CID about the abduction. Her dilemma was, did she call the local CID at Newark, or involve the MCIU because of the involvement of the small white van?

She grabbed the telephone and dialled a number. It was answered on the second ring.

'MCIU, DC Jefferies. How can I help?'

Sergeant Causer identified herself and quickly outlined the circumstances of the disappearance of Sir Anthony Pemberton before saying, 'The reason I've called your office instead of the local CID is because a small white van, one that looks like a Ford Escort, was seen leaving the car park immediately after Sir Anthony was assaulted. When that van disappeared, so did Sir Anthony.'

Fran Jefferies said, 'And you think he was somehow bundled into this van?'

'The quality of the video recording is awful, but the assault is quite clear. There's no real view of the van until it drives away, because it's parked up on the far side of Sir Anthony's Jaguar. So there's no way you can see if he's been shoved in the back of the van or not. But that's the most likely explanation.'

'Can you see the van's registration plate?'

'No.'

'Can you hold the line one second?'

Sergeant Causer chewed her bottom lip as she waited for the detective to return to the phone. After a few minutes she heard her approaching, and then the detective said, 'Sergeant Causer?'

'I'm still here.'

'I've just spoken to DCI Flint, and he's sending somebody out to see you at Southwell police station. He's asked me to ask if you've seized the video tape.'

'Yes. I've got it here.'

'Do you have the means of playing it at the police station so our detectives can view it when they get there?'

'We've got a video recorder linked to the TV in the refreshment room. So I should be able to play it on that.'

'Great. They'll be with you in about half an hour.'

Sergeant Causer replaced the phone and leaned back in her chair. She knew she'd made the right call. If she hadn't, the MCIU wouldn't have bothered driving out to Southwell. She was tempted to call Lady Pemberton, as she thought the old woman must be going out of her mind with worry, but she decided she should hold off until she had spoken to the MCIU detectives. After all, she might seem like a smart, demure old lady, but she could also be behind the assault and the abduction. Louise would let the detectives decide how they wanted to play it.

25

Rob Buxton drove into the car park at Southwell police station. As he stopped the car, he turned to DC Jane Pope and said, 'It's a few years since I was at this nick.'

'Did you work here?'

'When I first transferred down from South Yorkshire, I was stationed here as a sergeant in uniform. It was a great little nick back then.'

Sergeant Causer was waiting for them when they walked into the main foyer. She had already tried the video recorder before the detectives arrived to make sure it worked.

Rob Buxton took out his warrant card and said, 'I'm DI Buxton; this is DC Pope. I take it you're Sergeant Causer?'

She nodded. 'Yes, sir. I took a report this morning from

Lady Pemberton that her husband, Sir Anthony Pemberton, hadn't come home from work last night, and she was worried because it was so out of character. I took initial details for a missing from home report and started a few general telephone enquiries before I went to the golf course.'

Rob said, 'Why visit the golf course?'

'That was Lady Pemberton's idea. She told me that her husband sometimes called in there on his way home from work.'

'Okay, and what did you find out there that's caused you to have major concerns?'

'It might be quicker if you watch the video recording from the security camera that covers the golf course car park.'

'Right you are,' Rob said. 'Let's do that.'

She pressed play, and the grainy black-and-white images came on the television.

She pointed to the screen and said, 'That's Sir Anthony walking back towards his car.'

Jane Pope asked, 'How do you know that's him?'

'The golf pro at the club, Graeme Checkley, identified him to me earlier when I first viewed the tape. Keep watching as he moves from behind his car to the far side.'

Rob let out a low whistle and muttered, 'Jesus Christ,' as he saw the unknown man strike the old man over the head, knocking him down.

The tape continued until the lower half of the white van came into view briefly before disappearing again out of sight of the camera.

Rob said, 'Rewind to the van, can you?'

Sergeant Causer rewound the tape and then pressed play until the van came back into view.

Rob said, 'Pause it there, please.'

With the image of the van frozen, Rob stood and looked closely at the screen before saying, 'It's definitely a Ford Escort van. I take it this club pro didn't know the vehicle?'

Sergeant Causer shook her head. 'No. He said they get all sorts in there, as the driving range is open to the public.'

'Okay. Have you taken a statement from him yet?'

'No. I seized the tape, and I've exhibited that, but I wanted to report the possible abduction before I did anything else. I was worried that time could be of the essence.'

'Exactly right. Have you spoken to Lady Pemberton yet?'

'Not yet.'

'Good. Can you go back to the golf club and get statements from the club pro and anyone else who may have information. You mentioned that you became suspicious initially because the keys had been found still in the driver's door of the Jaguar. Have you got those now?'

'No. The keys were with the club captain for safe keeping, and he was out on the golf course this morning.'

'Okay. While you're at the golf club, I'll need you to seize the Jaguar car keys from him as well, as we'll need to recover the vehicle for a full forensic examination. We'll go and speak to Lady Pemberton and get a few more background details about her husband and his business interests. Do you have the missing person report to hand?'

Sergeant Causer handed over the handwritten document and said, 'She lives not far from here at Halam. The address is in the report, as is his workplace.'

Rob took the report and said, 'We'll see you back here at four o'clock. Sorry, I haven't asked you what shift you're working today.'

'I'm on the early turn. I should finish at two, but I'm okay to work a few hours overtime.'

'That would be a massive help. The van on the video might not be connected to the Sergeant Stringer investigation, but the assault and the abduction is serious enough for us to get involved initially. If it looks like the two offences aren't linked, we can always hand it over to the local CID later, and no harm done. Can I leave you to arrange a full lift for the Jaguar back to headquarters?'

'No problem, sir.'

'Thanks, and good work today.'

26

3.00 p.m., 24 July 1991
Ivy Lodge, Church Lane, Halam, Nottinghamshire

Rob looked down the driveway towards the large, detached house that sat in well-maintained gardens immediately adjacent to St Michael's Church.

He said, 'This is it, Ivy Lodge.'

Jane said, 'Might as well drive down to the house. The Merc's there, so she must be at home.'

Rob selected first gear and drove slowly onto the driveway, hearing the tyres crunch on the gravel.

As the two detectives got out, the front door was opened by an elderly woman who stood framed in the doorway, a fraught look on her face and her arms folded firmly across her chest.

She asked sharply, 'Can I help you people?'

Rob took out his warrant card as he approached. 'My name's Detective Inspector Buxton, and this is DC Pope. We're from the Major Crime Investigation Unit and would like to talk to you about the report you made to the police this morning, concerning your husband, Sir Anthony.'

Rob could see the colour drain from the woman, and he added hurriedly, 'We don't have any firm news, but we do need to talk to you urgently, as we have very real concerns about your husband's disappearance. May we come inside and talk?'

A look of relief flashed across the woman's features, and she said, 'Yes. Of course, come in.'

The two detectives followed her inside and were directed into one of the spacious reception rooms.

Lady Pemberton said, 'Please take a seat. What do you need to know?'

Rob said, 'Has your husband ever stayed out like this in the past?'

'Never. Only when he's away on business, but that's different. Whenever he's working from his office at Beeston, he always comes home at night.'

Jane said, 'What time would he normally get home?'

'Normally he's home for around six o'clock, but just lately he's been working long hours and hasn't been getting home until much later. He's retiring as chief executive of the company later this year, and he's ensuring everything about the business is in great shape for when he hands over. I have already told this to that police sergeant earlier.'

'I appreciate that, but I'd like to hear your information directly from you, Lady Pemberton. Does he know who will be taking his place when he retires?'

'The new CEO's going to be Jurgen Hauptmann. He's one

of the company's top scientists and currently head of Research, but he's no businessman. I think that's why Anthony's been doing so much work; he wants it to be a smooth transition when Jurgen eventually takes over.'

'You told our colleague this morning that Sir Anthony sometimes goes to a local golf club on his way home from work. How often does he do that?'

'Just lately, not very often at all. Do you know if he was there last night?'

'We believe so. Do you know who he would have met at the club?'

'I'm sorry. I haven't a clue. I never got involved with his friends at the golf club. I find most of them to be crashing bores.'

Rob asked, 'This is a standard question that we always ask, so please don't be alarmed. Does your husband have any enemies that you're aware of?'

'That's a ridiculous suggestion, Detective. He's a seventy-year-old businessman, not a member of the mafia.'

'He's also the head of a huge pharmaceutical company. Some people have strong views on pharmaceuticals. Are you aware of any threats your husband may have received?'

'No. There hasn't been anything like that, not to my knowledge anyway. I'm not sure he would say anything to me even if he had been threatened. He's not that sort of man. Anthony has a very stoic outlook on life.' She paused and then said, 'Have you found his car yet? I've been having this terrible vision of the car being upside down in a ditch somewhere. I've been worrying myself sick.'

'The car's been located at the golf club,' Rob said. 'We're currently trying to establish where Sir Anthony went after that. Who might he have got a lift with, do you know?'

'I'm sorry, I've no idea who might have given him a lift, or where else he would go.'

Jane said, 'Have you had any tradesmen working here at the house lately?'

'Not lately. The last person we had doing any work was a couple of years ago, when I upgraded the kitchen cabinets.'

'The gardens are beautiful.' Jane smiled. 'Do you look after them yourselves, or do you have a gardener to help?'

'Up until five years ago, we always used to do it ourselves. But as we both got older, the size of the task became too much for us. We've now hired a gardener, a lovely young man named John. He comes in twice a week and keeps the gardens beautifully.'

'What vehicle does John drive?'

'He's got a small van that he carries all his tools in.'

'What colour's the van?'

'Dark blue. Don't ask me what sort it is. I'm hopeless with that kind of thing.'

Rob said, 'My colleague here is going to take a quick written statement from you that covers the basics like when your husband left for work, and what his mood was like when he left. Is that okay?'

'That's fine. Anthony was always in good spirits when he left for work. He loved his job but was looking forward to handing over in the autumn so we could spend more time together. Do you think he's going to be all right?'

'I'm sure he's going to be okay,' Rob said gently. 'We're doing everything we can to locate him. Please try not to worry.'

27

8.00 p.m., 24 July 1991
MCIU Offices, Mansfield, Nottinghamshire

Danny had just finished debriefing the day's enquiries on both murder investigations and had returned to his office. He was about to put his jacket on ready for home, when Rob Buxton walked in.

'Have you got a minute, boss?'

'Is this about the Southwell job?'

'Yeah. It's a strange one, and if it's all right with you, I'd like to stick with it for at least one more day.'

Danny was thoughtful. 'I don't know, Rob. We've already got so much going on here, I don't know if we can afford to take on an abduction case as well. What are your main concerns?'

The experienced detective inspector shrugged and said, 'I can't put my finger on it exactly, but you know when a job seems bigger than it first appears – well, you get that feeling in your bones.'

Danny knew exactly what Rob was referring to. It was a feeling he had often experienced in the past and knew it was folly to ignore such instincts.

'Okay. I hear what you're saying, but I'm going to need a bit more than your gut feeling to keep you on that enquiry for another day. Talk to me.'

'Sir Anthony Pemberton is in his seventies and due to retire from his role as CEO of Future Visions later this year. He appears to have a perfectly happy marriage, yet for no apparent reason he's been assaulted and possibly abducted. The man has literally vanished into thin air.'

'I get all that, but the assault and even the abduction, if that's what it turns out to be, is a crime the local CID are more than capable of investigating.'

'You're always telling me that you don't do coincidences. Well, how about this for a series of coincidences. After the enquiries done by Jag and Sam today, we now have good reason to believe that Terrence McAvoy was abducted from Sheffield. Staff at that industrial unit found the shopping trolley with McAvoy's few possessions abandoned in the doorway of their premises. That's something he would never voluntarily leave behind. His tortured, acid-burned body is later found dumped on a golf course. A few days later a small white van is seen driving away from the scene where an off-duty police officer is murdered after disturbing a burglary. Although it hasn't yet been confirmed, the only thing believed stolen during that burglary is a large quantity of sulphuric acid. Then last night, at another golf course, Sir Anthony Pemberton was assaulted and abducted by a man using a small white van.'

Rob stopped talking and leaned back in his chair before adding, 'That's a few too many coincidences for this daft Yorkshire lad to accept, Danny.'

Danny was thoughtful for a few moments and then said, 'What do you still need to do?'

'We know that the last person to speak to Sir Anthony before his disappearance was a colleague at work. He was in a late meeting with his soon-to-be successor, Jurgen Hauptmann. I'd like to make enquiries at Future Visions at Beeston tomorrow morning and speak to Hauptmann to see if he can shed any light on who might want to do this to Sir Anthony. If I still haven't got anywhere after I've spoken to Hauptmann, I'll pass everything on to Newark CID to continue the investigation.'

'Okay.' Danny leaned back in his chair. 'I'm prepared to give you the benefit of the doubt. You and Jane can go to Beeston tomorrow and make your enquiries at the pharmaceutical company. I want you to keep me informed, one way or the other. I can't afford for you to be sidetracked from the two murder investigations we're already running. Is that understood?'

Rob grinned. 'Thanks, Danny. I won't spend any more time there than I need to.'

28

7.00 a.m., 25 July 1991
Future Visions Pharmaceutical Company, Beeston,
Nottinghamshire

Jurgen Hauptmann was feeling excited. Every day that passed meant he was another step closer to becoming the CEO of the company he had been employed by for over twenty years. He had joined Future Visions as a freshly qualified biochemist, with a top degree from the world-renowned Technical University of Munich, Germany.

A brilliant chemist, he had been awarded the Nobel Prize in Chemistry by the Royal Swedish Academy of Sciences over ten years ago, for the important work he had undertaken to identify the make-up of nucleic acids, specifically the determination of base sequences. The Academy of Sciences had recognised the significant value of this breakthrough in groundbreaking research into genetic profiling generally. The award made Hauptmann the second-youngest winner behind Frederic Joliot, who was just thirty-five years of age when he was awarded the prize in 1935.

The recognition and kudos the award gave Future Visions was the reason for Hauptmann's meteoric rise from scientific assistant to Dr Rebecca Haller to his current position as head of Research.

Even though his current role was extremely high status, he still yearned to be the top man in the UK operation of the company. He was desperate to become the new chief executive officer and to revel in the prestige of that position.

Jurgen Hauptmann was a man fuelled by his own giant ego.

He liked to be one of the first to arrive at the laboratories every day, and after the recent meetings he had held with Sir Anthony, there was a lot for him to understand before he took over the actual running of the laboratory operation.

Hauptmann was career obsessed and a single man. He never worried about the lengthy hours he spent at work. He preferred to spend his time at the laboratories rather than rattling around in the large house he owned on the outskirts of Nottingham.

He roared his silver Porsche 959 at high speed along the narrow country lanes that led to the sprawling Future Visions laboratories.

His familiarity with the route – he had driven along this road to work thousands of times – coupled with the knowledge that there would be very little traffic on the road at this time of day meant he was now driving way too fast.

As he steered the powerful sports car around one of the final bends, just before the laboratories came into view, he suddenly saw a small white van that had slewed sideways across the narrow lane, effectively blocking the road less than seventy-five yards ahead.

He slammed the gear stick into neutral and pressed both feet down on the clutch and brake pedal. He gripped the leather steering wheel tightly as the tyres locked with a loud screeching as the tyres skidded on the slightly damp tarmac. He grimaced as his Porsche continued to slide towards the stationary vehicle.

With less than a couple of yards to spare before it impacted the side of the van, the Porsche finally came to a shuddering stop.

A shaken but livid Hauptmann switched the ignition off. At over six feet tall, with long skinny limbs, it took him a moment to ease himself out of the compact, low-slung driver's seat.

He could feel his temper rising as he approached the van. 'You idiot!' he yelled. 'What the hell do you think you're playing at? You could have killed me!'

He yanked the door open and was shocked to find there was nobody in the vehicle. His anger rose even more when he realised his complaints had gone unheard.

Feeling more than a little frustrated and wondering how the hell he was going to manoeuvre around the obstruction to drive the short distance into work, he turned and stalked back to his car.

As he reached the vehicle, he heard a man's voice say, 'Jurgen Hauptmann?'

He spun around to see who had spoken his name.

The last thing he saw was a heavy wrench crashing down towards his head.

29

8.00 a.m., 25 July 1991
Future Visions Pharmaceutical Company, Beeston,
Nottinghamshire

J ane Pope stopped the CID car at the red and white drop barrier that formed the entrance to the Future Visions Pharmaceutical laboratories and waited for the security guard to approach the vehicle.

As the burly man stepped out of the gatehouse, casting a wary eye over the unfamiliar vehicle, Rob Buxton muttered, 'Bloody hell. I expected security to be tight here, but this all looks a bit extreme. Apart from the fact he isn't armed, this bloke's the size of a house and kitted out like a special forces soldier.'

Leaving the barrier down and blocking the entrance, the guard stood at the side of the vehicle and indicated for Jane to lower her window.

As she wound the window down, Rob took out his warrant card and said, 'I'm Detective Inspector Buxton, and this is DC Pope. We're from the Major Crime Investigation Unit. We need to speak with Jurgen Hauptmann.'

'What about?'

Rob said, 'We're investigating the sudden disappearance of the CEO of this company, Sir Anthony Pemberton, and we need to speak with Mr Hauptmann as a matter of urgency.'

A worried look descended on the security guard's face. 'The head of security is on his way,' he said. 'He's going to want to speak with you about that. Do you see the visitors car parking bays over by the fir trees?'

Jane replied, 'I see them.'

'Park over there, then come straight back here. Something strange is happening today, and what you've just told me about Sir Anthony tops it all off.'

The red and white barrier was raised, and Jane drove to the parking space the guard had indicated.

Rob said, 'That wasn't the reception I was expecting. Very weird.'

Jane replied, 'Something's going on. Did you see the worried look on that guy's face?'

As the two detectives walked back to the gatehouse, Rob said, 'Let's see what's up, shall we?'

30

8.20 a.m., 25 July 1991
Future Visions Pharmaceutical Company, Beeston,
Nottinghamshire

The security guard expertly stonewalled, blocking every question from the two detectives until his supervisor arrived.

The head of security, Alan Villiers, was a large man in every sense. Although in his late fifties, he still had a full head of thick, steel-grey hair. At six feet four inches tall and weighing just short of eighteen stone, Villiers was not a man to be messed with.

He walked into the gatehouse and said in a voice that carried a strong South African accent, 'I need to see your identification before we talk.'

Rob took out his warrant card and repeated what he'd said earlier to the guard. 'I'm Detective Inspector Buxton;

this is DC Pope. We're from the Major Crime Investigation Unit, and we're here to speak to Jurgen Hauptmann. Now what's the problem? Why all this cloak-and-dagger stuff?'

Villiers looked at the guard and said, 'You haven't told them what's going on?'

'No, sir. I thought it best to wait until you arrived.'

The head of security sighed and said, 'Okay. Go and do a perimeter check, Scott. Where's Gerry?'

'He's getting a brew. He'll be back soon.'

'Okay. Perimeter check, now.'

Appearing glad to be out of the gatehouse, the guard grabbed his heavy coat and went on his patrol. Rob got the sense he wouldn't want to be in Gerry's shoes when he returned.

Villiers looked at Rob and said, 'I thought you were here because of what's happened to Hauptmann. Not to speak to him.'

'What do you mean, because of what's happened to him?'

'We were all a bit shaken yesterday when word got out that Sir Anthony was missing.'

'Hang on a minute. How do you know he's missing?'

'His secretary, Moira, told me about the telephone call she'd received from his wife yesterday morning. I don't suppose I was the only one she told. Office gossip flies around a place like this in minutes. By home time last night, everyone here knew Sir Anthony was missing.'

'Okay, so what's happened to Hauptmann?' Rob said, wanting to get this conversation back on track.

'He's always at work for around seven o'clock every morning. The guards can set their watches by him arriving. He didn't show up today as normal. Then Scott, the guard you've just spoken to, arrived around seven thirty. He told the night-shift security guard, Gerry, that he thought he'd seen Hauptmann's silver Porsche in a ditch about a quarter of a mile down the lane.'

'Go on.'

'The two of them went out to investigate and did indeed find Hauptmann's Porsche in a ditch. There was no sign of Hauptmann with the vehicle.' The security chief paused and then said, 'And if that wasn't bad enough, the guards found a patch of blood on the road not far from where the car had gone in the ditch.'

'And they couldn't find Hauptmann? Do you think he was injured in the crash?'

Villiers had a worried expression on his face when he said, 'When they called me and told me what was happening, I instructed them to leave everything in situ, and to wait until I arrived before they did anything. They told me on the phone that the car wasn't badly damaged, that the keys were still in the ignition and that there was no sign of any blood inside the car.'

'Why didn't you call the police if you had concerns?' Rob said. 'I can see you're worried about something. Is it because your guards went inside the car and ignored your instruction?'

'It's worse than that, Detective. Initially, I did want to get here and see for myself what was happening, but my staff have royally fucked up this morning. They've gone way beyond ignoring my instructions. The idiots took it upon themselves to hook up the Porsche to their Land Rover and drag it out of the ditch. Then, to make matters worse, because the keys were still in the ignition, Gerry climbed in and drove it back here.'

Rob couldn't help but raise his eyebrows at that. 'Where's the car now?'

'I had it moved into the CEO's garage space so it's under cover in case it rains.'

Trying not to allow his anger at the guards' reckless actions to show, Rob said, 'Obviously, we would have preferred nobody to go inside the car and to leave it where it was, but it's happened now, and we can't turn the clock back. I'm still going to arrange for the vehicle to be towed to our headquarters for a full forensic examination. I'll need the details of the guard who got in and drove the car, as we may need to take samples and fingerprints for elimination purposes.'

'I can sort that. Don't worry, Detective. His name's Gerry Glazer, and I'll make sure he co-operates with you fully.'

'The other guard, Scott, looks quite young; is he new to the job?'

'He's been with us a few years; he just doesn't engage his brain as much as he should at times. The wages aren't the best, so it's hard to attract good-calibre personnel.'

'I take it you haven't yet notified the local police about the accident?'

'That was going to be my first call, but then you arrived, so I'm telling you rather than calling the local cops.'

'Don't worry,' Rob said. 'I'll call it in from here. If it is a road traffic accident, then potentially Hauptmann could be injured and still wandering around these fields somewhere. I'll need to get some manpower out here to start a search.'

'I've a full day shift of five men arriving for duty shortly, they can help with that, Detective.'

'Okay. Now, is there a phone I can use? I need to talk to my boss in private about this morning's events. Then we'll

need to have a detailed conversation with you about Sir
Anthony Pemberton, Jurgen Hauptmann and any threats
either man may have received over the last six months.'

'I'll call Taplow back in from his perimeter patrol so he
can man the gatehouse; then I'll take you to my office. You
can use the phone there. I'm not aware of any threats being
made to either man. All the scientists and staff who work
here know that all threats are to be taken seriously. They're
given strict instructions when they join the company that
any threat is to be reported to me immediately. There are
maniacs out there who have some very alarming and radical
views about the pharmaceutical industry. That's why security's so tight. You wouldn't believe some of the things that
have happened over in America. I know this is the UK, but
the threat level's the same. I'm ex-military and have seen
some things, but these nutters take things to extremes.'

'Are you talking about serious violence?' Rob said, interested in this man's perspective.

'Detective, scientists have been murdered in the United
States purely because of the type of work they're doing. This
threat is very real.'

31

10.00 a.m., 25 July 1991
MCIU Offices, Mansfield, Nottinghamshire

Danny placed the telephone back on its cradle, let out a deep sigh and sat back in his chair. Rob Buxton had described the circumstances surrounding Jurgen Hauptmann's disappearance this morning – it wasn't the news he'd been expecting to hear from Rob, and it was deeply worrying.

It appeared the instincts his experienced detective inspector had voiced the evening before were right; there was indeed much more to the disappearance of Sir Anthony Pemberton than a straightforward missing persons case.

Not only had the chief executive of Future Visions Pharmaceuticals disappeared in highly suspicious circumstances, now the company's head of research, and the man tipped to become the next CEO, had also seemingly vanished into thin air.

Rob had organised local officers to search the immediate area where Hauptmann's vehicle had been located; their aim was to ensure that the scientist wasn't lying injured in a field somewhere.

Danny had already formed the opinion that this latest disappearance was nothing to do with a road traffic accident. It was his view that both men had been snatched. The only thing that wasn't clear yet was the motive behind the abductions.

He grabbed his jacket and was about to walk out of his office to drive to Beeston when there was a sharp knock on the door. He turned just as Detective Chief Superintendent Mark Slater walked in.

'Have you got a minute, Danny?'

Danny gestured for Slater to sit down and said, 'What brings you out here, sir?'

'I want to know what you're doing about the assault and abduction of Sir Anthony Pemberton. I understand from the local CID that the MCIU are running the missing from home enquiry.'

'This office took a phone call yesterday from Sergeant Causer, who works at Southwell police station. She voiced serious doubts about this being a run-of-the-mill missing persons enquiry; she had formed the opinion there was something far more sinister going on. She'd viewed a CCTV recording from the golf course where Sir Anthony was last seen, and that footage clearly showed he was assaulted before disappearing.'

'Why didn't she simply pass her concerns on to the local CID? Why call the MCIU?'

'A small white van was seen to leave the car park immediately after the assault. Sergeant Causer was aware of our interest in such a van linked to Sergeant Stringer's murder, and she wondered if there could be a connection between the two incidents.'

'I see. What have you put in place so far?'

'Where's all this interest in a missing person report coming from, sir?'

Mark Slater held his hands up and said, 'When I arrived at work this morning, the chief constable was waiting in my office, demanding to know what was happening. He had received several telephone calls yesterday evening from Lady Pemberton, making clear her distress over her husband's unexplained disappearance.'

'She called the chief constable?'

'Apparently, Jack Renshaw's wife is a lifelong friend of Lady Pemberton. The two women were pupils at the same private girls school as youngsters. Ever since Renshaw took the chief's post here, the two ladies have rekindled that friendship, as they both now live in the county. That's where it's coming from,' Slater said sharply. 'So what have you got in place?'

'Up until fifteen minutes ago, I was ready to pass the investigation on to the local CID to deal with, as we already have two unsolved murders running.'

'What's changed?'

'Yesterday evening Rob Buxton voiced his concern that something bigger could be at work and requested that he be allowed to continue enquiries today at the Future Visions Pharmaceuticals premises in Beeston. He wanted the chance to see if he could find anything at their labs and offices that bore out his own suspicions before we handed it over to the local CID.'

Danny paused before continuing, 'When he arrived there this morning, he was immediately informed of a further suspicious incident. One of the company's top scientists, Jurgen Hauptmann, hadn't arrived at work at his usual time, and his sports car had been found in a ditch not far from the laboratory.'

'Couldn't that just be a coincidence? The man could have been involved in a road accident?'

'I said the same thing to Rob, but apparently there's very little damage to the car. A pool of blood has also been found on the road near the scene of the crash, but there's no trace of blood inside the car.'

Mark Slater spent a moment deep in thought; then he said, 'Two high-profile members of the board of this multinational pharmaceutical company go missing a day apart. They have got to be connected.'

'We must treat them that way until we know any different. Rob's been speaking with the company's head of security, who's a very worried man. There haven't been any incidents in the UK, but in the States where the parent company offices are, there have been several reported cases of radicals committing extreme violence against high-ranking company officials.'

'How extreme?'

'Two scientists and an executive have been murdered purely because of ethical concerns over the experiments they were undertaking.'

'Bloody hell,' Mark exclaimed. 'I take it the MCIU will be continuing the enquiries into these two missing from home cases?'

'I agree it's worrying. But the MCIU doesn't have the resources to run those two enquiries on top of the two outstanding murders we're already investigating.'

Slater shook his head. 'My question was a rhetorical one, Danny. The chief constable has indicated strongly to me that your priority investigations must be the murder of Sergeant Stringer and the abduction of Sir Anthony Pemberton. When he finds out that this scientist has also vanished in suspicious circumstances this morning, I think he will be even more insistent that this is the case.'

Danny could feel his temper rising. 'And what about the murder of Terrence McAvoy? What am I supposed to do about that, ignore it?'

'Jack Renshaw's of the opinion that the McAvoy murder was the work of a crank. He feels it was a one-off, a murder committed by someone with a personal grudge against a homeless man.'

'Whether it was or wasn't is immaterial; it still needs to be investigated properly. And for the record, I think this is someone who will kill again. The amount of time and effort it took to kill McAvoy in such an unusual and macabre way doesn't appear to be the work of a man intending to kill one apparently random homeless man. I think there's much more to it than that.'

Slater stood to leave. 'You run your investigations how you see fit, Chief Inspector, but it's always worth bearing in mind where your support lies. Do yourself a favour and concentrate on the two investigations we've spoken about.'

As Slater closed the door, Danny cursed under his breath.

32

10.30 a.m., 25 July 1991
Woodland near Welbeck, Nottinghamshire

Sir Anthony Pemberton had seen the big man carry somebody else into the tunnel and lock them inside one of the adjoining cages. All he could tell from the fleeting flashes of light from his captor's head torch was that the second captive was also a man. He had obviously been rendered unconscious before being brought into the tunnel, and that was why he was being carried.

Having unceremoniously dumped his hapless victim in the cage, the big man in the gas mask had left the tunnel without speaking a word.

Pemberton had sat in the darkness, waiting patiently for the other man to stir and regain his senses. He could now hear a rustling and groaning that suggested the man was finally stirring.

He heard a groggy voice ask, 'Is anybody there?'

Sir Anthony answered quickly, 'Yes. Are you injured?'

'Where is this place? What the hell's going on?'

'I recognise your voice from somewhere,' Sir Anthony said, struck by the familiarity of the man's tone. 'Do I know you?'

Sounding slightly incredulous, the voice in the darkness asked after a long moment, 'Is that you, Sir Anthony?'

'Yes, yes. Who's that?'

'It's Jurgen.'

As soon as the scientist spoke his name, Sir Anthony realised that the man in the next cage was Jurgen Hauptmann, the man destined to be his successor at Future Visions.

'I don't understand any of this, Jurgen,' he said. 'I've been down here for what seems like an eternity. Somebody attacked me at my golf club and brought me here.'

The scientist replied, 'I was attacked on my way to the lab. I believe it had been staged to look like a car accident on the lane that leads to the labs. When I got out of my car to see what had happened, somebody hit me and knocked me unconscious. Do you think this is connected with work?'

'It's got to be. It will be cranks, radical lunatics, trying to make a point that means nothing in the real world.'

'I haven't even seen who brought me here. I was attacked from behind. Have you seen them?'

'I've only seen one man,' Sir Anthony said. 'He was a big man but was wearing some sort of gas mask, so I couldn't see his face.'

'My God,' Jurgen said, his usual confident tone faltering. 'I think we're in serious trouble, Sir Anthony. Has this man you've seen said anything to you?'

'Not much.'

'Do they want a ransom? Do you think he's kidnapped us to steal industrial secrets?'

'He hasn't said anything at all about why I'm here. He just brought food and water and told me that I wouldn't be staying here long.'

'Was he English or foreign?' Jurgen pressed. 'Think, man, this could be important. The police are going to want to know this stuff.'

Before Sir Anthony could answer, he saw torchlight bouncing off the arched tunnel walls and realised their captor was returning. He whispered, 'He's coming back, Jurgen. If I were you, I'd pretend to still be out of it.'

Jurgen did not reply, but Sir Anthony heard a rustling sound, as though the other man was once again moving around in his small cage.

Sir Anthony curled up in a tight ball and closed his eyes, pretending to be asleep. Through his closed eyelids, he saw torchlight shine on his face and felt a sharp prick in his thigh. He instantly opened his eyes and squinted against the harsh torchlight shining directly in his face. As his eyes readjusted, he saw the man in the mask was holding a hypodermic needle, and he knew he had been injected with something.

Almost immediately, he started to feel light-headed. As his captor started to unlock his cage, he was struggling to focus but just managed to hear him say, 'It's your time to leave, Sir Anthony.'

Next he felt strong hands grip him and pull him from the cage, then lift him off his feet. He knew he was being carried along the tunnel. The last thing he heard was Hauptmann's voice screaming in the darkness. 'What about me?' he called. 'If you leave him here and let me go, I'll make you a very rich man. Don't leave me here, you bastard!'

33

6.30 p.m., 25 July 1991
MCIU Offices, Mansfield, Nottinghamshire

Having debriefed the day's enquiries made by the investigation teams, Danny had returned to his office. He needed to write up his notes on the progress made.

The meeting earlier in the day with Mark Slater had raised major concerns. He was worried about the abductions of two top staff from the pharmaceutical company but had also been loath to shelve the investigation into the death of Terrence McAvoy. He could not agree with the chief constable's assessment of that murder; he held a firm belief that McAvoy's killer would strike again in the future.

He had seen Rob Buxton return just as he finished the debrief and had asked his two detective inspectors to join him in his office. He needed to discuss the implications of what Slater had instructed earlier, and how it would impact on each detective's workload.

He had no intention of shelving the investigations, while he knew it would take a monumental effort from everyone at the MCIU to bring about a successful resolution to any of the cases.

Rob Buxton and Sara Lacey walked into the office, and Rob spoke first. 'It's not a road traffic accident. I've had traffic officers examining the scene all day. They found a long skid mark on the road immediately before where the car was found in the ditch. There was no debris or other signs that the Porsche had been involved in any kind of collision. The clincher is they believe the car had been driven slowly into the ditch. It was still in first gear when the security guard got in it, and the keys were still in the ignition. The traffic officers carried out an examination as the vehicle was raised onto the tow truck. They found minimal damage to its underside and are of the opinion the whole thing had been staged to look as though it had been driven off the road at speed.'

'I want you to stay with this inquiry, Rob.'

'It will mean a hell of a lot more work,' Rob pointed out, 'on top of what we're already dealing with.'

'I had a visit from Slater earlier. He wants us to prioritise the Sergeant Stringer investigation and the two abductions. He wants us to place the McAvoy murder inquiry on the back burner. I'm not happy about that, so it will mean long days and a lot of extra work for all of us.'

'Sorry I didn't come to see you straight after the debrief,' Sara Lacey said. 'I was on the phone to Dr Weaver at the Forensic Science Service. She's just faxed over her findings on the samples we sent from McAvoy's body. The report makes very interesting reading.'

'Go on.'

'The acid used to kill McAvoy was not only lethal, but also highly unusual. It was a mixture of hydrochloric and fluoroantimonic acid. According to Fay Weaver, the only reason it took so long to kill McAvoy was because of the high calcium content of the thick bone of the skull. It doesn't easily break down with either of those acids.'

'Bloody hell, Sara. I've never heard about any of this stuff.'

'I'll bring you her full report so you can get a better understanding of what they've found.'

'Thanks. Does she say anything else?'

'Apparently, mixing acids in this way can be an extremely risky thing, as they can sometimes react against each other. That reaction can manifest itself as a highly toxic gas being given off. She thinks the killer must have a scientific background to even attempt this.' Sara paused before continuing, 'She insisted that if other bodies killed in this way are located, then we must wear full protective clothing – and breathing apparatus if they're found in an enclosed space.'

'If that's the case, how come nobody fell ill when we recovered McAvoy's body?'

'I asked her that question, and she said we got lucky at the golf course simply because it was such an open environment, and it was a breezy day.'

'Make sure you brief all our staff and the scenes of crime teams immediately,' Danny instructed. 'I also want a bulletin sent to divisions to brief their staff of these dangers. They will be the first responders if any other bodies are discovered, and I don't want them walking into harm's way unwittingly.'

'I'll get straight on it, boss.'

'Before you go, Sara.' Danny held her gaze. 'I want you to lead the investigation into the death of Sergeant Stringer.'

Then he paused and turned to Rob. 'Rob, I want you to concentrate on these abductions. Before you leave tonight, I want you to draw up a list of immediate action points and let me know what staff you'll need to carry them out.'

'Okay, boss. What about the McAvoy investigation?'

'I'll talk to Jag Singh. He can lead that team, and that'll mean I'll have an overview of all three inquiries. Do either of you have any concerns?'

Sara said, 'No, boss.'

'No problem.' Rob shook his head. 'I'll draw up those lists before I leave for home.'

As Sara left the office, Rob looked at Danny and said, 'Shouldn't we be warning the public about the dangers of being in close proximity to this acid as well?'

'Good thinking.' Danny nodded. 'I'll contact the press office to get something out on the late bulletins tonight. I'll make it clear that members of the public are not to approach any bodies they may discover and are to contact the police immediately. I'll have it repeated on all the main news programmes tomorrow morning.'

'Do you think there's a likelihood of more murders, then?'

'I'm convinced of it,' a grim-faced Danny said. 'It's a hell of a lot of trouble to go to – to kill a homeless man. Make no mistake, there's more to come from this maniac.'

34

2.00 p.m., 26 July 1991
MCIU Offices, Mansfield, Nottinghamshire

S ara Lacey saw Danny walking in to the MCIU offices
and said, 'I've got an update from Addison's, boss.
They can now state for certain what was stolen
during the burglary.'

'It's about time,' Danny muttered. 'I don't know what
they've been dragging their heels over. Let's take this in my
office, Sara.'

Sara followed him in and said, 'I've spoken to Vanessa
Symonds, and she's given me the precise amounts stolen,
plus information on the containers it was held in.'

'So it is the acid, then?'

'There are six large containers of sulphuric acid that
cannot be accounted for.'

'How large?'

'Ten-gallon drums.'

'Six ten-gallon drums?'

Danny was thoughtful and then said, 'My schoolboy maths says a gallon of liquid is equal to roughly eight pounds in weight. That means each barrel would weigh around eighty pounds. That's a heavy load for one person to handle unless they were extremely strong.'

'True,' Sara agreed. 'Vanessa Symonds has sent photographs of the ten-gallon drums, so we know exactly what we're looking for.'

'Excellent.'

'It's right what you said about it being a heavy load for one person to move. Vanessa told me that for health and safety reasons, Addison's stipulate it should always be a two-person lift to carry those drums – when they're full. It does lend credence to the white van being involved. The thief would definitely need a vehicle to transport that amount of weight away from Addison's.'

'Do you have any update on efforts to trace the white van?'

Sara shook her head. 'Nothing positive so far. There are thousands of vans like that locally, not to mention similar vehicles registered in neighbouring counties.'

'Thanks for the update, Sara. I know you've had difficulty obtaining that information from Addison's, so well done for sticking with it. Make sure everyone sees the photographs of the stolen drums, and let's keep plugging away on tracing the white van.'

'Will do, boss.'

Danny had spent the previous evening at home reading and rereading the report from the FSS on the make-up of the acid used to kill Terrence McAvoy. Something had been troubling him, and now he had the update from DI Lacey, he could finally ask the question that had been niggling him.

He opened his diary, picked up the phone and dialled the number for the Forensic Science Service.

The call was answered on the third ring. 'Dr Fay Weaver.'

'Good afternoon, Dr Weaver,' Danny said. 'It's DCI Flint from Notts MCIU. I've been reading your report on the acid death we're currently investigating, and I have a couple of questions I'm hoping you can answer.'

'Of course. I tried to keep my report in layman's language, but I'm happy to answer any questions you have.'

'I appreciate that,' Danny said. 'In your report you state that the reason it took so long for Terrence McAvoy to die was because the acid used by the killer couldn't break down the calcium in the bone of the skull very quickly. I don't really understand that. I thought acid would eat through anything.'

'And so it will, given long enough. Every acid has a different strength. Even the two acids that were mixed for this attack have different properties. Both are extremely powerful and will do a lot of damage to soft tissue and other body structures, but the calcium in bone is resistant for longer.'

'I understand that. The question I need answering is this: which acid has the destructive properties needed to get through that calcium barrier the quickest?'

Dr Weaver remained silent for a while and then said, 'Probably something like common or garden sulphuric acid.'

'And could you mix sulphuric acid with the two acids you described in your report?'

'You could,' Dr Weaver said after a moment's considera-tion, 'but it would be fraught with danger to attempt it. I'm no chemistry expert, but even my rudimentary knowledge tells me that such a volatile mixture of acids would be likely to give off a toxic gas that would be extremely harmful, if not lethal, if inhaled.'

'You said you're not an expert, but do you think a person with a basic knowledge of chemistry could undertake something like mixing these acids?'

'I think it would take more than a basic knowledge of chemistry to safely do that. Not only mixing it, but handling it, storing it and finally using it would all be extremely hazardous operations. I think the person attempting all that would need detailed, practical knowledge of chemistry to stay safe themselves.

Danny said, 'Thanks, Dr Weaver. I appreciate you taking the time to answer my questions.'

'Any time, Chief Inspector. It makes a refreshing change to speak to you when you don't want something doing urgently.'

Danny squirmed a little and said, 'Fair comment, Doctor. I know it must seem that I always want things doing yesterday. Thanks again for the information.'

He replaced the telephone, sat back in his chair and puffed out his cheeks. He had already harboured thoughts about there being a link between the murders of Terrence McAvoy and Sergeant Gary Stringer, and now that Dr Weaver had confirmed his fears, he was an extremely worried man.

He didn't know it then, but his fledgling theory was about to be proved right.

35

6.00 a.m., 27 July 1991
Manor School, Mansfield Woodhouse, Nottinghamshire

Harry Ellis loved his job. He had spent eighteen years as a dog handler in the RAF, and when he retired, he was still a young man, so he wanted to do something that would mean working outdoors and staying active.

He had attended the Manor School when it was a grammar school and not the comprehensive it was now, so when the school caretaker vacancy was advertised, he applied. The job came with a lovely bungalow that would be perfect for him and his wife. He had no children, but he had kept his service dog when he retired.

Schaefer, his black and tan Alsatian, caused the only reservations the school board had about appointing the ex-serviceman for the position.

Harry had allayed their fears by convincing them that he would ensure his dog never encountered any of the school's pupils. The first thing he did after getting the job was to build a spacious, but secure, run for Schaefer in the bungalow's back garden. The school governors were more than happy with the arrangement and realised that the well-trained dog would also be an asset for the school's security.

Immediately prior to Harry's appointment, the school had suffered a series of damaging burglaries, where valuable equipment was stolen, and a lot of petty damage had been caused. Once appointed, Harry lost no time in placing signs around the school buildings warning that the property was now patrolled by a guard dog as well as an onsite caretaker.

His strategy worked: there had been no further burglaries during the five years Harry had worked at the school.

Having finished his morning mug of tea, he slipped the lead onto Schaefer's collar and said, 'Come on, lad, let's go and earn our keep.'

As soon as the lead was attached to the collar, the dog knew what was expected. He never barked, just walked obediently at heel next to Harry as he carried out his rounds, checking all the buildings on the school complex.

Once all the buildings had been checked and found to be secure, he took the battered and chewed tennis ball from his pocket.

As soon as the dog saw the ball, he strained just once on the leash.

Harry smiled. 'Patience, lad. Let's see the grass first.'

He walked the dog out onto the vast playing fields that surrounded the school. It was already starting to get light, but it was a dull day, and the sports fields were shrouded in a low mist. He could just about make out the two sets of rugby posts in the distance.

He slipped Schaefer off the lead but gripped the dog's collar as he said firmly, 'Wait!'

The dog settled patiently on its haunches as Harry threw the ball as far as he could into the mist. 'Go on then, fetch!' he shouted.

The big dog raced off in the approximate direction Harry had thrown the ball. He knew it would only take his smart dog seconds to locate and retrieve his toy.

When the dog didn't return as expected, Harry yelled, 'Schaefer!'

Harry called again, then listened as he realised he could hear urgent barking in the distance out on the rugby pitches.

Concerned his dog had located a trespasser on the field, Harry began to run towards the barking.

As he got closer, he could see the dog standing on guard in front of what looked like a person sitting down on the grass immediately between the posts of the first rugby pitch.

He slowed down to a walk as he approached the barking dog and said, 'Quiet, Schaefer. Heel!'

The dog immediately stopped barking and walked slowly back towards Harry. Harry slipped the lead back on and whispered, 'Good boy. What have you found, lad?'

As he walked towards the seated figure, Harry could now see it was an elderly man. His worst fears were confirmed when, as he got closer, he could see that the old man was dead and that he had the most horrendous injuries to the top of his head.

Harry hissed, 'Down, boy.'

The dog lay down on the damp grass and remained

motionless as Harry placed the lead on the ground next to him.

Once the dog was still, Harry moved forward to have a closer look at the body. He could now see that the reason the old man had remained in a sitting position was because he had been propped up with a wooden stake, which had been driven into the soft earth behind his clothing. The stake had prevented the body from toppling over.

Whoever had left him in the field, Harry thought, had gone to a lot of trouble to ensure he was found in this position.

He could now see that the man's hands were clutching his own throat, but that they had been tied with string to remain in that position. The wound to the top of the man's head was something Harry had never encountered before. During his military service, he had been trained in how to treat the most horrendous battlefield injuries. This injury looked as if something had gnawed the top of the old man's skull away. It was like a scene from a horror film.

A gentle breeze suddenly wafted noxious fumes from the man's body towards him. The stench made him gag and cough. He retreated from the body and picked up the dog lead. Having moved away from the foul-smelling corpse, he recalled a news bulletin he had seen the previous night, which had warned about approaching any bodies that were discovered in remote locations.

Harry turned away, and as he walked briskly away from the body, he looked down at Schaefer and said, 'Come on, lad. I need to get the cops out here before school starts.'

36

Danny stood next to his two detective inspectors, well back from the body, as Seamus Carter carried out his initial inspection. They were wearing full forensic suits and face masks. Tim Donnelly and his scenes of crime team were also standing a good distance away from the body and were dressed in a similar fashion, but also wearing full respirators as the pathologist carried out his basic checks.

Danny looked at Rob and said, 'Are you satisfied it's Sir Anthony Pemberton?'

'It certainly looks like him. And the clothing on the body is as Lady Pemberton described. We'll need a formal identification, but I think it's him.'

'I'll need you to arrange that identification as soon as you can, Rob.'

'Will do, boss.'

Danny glanced at his watch. Time was of the essence. The mutilated body of Sir Anthony would need to be removed from the school playing fields before pupils started to arrive. Not only did the body pose a real threat to health, but it would undoubtedly cause trauma to any youngsters unfortunate enough to glimpse the terrible injuries that had been inflicted.

A surge of anger rushed through him.

What sort of sick individual is capable of not only doing something like this, but then staging the body so it is likely to be found by children?

He was drawn from his thoughts as he saw Seamus approaching him, carefully removing the respirator away from his bushy beard. Immediately behind the pathologist he could see Tim and his team moving back in towards the body.

Danny said, 'I'm surprised you managed to get that respirator on over your beard, my friend.'

'It's not the most comfortable way to start the day. I'll grant ya that, Danny.'

Seamus paused before saying, 'It looks identical to the golf course death. An acid of some description has been slowly dripped onto the top of the man's skull until it's eaten through the bone and destroyed the brain.'

'Was he alive during that process?'

'I'll know for sure at the post-mortem, but looking at the ligature marks on his wrists, ankles and forehead, he was struggling against his restraints for a long time. I'd say the poor soul was alive for a lot of the process. The only mercy is that I don't think it took so long for this man to die as it did Terrence McAvoy.'

'Why do you say that?'

'Just going on the livid, red scarring at the edges of the wound. This was still quite fresh when the acid drips were stopped. I would estimate it took less than twenty-four hours for the acid to eat through the skull.'

'Any ideas why that could be?'

The big Irishman shrugged. 'I guess the obvious one would be that the acid used this time was a different mixture to that used on McAvoy. Every acid has a different destructive rate.'

Danny sighed. 'So I'm beginning to understand. I had a conversation yesterday on similar lines with Dr Weaver.'

'This killer is refining his methods, Danny. McAvoy obviously took too long to die for their liking.'

Danny folded his arms, thinking. 'Are there any other obvious injuries?'

'There's evidence of bruising to the flesh around the base of the skull, what's left of it. Until I get him to the mortuary and out of those clothes, I can't really get a proper look.'

'How long before we can move the body?'

'I've done all I need to do here. As soon as Tim and his team have finished, I intend to encase the head completely in a specialist Teflon bag that will resist the acid. The problem we have is that, just as I did with McAvoy, ideally I'd like to transport him in the same position as he is now. That way we won't lose the contents of the skull.'

'How are you going to manage that?'

'I've spoken to Tim, and I'll talk to the undertakers when they arrive. Two of Tim's technicians have volunteered to stay in their respirators and travel with the body in the back of the van. That way they can keep it upright as it's transported to the mortuary at King's Mill. There's no other way I can think of doing it, and it's vital we preserve the contents of the skull if we're to determine the type of acid used.'

Seamus now pointed at the black van being driven onto the field and said, 'The undertakers aren't happy. Another acid death means their van will be off the road for a day or two while it's cleaned.'

'Tough,' Danny growled. 'They'll no doubt send the bill to the police anyway, so they'd better not moan to me about it.'

He paused to let the brief flash of irritation pass, then said to Seamus, 'How are you going to carry out a post-mortem if the body's still in such a dangerous state?'

'Once I get to the mortuary, I'll be able to neutralise the acid residue and stop the release of toxic fumes.'

'By neutralising it, will we lose anything evidentially?'

'We shouldn't. The component parts of the acid used will still all be there, but the chemical reaction between the acids should stop.' He paused. 'It will mean, though, a significant delay before we can start the post-mortem. I think it's probably best if I call you when it's safe to proceed. I'm not entirely sure how long this process is going to take.'

As the undertakers' van came to a stop near the body, Danny shouted across to Tim, 'Have you got everything you need, Tim?'

Tim Donnelly nodded. 'We're good to go. Tony and Barry will travel with the body in the back of the van.'

'Okay. Be careful, but be as quick as you can, please. We need to get him out of here.'

Danny watched as the scenes of crime team staff worked

as a coherent unit to securely fasten the bag around the man's head before lifting the body and carefully placing it in the rear of the black van. The two undertakers remained in the front of the van, not wanting to get involved in lifting the dangerous body. It was left to the two scenes of crime technicians to climb into the back of the van to ensure the body remained upright while it was transported. The bag that had been securely fastened around the dead man's head would help to avoid any spillage.

Tim Donnelly gave strict instructions to the undertaker driving the van to take it extremely slowly and not to accelerate or brake sharply.

The entire delicate operation took twenty minutes under Seamus Carter's watchful scrutiny.

As the van started to crawl back across the field, Danny said to Tim, 'How long before you complete your search of this area?'

'We've already searched the perimeter of the scene, so it's just the immediate area that was beneath where the body was situated. Twenty minutes max.'

'Have you found anything yet?'

'It's something we haven't found,' Tim said, 'that's interesting.'

'Go on.'

'There were no tyre tracks on the grass. You can see where the undertakers' van has just been. Whoever brought the body here – well, they didn't drive a vehicle onto the field. There are drag marks on the grass that lead from the footpath over there. That footpath leads to Ley Lane and houses.'

'Okay, Tim, thanks. I hate to rush you, but this place is going to be crawling with very curious kids any minute now,'

Rob said. 'Do you think that's why this location was chosen? The killer knew we would be under severe time duress. He wanted us to find the body, but at the same time not have long to process the scene.'

Danny growled. 'I wouldn't put anything past this nasty bastard.'

Sara glanced at him as she said, 'Thoughts on priorities, boss?'

'The house-to-house on Ley Lane and the surrounding streets will need sorting out,' Danny replied. 'Keep the cordon around the playing fields in place for as long as you need it to be there. Brief the officers manning it that it's still important to keep the schoolkids away from the site for as long as possible. The caretaker will need to be interviewed and a full statement obtained. Then it will be down to what forensics and the post-mortem can tell us.'

As the three detectives made their way from the sports field back towards the car park, Danny said, 'I had a conversation with Dr Weaver yesterday about her report and the properties of different acids. She told me that the best acid to burn through bone, specifically the calcium in bone, is sulphuric acid. I think forensics will tell us that there's now sulphuric acid added to the mixture used on McAvoy.'

'Sounds likely,' Rob said. 'And are you linking Stringer's murder to these acid deaths?'

'If the FSS report tells us that sulphuric acid is now involved in this mixture, I'll definitely be thinking along those lines.' He paused and then said, 'I've been asked several times, who would want to steal a large quantity of sulphuric acid? I think we now have the answer to that question.'

'So, are we linking all three murders?'

'We can link the two acid deaths right now, but I want to wait until we have the results of the acid tests before we officially link into these the murder of Sergeant Stringer.'

37

3.30 p.m., 27 July 1991
King's Mill Hospital, Mansfield, Nottinghamshire

I t had taken Seamus Carter almost two hours to complete the post-mortem examination of Sir Anthony Pemberton.

It would rank as one of the worst such examinations Danny had ever witnessed. There was something that felt dreadfully wrong about the way the skilled pathologist had to empty the liquified contents from the dead man's tortured skull before he could even lay the body down from its propped position and start the examination.

The mortuary wasn't its usual hive of activity. Because of the toxic nature of the substance used to kill Sir Anthony, the numbers inside the examination room had been kept to the bare minimum. For Danny, this had made the entire process seem even more desolate and depressing.

The only other detective in the room was DC Nigel Singleton performing the task of gathering all the exhibits. After him, the only other people in the room were two scenes of crime technicians. They had been responsible for assisting Seamus and for recording the examination on video and with still photographs.

There had been a long delay before the post-mortem could commence as the pathologist waited for the acid residue still around the wound of the skull to be successfully neutralised. Only when Seamus Carter had deemed it to be a safe environment had they entered the examination room.

Now that he had completed his detailed examination, Seamus stepped away from the cadaver and ushered Danny towards the far wall. 'I've found no great surprises, Danny. It's very much as I described while making my appraisal at the scene.' He continued, 'I can confirm that death occurred a lot faster on this occasion, but I would still estimate that the entire drip process lasted for at least twenty-four hours.'

Danny winced and said, 'Was he alive while this was happening?'

Carter nodded grimly. 'Very much so. I can only hope that he lost consciousness quickly. The pain initially, as the first drops of acid hit his flesh, would have been excruciating. There was no evident damage to the heart, so it's unlikely his heart gave out under the stress of it all. I believe the cause of death would have been the significant brain injury caused by the acid.'

'You said *the drip process*; is that how this happened?'

'There's evidence of acid burns caused as the liquid hit the man's bald head and splashed. There's a distinct pattern to demonstrate this. Each one of those individual burns on his head would have been agony.'

'I understand you won't know for sure until after the samples have been tested at the lab, but do you have any ideas on the acid used this time?'

'It's obviously not the same as McAvoy. The colour of the residue and the stench is completely different. If I was to make an educated guess, I'd say sulphuric acid is involved. There's that overpowering smell of rotten eggs that would suggest sulphuric acid, but as you say, we'll need to get the samples analysed to be certain. The lab will confirm exactly what type or types of acid have been used.'

Danny nodded. 'You mentioned, at the scene, bruising to the remaining flesh on the back of the man's head. We have a CCTV image of Sir Anthony being struck with a heavy object across the back of the head just above the nape. Is it possible that's the blow that caused that bruising?'

'How long ago did that happen?'

'This was four days ago.'

The pathologist pursed his lips. 'The bruising is consistent with that amount of time passing.'

'Is it possible that the blow killed him?'

'I didn't find any fracture of the skull beneath the bruising, so it's unlikely the blow proved fatal.' Carter now pointed at the jug he had used to empty the dead man's skull and said, 'Obviously, we'll never know if there was any brain injury, because what's left of the man's brain is little more than a congealing jelly now.'

Danny felt bile rise in his throat, and he swallowed hard before saying, 'Did you find any other injuries?'

'Internally, I found considerable damage to both lungs and the airway tract. There's also severe inflammation to the soft membranes of the mouth and the nostrils. I think these injuries are consistent with time spent inhaling the fumes given off by the acid used to kill him.'

'Would the damage to his lungs have been sufficient to kill him?'

Seamus Carter shook his head. 'It wouldn't have killed him. The injury to the brain is your cause of death. The damage to the lungs would have been more than enough to cause severe respiratory difficulties had he survived the acid attack. This is lethal stuff, Danny.'

Danny pondered the pathologist's words before saying, 'Did you find any other injuries externally?'

'The only other marks on the body were the bruises caused to his wrists, ankles and forehead, where he struggled against some kind of restraints.' He took a breath, gathering his thoughts. 'I also found, and I've had photographed, what looks like a needle-prick injury on the man's right thigh. It's possible he was drugged at some stage while he was held captive. I've taken samples for a full toxicology report, but whether it will still show up depends on when the drug was administered.'

'I see,' Danny said, considering these new implications. 'And how soon can you let me have your full report?'

'I'll send you over a preliminary report in the next couple of days. The full report will take a little longer because of the toxicology work.' The pathologist clapped a large hand on Danny's shoulder. 'I think we both need some fresh air.'

Danny half smiled. 'I know I do. I thought you were used to all this?'

'I'll be honest with you, Danny. I've never seen anything like this before. I've seen bodies that have been eaten away by acid in an effort by the killer to dispose of them. But I've never seen acid used purely as a murder weapon. All murder is abhorrent, but this monster's method is designed to make his victims suffer a long, slow and agonising death.'

38

Danny ended his careful and methodical debriefing by saying, 'I carried out a local press briefing late this afternoon, and there will be a headline piece in tonight's *Evening Post*. I expect the national press to pick this up because of Sir Anthony Pemberton's high profile, so we can expect a higher volume of calls coming in this evening and tomorrow morning. I'm now officially linking the deaths of Terrence McAvoy and Sir Anthony Pemberton. As a top priority we need to focus on establishing a link between the two men.'

'That's a link that could take some finding, boss,' Rob said. 'What do a homeless drug addict from Sheffield and a wealthy industrialist knight of the realm have in common?'

'Granted, it's unlikely to be anything obvious, but there'll be a link somewhere.'

Danny saw Jag Singh walk into the office. The newly promoted DS said, 'Apologies for missing the briefing, boss. I was in the middle of obtaining some interesting information about the scientist, Jurgen Hauptmann, and I didn't keep an eye on the time.'

'No problem, Jag. Rob will fill you in on the main points of the briefing. What's this information?'

'Eleven years ago, when Hauptmann was forty-one, he was awarded the Nobel Prize in Chemistry by the Royal Swedish Academy of Sciences. I made a note of the work he'd done to earn the award. Even if I read it out to you, it won't make much sense. It was best described to me as something relating to the make-up of nucleic acids.

Danny said, 'DNA, then?'

'Exactly.' Jag nodded. 'Identifying the matter that makes up the acid that forms part of DNA.' Jag looked around before he went on. 'The interesting part is that there was a major controversy at the time the prize was awarded.'

'In what way?'

'According to the Future Vision members of staff I've spoken to today, a female scientist working alongside, but senior to Hauptmann at the time, claimed that she had been the one who made the significant breakthrough, and that Hauptmann wrongfully claimed the credit for her pioneering work. It seems she had taken an extended leave of absence from the laboratory at the time Hauptmann made his breakthrough, and later claimed that the notes Hauptmann provided to prove his work were in fact hers. Her claims were dismissed as professional jealousy. The reasoning being that her claims were made from a sense of embarrassment because it had been the junior scientist, supposedly assisting her, who had made the discovery.'

'This is good work, Jag.' Danny was intrigued by what Jag had discovered. 'This is exactly the kind of background information we need. Did you speak to the other scientist involved, to get her version of the events?'

'I'm afraid that wasn't possible. Rebecca Haller left Future Visions Pharmaceutical, as a bit of a pariah figure, shortly after the controversy.'

'Did she resign, or was she sacked?'

'She was sacked after refusing to withdraw her claims against Hauptmann, who by now was being lauded as something of a genius by the scientific community.'

Danny looked for Sara Lacey and said, 'Sara, I want you to concentrate your efforts tomorrow on tracing Rebecca Haller. I want to know exactly where she is and what happened to her following her dismissal from Future Visions. It's quite possible she's now working for one of Future Vision's rivals.'

Sara nodded. 'On it, boss.'

He faced Jag and said, 'I want you and Jane back at Future Visions tomorrow morning. I want you to speak to as many of the company's scientists as you can. It doesn't matter how junior they are; when something like this happens, people always have an opinion.'

'No problem, sir. This all happened eleven years ago, so some of the younger staff members won't remember the furore it caused back then.'

'That's true, but you can guarantee they will have heard about it from their older colleagues. Let's see what the consensus on Jurgen Hauptmann is.'

39

7.00 p.m., 27 July 1991
Woodland near Welbeck, Nottinghamshire

Standing at the overgrown entrance to the tunnel, he read the newspaper article again. Once more he scowled as he reread the phrase that had enraged him the first time he'd read it. The printed words now appeared to taunt him from the page.

He read aloud, 'Brilliant scientist Jurgen Hauptmann missing'; then he finished the article and exclaimed loudly, 'Hah!' before screwing the newspaper up into a tight ball and hurling it into the woods in disgust.

He strapped on the gas mask and made his way inside the black tunnel, allowing his eyes to become accustomed to the low level of light.

He walked carefully, avoiding debris and any fallen bricks that had come down from the arched ceilings. The tunnels were a masterpiece of Victorian engineering that had been constructed by John William Bentinck, the 5th Duke of Portland and heir to the Welbeck estates, but years of neglect had taken their toll, and now the tunnels were a dark and dangerous place.

The duke had held a keen interest in the social and technological advances of the time, but in essence he was a loner obsessed with camouflage and concealment. Over several years during the 1850s, he had constructed a labyrinth of tunnels that stretched over six miles in length and afforded him the luxury of being able to move around his estate, away from the gaze of the public.

Some of the tunnels were large enough for a horse-drawn carriage to be driven along. He had dedicated his life to the design and construction of these mysterious underground spaces, hidden from view beneath the sprawling woodlands of Sherwood Forest.

Those same mysterious, long-forgotten spaces, although now in a state of disrepair, were the perfect location to carry out his dreadful plans.

As he made his way deeper into the tunnel and the light from the entrance completely disappeared, he flicked on the torch he was carrying.

Ahead he could see the row of wire-mesh cages and saw his one remaining prisoner fidgeting in the second of those cages. He heard the prisoner bellowing abuse and threats from the cage as he approached.

Without saying a word, he unlocked the cage, reached inside and launched a vicious assault on the cowering man, raining heavy punches down onto his head.

Once the scientist lay groaning and semi-conscious on

the cage floor, he dragged him out and started to haul him along the tunnel towards the killing room.

The newspaper article describing his prisoner as a brilliant scientist had tipped his already disturbed mind over the edge.

He needed to bring his plans forward.

40

7.00 p.m., 27 July 1991
Woodland near Welbeck, Nottinghamshire

As soon as he had seen the torchlight approaching, Jurgen Hauptmann had begun shouting obscenities at the man who had the audacity to hold him in these inhumane conditions.

Initially, he thought that his demands to be released immediately had been listened to, as the man reached down and unlocked the cage,

Any such thoughts were quickly dispelled as his captor launched a vicious assault. He felt hard, heavy punches landing on his face and head. One punch that landed on his right temple totally dazed him, and he could no longer protect himself from further blows.

He felt himself being dragged out of the cage and then hauled along the filthy stone floor of the tunnel.

In his dazed state, he couldn't really process what was happening to him, but he felt himself being lifted from the floor and placed in a sitting position on a hard unyielding surface.

He could feel strong hands manipulating his own arms and legs, and felt a biting pain as something sharp dug into his wrists, then his ankles.

As his concussed brain finally started to clear, he felt those same strong hands pushing his head back against the hard back of the chair. He then felt a strap being tightened around his forehead until he could no longer move his head in any direction.

A feeling of intense panic blasted through his body as he realised he could no longer move his arms or legs, and that he was now totally immobilised.

A single torch on the other side of the small room offered the only light. Every so often, he caught a glimpse of his captor. It was a terrifying sight. The man was huge, towering over him. Seeing those enraged eyes staring wildly out from behind the black rubber gas mask filled him with a mind-numbing fear.

He managed to splutter, 'What the hell are you doing?'

As he breathed in to speak, he could almost taste the strong chemical odour that filled the room and almost made him gag.

His initial abject fear rapidly turned to frustration and then to anger as he repeatedly tried and failed to loosen the straps that bound him.

He screamed, 'Let me out of this thing!'

The man standing in front of him slipped two fingers beneath the gas mask, just enough to raise it away from his face, before growling, 'Don't worry, Hauptmann. You won't be here much longer.'

Now Jurgen watched as his captor retightened the straps on the gas mask and turned away, picking up the torch. He began shouting at the man again, demanding to be released.

He could hear the man cackling under the mask before the maniacal sound of his laughter was drowned out by the hum of a generator being switched on.

With his head strapped to the chair, only his eyes followed the man as he left the room.

Plunged into darkness, he was about to shout after the man when he felt the first drip of liquid hit the top of his head. The sensation of feeling the droplet land was instantly replaced with a searing bolt of pain as the liquid began to burn its way into his flesh.

His brain had just about accepted that first flash of searing pain when he felt the second droplet land.

He screamed in agony, and as his screams died to a whimper, he began waiting for and dreading the fall of the next droplet.

He was a man of science and knew exactly what the burning liquid was and what it would eventually do to his flesh and bones.

He knew he was going to die in this foul-smelling room, powerless to do anything. He whimpered, and tears streamed down his face.

As a third bolt of pain seared through his head, that whimper turned into another blood-curdling scream.

41

10.00 a.m., 28 July 1991
Future Visions Pharmaceutical Company, Beeston,
Nottinghamshire

Jag Singh and Jane Pope sat in front of a group of four young scientists, all employed at Future Visions. The detectives knew the two men and two women were some of the latest people to be employed by the company, but they needed to speak to everyone who had worked with Jurgen Hauptmann.

Jag asked a general question, 'What was Dr Hauptmann like to work for?'

One of the men shifted uncomfortably in his seat, obviously reluctant to comment.

Jane had obviously spotted his body language too and said, 'We want to hear your opinion, not a character reference. It will help us enormously if we can get a clearer picture of what he was like as a person.'

The same young man said, 'We had all heard about this brilliant scientist. One of the reasons I was so keen to get a research job here was Jurgen Hauptmann's reputation. It's not often you are given the opportunity to work with a Nobel Prize winner.' He paused as though carefully considering what to say next. Eventually he continued, 'Let's just say his reality doesn't live up to the hype.'

One of the two young women nodded in agreement and said, 'Frankly, I'm amazed at just how clueless he is around some of the most basic procedures.'

The other man in the group said, 'And the arrogance of the man knows no bounds. At least in his own mind he's a brilliant scientist.'

The final member of the small group bucked the trend when she said, 'I really enjoy working with him. You can think what you like about him as a person, but you can't take away his research and his achievements.'

The man who had called him arrogant scoffed and said, 'Oh yeah. We've all heard about the Nobel Prize. He never lets anybody forget that.'

The woman retorted, 'And that's your problem right there, Simon. Jealousy, pure and simple.'

Simon coloured up a little and said angrily, 'Of that arrogant prick, never. You're so wrong, Fiona.' He stood up and said to the detectives, 'Are we done? I have nothing else to say about Jurgen Hauptmann, and I've a mountain of work to get through today.'

Jag said, 'If you feel you've got nothing else to add, that's fine. I don't want to keep you from your work.'

Two of the other scientists also stood and left the room,

stating they all had work to finish, leaving just the young woman who had defended Hauptmann sitting opposite the detectives. As she stood to leave, she said, 'You shouldn't worry about Simon. He and Jurgen don't get on, but I know he respects him as a scientist.'

Jane said, 'It didn't sound like that to me.'

'Simon came to us from Cambridge University two years ago. He came with an impeccable chemistry doctorate and an ever-burgeoning reputation. For such a young man, he's already a brilliant scientist. Between Dr Hauptmann and Simon, it was always more to do with male ego rather than science.'

Jane said, 'Ah, the old male ego.'

The young scientist chuckled. 'Afraid so. Both are brilliant men; both could bicker like schoolboys in the playground.'

'Thanks for that insight.'

As she left the room, Fiona added, 'When he's away from the lab, Simon's a lovely man. He just gets intense when he's working.'

42

1.00 p.m., 28 July 1991
Nottingham Social Services, County Hall,
Nottinghamshire

Sara Lacey had spent the morning researching
Rebecca Haller, the female scientist who had also
claimed to be responsible for the scientific discovery
for which Jurgen Hauptmann subsequently received the
Nobel Prize for Chemistry.

Her research into Haller had unearthed a sorry tale of
breakdown and loss. Following her dismissal from Future
Visions Pharmaceutical, there was no record of her ever
having worked again. Enquiries at the address listed in the
company's records revealed that she had lost her home six
months after her dismissal. The mortgage company had
repossessed the four-bedroom detached house in Beeston
after she failed to keep up the monthly repayments.

Sara had then made enquiries with Nottingham City Council emergency housing to try to establish where Haller had lived following the house repossession, which effectively left her homeless. This line of questioning revealed that at the time of the repossession, she still had her teenage son living with her.

The council had provided her and her son a room in a hostel, where she had lived for almost six months before she was evicted for alcohol abuse. Her son was then taken into care by the local authority, and Rebecca was left to find her own accommodation.

The trail for Rebecca Haller had then gone stone cold. Sara had found a few reports of her sleeping rough for a while in the Beeston area, but then nothing.

She was now at the social services offices to see if the social worker responsible for Rebecca Haller's teenage son could shed any light on Rebecca's current circumstances.

A basic enquiry at the reception desk had identified that the social worker she needed to speak to was Miriam Jackson.

Miriam was now working from the Carlton office but had agreed to drive to County Hall to speak with the detective.

After a forty-minute wait, Sara saw a middle-aged woman wearing a smock top and jeans approaching. The woman had a personality that matched her curly hair and vibrant clothes. As she noticed Sara, she said, 'I take it you're Detective Inspector Lacey?'

Sara stood to greet the social worker and said, 'Is it that obvious?'

Miriam Jackson smiled. 'I'm afraid so, Detective. The power suit clinched it. How can I help you?'

'I'm trying to trace Rebecca Haller, and I understand you

were the lead social worker when her son, Sebastien Haller, was taken into care.'

The social worker was deep in thought for a minute or two, then said, 'Are you talking about the woman who was the scientist?'

'Rebecca was a scientist, yes. After the mortgage company repossessed her home, the council provided her hostel accommodation. My understanding is that she lived in that hostel with her son, Sebastien, for almost a year before being evicted for issues relating to alcohol abuse. Her fourteen-year-old son was taken into care at that time. We urgently need to speak with Rebecca, so anything you can tell me about her would be a massive help.'

'I'll have to check our records, but if we are talking about the same woman, I'm afraid you're not going to be able to talk to her.'

'Why?'

'The scientist whose son I helped place in the care system took her own life a few months later.'

'And you think this could be Rebecca Haller?'

'Come with me to the records department, and we'll make sure. This all happened a long time ago, but the more you say her name, the more it rings a bell. I'm sure the woman who killed herself was Rebecca Haller.'

43

4.30 p.m., 28 July 1991
MCIU Offices, Mansfield, Nottinghamshire

Sara sat down wearily in the chair opposite Danny. It had already been a long day and she still had to appraise him of all the enquiries she'd carried out to trace Rebecca Haller.

Those enquiries had taken her from Nottingham to Beeston and then back to Nottingham.

After detailing all the information she had gleaned from the council's housing department, she spoke of her conversations at the social services offices, saying, 'I discovered that Rebecca Haller was known to a social worker named Miriam Jackson. Jackson was the lead social worker responsible for placing Haller's son, Sebastien, into care after her behaviour at the hostel had caused them both to become homeless. It seems the council didn't mind a vulnerable woman living alone on the streets, but they weren't prepared to allow a juvenile to do the same.'

Danny said, 'We all know the system isn't perfect, Sara. But hang on, you said, "was known", past tense.'

'Rebecca Haller's dead, sir. Ten weeks after being left to survive alone on the streets, she took her own life; so no, the system isn't perfect.'

'I hear what you're saying, Sara.' Danny felt pity, too, for this woman; what an awful end to her life, he thought. 'How long ago was that?'

'About ten years ago.'

'Is there any connection between Rebecca Haller and Terrence McAvoy, do you think? Seeing as both have spent time living on the streets?'

'None that I've found. Rebecca was known to frequent the Beeston area when she was homeless. She never strayed far from her original home, by all accounts. It's all very sad.'

'What do we know about her son, Sebastien?'

'He was fifteen years old when he was taken into care.'

'Why the care system? What about his father?'

'There's no record anywhere of his father. Rebecca Haller raised him on her own, as well as holding down a top job at the pharmaceutical company.'

'Until it all went wrong.'

'The more I've researched this woman today, the less I've understood her motives for kicking so hard against the company that had employed her for over twelve years. Sebastien was only three years old when she started work at Future Visions. Up until the furore over the award for Hauptmann, she was seen as a model employee. Even having a young son to care for didn't seem to impact on the quality of her work. But from what I've heard today, she just wouldn't let this award controversy disappear. In the end the company felt they had no choice but to let her go. She virtually forced them to choose between her and Hauptmann. Once she lost her career, everything just unravelled.'

'It does seem a strong reaction – even to such a prestigious award.'

'Unless she knew she was right,' Sara countered, 'and it had been her work that Hauptmann plagiarised for his own gain.'

Danny pondered that notion before saying, 'What became of Sebastien Haller after he was taken into care?'

'Because of his age, Miriam Jackson decided he would be best served by being cared for by long-term foster parents, rather than going into the care system proper, as it were, at a children's home.'

'Do we know who the foster parents were?'

'Janice and Stuart Wainwright. I've made an appointment to visit them tomorrow.'

'Are they local?'

'Retford.'

'Good work, Sara. Stay on track.'

44

5.30 a.m., 29 July 1991
The Carrs, Church Road, Warsop, Nottinghamshire

The early morning sun had just slipped over the horizon, and Sid Farmer could already feel its warmth on his back as he continued his daily run.

He was sixty-seven years of age, and ever since the death of his wife, he had completed the same two-mile run, whatever the weather. A keen runner for most of his adult life, Sid was determined not to allow old age to creep up on him. He needed to make the effort now he had finished working and was on his own.

He had been a park keeper employed by the council all his working life, and as a native of the small town of Warsop, this had always been his favourite park.

The Carrs Park was a vast swathe of grass and mature trees bordered by the River Meden. The narrow river had been structured at this point, sometime in history, to form a mill pond. This expanse of water was now edged with magnificent, mature willow trees, whose branches reached down and kissed the still water.

This part of his daily run was always his favourite, and it was even more superb this morning, as the early sunlight at his back lit up the beautiful St Peter and St Paul Church. The ancient stone building stood proudly on the hill overlooking the mill pond and the parkland.

His circular run always took him back along the footpath towards the parking area on Church Road. When he had first started running, he planned his route so that every morning he would see this beautiful view of the church in the distance, rising above the mill pond, where the swans would move serenely across its tranquil waters.

It was such a stunning, peaceful view that he had never considered changing his route. This view of the church where he had married the love of his life made his heart rejoice every morning.

As he neared the car park, his mind turned to less spiritual matters as he thought about his mug of hot tea and breakfast of porridge and honey.

Sid was a man who liked routine; it gave a purpose to his life and had helped him overcome the double blow of compulsory retirement from a job he loved, and the death of his wife of forty-five years to cancer, just weeks after that retirement. The plans they had spent years talking about were suddenly dashed, and he'd felt totally alone, bereft and vulnerable.

Even though he was in his sixties, he had turned back to the simple pleasure of running, and it had been his salvation. It had given him both the strength and peace of mind to once again enjoy his life.

As he jogged onto the tarmac of the car park, he gradually slowed his pace until he was walking. Still in his routine, he started doing the stretching exercises that helped his ageing muscles to warm down and stay limber.

He felt inside his tracksuit top for his keys and was about to unlock his car door when he glanced up towards the church in the distance.

He squinted, trying to focus on the object that had caught his eye. His eyesight wasn't as sharp as it had once been, but leaning against the stone wall at the bottom of the hill in front of the church, he could see what he thought was a person sitting very still on the grass.

He slipped his car keys back into his tracksuit pocket and started to stride across the field towards the seated figure.

As he walked, he stared at the person, and at no time did he see them move.

The closer he got, the more convinced he became that it was someone sitting on the damp grass, and that there was something seriously wrong with that person.

Once he was within ten yards, his increasingly bleak fears were confirmed. The seated person was in fact a middle-aged man who was wearing a dark suit, white shirt and tie. He had what looked like a serious injury, some sort of terrible burn, to the top of his head.

Sid knew the man was undoubtedly dead.

He had seen several dead bodies in the past. Vagrants who had slept rough in parks had sometimes succumbed to freezing temperatures as they slept. Drunks who had been involved in pub fights had staggered into parks to escape their attackers, before collapsing and dying of their injuries.

As he stood, staring transfixed in pity and horror at the dead man, Sid caught a whiff of a strange pungent smell that emanated from the body as the softest of breezes drifted across the parkland.

It was a strong unpleasant odour that immediately caused Sid to involuntarily take a step back.

That brisk movement away from the body galvanised him into action. He knew there was a public telephone box on Eastlands Lane that he could use to call the police.

He set off running.

Slowly at first and then gradually picking his pace up. He didn't want to overdo it, as he could feel his heart thumping frantically in his chest after the shock of finding the dead man.

He jogged onto Eastlands Lane and breathed a sigh of relief as he saw the red phone box less than a hundred yards away.

Help would soon be on its way.

45

6.30 a.m., 29 July 1991
The Carrs, Church Road, Warsop, Nottinghamshire

Danny parked his car on Church Lane about fifty yards further on from the now cordoned-off entrance to the car park that serviced the Carrs. The only vehicle in the car park was the Ford Escort owned by Sid Farmer. Parked on either side of Church Lane, Danny could see several CID cars, scenes of crime vans and the Volvo estate owned by Seamus Carter.

As he got out of the car, he was met by Tim Donnelly, who said, 'Morning, boss. It's another acid death. I've put screens around the deceased rather than a forensic tent. The weather looks set to be fair, so rain shouldn't be a factor, but this area will soon be busy with people going about their business. I'm conscious of the lung damage that could be caused by the fumes still being given off from the body, so I didn't want to enclose it in a tent.'

Danny nodded as he donned the forensic suit that Tim handed to him. He looked past the scenes of crime supervisor and could see the white screens at the top of the small hill next to the low wall that bordered the churchyard. He could see Rob Buxton and Helen Bailey standing a few yards back from the screens.

He said, 'Is Seamus Carter examining the body?'

Tim nodded. 'Yes. He arrived about ten minutes ago. He's behind the screens.'

Danny gave his details to the uniformed officer guarding the approach across the field and made his way towards the screens.

As he reached Rob, he asked, 'Is it Jurgen Hauptmann?'

Rob held a solemn expression and replied, 'It certainly looks like him. Whoever it is has had a bit of a beating as well as the damage the acid has caused. Hauptmann has a brother, Dieter, who works in banking and lives in London. I've arranged for the City of London police to contact him and request he travel to make an official identification. He was contacted by Future Visions and made aware of the circumstances of his brother's disappearance, so he knew receiving news like this was a possibility.'

'That won't make it any easier.'

'I know, boss.'

'Have you seen the body?'

'Only from this distance. The fumes are extremely strong, and there's very little breeze. I thought it best not to take any chances after hearing about the damage caused to Sir Anthony Pemberton's lungs. Seamus is wearing a respirator to make his initial examination. Once he's done that, he's going to place one of those Teflon bags over the head. He hopes it will lessen the toxic fumes before the body is transported to the mortuary.'

Danny swore under his breath. 'I know I've said it before,' he said, 'but what sort of twisted, warped brain comes up with this method of killing?'

Rob shrugged. 'Part of me doesn't want to meet a person who's capable of such a cruel, sadistic act, but I also think that until we stop him – or her – this is going to keep happening.'

'I'll be honest, Rob. I've thought that ever since Terrence McAvoy's body was found. This is a killer who's refining his technique and who appears to have developed a taste for it now.'

The screen was moved to one side, and Seamus Carter stepped out.

After stepping away a few yards, he took his respirator off, took a deep breath of fresh air and said, 'It's the same as the other two.' He paused as if reconsidering that comment and then said, 'Well, it's identical to Sir Anthony Pemberton, not both. It looks like the same acid has been used on this body as on Pemberton and with the same devastating effects. This man has also suffered a severe beating prior to being subjected to the acid torture. There's a lot of bruising visible on what's left of his face. Identical ligature marks on his wrists and ankles are present. Looks like the same person's handiwork to me.'

'That's three now, Danny,' Rob said. 'We're dealing with a serial killer.'

Danny didn't answer his inspector's matter-of-fact statement, but it did give him an idea. There was someone he could call who just might be able to make sense of this madness and possibly provide him with an insight into what the hell was going on.

He said, 'Thanks, Seamus. Are we good to move the body?'

'All set as far as I'm concerned. The head is now contained, and we'll have to move the body in a similar way to Sir Anthony. I've contacted Tim to call out the same firm of undertakers before I travelled here. Once the control room informed me it was another acid death, I thought we may encounter similar issues.'

'That's good; they did a great job last time.'

'As far as I'm concerned, as soon as they arrive, we can move the body. I believe Tim has everything he needs from the scene as well. I'll ask him to use the same two technicians to transport the body, as they already know what's involved. We just need to somehow get the undertakers' van as near to these screens as possible.'

Rob said, 'Even though it's a bit uneven, the ground's quite firm, so we should be okay to drive straight over the grass.'

Danny turned to face the pathologist. 'Assuming we can get the body moved without a hitch, how soon before you'll be ready to carry out the post-mortem?'

'There will be the same neutralising process on the acid residue to complete before it will be safe to do the examination. I think it's better if I call you again on this one. I can't rush that neutralising process.'

'Okay, Seamus, thanks.'

Danny then invited Rob and Helen to walk back with him to the vehicles parked on Church Lane.

As they walked, Danny outlined the priority enquiries he wanted completing in and around the scene. Including searches and house-to-house enquiries in any property that overlooked the Carrs.

As he signed out from the scene and placed his forensic suit in the bin bag provided, he said, 'Rob, I want you and Helen to work the scene with Tim. I need to get back to the office and start getting things organised. I've no doubt Chief Superintendent Slater will want to be involved as soon as he's notified that we now have a third victim and all that entails, media-wise.'

'No problem, boss. I've got plenty of staff here. What time do you want a debrief?'

'I'll notify you as soon as I know when the post-mortem's being carried out. There's plenty to be going on with here, so I don't see the point in dragging everyone back to Mansfield until after the post-mortem's done. You sure you've got enough staff?'

'Positive. Special Ops are on their way to carry out a search of the field, the churchyard and the car park. I've got Lisa Bettridge getting a statement from Sid Farmer, the man who found the body, and teams already allocated to look for any cameras and to start surveying any possible extension to the house-to-house enquiry. Detectives have already visited the properties that look directly out over the Carrs and the car park.'

'Anything from that round of door knocking?'

'Nothing as yet.'

'Tell me about Sid Farmer?'

'Retired, a widower, in his mid-sixties. He likes to keep himself fit, so does the same two-mile run every morning.'

'Impressive.'

'He comes over as being a very genuine man. Wasn't too

shaken by seeing the body, but I think that can be expected from someone his age who's had a lot of life experience.'

'Did he see anybody else on the park or any other vehicles in the car park?'

'When he was first spoken to, he said he couldn't recall seeing anyone else during his morning run. Hopefully, Lisa will be able to jog his memory as she gets his statement. She's taken him home, as we couldn't afford to let him move his car out of the car park until after the Special Operations Unit have carried out their fingertip search.'

'If you turn anything up during the day, I want to know straight away,' Danny instructed as he set off.

He shuddered involuntarily, feeling an awful mix of relief and horror at getting away from yet another gruesome scene.

46

9.30 a.m., 29 July 1991
MCIU Offices, Mansfield, Nottinghamshire

Danny picked up his phone on the second ring. 'Chief Inspector Flint.'

Detective Chief Superintendent Slater sounded agitated. 'I want you at headquarters no later than eleven o'clock, Danny. The chief's asked me to brief him as soon as he gets into his office this afternoon, about this body found in Warsop.' He paused. 'All the control room are saying is that it's being treated as a suspicious death. Please don't tell me it's another murder?'

'I'm afraid it's looking that way, sir. I've a couple more priority enquiries to set in motion first; then I'll drive over to headquarters and update you fully.'

Danny terminated the call and then dialled a number for Durham University. He'd located the number in his 1987 diary, which detailed the actions from the Stephen Meadows and Mike Grant murder inquiries.

The phone rang incessantly, and an exasperated Danny was just about to hang up when he heard a woman's breathless voice say, 'Professor Sharon Whittle. Can I help you?'

Danny said, 'Good morning, Professor. It's Chief Inspector Flint. You sound a little out of breath.'

'Hello, Danny. I could hear the phone ringing, but I was way down the corridor. I've literally had to sprint to catch it before it stopped. I've found in the past that when a phone rings and rings like that, it's usually something important. Is it important?'

'I'm currently dealing with the deaths of three men who have all been killed in an identical and bizarre manner.'

'You now have my full attention. I saw a piece in the newspaper about the two acid deaths in Nottinghamshire. Has there been a third?'

'A third body was discovered this morning. He was also killed in the same unusual way.'

'How sure are you that it's the work of the same individual?' She took a deep breath. 'Three deaths, three different locations, three different times. If you're convinced they've all been committed by the same person, then you know you're dealing with a serial killer, Danny.'

'I'm convinced all three murders are the work of the same twisted individual. I've never known a killer to use such a barbaric method as this one. It's like ritualistic torture, one that leads to a slow and excruciating death. He really wanted these men to suffer before they died.'

There was a long silence before Sharon said, 'I've checked my diary for the next few weeks, and I've no pressing engagements. If you think I could assist your investigation, I'm sure I could clear my absence for a couple of weeks with the university's vice chancellor.'

'That would be really helpful.'

'Let me make a couple of phone calls. Hopefully, I'll have my absence granted in time to catch the next train to Nottingham.'

Danny clenched his fist, punched the air and mouthed a silent, "Yes."

His reaction was hardly surprising.

Professor Sharon Whittle already had a reputation in the field of forensic psychology. She had previously worked on several high-profile serial killer cases in America, alongside federal agents from the Behavioural Science Unit at the FBI training division at Quantico, Virginia.

Danny was smiling broadly as he said, 'That would be fantastic, Professor Whittle. I could really use your input on this one. I've never seen anything like this before. There's quite a bit more I need to tell you, but that's not a conversation we should have on the telephone.'

'Why don't you fax me all the paperwork you have on the murders and anything else you think I might find useful. That way I can read it on the train down to Nottingham and familiarise myself with exactly what you're dealing with.'

'I have a fax number for you in my notes; is it still the same?'

'It's the same.'

'Okay. I'll get those documents sent to you straight away, and I'll look into accommodation for you as well. How long do you want to stay?'

'If needed, I can stay for at least a couple of weeks, no problem.'

'Thank you for this, Professor. Let me know when you've

cleared everything and what time your train's arriving at Nottingham. I'll then confirm your accommodation and make sure I'm at the train station to pick you up myself.'

'I'm sure it won't be a problem, but I'll call you when I know the train times. Opportunities to work a serial killer case in the UK are thankfully few and far between, so I'd love to be involved in this inquiry.' She paused and then said with a smile in her voice, 'There's one other thing, Danny. If we're going to be working together on this, please call me Sharon. Only my students refer to me as professor.'

'Thanks, Sharon. I'll send that paperwork, and I look forward to seeing you soon.'

47

11.00 a.m., 29 July 1991
Force Headquarters, Nottinghamshire

Danny could see that Mark Slater was unusually stressed. It was the first time he had seen him so animated. His usual laid-back attitude was nowhere to be seen as he paced up and down behind his desk.

Danny knew his supervisor was worried about briefing the chief constable on the morning's developments. The very thought of a serial killer at large in the county was horrendous enough. When one of the victims was such a high-profile figure as Sir Anthony Pemberton had been, then the ongoing situation had disaster written all over it.

Choosing his moment carefully, Danny said, 'I'm sorry I haven't got more positive news. But we now have three victims all killed in an almost identical fashion, and I'm convinced these murders are also linked to the murder of our colleague Gary Stringer.'

'Why on earth would you think that? Sergeant Stringer was shot dead with a twelve-bore shotgun as he disturbed a burglary in progress. That's nothing like these other deaths.'

'Our enquiries show that the only item stolen during that burglary was a large quantity of sulphuric acid.'

Slater interrupted impatiently, 'Yes, yes. I've read the reports.'

'Before I came to meet you, I took a phone call from Dr Fay Weaver at the Forensic Science Service. She confirmed my fears that the acid used to kill Sir Anthony differed in one specific way from that used to kill Terrence McAvoy. Sulphuric acid had been added to the volatile mixture of acids being used by this killer. I fully expect the acid used to kill Jurgen Hauptmann last night will also contain sulphuric acid.'

'I'm sorry, Danny, but that still doesn't convince me these four murders are all linked. I just don't see the death of Gary Stringer as connected in any way.'

'I believe the sulphuric acid was stolen by Terrence McAvoy's killer because the whole process of the acid dripping was taking too long to work.'

'I don't understand.'

'Nor did I until Dr Weaver explained it to me. Each acid has a different strength. The reason it took so long for the first acid to kill McAvoy was because it couldn't break down the calcium in the bone of the skull. Sulphuric acid can do that. The killer needed to get his hands on a large quantity of sulphuric acid to speed up the killing process.'

'And now you think he's got the right mixture?'

'Seamus Carter is of the opinion that the acid used on

Hauptmann is identical to that used on Sir Anthony Pemberton. Obviously, we'll need the lab to confirm that.'

Mark Slater finally stopped pacing and sat down heavily in his chair. 'What you're telling me is that we definitely have three linked victims, and that potentially Gary Stringer is a fourth.'

Danny nodded. 'I believe so.'

'Which means we're dealing with a serial killer.'

'Yes, sir, and I don't think he's finished yet.'

A look of abject horror descended on the senior officer's face. 'What makes you think that?'

'If he only intended to kill Pemberton and Hauptmann, he wouldn't have needed to steal so much sulphuric acid.'

'Bloody hell.' Slater blew out a long, despairing breath. 'The media are going to be all over this when it breaks later today. The local newspapers have already labelled this nutter as "the Acid Killer". Once this third death is made public, the national media spotlight will be well and truly on us. Have you any idea at all how he's selecting his victims?'

'Yes, sir,' Danny said, 'but the problem I have is Terrence McAvoy. There's a definite and obvious link between Pemberton and Hauptmann, as they are both prominent figures in Future Visions Pharmaceutical. McAvoy was a homeless drug addict from Sheffield with no connection that we can find to either man or the company. None of it makes any sense with McAvoy in the mix.'

'Well, you're going to need to start making sense of it, Danny. Because if you can't stop this lunatic, a lot more people could die. So, what are you doing to sort out this mess?'

'I've invited Professor Sharon Whittle from Durham University to come and assist us with the case.'

Slater lifted his eyebrows in evident disapproval. 'Why didn't you feel the need to run this by me before you made the invitation?'

Danny felt his hackles rise. 'I didn't think you'd have a problem with it, sir.'

'There's such a thing as protocol, Chief Inspector. That invitation should have come from me.'

Struggling to keep his surging anger in check, Danny tried not to snarl as he spoke. 'With respect, sir, right now, I don't think any of us have time for the luxury of protocol. We're going to need all the help we can get to catch this killer. Now, what's the problem with using Professor Whittle's expertise to hopefully achieve that?'

Slater raised his hand in a gesture of appeasement. 'You're right, I'm sorry. This whole business has left me a little rattled. I don't have a problem with Professor Whittle. In fact, the opposite. I've never met her, but when I did an attachment to the FBI, the trainers at Quantico spoke extremely highly of her. They all thought she was one of the best in her field of expertise. I wasn't aware you knew her.'

'I worked with Professor Whittle on two previous murder inquiries, sir. I'll be honest, I was sceptical at first, as she had been rather foisted upon me by your predecessor, Chief Superintendent Potter. But in working with her, I found her input and insight invaluable in the Stephen Meadows and Mike Grant inquiries.'

'I'm not familiar with either of those. Tell me more,' Slater said.

'Meadows and Grant were two killers, acting separately, who terrorised Nottinghamshire in the long hot summer of 1987. Meadows abducted and drowned his victims in the River Trent, and Grant was a serial arsonist who set several fatal house fires. It was largely due to Professor Whittle that we were able to understand how those killers were selecting their victims. Once we understood that, it made the job of catching and stopping them easier.'

'I can see you were impressed, Danny. Let's hope she can do the same again, and then we can find this killer before he strikes again.'

They both sat in silence for a moment before Slater added, 'Have you any thoughts on what to disclose to the media?'

'I think we should tell them that we're now linking the three acid murders. I don't think there's any benefit in publicly linking the murder of Sergeant Stringer, not currently. I think if the public realise this killer is prepared to kill a police officer with impunity, it will heighten the growing sense of unease and panic that already exists.'

'That makes sense. So, when do you intend to do a press release?'

'That will depend on what time the post-mortem is completed today. As you know, there will be a delay because of the time it takes the pathologist to neutralise the acid used on the victim.'

'Do you have any good news for the chief?'

'Now that I can link all three murders, it will help to streamline the enquiries we're already doing. The assistance of Professor Whittle is also a massive positive. If she can help us understand why he's selecting and killing these people, it will give us ways to identify and eventually stop him.'

'Let's hope so, for all our sakes. Keep me informed of any developments, day or night. Any problems with the media, I want to know. I'm happy to take the burden of dealing with them from you. It's my field of expertise, after all.'

48

S ara Lacey parked her car directly opposite the detached bungalow located just outside the market town of Retford. She was relieved to see two cars on the driveway. She had phoned ahead to let Janice and Stuart Wainwright know that she would be arriving a little later than arranged. She had made the call out of courtesy, as she knew people sometimes had urgent commitments, ones they couldn't rearrange.

It was important she gather as much information from the foster parents of Sebastien Haller as possible.

As the front door was opened by Stuart Wainwright, Sara took out her warrant card and said, 'I'm DI Lacey from the MCIU. We spoke earlier on the phone. I hope I haven't disrupted your day too much?'

'Not at all,' Stuart said. 'My wife's in the lounge; we can talk in there. Please come through.'

The bungalow was warm, clean and tidy, but the décor matched the age of its occupants.

Once inside the lounge, Stuart introduced his wife.

Sara shook the woman's offered hand, and Janice said, 'Please sit down, Detective. Can I get you a drink?'

Realising that she had already taken up most of the couple's morning, Sara said, 'I'm fine, thanks. The sooner we have a chat about Sebastien, the sooner I can leave you good people in peace.'

Stuart sat down next to his wife and asked, 'What do you want to know?'

'My understanding is that Sebastien was taken into care when he was fifteen years old. Is that right?'

'He had only just had his fifteenth birthday when he came to us. He was very troubled at first,' Stuart said.

'In what way?'

'He couldn't understand why he needed to live with us at all and couldn't simply remain at the school he was attending.'

'I'm sorry. I thought he was living in the hostel with his mother?'

'No. He was a boarder at a private school, but their rules stated he had to have a permanent home address. There were no exceptions.'

'Okay. This is all new information for me. The social services never mentioned anything about a private school.'

'Well, no,' Stuart said. 'It was highly unusual for a private school boarder to need to be taken into the care of the local authority.'

'What school was it exactly?'

'Sebastien was a full boarder at the Welbeck College, just outside Worksop. It's a very prestigious school.'

'And after he came here to live, which school did he attend?'

Stuart smiled amiably. 'It wasn't like that, Detective. Once he was settled here and we could register this address as his home address with the school, Sebastien was allowed to resume his studies at the boarding school. They were extremely pleased to have him back, as he was a quite brilliant student, by all accounts.'

'I see.' Sara tried not to let how surprised she was by all this show. 'So, how much time did Sebastien spend here?'

'He was here throughout any school holidays and for the odd weekend. He was never any bother once he was back at the school. He was a pleasure to have around the place. Such a studious and caring boy.'

'Are you aware what happened to his mother?'

Janice spoke for the first time. 'The social worker told us she had fallen on hard times and had ended up taking her own life. That's all we were told. We were never told all the hows and whys of the dreadful situation.'

Sara nodded in sympathy and was quiet for a moment before she said, 'I expect the fees for Welbeck College didn't come cheap. Were you expected to pay for his continued private education?'

'We couldn't have afforded that, Detective.'

Stuart added, 'We were told that the bills for his education had been taken care of by his mother's former employers.'

'Future Visions Pharmaceuticals paid for Sebastien's education?' Again, Sara felt a little wrongfooted by how this conversation was going; none of it was what she might have expected.

'The social worker told me not to worry about the school bills, as the head of the company was keen to pay them.'

'Sir Anthony Pemberton?'

'If that's who the head of the company is, then that's who paid for his schooling.'

Sara felt thoroughly shocked by this disclosure, but continued, 'Did Sebastien ever talk about his mother and what had happened to her?'

Janice said, 'He obviously loved his mother very much but never wanted to talk about her or discuss with us what she was like. I put it down to the shock of losing her in such awful circumstances when he was still relatively young.'

'Was there a funeral?' Janice asked, wondering at this child trying to process the reality of his life.

'His mother's funeral had already taken place by the time he came to stay with us. It was all very sad.'

'And I have to ask, are you still in contact with Sebastien?'

Her voice tinged with sadness, Janice said, 'We haven't seen him since the day he left for Cambridge University over eight years ago.'

Stuart said more positively, 'Well, he was a young man by then, ready to make his own way in the world. He didn't need us anymore.'

'Haven't you had any contact with him?' Sara persisted, not wanting to hurt this good-hearted couple's feelings, but determined to gather as much information as she could. 'Maybe a letter or a phone call?'

Janice shook her head, but Stuart said proudly, 'I did hear that he'd done extremely well at Cambridge and achieved a doctorate in chemistry. However, that was from a third party, so I don't know if it's true. It wouldn't surprise me, because he was always such a brilliant, hard-working student.'

Sara glanced at Janice, who was staring solemnly down at the floor. Gently, she asked her, 'What was he like as a teenager? Your husband has said what a brilliant student he was, but all teenagers, especially boys, have their moments. Did Sebastien have any such moments?'

Janice looked up and said, 'There was only the one time he got into trouble at the school. It was serious enough for us to be called in to speak with the housemaster.'

'What was that all about?'

'He had been warned about frequenting the disused tunnels that run under the school.'

'Tunnels?'

Stuart interjected, seeing Sara's blank face. 'The entire Welbeck estate, including the college, sits on a honeycomb of miles of man-made tunnels. A lot of the boys thought it was a great adventure to explore them.'

'This has been very useful, thank you. But you're sure you haven't had any contact with him lately?'

Stuart said, 'Not since the day he left for university.'

With a distinct tone of deep sadness in her voice, Janice added, 'That was the last time either of us saw or spoke to him.'

49

4.00 p.m., 29 July 1991
Midland Railway Station, Nottingham

Danny had instructed Rob Buxton to attend Jurgen Hauptmann's post-mortem and had arrived at the railway station in plenty of time to meet the train. He heard the muffled announcement over the Tannoy: the next train to arrive at platform four would be the express service from Newcastle Central.

He drank the last of his coffee from the paper cup before hurling it into a waste bin and making his way to platform four.

He positioned himself between the final carriage and the exit so the passengers leaving the train would have to pass him.

As the carriage doors flew open and the passengers

began to empty onto the platform, he scanned the crowd for one person.

He spotted Professor Sharon Whittle almost imme-diately.

She hadn't changed much in the four years that had passed since he had last worked with the criminal psycholo-gist. She was still a very smart, petite woman with the same ash blonde hairstyle and round rimless spectacles that made her eyes appear large, giving her face an almost doll-like look.

She was dragging a suitcase behind her along the plat-form and struggling to carry her briefcase and a large handbag at the same time. Danny raced forward to help and saw the professor's face break into a wide smile. 'Thank goodness you're here, Danny. I was beginning to wonder how I was going to get my bags up to street level. I can still remember all those steps from the last time I was here.'

Danny took the heavy suitcase from her and said, 'I really appreciate your coming so promptly. I could really use your input on this case, Sharon.'

'I can't believe four years have flown by so quickly. After your phone call yesterday, I looked at my case study notes for the Stephen Meadows and Mike Grant inquiries. I was totally shocked to see those were back in eighty-seven.'

Danny remembered that slight American accent from their last meeting and asked, 'Have you been working in the States recently?'

She laughed and said, 'You heard my western drawl. It slips out every now and then. I do seem to spend a lot of time over there. When I told my husband I was going to Nottingham for a few weeks, he just laughed and said it would make a nice change from Washington or Los Angeles.'

They had been walking as they talked, and Danny said, 'The car's just over here. It's only a half-hour drive, maybe forty minutes at this time of day, from here to Mansfield. I've booked you into the Park Hotel again, if that's okay?'

'That's fine. The room was very comfortable, and if I remember correctly, it's in a quiet part of town. Unless they've built a couple of nightclubs since I was last here.'

'No nightclubs, and it's the same people who run it. I'm sure you'll be happy there.'

As Danny began the drive back to Mansfield, he said, 'Did you manage to read any of the reports I faxed you?'

'I've speed-read them all, and I do have one or two initial thoughts. I'll have a much better insight when I've had time to study the information carefully.' She paused. 'Before I tell you my thoughts, I do have a question for you.'

'Go on.'

'Have you had any update from the lab on the type of acid used to kill Sir Anthony Pemberton? Does it differ from the acid used to kill Terrence McAvoy?'

Danny was amazed at how deftly the professor had grasped the crux of the case. 'It was a different combination of acids,' he said. 'How did you know that?'

'Try as I might, I couldn't envisage any connection between McAvoy and Pemberton. They were such opposites in life. Then it dawned on me that the person doing these killings has a broad knowledge of the sciences, in particular chemistry. And what do scientists do, Danny? They experiment.'

'I don't understand.'

'I think McAvoy was the final experiment, the acid test if you will, before this killer started on his real purpose. With the subsequent abduction and death of Jurgen Hauptmann, I think the link is now evident, and it's Future Visions Pharmaceutical. The answer will lie within that company somewhere.'

'We've already started interviewing the staff there.'

'The connection to the company may not be as obvious as that, but it will be there, for sure.'

'Any thoughts on the relevance of using acid to kill?'

'I'm not sure yet, but I think you're on the right track; the acid will have real relevance for this killer. Have you looked at previous murders linked to acid?'

'I did after McAvoy's body was discovered, but murders involving acid are very few and far between.'

'Broaden that search, Danny. I think maybe we should be researching all deaths involving acid over the last ten to twenty years, depending on the numbers that are found.'

'All deaths?'

'Why not? You said yourself, acid holds real relevance for this killer.'

Danny was now deep in thought. He already held Sharon Whittle in high regard, but the way she had so quickly highlighted gaps in his own enquiries and thought processes felt nothing short of remarkable.

He said, 'Once we've got you settled in at the hotel, I want you to be our guest for dinner tonight. Sue can't wait to meet you. I've told her so much about you in the past that when I told her you were coming to work on this case, she insisted that you come for dinner.'

'That would be lovely, thank you. I'm famished after the journey and didn't really fancy a pizza tonight.'

'I don't know what Sue's preparing,' Danny said with a grin, 'but I can guarantee it won't be pizza.'

'Have you got time to show me the three deposition sites? I've seen photographs of the first two, but I always like to get a sense of the locations and the surrounding areas by visiting them physically.'

Feeling pleased he had made a contingency plan for Hauptmann's post-mortem, Danny glanced at his watch and said, 'It will take around an hour to drive to Worksop at this time of day. The other two sites are at Mansfield Woodhouse and Warsop, which are on the way back to Mansfield. I take it you want to see them in the order they were used?'

'Yes, please. That way I can gauge if he's changing his methods.'

'As you've seen in the photographs of the first two, the bodies were staged in an identical manner. The third was also staged the same way, so that part at least hasn't changed.'

She stared out the window at the countryside hurtling past and then, with genuine concern in her voice, said, 'I read about that awful business in Dunstanburgh last year, Danny. That must have been a tough time for you and your family. How are you now?'

'I'm okay. It was a close call, and I count myself very fortunate to have got out of that caravan unscathed. It's not every day an unhinged woman tries to fire a gun at you.'

'Have you had any therapy?'

Danny smiled. 'And now you really are sounding American. I'm okay, and I believe I've dealt with it. I have a wonderful wife, who's a doctor and who understands the possible repercussions from an incident like that. I've had the opportunity to talk the incident through at length. As far as I'm concerned, it's now dealt with.'

'That's good to hear.' Sharon paused, then asked, 'Would you mind if I don't stay long after dinner tonight? I really want to have a deeper read of the documents you sent me.'

'No problem at all; you stay as long as you like. I'll drive you back whenever you're ready.'

'Thanks, Danny. And I can't wait to see how your little daughter is.'

'Hayley's not so little and full of mischief now. You can see for yourself later.' Danny smiled at the thought. 'Thank you for taking the time to come and help us. I really appreciate it.'

'As I said on the phone, I do have a selfish reason as well, Danny. Serial killers operating in the UK are a rare commodity. So to get the opportunity to work on such an investigation, without having to travel thousands of air miles, is something of a gift horse for me.'

50

6.05 p.m., 29 July 1991
The Carrs, Church Road, Warsop, Nottinghamshire

Professor Sharon Whittle stood with her back to the low stone wall that bordered the churchyard of St Peter and St Paul Church. There was still a lot of police activity on and around the parkland of the Carrs. The blue police tape, which had been erected around the deposition site where the body of Jurgen Hauptmann had been found, fluttered in the soft breeze. The noise of the tape, and the horrors it evoked, felt at odds with the peace and tranquillity of the surrounding parkland.

She slowly turned a full three hundred and sixty degrees, taking in the view at every angle.

Maintaining her view and without looking at Danny, she said softly, 'This one's extremely considered in everything he does, Danny.'

'I know he's a planner, if that's what you mean.'

'Oh, yeah. He's that all right. Everything has been planned down to the finest detail. I'm even more convinced now I've seen all three sites that Terrence McAvoy was an experimental killing, carried out purely to satisfy this killer's need to plan and calculate everything.'

'You think he's that cold?'

'I believe you are dealing with a true psychopath. This is someone who thought nothing of taking a life purely because he saw that life as a disposable commodity that he needed. That displays a complete lack of empathy and a great deal of ruthless objectivity.' She paused, observing the scene below. 'Look around you, Danny. Even now there are people still using the park. Families with young children. On a nice day like this, I bet it's busy from an early hour.'

'The body was found by an early morning jogger. There are always people running here, in all weather at all times of the day.'

'Exactly. It's the same as the other sites; he's desperate for his handiwork to be viewed. He wants the world to see what he's done, what he's capable of, how strong and powerful he is. I don't think he's finished yet, not by any means.'

'You think there's more to these sites than just being dark at night and easily accessible with a vehicle?'

'Those two points will certainly be part of his selection process, but another important consideration for him is knowing the bodies will be found quickly and by numerous people. Not only does it illustrate his work, but crucially it limits your time to process the scene. The school was the best example of that; he would have known the body would have to be removed from the crime scene quickly, before curious schoolchildren started traipsing all over it.'

As they walked back to the car, a thoughtful Danny asked, 'Why do you think the killer hasn't finished yet?'

'There's something telling me that there are others he feels he needs to punish for being involved in whatever this great wrong is, the great wrong he perceives has been done to him.'

'Revenge is the motive?'

'Everything I've seen and read so far points me towards that conclusion. The method of killing, the pain and suffering he's subjecting his victims to before they are killed, the deposition sites that all scream out *look at me, look what I can do*. You need to understand what he's seeking revenge for. If you can understand that, you'll identify this killer, I'm convinced of it.' A moment passed, with them both deep in thought. 'Nothing about any of these killings is random. I believe the reasons behind this killing spree are extremely deep rooted. This is something he's been fixated on for years. I think his every waking moment has been consumed by his need to get even, to make these people pay. Everything he will have ever done in his life has been geared around achieving this end goal.'

Danny opened the car doors. He had just started the engine when the radio crackled:

'Control to DCI Flint. Over.'

He snatched up the handset. 'DCI Flint. Go ahead. Over.'

'Sir, I have a message from DI Buxton. The post-mortem has been completed, and the debriefing is scheduled for seven o'clock this evening.'

'Received. Contact the MCIU office and let DI Buxton know I'll be there. Over.'

Danny replaced the handset and said, 'I've just got time to drop you off at the hotel before I go to the debrief.'

'Would you mind if I sat in on the debrief?'

'Not at all. But I thought you might want to get settled in after your journey.'

'Plenty of time for that,' Sharon said briskly. 'I'd prefer to meet everyone and listen first-hand to the debrief, then dinner, then reading and finally sleep.'

Danny smiled. 'Sounds like a plan.'

51

7.00 p.m., 29 July 1991
MCIU Offices, Mansfield, Nottinghamshire

D anny was flanked by Rob Buxton and Sharon Whittle as he brought the room to order. 'Settle down, everyone. The sooner we go through every-thing, the sooner we can all go home.'

The room instantly fell silent.

Gesturing to his right, he said, 'I want to introduce you to Professor Sharon Whittle. Some of you will remember her valuable input in the cases of Stephen Meadows and Mike Grant four years ago. For those of you who are new to the unit, Professor Whittle is a world-renowned forensic psychologist who has worked numerous murder cases alongside the FBI in America. She is here to assist us by creating a profile of this offender and to give us all a greater understanding of what his motivation might be for carrying out these horrendous murders. If we can understand that, we'll be another step closer to identifying him – and to stopping him. I want you to afford her your upmost respect, and I will always expect your full co-operation towards any requests she makes.'

He stared out at the faces of his team of experienced detectives to emphasise his words and was met with nods of approval.

'Okay. Let's get started. DI Buxton will give us all an overview of the post-mortem examination carried out earlier this evening.'

Rob stood to address the room. 'I can now confirm that the victim of this latest murder is Jurgen Hauptmann. His body was formally identified by his brother before the start of the post-mortem. The pathologist, Seamus Carter, is of the opinion that cause of death was the catastrophic brain injury caused by the slow and gradual application of acid to the top of the skull. He believes it's the work of the same man.'

Rob held a serious expression. 'What this means, people, is that we are now officially dealing with a serial killer, so you can expect the national media to be breathing down our necks. This is a gentle reminder for you to be aware of your every move while carrying out any future enquiries. Your manner will be subject to constant and sometimes intrusive press attention. I shouldn't have to tell you this, but I'm going to anyway. Always conduct yourselves in a professional, courteous manner. Let's not give them any ammunition, understood?'

He paused to allow that message to sink in.

'As far as the post-mortem goes,' Rob continued, 'there were significant injuries also found to the face. The pathologist stated this bruising is consistent with Hauptmann being beaten before death. However, none of these blows contributed to his death. I've spoken to scenes of crime, and the full album of photographs from the examination will be available to be viewed tomorrow morning. I want all of you to familiarise yourselves with them at the earliest opportunity.' Rob looked at Danny and said to conclude, 'The pathologist's full written report will be ready by tomorrow afternoon, boss.'

'Thanks.' Danny scanned the room for Helen Bailey. When he saw her, he said, 'Helen, what progress has been made at the Carrs?'

She stood to reply. 'The search of the scene has now been completed. Nothing was found either at the deposition site or in the car park. The only witness to come forward so far is Sidney Farmer, the man who discovered the body. His witness statement has been obtained and is on your desk, sir.'

'Thanks. How about the house-to-house enquiries?'

'We've made good progress today and have now spoken to the occupants of all the houses directly overlooking the Carrs.'

Danny nodded. 'That's impressive work, Helen.'

'There's still more to do tomorrow,' she continued. 'I hope you don't mind, but I thought it prudent to extend the house-to-house to cover the houses on all the approach roads leading to or from the Carrs. It's not a huge amount of work, and if there are any witnesses to a vehicle being driven in the area during the early hours of the morning, I think they'll be found in one of those houses.'

'That's an excellent call, well done.'

He faced the room again and said, 'Does anybody have any questions?'

The room remained silent.

'We all know what we're dealing with by now,' Danny said. 'There's going to be plenty more to do tomorrow, and I want everyone back on duty at eight o'clock. It's been a long day already, so finish up what you need to do this evening, then get off home. We go again tomorrow, so expect another long day, and thanks for all your efforts today.'

As the assembled detectives stood to finish writing the reports generated by the day's enquiries, Danny faced Sharon and said, 'You must be famished. Are you ready for some food?'

'I'm starving, Danny. Your team all seem as keen as ever. Would you mind if I spend most of tomorrow here, reading the paperwork? I only managed to speed-read it on the train, and I'd like to get a better understanding by going over everything properly.'

'Whatever works best for you, I'm happy with,' Danny said. 'I'm here to be guided by you, Sharon.'

52

7.00 p.m., 29 July 1991
Nottingham Social Services, County Hall,
Nottinghamshire

I t had been another long and tiring day for Miriam
Jackson.

As she wearily made her way down to the almost
deserted car park, she cursed the fact that she still had an
hour's commute before she got to her home in Gunthorpe.

At least the traffic wouldn't be as heavy as it usually was
when she set off for home.

Her arms were laden with folders and documents from
the strategy meeting that had made her so late finishing, and
as she stood at the side of her car, she struggled not to drop
any as she searched her pockets for car keys.

Finally, she located the key, and after another struggle,
she managed to unlock the boot of her Ford Fiesta. Being

careful not to spill any of the sensitive documents onto the ground, she placed them into the boot.

As she closed the boot, she heard a man's voice say, 'Is that you, Ms Jackson?'

The social worker spun around, alarmed at suddenly hearing a voice behind her in what she had assumed was a deserted car park.

As she turned, she came face to face with a giant of a man standing directly in front of her. He growled, 'You are Miriam Jackson, aren't you?'

With a note of indignation in her voice at this unwelcome intrusion, she said abruptly, 'That's me. Now, do I know you?'

The man stepped forward, crowding her until she felt the back of her car immediately behind her.

He growled again. 'You're going to.'

Miriam started to squirm, trying to force a way out from under the big man's weighty presence. She opened her mouth to scream but felt a large, calloused hand clamp over her face, preventing any sound escaping her mouth.

Her eyes widened in horror as she saw the man was holding a hypodermic needle in his other hand as he used his considerable body weight to trap her against the car. She felt a sharp scratch on the side of her neck and realised that the man had thrust the syringe into her neck, emptying the contents.

Miriam felt her head spin and her eyesight shudder. She felt his rough hands grabbing at her as her legs buckled.

The last thing she felt was the strength of his hands under her armpits as he dragged her roughly across the car park.

53

2.00 a.m., 30 July 1991
School Lane, Kirklington, Nottinghamshire

The big man had patiently observed the red-brick, detached house for almost five hours. When he had started researching Dr Greg Thornhill, he had been delighted to find that the consultant lived in such a secluded location.

He had initially thought about abducting the doctor from the Queen's Medical Centre emergency care department, where he worked. But he had quickly realised that the area around the emergency care department was always busy, and had decided it was far too risky. Instead, he had turned to scoping out the possibility of lifting him from his home address.

Had Dr Thornhill not recently gone through an acrimonious divorce, the house would probably have been deemed unsuitable too.

His long-suffering wife had taken their two children with her when she had moved out. Which meant, for the time being at least, the doctor would be living at the palatial house alone.

He had parked his van on a small lane near Edingley Beck and made his way across the fields to the rear of the house on School Lane. The only unplanned detour he had been forced to make was skirting briefly back onto the road to cross over the River Greet.

Once in the rear garden, he had secreted himself in bushes and observed the doctor moving around the house. Throughout the time he had been there, he hadn't seen anybody else inside.

Checking his watch, he realised that it had now been two hours since the last light was switched off inside the house. He decided it was time to act.

Moving stealthily, he made his way towards the rear of the house. He could see the alarm box on the wall. He knew that if all went well, he would be long gone before the first police officers arrived at this secluded location.

He took the crowbar from his jacket and got to work on the patio doors. With his enormous strength, it took him no time at all to force the lock, and the door flew open.

He crouched in the kitchen for a few seconds to see if any audible alarm would sound. When the house remained deathly quiet, he began making his way up the stairs to the bedrooms. He didn't know if the burglar alarm had a silent activation, so he knew he needed to act fast.

After opening the third door on the gallery landing, he

found the master bedroom and could see Greg Thornhill asleep in the vast bed.

Stepping forward silently, he slipped the hypodermic needle from his pocket and plunged it into the doctor's bare arm.

He studied the man's face and saw Thornhill stir momentarily. He saw him open his eyes once before closing them again.

He pinched the man's fleshy cheeks hard, and when there was no reaction from the drugged doctor, he flung the covers back and dragged him from the bed. Grabbing the semi-naked doctor, he lifted him over his shoulder, carried him down the stairs and out into the cold night air.

Although Thornhill was short in stature, he was considerably overweight, and the man grunted with the effort as he carried the unconscious doctor across the garden. As he reached the hedgerow, he listened intently for the telltale sounds of approaching sirens or the diesel engines of police vehicles. The air remained still and silent as he slipped through the hedge and across the fields, back to his waiting van.

Ten minutes after abducting Greg Thornhill from his own home, the big man opened the back doors of the van and threw the unconscious doctor into the rear of the vehicle. He smiled as he heard a sickening thud as the man's head smacked against metal.

He allowed himself a few deep breaths, after the exertion of carrying the doctor across the fields, before stepping inside the van. He slipped plasticuffs on the doctor's wrists and a gag around his face.

As he walked from the back of the van and got into the driver's seat, he whistled a low, almost celebratory tune.

After the successful abduction of the social worker earlier, Dr Greg Thornhill was another name he could now tick off his list.

Four down, two more to go.

54

When Danny walked into the office, he saw Jag Singh and Fran Jefferies already at their desks. 'I need a word with both of you now,' he said, taking his jacket off, ready to start work.

Jag said, 'What's up, boss?'

Danny replied, 'When you did the interviews with the staff at Future Visions, was there anybody you weren't a hundred per cent happy with?'

Jag thought back to all the interviews he'd carried out at the labs with Jane Pope, and after careful consideration, he said, 'There was one guy who was a bit arsey. He really disliked Hauptmann and wasn't afraid to say so. One of the other scientists called him out for being jealous of Hauptmann's achievements. I do recall thinking that the way he responded to his fellow scientist's accusation showed he had quite a nasty temper on him. That said, neither Jane nor I thought too much about it at the time because he's a relatively young bloke who hasn't been with the company that long.'

'Did you ask him about Rebecca Haller?'

'Standard. We've asked everyone that question. He said he didn't know anything about her or any of the controversary that surrounded her claims over the Nobel Prize, as it was before his time.' Jag could tell by Danny's expression that he was leading up to something and said, 'Do you want me to go back and reinterview him?'

'I think I do, Jag. Talk to him on his own this time and delve a little deeper into why he dislikes Hauptmann so much.'

'Okay, boss. No problem.'

'What's this guy's name, Jag?'

Jag flicked open his notebook and said, 'Simon Archer.'

Danny then turned to Fran and said, 'I've a very specific enquiry for you, Fran. I want you to start researching all deaths that have involved acid, in any way, throughout the county.'

'We've already done that, boss.'

'Not just murders. Any deaths at all. Industrial accidents, suicide, anything that involved acid in any capacity.'

'Okay. How far back do you want me to go?'

'Depending on the numbers you turn up, at least ten years, and if it isn't too laborious, I'd like you to go as far back as twenty years.'

Fran raised her eyebrows and said, 'That's quite a tall order, boss.'

Danny nodded. 'I appreciate it could be, Fran. Go back

ten years to start with, and see what the numbers are like. I don't think there will be that many, but I appreciate they may not be easy to identify.'

'That's what I was thinking. I don't think there will be hundreds, but there could be some that are recorded as something else even though acid was involved.'

'I know you'll do your best. Keep me informed on the numbers, please.'

As the two detectives got up to leave, Danny said, 'Jag, after you've seen Simon Archer, I want you to pull all new reports of missing persons that show anything that could suggest something more sinister. I think this killer will be targeting more people, and he seems to have developed a favoured method of abducting his chosen victims.'

'No problem. I'll update you as soon as I get back from Future Visions.'

'Fran, I want to see DI Lacey as soon as she arrives this morning.'

'Okay, sir.'

'And has Professor Whittle arrived yet?'

'She's been here over an hour already. She's in the back office, wading through all the paperwork generated so far.'

'Thanks. I'll go and say hello and see that she's got everything she needs.'

'There's two full days of reading in that room already, boss!'

Danny had read the first three reports on his desk when Sara Lacey knocked once and walked into his office, saying, 'You wanted to see me, sir?'

'I never got the chance to ask you yesterday. How did you get on speaking to Sebastien Haller's foster parents?'

'It was okay. I found it a little strange that they haven't

had any contact with Sebastien Haller, not since he left their home to study at university.'

'Nothing at all? Not even a phone call?'

'They say not.'

'Do you believe them?'

'Yeah. Mrs Wainwright got quite upset when she was talking about it. I could see she was hurt by his lack of contact.'

'Did they tell you anything of note about what he was like as a teenager?'

'A model student, by all accounts, who worked hard at school and was no bother. What I didn't know until yesterday was that Sebastien Haller continued his private school education after being taken into care.'

'How did that work? Did the Wainwrights pay?'

'No. The school fees for Welbeck College were paid by the head of Future Visions, Sir Anthony Pemberton.'

'Bloody hell!' Danny exclaimed, genuinely surprised. 'I wasn't expecting that.'

'I know, sir. Another thing that's more than a bit odd is that when I phoned Cambridge University, to confirm what the Wainwrights had told me, the man I spoke to couldn't find any record of Sebastien Haller ever attending the university.' She paused, as if still puzzled. 'I think that has to be an error because the Wainwrights were adamant that Sebastien had gone to Cambridge and achieved a doctorate.'

'Strange,' Danny agreed as he listened carefully. Then he weighed up his options before saying, 'Have you got much on today?'

'I've always got plenty on, boss. What are you thinking?'

'I want you to drive to Cambridge University, speak to

somebody in their records department and bottom this enquiry out once and for all.'

'Okay, sir. Can do. Did the psychologist arrive yesterday?'

'She's here. She's spending today reading everything we've done so far. I'll introduce you to her tomorrow morning. Let me know what you find out at Cambridge.'

55

1.30 p.m., 30 July 1991
Future Visions Pharmaceutical Company, Beeston,
Nottinghamshire

J ag had been pleased when Danny suggested he speak to Simon Archer again. There had been something about the scientist that seemed at odds with his colleagues. He had thought about it on the drive to the labs that morning and had concluded that his misgivings were probably down to something as simple as the way the young scientist presented himself.

If you met Simon Archer for the first time, Jag thought, you would never guess he was a brilliant scientist, with an impeccable qualification achieved at the prestigious, world-class Cambridge University.

Jag wasn't sure if it was the man's sheer physical presence or the way he dressed. Archer had the build of an Olympic weightlifter, and there were no scientist-stereotype tweed jackets or corduroy trousers for him. He wore designer-label clothing, his long, dark hair was tied back in an on-trend ponytail style, and his beard was well trimmed.

Jag arrived at the Future Visions laboratory just after eleven o'clock, only to be told that Archer wouldn't be coming in to work until two o'clock that afternoon. He had decided to wait, and now sat in reception, waiting for the scientist to arrive.

The glass doors suddenly swung open, and Jag saw Simon Archer walk into the main reception area.

He approached him and said, 'Hello again, Simon. I don't know if you remember me, Detective Sergeant Singh from the Major Crime Investigation Unit. I need another quick word with you, but in private this time.'

Archer looked flustered and said sharply, 'It's not convenient. I have a lot of work I need to complete this afternoon.'

Jag spoke more firmly now. 'I spoke to your supervisor earlier, and he told me that you were only coming in this afternoon for a few hours, as you had already completed your work and just had a small report to file on the outcomes of your latest experiments. So, Mr Archer, this won't take long.'

Archer shifted his weight from foot to foot and said nervously, 'What do you want to talk to me about?'

Jag said, 'Not here. I've arranged with the receptionist for us to talk in the conference room; it's free this afternoon.' He indicated with his outstretched hand and said, 'I believe it's over there.'

As Jag closed the door and sat down, he said, 'I was told to talk to you about the dangers of combining different acids.

Some of the things that could go wrong playing with that stuff.'

'Why me? Anyone could have spoken to you about that; it's basic chemistry.'

Jag persisted. 'Humour me, Simon. I don't understand chemistry at all.'

Archer let out a resigned sigh. 'The main danger would be if the acids reacted to each other in an adverse way and gave off noxious gasses.'

'Do all acids behave that way when mixed, or just some of them?'

'That's the big unknown. It would depend on the quantities, temperatures, types of acid, etcetera. There are any number of variables that could cause an unexpected reaction.'

'Did you always want to be a chemist?'

'Excuse me?'

'It's quite an unusual occupation. I just wondered if it was something you felt drawn to do.'

'I don't know. Did you always want to be a detective?'

'There are lots of detectives, not so many chemists. Did your parents encourage you to be one?'

'No. Not really. Are we done here?'

'Just a couple more questions. Why didn't you like Jurgen Hauptmann?'

'I didn't dislike him as a person. I just thought that as a scientist he was overrated.'

'That's a bold statement to make about a man who attained the Nobel Prize for Chemistry.'

'That was a long time ago, Detective. He was a man living on past glories, who wasn't up to date on any current pioneering work. As far as I'm concerned, Hauptmann was an arrogant fraud.'

'If you'd already formed the opinion that he was a fraud, what did you think when you heard about the controversy surrounding the scientist who worked with Hauptmann when he was awarded the Nobel Prize?'

'Do you mean the claims made by Rebecca Haller?'

'Yes. Precisely,' Jag said.

'I thought she was probably telling the truth back then.'

'Do your colleagues agree with your point of view?'

'If you asked the same question directly to any of the scientists here, in private, I honestly believe that ninety per cent of them would give you the same answer I've just given you.'

56

1.30 p.m., 30 July 1991
University of Cambridge, Trinity Lane, Cambridge

Sara Lacey walked up to the reception desk at the records and administration centre of Cambridge University. She used her warrant card to identify herself and said, 'I spoke to Keith Jones on the phone yesterday about one of your previous students, Sebastien Haller. Is it possible to speak with him in person today? I've new information that may assist us in identifying Haller.'

The young receptionist picked up the telephone on her desk and dialled a number before saying, 'Just the person. That detective, who you spoke to on the telephone yesterday, is here to see you. She says she needs to talk to you again.'

She paused and then said, 'Thanks, Keith.'

Replacing the handset, she said, 'He's on his way down. You can wait on the chairs over there.'

'Thank you.'

Five minutes later Sara saw a middle-aged man, with receding grey hair, wearing an Aran wool sweater and dark corduroy trousers approaching. He sat down opposite Sara, peered over his rimless spectacles at her and said, 'Detective Lacey, what can I do for you?'

'You told me on the telephone yesterday that your records here have no trace of Sebastien Haller ever attending this university.'

'I certainly couldn't find that name in any of the databases I checked. Is there a problem?'

'It's hard for me to reconcile that because his foster parents are adamant he did come here and achieved a doctorate in science.'

'Science is a very broad term, Detective. Do you know what branch of the sciences Haller studied?'

'His foster parents believe he studied chemistry.'

'If you know the year he would have started his studies, I may be able to search a different way.'

'He would have studied here from 1983.'

'Well, a chemistry degree can take three years to achieve, so his graduation would have been in 1986. His doctorate would have taken another two years. Let's go back to my office so I can check the systems and see exactly who studied chemistry at this university between those dates and who successfully graduated.'

Sara duly walked into the heart of the cool, stone university building behind Keith Jones looking for evidence of Sebastien Haller.

57

5.00 p.m., 30 July 1991
MCIU Offices, Mansfield, Nottinghamshire

J ag spotted Sara striding back into the main office and
said, 'Hello, boss. Did you get anywhere at the
university?'
'It's a bit of a puzzle. There's no trace of Sebastien
Haller ever going to Cambridge University, but the foster
parents are both adamant that's where he studied.'

'Did you get a list of students who studied at the time
Haller should have been there?'

'I did. There're twenty-five names on this list. All but five
of them are men. They all achieved a doctorate in chemistry
in 1989.'

Jag took the list from her and quickly scanned it.

He pointed at one of the names and said, 'That's odd.

You've got the name Steven Archer on here, and I've been speaking to Simon Archer at Future Visions today.'

'How old is Archer?'

'Mid to late twenties, I suppose, why?'

'Do you think it's possible that Sebastien Haller changed his name before entering the university?'

'It's a bit of a stretch, boss. Surely his foster parents would have known if he'd done something like that?'

'They haven't had any contact with Haller since the day he left for university.' Sara's mind was racing now. 'What does Archer look like?'

'Long dark hair in a ponytail. He's a very trendy guy, but he's a big unit too.'

'What, fat?'

'No. The opposite, he's obviously a gym monster who likes weight training.'

Sara looked her colleague in the eye. 'We need to take this to the boss, Jag,' she said, the urgency thrumming in her voice. 'We could be onto something here.'

58

6.00 p.m., 30 July 1991
Woodland near Welbeck, Nottinghamshire

Miriam Jackson had waited patiently in the darkness for the man in the next cage to wake up. She had only just woken up herself from her drug-induced sleep when she'd seen the man in the gas mask carry in his new prisoner.

The man dumped unceremoniously in the small wire cage had been dressed only in pyjama bottoms and seemed totally out of it when he was carried in. Miriam guessed that he'd probably been drugged too.

As soon as she heard the man stirring, she called out in a low, urgent voice, 'Are you awake?'

The man still sounded groggy, and he shivered as he said, 'Where am I?'

In no more than a whisper, Miriam said, 'I don't know where we are. In a tunnel of some kind.'

The man sat up, his head brushing the top of the cage. He started to rattle the cage door, trying to loosen the lock.

Miriam hissed, 'Be quiet. You can't get out; it's padlocked. If you make too much noise, he'll come back.'

The man said, 'This is madness. Who will come back?'

'The lunatic who brought us to this Godforsaken place.'

'I don't understand any of this. Who is he?'

'I don't know. He snatched me from work.'

'How long have you been here?'

'I was drugged, so I've no clue how long I've been down here.'

'What's your name?'

'Miriam Jackson. I work for social services.'

'Do you think this is connected to your work?'

She stifled a sob and said, 'I don't know. I just want to go home.' She pulled herself together a little and spluttered, 'What about you?'

'Greg Thornhill,' the man whispered. 'I'm a doctor at the Queen's Medical Centre. I was taken from my house. I can remember going to bed, and that's it. My arm's aching, so I think he must have drugged me too. Have you seen this man?'

'Not really. I remember him being very big, but I didn't get a good look at his face when he snatched me. When I saw him down here, he was wearing a mask of some kind.'

'A mask?'

'It looks like a gas mask from the war.'

Suddenly, a torch beam splashed across the tunnel walls, and Miriam said, 'He must have heard us talking. Shit. He's coming back.'

59

6.00 p.m., 30 July 1991
Woodland near Welbeck, Nottinghamshire

The big man slipped on the gas mask and made his way into the tunnels. The tunnel had cleared of the fumes given off from Jurgen Hauptmann's mutilated body, but it didn't hurt to wear the mask when he was going to feed the prisoners. He knew it added to their fear and would make them even more compliant.

He was worried about the detective who kept coming back to the labs. He couldn't understand why he was still poking his nose in, asking stupid questions and wanting to interview people.

He knew he had covered his tracks when he had snatched Hauptmann. There was no way the cops had any evidence against him. He just needed to take some time away from work. They would soon forget about him, especially when new bodies started turning up.

They wouldn't have to wait long.

There were still two more names on his list. Two more people he needed to snatch up and put in cages, then make them all pay for what they had done.

As he got deeper into the tunnel and the faded light turned to complete darkness, he switched on the torch to light his way. As he approached the cages, he thought he could hear muffled voices.

He saw both his captives sitting bolt upright, staring out from behind the wire mesh, fear written large across their features.

He bent down and growled at the man in the cage, 'Turn around and face the wall if you want to eat and drink.'

The man immediately shuffled around on his bottom until he was seated facing the wall.

He unlocked the cage and placed a bottle of water and a pack of sandwiches inside before closing and padlocking the door.

He repeated the process with the woman.

As he snapped the padlock shut on her cage, she suddenly yelled, 'Why are you doing this to us?'

He squatted down in front of her and hissed from beneath the mask, 'Because I can, and because you both deserve everything that's coming your way.'

The man said, 'We've done nothing wrong to you. You can't hold us down here like this; it's inhuman. I'll freeze to death like this.'

'Don't worry, Dr Thornhill, you won't be here long, and trust me, being cold is the last thing you should worry about.'

60

6.00 p.m., 30 July 1991
MCIU Offices, Mansfield, Nottinghamshire

Danny was talking to Rob about forensic progress and updates.

He said, 'What about the Future Visions abduction? Did we get anything from Jurgen Hauptmann's car when that was examined?'

'I spoke with Tim about that yesterday,' Rob replied, 'and it's all rather disappointing. The only fingerprints they found inside the car were Hauptmann's. There were glove marks found on the steering wheel, but they could have been left by that dopey security guard. The one who drove the car back to the lab after it had been pulled out of the ditch.'

'Bloody hell. Any blood found inside the car?'

'As we thought before, sir.' Rob shook his head. 'No.'

There was a knock on the door, and Sara Lacey and Jag

Singh walked in. Sara said, 'Sorry to interrupt. Have you got a minute for us to run something by you?'

Danny sat back in his chair. 'Only if you've got something positive to tell me. I've had enough negativity for one day.'

Undeterred, Sara said, 'It might be nothing, but we think there's a possibility that Rebecca Haller's son is now working as a scientist for Future Visions and is using the name Simon Archer.'

Danny turned to Jag and said, 'Isn't Simon Archer the guy you spoke with again today? The one you weren't completely happy with?'

'That's him, boss.'

'How was he today?'

'He was still a truculent sod, but he did speak to me about Rebecca Haller this time. He told me he believed her version of events. He feels that she was probably telling the truth about the scientific discovery Hauptmann claimed all the credit for. He believes it would have been Haller who made that discovery, because Hauptmann was such an inept scientist.' He paused. 'He also told me that if I asked ninety per cent of the scientists who work there, in private, they would all be of the same opinion. Apparently, none of the scientists who have ever worked with him believe it was Hauptmann who made that giant leap forward in chemistry.'

'Was he really that poorly thought of by his colleagues?'

'According to Archer, he was.'

'That's interesting to know. The company gave us the impression that Hauptmann was some sort of genius.'

'From what Archer told me today, he sounds far from that.'

Danny now faced Sara and said, 'What did you find out

at Cambridge today to make you think Archer could be Sebastien Haller?'

'As you know, I went to the university in person after a telephone conversation revealed no trace of Sebastien Haller ever attending. I sat down today with Keith Jones, their head of admissions, and we searched the records for anybody who graduated with a doctorate in chemistry at the same time as it's believed Haller attended Cambridge. I ended up with a list of twenty names, and one of those was a student named Steven Archer.'

'Not Simon Archer?'

'No. He's listed as Steven Archer, but like the others on the list, he achieved a doctorate in chemistry.'

'Everyone I've spoken to at Future Visions says what a brilliant scientist Simon Archer is,' Jag added, 'and how highly rated he was at Cambridge.'

Danny asked Sara, 'Did you do any other enquiries with the university records? A next of kin? Any relevant addresses?'

'I went through everything with Keith Jones. There's no next of kin listed for Steven Archer, and Keith told me that could be for several reasons. Apparently, it's not that unusual for students to fail to provide such personal details, and the university policy is to respect that right of privacy.'

Danny stroked his chin, deep in thought as he weighed up what the two detectives had told him. After a few minutes he said, 'I want this finalising one way or another. Sara, I want you to go back to Cambridge first thing in the morning. We're going to need a good description of Steven Archer, a photograph if they have one. Try to establish if the university have sent any references to Future Visions on his behalf.'

'Okay, boss.'

Danny said to Jag, 'I want you to go back to Future Visions first thing tomorrow and speak with Simon Archer again. I want to know what's going on with him. See what his reaction is about the possibility of a name change. If there's anything he says that you're not comfortable with, I want him arrested and brought in so we can interview him under caution at the police station. Understood?'

'Yes, sir.'

As soon as the two detectives left his office, Danny said, 'Rob, I want you to accompany Jag when he sees Archer tomorrow morning. I trust his judgement, but I know it's a big ask for someone so new in the rank. Basically, I want you to watch his back. I don't want to delay anything that could stop this maniac killing again, but I don't want to give a company like Future Visions an excuse to sue the force. You know exactly what's required, and Jag doesn't, not yet.'

61

8.00 a.m., 31 July 1991
MCIU Offices, Mansfield, Nottinghamshire

Danny had arrived at the office early so he could brief Rob and Jag at seven thirty before they left for the Future Visions labs at Beeston. He was just making himself a coffee when he saw Professor Sharon Whittle walk in behind Jane Pope.

Jane said, 'We arrived at the same time, so I thought I'd show the professor up here rather than leave her waiting in reception.'

Danny said, 'Quite right too. I'm glad you're here early, Sharon. I've got some fresh information I need you to hear.'

The electric kettle clicked as it boiled, and he said, 'Can I get you a coffee?'

She said, 'No, thanks. I've not long had one with my breakfast. What's this new information?'

As they walked into his office, he said, 'There's a possibility that Rebecca Haller's son is now working as a research scientist at the Future Visions laboratories, but under a different name.'

Sharon gave him a sharp look. 'I read about the controversary surrounding the claims made by Rebecca Haller, that she had made the discovery that Hauptmann got all the credit and kudos for. I didn't see anything in the paperwork referring to her being a mother or anything about what became of her after Future Visions fired her.'

Danny gave her a brief update. He explained how, shortly after being fired from her job, Rebecca had lost the family home and that she and her teenage son had ended up living in a hostel. He went on to describe how she had turned to alcohol, and after one incident too many at the hostel, she was evicted and made homeless.

He said, 'It was at that point that social services stepped in and placed her son, Sebastien, in care.'

'Where's Rebecca Haller now?' Sharon asked.

'Unfortunately, she's dead. Suicide.'

'Do you know how she killed herself?'

'I don't. Give me one minute.'

Danny walked into the main briefing room and saw Fran Jefferies already at her desk. 'Good morning, Fran. I need you to get onto the coroner's office and find out how Rebecca Haller died. We know it was suicide, but we don't know any of the details.'

Danny returned to his office and said, 'I've asked Fran to make a quick call to the coroner's office. We should know exactly how she took her own life very shortly. Any thoughts?'

'I have an idea, but I'd prefer to wait until we get that information from Fran.'

'Okay. And what are you thinking after reading all the information yesterday?'

'Only that I fully agree with your assessment so far. I think your sergeant was probably killed by the same person responsible for the acid murders. I'm also convinced that he hasn't finished yet and that he intends to kill again. Did you start looking out for any suspicious missing from home reports or reports of possible abductions?'

'Yes. But I only set that in motion yesterday. Any such reports will start filtering into this office today.'

There was a knock on the office door. Fran walked in clutching her notepad and said abruptly, 'Rebecca Haller took her own life by ingesting a caustic liquid.'

Sharon asked, 'Do you know, for example, if it was bleach or a drain cleaner?'

Fran glanced at her pad. 'A bottle of Drainclear was found next to her body, so the assumption was made that she'd drank it to kill herself.'

'That would have been such a terrible, agonising death,' Sharon said, her face full of empathy. 'Two of the main ingredients in any domestic drain cleaner are hydrofluoric acid and sulphuric acid. That's why they're sold with such strict guidelines on how they are used.' She looked thoughtful for a long minute or two. 'If this is her son, now working at Future Visions, he's only there for one purpose. To exact hideous revenge against the people he believes are responsible for his mother's death.'

'Is that the reason these people are being killed with acid?' Danny said, thinking that he knew the answer already, 'The slow release of acid onto the victims is intended to make them suffer a lingering, painful death. The same pain and suffering his mother would have felt in her final moments. It all fits for a revenge motive.'

Fran said, 'There's something else, boss.'

'Go on.'

'The control room have just telephoned through two suspicious reports of missing persons. The first one is a social worker, Miriam Jackson. She never returned home on the night of the twenty-ninth, and her car is still where she left it parked outside the council offices.'

'Miriam Jackson?' Danny almost jumped out of his seat. 'That name rings a bell. Just a minute.'

He flicked through the pages of his personal record of investigation. 'Here it is,' he said. 'Sara spoke to Miriam Jackson just the other day. She was the social worker responsible for placing Sebastien Haller into the care system.'

Sharon said, 'You need to consider her as a potential victim of this maniac, Danny.'

Danny nodded, his expression grave, and said to Fran, 'What's the other report?'

'A break-in was discovered at a house in Kirklington this morning, but the car used by the doctor who lives there was still parked on the driveway. The house is remote, but neighbours saw him return home last night. He's nowhere to be found this morning.'

'Does he have any connection with Rebecca or Sebastien Haller?'

'Nothing that's obvious.'

'Look into it, please, Fran. I must know if we need to treat his disappearance as a potentially life-threatening situation as well as Jackson's. Oh, and Fran, make sure we get a full copy of the coroner's file that was prepared for the inquest into the suicide of Rebecca Haller.'

62

When Sara Lacey arrived at the main reception at the Cambridge University college, she had been met by an extremely nervous and reticent Keith Jones, who informed her that any further information she required would need to be authorised directly by the vice chancellor.

As he walked her through the grounds of the prestigious university to the vice chancellor's office, Jones explained that it was nothing personal and that he was merely observing the strict privacy rules the university followed when any outside agencies were attempting to access personal details of students from the university files.

After carefully inspecting Sara's identification, Vice Chancellor Professor Deirdre Bateson apologised. 'I'm sorry

I need to ask you so many questions, but as a university we follow strict rules on the divulgence of personal data and information. Keith really shouldn't have disclosed the amount of information he has already. Previous students are also entitled to that high level of protection from any intrusion.'

Sara countered, 'I fully understand your obligations to students past and present, but I need to point out that the information we are seeking is in respect of an ongoing murder investigation where people have already died in the most horrendous fashion, and others could still be at risk of suffering a similar fate. That is why this information is not only necessary but also extremely time critical.'

'My understanding from Keith is that you now require a photograph of Steven Archer on top of the information you have already obtained in respect of students graduating with a doctorate in chemistry in the same year as Archer. You have made mention of a murder investigation. How will a photograph of Steven Archer be useful to such an enquiry?'

Sara could tell from Deirdre Bateson's belligerent tone that unless she told the professor everything, there was no way she would release the photograph.

Sara took a deep breath and patiently outlined the facts of the three acid murders and then said, 'Our enquiries have revealed that a man by the name of Sebastien Haller attended this university but may have used the name Steven Archer while he was here. Haller's mother committed suicide by ingesting acid after being sacked from her role as an investigative scientist at Future Visions Pharmaceutical. Two of the victims in this murder investigation were employed by that company, and we believe that Haller has a strong motive to be involved in the deaths of those two men.'

Sara maintained eye contact with Bateson as she concluded firmly, 'A photograph will help us prove that Steven Archer is the same person as Sebastien Haller. Once we've established that fact, we wouldn't need to use the image supplied by you in evidence, and it will be returned to your records. That way the university can be assured there will be no comeback on its strict privacy rules.'

Deirdre Bateson leaned back in her chair, and after careful consideration, she said, 'Very well, Detective. The university will supply your investigation with a photograph of Archer. We always strive to assist the police whenever we can.'

Sara doubted that was the case but said nothing.

Deirdre Bateson picked up a folder from her desk and said, 'I'm afraid there isn't much choice; we only have one photograph of Archer in our records. By all accounts, he wasn't a very sociable chap while he was here, too focused on his studies. Which is probably why he achieved such a fabulous outcome to his studies. I'm afraid far too many students embrace the social side of university life with twice the vigour they devote to their actual studies.'

'May I see the photograph?'

Bateson handed over the envelope. Sara took out a grainy photograph of Steven Archer resplendent in mortar board and gown.

As Sara studied the image, Professor Bateson said, 'This is the only picture of Steven Archer we have on record. It was taken by the university's official graduation day photographer. Archer never purchased any copies.'

Sara turned the photograph over and read the printed inscription on the back.

Steven Simon Archer – 1989

She said nothing to Deirdre Bateson but noted the fact that Steven Archer's middle name matched the name of the man now employed by Future Visions as Simon Archer.

Replacing the photograph, she said, 'Thank you for your co-operation, Professor Bateson. It's very much appreciated.'

63

11.30 a.m., 31 July 1991

Future Visions Pharmaceutical Company, Beeston,

Nottinghamshire

I t had been a frustrating morning for Rob Buxton and Jag Singh. Simon Archer was not at the Beeston laboratory when they arrived.

After being met with resistance to any questions, both at the security gatehouse and again subsequently at the main reception area, Rob had insisted on speaking with the head of security, Alan Villiers.

After being forced to wait for a further thirty minutes, Rob was trying hard to contain his rising anger at the continued obstruction when he finally saw the giant Villiers approaching.

He took a deep breath and said, 'Mr Villiers, if I don't get some co-operation around here in the next five minutes, I'll be taking this matter up with your head office.'

Villiers held up both hands in a gesture of apology and said, 'I can only apologise, Detective. Everyone's frightened to death of disclosing the type of personal information you're asking for. Let me see if I can help.'

Rob repeated what he had been saying since they arrived. 'We need to speak with Simon Archer as a matter of urgency. We arrived here this morning fully expecting him to be at work, only to be informed by your security guard at the gatehouse that he hadn't arrived at work as expected. It has then taken us almost an hour of back and forth with the secretary on reception to finally establish that Archer isn't the latest scientist employed by this company to be abducted but has phoned in and booked time off from work.'

'I'm sorry for the misunderstanding. If Archer isn't here, what is it you need from me?'

'What I need is a current home address, any vehicle details and any photograph you may have of Simon Archer.'

'The only photograph we have will be a copy of his security pass. I can sort that out for you in next to no time. If you come with me to my office, I'll access the computer system and get you the other details you need.'

As the two detectives followed Villiers, he asked, 'Can I ask why you need to talk to Archer so urgently? My understanding is that he's simply booked a week off.'

Rob gestured towards Jag and said, 'There are a few anomalies in some of the things Archer told my colleague previously. We need to iron those out.'

As they walked into his office, Villiers said, 'Grab a seat. This won't take a minute.'

As he waited for his computer terminal to go live, he picked up the telephone and rang the gatehouse.

'Scott, it's Mr Villiers. I want you to run off a copy of Simon Archer's security photograph and bring it up to my office.' There was a pause, and then Villiers snapped, 'I want it now. Be as quick as you can.' He replaced the phone and started hitting the keys in front of his computer terminal.

He said, 'Here it is. Simon Archer's home address is twenty-eight Ash Grove, Stapleford, Nottinghamshire.'

Jag made a note and said, 'What about his vehicle?'

After tapping a couple more keys, Villiers said, 'There's no vehicle listed.'

An incredulous Jag said, 'How the hell does he normally get to work, then? I don't suppose the buses run all the way out here?'

'Scott will probably know better than me. He's usually the one booking people in and out of the gatehouse.'

Just at that moment there was a knock on the office door, and a breathless Scott Taplow walked in.

'I've got that photo you wanted, boss.'

'Thanks, Scott. Maybe while you're here, you can answer the detective's question. How does Simon Archer usually get to work?'

The shaven-headed security guard grinned. 'He travels in with his girlfriend.'

Villiers waited before letting out a sigh. 'And who's his girlfriend, you big dope?'

'Oh, sorry, boss. Fiona Foster.'

Villiers dismissed the guard. 'That's all, Scott.'

Rob waited for the man to leave and then said, 'Is Fiona Foster at work today?'

64

12.15 p.m., 31 July 1991
Future Visions Pharmaceutical Company, Beeston,
Nottinghamshire

'Hello again, Fiona,' Jag said. 'This is my boss, Detective Inspector Buxton. We need to ask you a couple of questions about Simon.'

The young scientist frowned seriously. 'Questions?'

'Yes, questions,' Jag continued. 'There's nothing to worry about. I didn't realise when we spoke the other day that you and Simon were close.'

The frown was instantly replaced with a look of incredulity. 'Close? Me and Simon Archer? I don't know where you've got that crazy notion. I'm friendly with the guy, and I give him a lift to work most of the time, but that's it. We are *not* an item.'

Jag noticed how strongly she emphasised the word *not* as

she spoke, and he raised both hands in an apologetic gesture. 'I'm sorry,' he said. 'Our information is obviously wrong. Someone was reading a little more into the car share than is there.'

'Dead right. Do you mind if I ask where you got that?'

Rob interjected and said in general terms, 'It was an assumption made by security, that's all. They see two people arriving to work together every day, and they start to assume. I wouldn't read too much into it.'

He waited for Fiona to calm down and then said, 'Just out of interest, why do you both car share? Does Simon not drive?'

'He can drive.' She scoffed. 'But he drives a clapped-out old van that's more like a waste skip than a road-worthy vehicle.'

'Do you ever come to work in his van?'

'We haven't so far, but I suppose if my car was ever in the garage, we would.'

Jag said, 'Don't you mind driving him every day? It's a bit of an imposition, isn't it?'

Fiona shook her head. 'Not really. He gives me petrol money every week, and it helps with the travel costs.'

'So, what sort of van does he own?'

'I've no idea. It's small, white and scruffy as hell inside. You wouldn't want to take your dog for a ride in it. I'm not joking.'

Jag said, 'I was here yesterday to talk to Simon, and he didn't arrive until later in the day. How did he get to work?'

'We both worked half a day yesterday, as we both had stuff to do. He didn't tell me he had spoken to you again when I took him home.'

Rob said, 'Do you know what Simon's doing with his time off the rest of this week?'

'He mentioned yesterday about doing some walking in Derbyshire and that he wouldn't need a lift until next week. He's mad on fitness, and when he's not weight training, he likes to get out into the countryside.' Now she looked thoughtful and said, 'Why are you asking all these questions about Simon? Is he in some sort of trouble?'

'We're just checking a few things out. We don't think he's in any bother, but there are a couple of discrepancies, that's all.'

He paused and then said, 'Did you know Simon when he was at Cambridge?'

'No. I did my degree a year before him, and I was at De Montfort University, in Leicester. I never met him until he started working here. We live not far from each other in Stapleford; that's why we started to car share. Or rather that's why I started driving him to work.' She shrugged. 'You can't really call it car sharing.'

'Does he ever talk about his time at Cambridge?'

'Not really. Simon's a bit of a closed book. He's hard to hold a conversation with. He will answer a direct question but never wants to elaborate. Most of our car journeys are spent listening to music. He never wants to talk about his family or his upbringing. The only things he's happy to discuss at length are fitness and science. He could talk to you all day about chemistry; he's obsessed.'

'That's covered everything,' Rob said. 'Thanks for your help this morning.'

As she stood to leave, Jag said, 'Sorry, Fiona. There's just one more thing. Have you ever been inside his house?'

Fiona thought for a second and then said firmly, 'No, I

haven't. I've known him for a long time now, and he's never invited me inside when I've dropped him off. I'm not saying I would have gone in, but thinking about it now, that does seem a little odd.'

'Does he have a girlfriend?'

'If he does, he's never spoken about her to me. I told you, Simon's very much a closed book.'

65

3.00 p.m., 31 July 1991
MCIU Offices, Mansfield, Nottinghamshire

Danny, Rob, Sara and Jag were sitting in the briefing room comparing the two photographs of Steven and Simon Archer.

Rob finished telling Danny what Fiona Foster had told them about the man she knew as Simon Archer, and then said, 'The two photos look the same to me, boss.'

Danny was undecided. 'I don't know, Rob. They look similar, but I wouldn't want to say for definite that they're the same man. They've got the same long dark hair and the beard, and they are about the same size, but it's difficult to call for certain. And even if they are, we still won't know if Archer's the same man as Sebastien Haller.'

Sara said, 'Why don't I take the photos of both Archers to

the Wainwrights? They lived with Haller for a couple of years; surely they're the people who would know for certain.'

Danny handed the two images to Sara and said, 'Good idea. Call them first to make sure they're at home. It's a long drive to Retford if they aren't going to be there when you arrive.'

'Will do, boss.'

Danny looked at Rob and Jag. 'In the meantime, I want you two to start researching Archer's home address. If we get confirmation that Archer is Sebastien Haller, I want us to be ready to detain him and search the property. I'm conscious that we've got two new missing persons reports that fit the general pattern employed by this maniac. I think it could be significant that Archer's never invited his colleague into his home. And don't forget he's driving a small white van – which he doesn't want people to see.'

'Do you think his house is where he's killing these people?'

'I don't know, but I want to find out before we have more bodies piling up.'

There was a single knock on his door before it was opened.

Fran Jefferies stepped inside and said, 'Have you got a minute, sir?'

'Yes, of course.'

Fran glanced at her notepad before saying, 'I think I've found something that links Dr Greg Thornhill to Rebecca Haller.'

'Go on.'

'I didn't get anywhere with hospital records – they just refused to disclose anything to me – so I've been trawling through police reports centred around the hospital. I found a report where the local police had been called to deal with a disturbance in the emergency department.'

She paused. 'Dr Thornhill had made the call. He insisted the police officers attending eject a drunken woman who had been causing a disturbance after she was refused medical care because of her abusive nature.'

'Don't tell me. That woman was Rebecca Haller.'

'Yes, sir. She was ejected. According to the officers' reports, she calmed down once she was outside the hospital, so her conduct didn't warrant an arrest. But she didn't get the medical care she was seeking.' Fran took a breath, her expression sombre. 'Sir, she took her own life the following day.'

'This is magnificent work, Fran,' Danny said. 'I want you to make sure that Dr Thornhill is now considered to be an acute risk missing person. Update the PNC accordingly, please.'

66

5.00 p.m., 31 July 1991
Retford, Nottinghamshire

Sara Lacey parked her car directly opposite the detached bungalow.

As she approached the front door, Janice Wainwright opened it. 'Please come inside, Detective. How can we help?'

Sara followed Janice through the bungalow and into the lounge, where her husband, Stuart, sat by the window, reading the newspaper.

She said abruptly, 'Stuart, put the paper down. We have a guest.'

Stuart immediately folded the newspaper and placed it on the coffee table. 'How can we help this time?'

Sara reached into her briefcase and removed the envelope containing the two photographs. 'I want you to take a look at these photographs and tell me if you think they could be Sebastien.'

Janice took the photographs first. She smiled as she said, 'He looks so handsome in his cap and gown. I wish we could have been there for his graduation ceremony.'

Sara said, 'You're sure that's Sebastien?'

'He's exactly how I remember him. The same long dark hair and the beard always trimmed so neatly.'

She passed the photos to her husband and said, 'That's definitely Seb, isn't it, Stuart?'

The husband studied the image of the man on the security pass and said, 'This could be him, but he looks bigger than I remember. The graduation photo is definitely Sebastien though.'

Sara said, 'Bigger in what way?'

'Bulkier than I remember. He looks like some sort of bodybuilder here.'

'Apparently he still likes to use weights regularly.'

The man stared through his spectacles at the two images and said, 'That would explain his bigger build, I suppose, and facially he looks the same. If Janice thinks it's him, I'm happy to go along with her. It certainly looks like Seb to me.'

Sara took the photographs and replaced them in the envelope. 'That's been a massive help, thank you.'

Stuart said, 'Is that it, Detective?'

Sara stood to leave. 'That's it, thanks.'

Janice jumped up and said, 'I'll show you out.'

As they reached the front door, Janice whispered, 'You know when you've finished your investigations, would you mind if I had a copy of the one with Sebastien in his cap and gown? We don't have any photographs, and I would love to have that one. He was such a lovely boy.'

Sara nodded. 'I'll talk to my boss, and if he says it's okay, I'll drop a copy off for you. Thanks for your time, Mrs Wainwright.'

As soon as she was in her car, Sara reached for the radio handset and said, 'DI Lacey to control. Over.'

The response was instant. 'Go ahead, DI Lacey. Over.'

'Could you contact DCI Flint at the MCIU and let him know that I've confirmed the graduation photograph of Steven Archer is Sebastien Haller. Over.'

67

6.00 a.m., 1 August 1991
28 Ash Grove, Stapleford, Nottinghamshire

Danny was feeling exhausted.

As soon as he received confirmation that Simon Archer had been positively identified as Sebastien Haller by Stuart and Janice Wainwright, many hours had been spent planning and finalising the raid on Archer's home address at Stapleford.

Danny was sitting in the passenger seat of the CID car alongside Jag Singh, and they both watched as armed SOU officers began stealthily approaching the neat semi-detached house.

There was no sign of any white van parked outside the address, and Danny was praying they hadn't already missed their target.

Ash Grove was an ordinary street, made up of houses

constructed in a similar build. Neat, red-brick homes with small front yards and alleyways running between the properties.

The only thing that differentiated Archer's house from all the others was the brand-new, cream-coloured uPVC double-glazed windows. There was also a large extension and a metal shed out in the back garden.

Danny glanced at his watch, and as the second hand ticked round to the twelve that signalled six o'clock, he heard the front door of the property being forced by the SOU. From the vehicle, he could hear shouts emanating from within the property. Less than a minute later his radio crackled into life, and he heard the officer leading the raid: 'Sergeant Turner to DCI Flint. Property clear. One person detained. You can come forward now, sir.'

'Chief Inspector Flint, received. Over.'

Danny and Jag immediately got out of the car and walked briskly to the property.

Sergeant Turner met them at the front door and said, 'Simon Archer's been detained in the kitchen. He was finishing breakfast and is dressed for a day's hiking by the look of him. There's an already packed rucksack in the kitchen as well.'

Danny asked, 'Has he said anything?'

'Nothing incriminating. He looked shocked when he saw armed cops storming in, but most people do. Once he got over that initial shock, he became aggressive and abusive. He's calmed down again now.'

'Good work, Graham. Is he still in the kitchen?'

'This way, boss.'

Danny and Jag walked through into the kitchen and saw Simon Archer still sitting in handcuffs at the breakfast table.

He looked red in the face and was staring down at the half-eaten bowl of porridge in front of him.

Danny noticed he was wearing warm clothing; there was a waterproof cagoule on the back of the chair and a pair of muddy walking boots next to the full rucksack near the back door.

Danny identified himself and said, 'Simon Archer. I am arresting you on suspicion of the abductions and murders of Sir Anthony Pemberton and Jurgen Hauptmann.'

He cautioned Archer, who responded by laughing out loud and saying, 'This has got to be a joke, right? I've absolutely no idea what you're talking about.'

Jag said, 'Our information is that you're the owner of a white van. I can see you intended going out today, so where's that vehicle now?'

'It's in my lock-up, two streets away. What's my van got to do with anything?'

'Where are the keys?'

Archer indicated the cagoule on the back of the chair. 'In the pocket.'

Jag picked up the jacket and removed the bunch of keys. 'Are you willing to show us where your vehicle is?'

Archer nodded. 'Look. I want to co-operate in any way I can, but this is all nonsense and more than a little over the top. I haven't killed anybody. I'm a scientist, for God's sake. Of course I'll show you where the van's kept, but are these handcuffs really necessary?'

Danny said, 'It's safer for everybody if they remain on for now. We can cover them when we leave the house. How far away is the lock-up?'

'Like I said, just a couple of streets. A five-minute walk.'

'Okay. On your feet.'

Danny slipped the cagoule over Archer's wrists, effectively hiding the handcuffs, and said, 'We'll drive you there.'

As the two detectives walked out of the house with Archer, Danny looked at Sergeant Turner and said, 'I'm going to need one of your men to accompany us to this lock-up.'

Turner turned and barked an order, 'Matt, go with the chief inspector and watch Archer.'

As the burly Matt Jarvis walked behind Archer, the SOU sergeant said, 'Do you want us to hold off our search until scenes of crime have been through, sir?'

'Have you found a firearm of any description?'

'No firearm and no ammunition, but as I say, we've only made a cursory search so far.'

'Have you gained access to the metal shed?'

'Yes, sir.'

'Anything of interest?'

'Nothing obvious. Tools and old decorating stuff. The usual crap people gather over time.'

'Okay. Let scenes of crime do their sweep first, and then I want this place thoroughly searched. I want every piece of paper read and every possible hiding place explored. If Archer has premises elsewhere, there will be documentation in here somewhere.'

'No problem, boss. I'll radio the scenes of crime team on standby and instruct them to come forward.'

'Thanks, Graham. Can you also instruct them we'll need to arrange for a full lift on a vehicle as well. They can put the vehicle examiners on standby.'

Two minutes later Jag parked the car alongside a row of garages a couple of streets away.

Archer, who was sat with his head bowed in the back of

the CID car, looked up and said, 'That's my one. The one with the blue door that's got graffiti sprayed all over it. The key for the padlock is on the bunch you took from my jacket.'

Danny turned to face Matt Jarvis. 'Are you going to be okay with him in the car on your own while we have a quick look?'

Matt looked hard faced at Archer and said, 'I don't think we're going to have any issues, boss.'

Archer shook his head as though agreeing with the muscular SOU officer.

It took Jag less than a minute to work his way through the bunch of keys until he found the right one for the padlock. As it sprang open, he dropped the hasp and swung open the double wooden doors.

As the doors opened, Danny saw the back of a dirty Bedford Astra van. Slipping on a pair of gloves, he took the keys from Jag, and the two detectives approached the rear of the vehicle. He tried the handle and found it was unlocked.

The interior of the van was a mess. There was all manner of junk in the back. He walked into the garage and tried the driver's door, which was also unlocked. The interior of the cab was equally messy, and there was a strange, unpleasant odour that was almost overpowering.

He turned to Jag and said, 'What do you think's causing that stench?'

Jag stepped forward and stuck his head inside the vehicle. 'God knows. It smells like something died in there.'

The two detectives exchanged glances before Danny closed the doors.

There was nothing he could see that was obviously incriminating, but the stench was more than a worry. As the two detectives walked back outside the garage, Danny said, 'Arrange for a lift to headquarters, Jag. I want this vehicle to undergo a full forensic examination.'

Jag added a note of caution. 'It's white, but it's not a Ford Escort van, boss.'

'True. But it would be an easy mistake to confuse the two types of vehicles, especially at night on an average CCTV system. I want it removed and examined. I want you to remain here and supervise that.'

'Okay, boss.'

As Danny took the CID car keys from Jag, he said, 'I'll make sure you're not waiting out here long.'

As he got back in the car, he turned to Archer and said, 'What's causing that stench in your van?'

Archer didn't make eye contact as he said, 'I think it's best I don't say anything else until I've spoken to a solicitor. I don't understand exactly what's going on here, but I do know I've done nothing wrong.'

'No explanation for that awful smell, then?'

Archer growled. 'Listen. I've never broken the law in my life, yet this morning I've been arrested at gunpoint and accused of murder. I think it's best I get some legal advice before I say anything else.'

He then swivelled in his seat and stared out the car window, effectively shutting down any further conversation.

68

Danny and Rob were discussing the arrest of Simon Archer. Sharon Whittle sat alongside listening to their conversation.

Rob said, 'The fact that the vehicle used by Archer is a Bedford Astra van and not a Ford Escort has to make it less likely that he's our man.'

'I agree, but don't you think it's strange how he clammed up as soon as I mentioned the stench in the van. We need to question him thoroughly and find out what he's got to say about these allegations.'

'I hear what you're saying, Danny, but you know what it's like. I don't think he'll talk to us at all, not once he's spoken to his solicitor.'

'I at least need him to account for his movements around

the dates of the abductions and the depositions of the three bodies. And I want to know exactly how long he's had that vehicle.' He looked at Rob, determined to make his point. 'We need to know where he was yesterday and why Cambridge University have him on record as Steven Archer, yet he uses the name Simon at the laboratories.'

'True,' Rob said. 'But he's asked for Bhatia Best solicitors in the city. I don't expect much co-operation from them. I think they'll instruct him to make no comment at this stage and wait to see exactly what evidence we can offer.'

'Who's going to be carrying out the interview?'

'Me and Glen.'

'Have we heard from the search team at Ash Grove yet?'

'I spoke with Graham Turner before I came to see you. They're about halfway through but haven't found anything startling yet.'

'Bloody hell!' Danny cursed. 'Has Jag returned from headquarters yet? Did he say how long it will take scenes of crime to forensically examine the van recovered from the lock-up?'

'He's back, but even that news isn't great. Tim Donnelly thinks it will take days, not hours, to thoroughly examine everything in the van and to then process the interior.'

Danny pinched the bridge of his nose and screwed his eyes shut as another wave of tiredness, which was starting to feel like despair, swept over him.

'And how long before Archer will be ready for interview, Rob?'

'He's with his solicitor now. They've already been in consultation for over half an hour, but we all know how Bhatia Best drag things out. Hopefully, it won't be much longer.'

Danny turned to Sharon Whittle and said, 'Any thoughts on interview strategy for this first interview?'

She replied, 'If he does talk to you, it might be an idea to go in at a low level and firstly probe his connections with Hauptmann and Pemberton. Try to establish exactly why he chose Future Visions Pharmaceutical to work for, when presumably he could have had his pick of any of the major pharmaceutical companies after achieving a doctorate at Cambridge.'

Rob nodded. 'We'll do our best to get him talking, but it won't be easy.'

Danny grimaced. 'It never is, Rob.'

69

10.00 a.m., 1 August 1991
Mansfield Custody Office, Nottinghamshire

Rob completed the introductions of everyone present in the interview room and reminded Simon Archer that he was still under caution.

He paused before saying, 'Do you understand the reason for your arrest this morning?'

Archer maintained steady eye contact with the detective as he said, 'My understanding is that I was arrested on suspicion of the murder of my two colleagues Sir Anthony Pemberton and Jurgen Hauptmann. Which I have to say is a ridiculous accusation.'

Rob breathed out; he always felt a sense of relief when the person he was interviewing answered the first question.

'One of the reasons for your arrest is to ascertain your whereabouts on certain dates and for you to be questioned while you have legal advice. This is your interview, and your solicitor is here to both advise you and ensure that your rights are upheld. Do you understand that?'

'I do, and to that end my solicitor has advised me not to answer any of your questions. I have made the decision that it would be far more prudent for me to co-operate fully with your enquiries so this nonsense can be quickly dealt with. That way you and your colleagues can concentrate on finding the person responsible for these crimes.'

Glen Lorimar now took over the questioning. 'I appreciate that, Simon,' he said. 'Do you mind if I call you Simon?'

'Not at all.'

'Okay, let's start with the van we seized from your lock-up in Stapleford. How long have you owned that vehicle?'

'Around three years now. Every year I think about swapping it, but then it passes the MOT, so I keep it for another year.'

'Do you possess or have access to any other vehicles?'

'No.'

'When we recovered that vehicle, there was a noticeably strong smell emanating from the interior. Can you explain that smell?'

'I wish I could. I noticed it about a month ago, and I must admit it's gradually got worse. I suppose I've stopped smelling it now, as I've got used to it.'

'Haven't you searched the van to try to establish what's causing it?'

'I haven't had time. You've seen the van; it's that full of rubbish in the back, it would be a full day's work.'

'We're having the vehicle forensically examined as we speak, so hopefully we'll find out what's causing it.'

Glen waited to see if there was any reaction from Archer

to the news that the vehicle was being subjected to a full forensic examination. When there was no change in his expression or demeanour, he continued with his next question.

'Can you tell me why your chemistry degree and doctorate were presented under the name Steven Archer, but you use the name Simon Archer at Future Visions Pharmaceutical?'

'That's an easy one, Detective. My full name is Simon Steven George Archer. When I started my degree course, I noticed that the university admin had mixed my first two names up. I was always known as Steven Archer at uni. That's the reason my degree was issued to Steven Archer and not Simon. When I started my job at Future Visions, I thought it best to revert to my first name.'

'Tell me about your family background. Where are you from originally?'

'Is that relevant?'

'I'm still trying to understand the reasoning behind you using different names, that's the relevance.'

'There are no big secrets. I was born in Stockport, just outside Manchester. My parents were both science teachers at the local grammar school.'

'You said were and not are. Have your parents retired now?'

'My parents died when I was ten years old. I was effectively raised by my grandmother in Surrey. She was a lecturer in chemistry at the University of Surrey in Guildford. She nurtured my already strong love of science. I think she's the main reason I did so well at school and was accepted into Cambridge. I owe her everything and was devastated when she too passed before I graduated. I have no family now, Detective.'

'I'm sorry for your loss, Simon. What was your grandmother's name?'

'Patricia Harvey. She was my maternal grandmother. I never knew my grandfather or my paternal grandparents.'

'That must have been a huge upheaval for you at the time. New schools are always hard to settle into, at any age.'

'I didn't have any issues at my new school. I've always been big for my age, so bullies steered well clear, thankfully.'

'What schools did you attend when you moved to Guildford?'

'Kings Road Junior School for a year and then Larch Avenue private school.'

'Is Larch Avenue a boarding school?'

'It is, but I didn't board, as it wasn't far from where my grandmother lived.'

'When you applied for the job at Future Visions, who conducted the interviews?'

'I was interviewed by Jurgen Hauptmann and the head of personnel, Gillian McMaster.' He paused before adding, 'It wasn't really an interview. I met with them both at the Beeston premises, and they offered me the job virtually straight away. I'm not bragging, but they were both aware that after the research work I had already conducted during my postgraduate studies at Cambridge, I could have gone to any of the big pharmaceutical companies. The main reason I applied for the job with Future Visions was because of the reputation of Hauptmann.'

'I understand from a colleague that your opinion of Jurgen Hauptmann may have now changed?'

Archer was tight lipped and thoughtful before he said, 'I

think that's a fair comment, Detective. Since collaborating with him and watching him work alongside other young scientists, I now believe he's a man living on past glories. I've found that his knowledge of recent discoveries and techniques is sadly lacking.'

'If that's the case, are you still happy about working at Future Visions?'

'I can't say it will be my life's work, but for now it suits me.'

'Can you tell me what you were doing on or around the thirteenth of July?'

'That's six weeks ago, Detective. How am I supposed to remember that?'

'Have you had any other time off work apart from this week?'

'I did have a couple of days off around the middle of July. I went to Scarborough for a few days to make the most of the sunshine. It was somewhere I used to go with my gran.'

'Can you remember where you would have stayed?'

'I booked the same bed and breakfast we always stayed in when I went with her. Like I said earlier, I owe her everything, and I miss her badly.'

'What's the name of the B&B?'

'The Haven Guest House, on the Esplanade.'

'How many nights did you stay?'

'Just a couple. It was a quick break from work, that's all.'

'Was anybody with you?'

'No.'

'Where were you on or around the twenty-third of July?'

'I would have been at home, at work, or at the gym. I don't really go anywhere else.'

'How often do you go to the gym?'

'I try to train every day. I guess I'm pretty much addicted to weight training. It helps me to wind down. After using my brain all day, it's nice to let my body do some physical work.'

'What gym do you use?'

'Atlas Body Sculpture in Stapleford. It's not a posers' gym. Most of the people who train there are serious. A lot of the guys compete.'

'How long have you been a member?'

'Ever since I started at Future Visions.'

'What's the system when you use the gym? Do you have to sign in?'

'You should, but not everybody does. It's a fire safety thing because the gym is in a cellar, and there's only one way in and one way out.'

'Do you always sign in?'

'When I remember. The staff all know me as a regular anyway. They will tell you what time of day I'm there.'

'And what about the twenty-fifth of July? Where would you have been?'

'The same. At home, work, or the gym.'

'Okay. That's all we need for the moment, Simon. Is there anything you want to ask me?'

'Have you any idea how long I'm going to be here?'

Rob said, 'You've just given us a lot of information to check. As soon as we've done that, then a decision will be made as to how we proceed.'

Archer's solicitor said, 'I want to echo my client's question. He has co-operated fully and answered all your questions. I take it your enquiries will be done expeditiously.'

'We'll do them as quickly as we can.'

'Would bail, to return to the police station, be an option?'

'Let's get done what we can, and then see where we're at, shall we?'

70

3.00 p.m., 1 August 1991
MCIU Offices, Mansfield, Nottinghamshire

R ob walked into Danny's office and was surprised to see Andy Wills sitting there.

He smiled and said, 'Detective Inspector Wills, you're back quicker than I expected. Surveillance not right for you?'

Andy stood and shook hands with Rob and said, 'I'm loving it. It's all very different to what I'm used to, and it's also extremely challenging.'

'So, what brings you here?'

'I've asked him here to see if his unit is ready for a live job,' Danny said. 'I don't think we're going to find anything to hold Archer, and I'm conscious that his detention clock is ticking. I'm considering bailing him to return to the police station at a later date. In the meantime, I want him watched twenty-four seven.'

Rob looked at Andy. 'Could you do that?'

'There's a lot of experience already on the unit, and a live job is just what we need to evaluate our capabilities. I have several ex-crime squad detectives who are already more than capable of doing foot and vehicle surveillance, and special ops officers who are experienced in manning covert surveillance premises to give us the off.'

Danny said, 'How long would you need to set things up?'

Andy said, 'Ideally, I'd like to find premises that overlook Archer's home address. If we can't, we do have observations vans we could use. Once that's in place, we'd be good to go.'

'What sort of time?'

Andy glanced at his watch. 'It's three o'clock now. If you bailed Archer at six o'clock, we should be in position to start the surveillance.'

Rob grinned. 'It will take me the best part of an hour,' he said, 'if I take the slow road, to drive him back to his home address in Stapleford, so you've got the best part of four hours to prepare. Will that be enough time?'

'That should be plenty. I'll get going and call you when everything's set up.'

Danny said, 'Thanks, Andy.'

'No, thank you. The unit needs a live job, and this could be the perfect opportunity to show what we can do. It will also help me iron out any shortfalls in our procedures. I'll call you as soon as we're ready.'

As Andy closed the door behind him, Rob said, 'I thought I'd update you on progress so far.'

'Fire away.'

'Both the schools in Guildford check out.'

'No issues at all?'

'None. His next of kin at that time was Patricia Harvey. The enquiries we've conducted with the University of Surrey records office have Patricia Harvey working there as a lecturer until she retired in 1986. She passed away in 1988, the year before Archer graduated from Cambridge.'

'Okay. So that's his childhood squared away. What about the relevant dates?'

'I've asked North Yorkshire CID to visit the Haven Guest House in Scarborough to check the dates Archer stayed there in the middle of July. They haven't got back to us yet.'

'And the other two dates?'

'I've still got people checking the Atlas gym in Stapleford. To say their fire safety book is less than perfect would be an understatement. It's extremely slapdash. There are dates where Archer has signed in, but there are plenty where he hasn't, including the two later relevant dates.' Rob flicked the page of his notebook. 'The staff do all remember Archer as a daily user of the gym. They have confirmed that he always arrives around the same time, between five and six in the evening, and that he trains seriously for at least a couple of hours each session.'

'What about work?'

'He's shown as being at work on those dates, but the abductions of Pemberton and Hauptmann happened outside his working hours, so that doesn't take us any further forward. He could have abducted Pemberton after work and Hauptmann before he started work.'

Danny was uneasy that none of the dates could be satisfactorily alibied away, but he knew that time constraints meant he would have to release Archer due to lack of evidence, sooner rather than later. His solicitor was already complaining about the length of time her client had spent in custody.

The search of his home address by the Special Operations Unit had revealed nothing suspicious.

He said, 'Any update from Tim about the examination of Archer's van?'

Rob shook his head. 'Nothing yet, boss. The last time I spoke to him, he was talking about it being late tomorrow before the job was completed.'

Danny threw his pen on the desk in frustration, then leaned back in his chair. 'Start making the preparations to release Archer on bail for six o'clock this evening.'

'How long a bail date should we put on him?'

'I don't think Andy will want to run a twenty-four-hour surveillance for any longer than a fortnight, and we will have all our answers by then. Bail him to return here on fifteenth August, and let's continue working on those alibi dates first thing tomorrow morning. If the surveillance shows nothing suspicious or doesn't identify other premises or vehicles by the time we have completed our checks on his alibis, we can always cancel his bail.'

'Are you starting to think he may not be our man?'

Danny shrugged. 'Let's keep an open mind and see what the surveillance turns up.'

Rob stood. 'I'm sure they'll turn something up, boss,' he said as he left the office.

Alone with his thoughts, Danny saw that he had printed the name Simon Archer in block capitals on the notepad in front of him. He picked his pen up, struck a line through the name and muttered, 'I'm not holding my breath, Rob.'

71

Danny and Rob were discussing the progress that had been made after a full day of enquiries into the alibis provided by Archer.

Rob said, 'It's looking increasingly like he isn't our man. His alibis for the time when Pemberton and Hauptmann were abducted are watertight.'

'How so?'

'We know from the CCTV tape at the golf course that Sir Anthony Pemberton was abducted at nine o'clock at night. We now have a witness who can place Archer still at the gym at eight thirty that night. There's no way he could have driven to the golf course at Oxton in time to abduct Pemberton.'

'Who's the witness?' Danny asked.

'A young woman who's worked at the gym for the last three years. She knows Archer well but has no connection to him outside of the gym, not that we can find. There's no reason for her to lie about his whereabouts that night.'

'Okay. What about Hauptmann?'

'Archer arrived at work on the morning Hauptmann was abducted at seven forty-five. We never spotted it before because Fiona Foster signed the log. She had driven Archer to work, which means there's no way he could have set up Hauptmann to abduct him that morning.'

'That's two down.' Danny sighed. 'What about the date Terrence McAvoy's body was discovered at Worksop?'

'On the night of the twelfth and the morning of July the thirteenth, Archer was staying at the Haven Guest House in Scarborough. He was there all night and had an early breakfast at seven o'clock. This has been statemented by North Yorkshire CID, which makes it highly unlikely he would have been able to deposit McAvoy's body at Worksop golf course.'

'Any update on his vehicle?'

'That rancid stench has now been identified.' Rob allowed himself a wry smile. 'Under a pile of other junk just behind the front of the driver's seat, a half-eaten pot of strawberry yoghurt was found. Some of the contents had spilled onto the mats in the back of the van. I think it's a smell that will stay in that vehicle for ever.'

'Anything of any evidential value found in the van?'

'Nothing. The van has been released, and Archer picked it up from headquarters today.'

'Is there any good news?'

'Andy and his team are still working the surveillance and have had no issues at all. Archer is oblivious to the fact he's under constant observation. Considering the enquiries already completed, how long do you want to continue with the surveillance?'

'It's only been twenty-four hours.' Danny leaned back in his chair. 'Let's run the surveillance for at least a week. If we've found nothing by then, I'll abort the operation and have his bail cancelled. This killer is an expert at long-term planning and preparation. There's still a possibility Archer could have another vehicle stashed somewhere, and that he also has access to other premises.'

'If your thinking's correct, why don't we maintain the surveillance operation but cancel his bail tomorrow. That will give him the green light that he's no longer a suspect. And if he's as devious as you suspect he is, I think he's more likely to slip up and make a mistake if we do things that way round.'

Danny was thoughtful for a couple of minutes. 'I think you're right. Contact his solicitor and inform her what we're proposing. Inform her there's no evidence to connect her client in either of the abductions and murders, and that we need her client to return to Mansfield police station so the custody sergeant can formally cancel his bail. In the meantime, I'll contact Andy and tell him what we're planning. Hopefully if he's going to do something, it will happen after his bail is cancelled.'

'I'm on it, boss.'

'Rob,' Danny said as the detective inspector opened the office door, 'good thinking, mate.'

72

6.00 p.m., 3 August 1991
Queen's Medical Centre, Nottingham

I t was the third full day of surveillance on Archer, and the first since his police bail was cancelled. At just after five o'clock he had driven to the gym and started his daily workout. He left thirty minutes later, still dressed in his training gear. He walked out the front door of the gym, ignored his parked van and got straight into a waiting taxi. He appeared in a hurry.

As most of the surveillance team followed the taxi, one pair were left to maintain observations on the parked van. This meant the follow team was restricted in the number of times they could effectively change over. It was risky, but Andy took the decision to maintain the follow, hoping that Archer remained oblivious to his unit's presence.

After twenty minutes the taxi turned onto the slip road

that led to the emergency department entrance of the Queen's Medical Centre. As the surveillance lead car followed, it was suddenly stopped by a road construction worker using a stop/go signal board. The driver had no option but to stop. The driver of the surveillance vehicle cursed under his breath as the taxi disappeared.

DC Sanderson, who was the passenger in the lead car, picked up the radio and said, 'From the eyeball, it's a loss, loss. We are baulked at a manual traffic control and have lost sight of the target. I'm deploying on foot to see if I can locate the taxi.'

A series of clicks came over the air as other officers engaged in the surveillance acknowledged the message.

DC Sanderson got out of the car and sprinted down the service road, following the direction of the taxi. In the distance he saw the taxi pulling up directly outside the emergency department. As he slowed to a jog, he saw Archer get out of the taxi and walk into the hospital.

Slightly breathless from his exertions, he said over the radio, 'Target has entered the emergency department of the hospital. I'm going to follow him inside but will need backup as soon as possible. Over.'

The detective slowed to walking pace and took deep breaths to steady himself before walking through the revolving door that led into the emergency department of the hospital. It was extremely busy, and he frantically searched the sea of faces to locate Archer.

He was nowhere to be seen.

Five minutes later Andy Wills walked through the revolving doors and found DC Sanderson.

He whispered, 'Where'd he go?'

'I don't know. I virtually walked in right behind him, and

he was nowhere to be seen. It's not like he wouldn't stand out; he was still wearing his gym kit, for Christ's sake. I just couldn't see him.'

'Okay. Have you checked the cubicles?'

'Yes. He's not in any of them. I've even had a discreet word with one of the nurses to see if she'd seen anyone in gym gear, and she said not. He's vanished, boss.'

'People don't just vanish. Stay here and keep your eyes peeled. If he does show up back in here, I want to know immediately.'

'Yes, boss.'

Andy Wills walked back to the car and got in the passenger seat. He picked up the radio and said, 'From DI Wills to the team. We have a total loss, repeat a total loss. I want every entrance covered. I want to know if any taxis come onto the site. Let's get looking. He's here somewhere.'

73

6.30 p.m., 3 August 1991
Queen's Medical Centre, Nottingham

I t had been a long and stressful day for Seamus Carter.
It had been a day of back-to-back post-mortem examinations at the hospital. As he walked up the stairs of
the multi-storey car park, he could feel his legs and back
aching. He longed to get home to his cottage, located just
outside Newark, have a nice warm bath and some food. He
grimaced at the thought of the forty-minute commute, but
then smiled as he remembered that his fiancée, Gemma,
would be there waiting for him.

Although it was still light outside, the car park was a
myriad of deep shadows. Most of the lighting inside had
been smashed by vandals, which meant the only light in the
parking area was the gloom filtering in from the outside.

After climbing four flights of concrete steps, carrying his

heavy briefcase, Seamus felt slightly breathless. There were cars dotted around this level of the car park, and he could see his Volvo parked at the far end.

It was sitting in deep shadow.

As he walked towards it, he fumbled in his jacket pocket for the keys. As he went to place the keys in the lock on the driver's side, he heard a man's voice behind him say, 'Seamus Carter?'

Shocked, he spun around and was confronted by a man of a similar height and build to himself.

He was about to say something when he saw the man swing a heavy spanner towards his head. He had no time to evade the blow and felt it crash onto the side of his head. He immediately dropped his briefcase and sank to his knees. He saw the concrete floor rushing towards his face before everything went black.

74

6.30 p.m., 3 August 1991
Queen's Medical Centre, Nottingham

The man had waited patiently in the shadows of the car park and had been pleased to see the pathologist's dark blue Volvo was still in the car park when he arrived.

He had felt a familiar surge of adrenaline as he saw the big man with the bushy beard approaching his vehicle. His research into the Irish pathologist had been as thorough as always. He knew the man's vehicle, he knew where he lived, he knew his description, and he knew his work schedule. It was amazing what you could find out with a lot of patience and a little know-how.

Walking to the back of Carter's Volvo, he unlocked the boot and raised it. He was pleased to see it was completely empty and was spacious enough to get the burly pathologist in.

He dragged the now unconscious Seamus Carter to the back of the vehicle and grunted at the effort it took to lift him into the boot. Once he was inside, he checked for a pulse and smiled as he felt a strong rhythmic beat in the pathologist's neck. He took a roll of gaffer tape from his pocket and wrapped it around the man's wrists and ankles, effectively binding him. He then stuffed a rag in his mouth and wrapped the tape around his head to form a makeshift gag. It was a struggle getting the sticky tape to adhere to the beard, and he needed to wrap several layers around his head before it stayed in place.

Scanning the area around the car, he spotted the dropped briefcase and placed that in the boot alongside the pathologist.

He closed the boot quietly, unlocked the driver's door, slipped the key in the ignition and started the engine.

He smiled again when he saw the car had a full tank of petrol.

He selected first gear, flicked the lights on and drove slowly out of the car park.

75

8.00 p.m., 3 August 1991
Woodland near Welbeck, Nottinghamshire

The big man grunted as he hoisted the unconscious pathologist out of the boot of the Volvo. He allowed Carter to drop to the floor before closing the boot.

He adjusted his gas mask and then gripped the man's jacket lapels before hauling him off the ground and lifting him over his shoulder into a fireman's lift.

He allowed his powerful legs to take the weight of the big Irishman; then he stepped inside the tunnel.

He flicked the handheld torch on as the darkness of the tunnel closed in around him. It was challenging work carrying the heavy man through the tunnel, and he was relieved to see the wire cages come into view.

He unceremoniously dropped Carter in front of one of

the empty cages and unlocked the door. It was awkward trying to stuff a man the size of Seamus Carter into the small wire cage. Eventually, after a long struggle, he managed to close and lock the door. The pathologist had been bent into a grotesque shape, which enabled him to fit inside the cramped space of the cage.

Now the big man shone the torch in the direction of the other cages and could see his other two captives sitting wide eyed in the darkness, terrified at what they were witnessing.

After the physical exertion of carrying the pathologist along the tunnel, he was now breathing heavily behind the gas mask, so he chose not to say a word to the two conscious captives. Instead, he bent down and moved his face closer to the cages until his captives could hear his rasping breaths from behind the mask. He revelled in seeing the fear on their faces as they stared unblinking at the monster standing before them.

Without saying a word, he stood up and walked away, knowing their eyes would follow him until he was completely out of sight.

After a ten-minute walk, he reached the entrance of the tunnel. He switched off the torch and ripped the claustrophobic gas mask from his face, greedily sucking in deep lungfuls of the fresh night air.

He would check on the three captives tomorrow morning. Right now, he had an unwanted car to dispose of before making his way home.

76

10.30 p.m., 3 August 1991
28 Ash Grove, Stapleford, Nottinghamshire

Andy Wills had waited until the night shift were due to start the observations before standing down the team. Even though his detectives had been frantically searching the hospital and the grounds for hours, there had been no further sightings of Archer. Andy felt the situation was now beyond redemption; he had no choice but to abort the operation.

He wasn't relishing the telephone call he would need to make to Chief Inspector Flint, informing him that his fledgling team had lost the target on their first live operation.

Feeling bitterly disappointed, he decided to make one more attempt to locate Archer before he allowed the team to go off duty.

With the night shift waiting on standby at police headquarters, Andy turned to DC Mitchell and said, 'Before we go back to HQ, let's take a drive over to Stapleford. I want to take another look at Archer's home address.'

DC Mitchell gunned the engine and accelerated away from the hospital grounds.

Fifteen minutes later, the detective slowed the vehicle, extinguished the lights and stopped directly opposite the semi-detached house. The downstairs lights of the property were on, and the curtains were drawn.

Suddenly, the unmistakeable, bulky figure of Simon Archer came into view as he walked across his lounge, passing in front of the bay window.

DC Mitchell let out a low whistle and said, 'The slippery bastard's inside, sir. How the hell has he got back here from the hospital without one of us seeing him?'

Andy grimaced. 'I don't know, Terry. That will be a question for the debrief later. Did you notice his left wrist?'

'Yeah. It looked to me like it was either in a plaster cast or heavily bandaged.'

Andy picked up the car radio and gave orders for the night shift to travel to Ash Grove immediately. They would need to re-establish observations on the home address again and set up a perimeter to contain Archer, in case he decided to go anywhere during the night.

Having ensured the surveillance team were now on their way, Andy said, 'As soon as the team arrive, get me to Stapleford police station. I need to make an urgent phone call.'

77

12.10 a.m., 4 August 1991
Mansfield, Nottinghamshire

D anny had been in bed for over an hour. He was having one of those nights where much-needed sleep just wouldn't come. As he lay staring up at the ceiling, his mind was full of images of victims mutilated by acid burns. He was about to get out of bed and make himself a coffee when the telephone on the bedside cabinet started to ring.

He snatched the receiver off the cradle and said quietly, 'DCI Flint.'

Andy Wills said, 'I'm sorry to call you at this time of night, boss.'

'Andy? What's happened?'

'Archer left the gym early and caught a taxi to the

Queen's Medical Centre. We followed the taxi but were baulked by a manually controlled traffic signal. Repairs are being done to the surface of the slip road at the entrance. The construction worker stepped into the single lane and spun the board just after the taxi went through. My detective had the choice of either stopping or running the guy over.'

'No choice at all, then. Did you manage to get eyes on Archer subsequently?'

'We have now. Archer has somehow got from the hospital back to his home address. Unfortunately, we had a total loss on him for just over four hours. I'm sorry, but we just couldn't locate him at the hospital.'

Danny silently cursed but said, 'Don't worry, Andy. That's the nature of surveillance work. It's never an exact science; way too many variables for that. The main thing is you've got him back under observation now.'

'Apart from keeping the observations running, I thought some of my team could go back to Queen's and start asking questions to see if we can establish what he was doing there.'

'I've no objection to you doing that, but it's like looking for a needle in a haystack. That hospital is huge.'

'When we spotted him back at home, it looked like his left wrist is either heavily bandaged or in a plaster cast. I thought we could ask some questions at the X-ray department and the A&E fracture station.'

'That's a good call. What time does the gym open?'

'It opens at six o'clock every morning.

'Excellent. As soon as the doors open, get someone down there and see if Archer had some sort of accident at the gym last night. I want to know why he got a cab to the hospital, instead of driving his van. Talking of which, where's his van now?'

'Where he left it last night. Still parked behind the gym.'

'When the enquiries have been made at the hospital and the gym, make sure you call me again if you find anything that troubles you. Okay?'

'Okay, boss. Thanks for understanding the situation.'

Danny replaced the handset, got out of bed and slipped on his dressing gown. He had been struggling to sleep before, and now that he had taken that disturbing phone call, he knew there would be no chance of him getting any rest tonight.

As he reached the bottom of the stairs, he was startled by an urgent knocking on the front door.

He stepped forward, slipped the two deadbolts back and unlocked the door.

As he was about to open the door, he heard Sue's voice behind him. 'Be careful, Danny.'

He turned and saw his wife standing at the top of the stairs in her nightdress.

He whispered, 'It's okay. Go back to bed.'

Sue didn't move a muscle. 'Who would come knocking at this time of night?'

Only one way to find out, Danny thought as he turned the Yale lock and opened the door.

Of all the people he might have expected to see standing there, Gemma Coleridge was not one of them.

There was a panicked expression on her face, and her eyes were red rimmed. It was obvious she had been crying.

He said, 'Gemma? Come inside; whatever's the matter?'

Danny could hear Sue coming down the stairs behind him as Gemma stepped inside the house. As soon as she was in the hallway, she blurted out, 'Seamus hasn't come home. I phoned work, and they say he left just after six o'clock. He should have been home hours ago.'

Danny's blood ran cold. 'Was he working at the City Hospital yesterday?'

'No, he was at the Queen's Medical Centre all day. We normally travel home together when he's working there, but he had a particularly busy day, so he told me not to wait for him, as he would be late finishing.'

'Who did you talk to when you phoned the hospital?'

'I have the mortuary direct line. One of the attendants who works overnight told me Seamus left just after six o'clock. I'm frightened to death he's had an accident and is trapped in his car in a ditch somewhere. I'm sorry for turning up here so late, but I didn't know who else to ask for help.'

Sue stepped forward and put her arm around Gemma's shoulders. 'Come in, Gemma. I'll put the kettle on. You're shaking like a leaf.'

As Sue took Gemma through into the kitchen, Danny picked up the phone in the hallway and dialled the control room number.

The phone was answered on the third ring. 'Inspector Harvey, Force Control Room. Can I help you?'

Danny said, 'Bill, it's Danny Flint. I've got the fiancée of Home Office pathologist Seamus Carter at my house. She's frantic with worry, as Seamus hasn't arrived home as expected from work. He should have been home by seven o'clock at the latest. Have there been any call-outs for him this evening?'

'Just a minute, sir.'

After a brief delay, the inspector returned to the phone

and said, 'No, sir. No call-outs from this force or neighbouring forces. He's not on our call-out list for either yesterday or today.'

'Okay. Have there been any reports of road traffic accidents between the Queen's Medical Centre and Rolleston?'

The inspector answered that question immediately. 'No, sir. It's been a quiet night so far.'

'Thanks, Bill. If you do get a report of that nature, please contact me at home.'

Danny put the phone down and walked into the kitchen.

He sat on the chair next to Gemma and said, 'I've just spoken to our control room. Seamus hasn't been called out by the police, and there are no reports of any accidents between the hospital and Rolleston. I'm going to go into the office. It will be much easier for me to make enquiries from there, as I've got all the necessary numbers to hand. I want you to stay here with Sue. I'll call as soon as I find anything out.'

Gemma stared at him through bloodshot eyes. 'Do you think he's all right, Danny?'

'I'm sure he's fine.' He smiled at her. 'That grizzly bear of yours is indestructible.'

Danny went back upstairs and quickly got dressed. As he was about to leave the house, he kissed Sue on the cheek and said, 'I won't be long, sweetheart. Look after Gemma, and I'll call you as soon as I know anything.'

'I will do. Drive carefully, Danny. You've had hardly any sleep yourself.'

As Danny closed the front door and walked to his car, he had an uneasy feeling in the pit of his stomach. Simon Archer had given the surveillance team the slip at the

Queen's Medical Centre, after which he had gone missing for four hours. At around the same time Seamus Carter had seemingly disappeared after leaving the same hospital.

It could just be a coincidence, but Danny never did like coincidences.

78

6.30 a.m., 4 August 1991
MCIU Offices, Mansfield, Nottinghamshire

Danny had spent the early hours of the morning reading and rereading the reports of the abductions. There were alarming similarities in the circumstances of the methods used in those abductions and the circumstances now surrounding the disappearance of Seamus Carter.

He was starting to feel desperately worried for his friend and colleague.

Rob Buxton and Sara Lacey arrived in the office at the same time and were surprised to see a dishevelled and unshaven Danny sitting in front of a vast pile of paperwork in the briefing room.

Rob asked, 'Have you been here all night, boss? Has something happened?'

Danny looked up, anguished. 'I don't know. Seamus Carter didn't arrive home last night. He left the Queen's Medical Centre around six o'clock yesterday evening. I've had hospital security check the CCTV on the main car park, and it shows his Volvo leaving just after six fifteen. The journey to his cottage in Rolleston should take forty-five minutes at the most, but he never arrived home.'

Sara asked, 'Why are you looking at the reports of the abductions of Pemberton and Hauptmann? Do you think Carter is somehow connected to all of this?'

'That's what I'm trying to find out. I've been trying to locate the coroner's file that was prepared for the suicide of Rebecca Haller, but I can't lay my hands on it.'

Rob said, 'That was one of the files Professor Whittle was studying before she left last night.'

Danny snatched up the nearest phone and dialled the number for the switchboard, saying sharply, 'Get me the number for the Park Guest House in Mansfield, please.'

There was a brief delay, and then Danny scribbled a number down on the blotter in front of him. He replaced the phone, lifted the receiver again and dialled the number.

The telephone remained unanswered for a long time, but Danny stayed on the line. Eventually, it was picked up, and a woman's voice said, 'Park Guest House. Can I help you?'

'You have a guest staying there, Sharon Whittle. Can you put me through to her room, please?'

'No need, she's in the dining room, about to have breakfast. Who's calling?'

'It's Chief Inspector Flint. I need to speak with her urgently.'

A few seconds later, Danny heard Sharon's voice. 'Is everything okay, Danny?'

'Do you have the coroner's file for the death of Rebecca Haller with you?'

'Yes. It's in my room. You authorised me to take reports out of the office to study them, remember.'

'There isn't a problem, but I need to see that file urgently. I'll send a car to pick you up in ten minutes.'

'Okay. I'll be waiting.'

He put the phone down and said, 'Sara, grab some car keys and pick the professor up as soon as possible – please?'

'On my way, sir.'

As Sara left the office, Rob said, 'What are you thinking?'

'I've been racking my brains all night, and the only reason I could think of why Seamus would be connected to any of this madness was if he carried out the post-mortem to determine the cause of death of Rebecca Haller.'

'I'm not sure if Seamus was even working here back then.'

'Me neither, but it's something we need to check.'

Both men continued to check the details of other reports while they waited for Sharon to arrive with the coroner's file.

Danny picked up the list of graduates who had all achieved a chemistry degree on the same course as Simon Archer. 'I've been staring at this list of names off and on all night,' he said. 'There's a name on here I'm sure I've heard, or read about, before or during this investigation. I just can't put my finger on where.'

Rob took the list and said, 'What's the name?'

'The fifth from the bottom, Scott Taplow.'

Rob mused, 'Yeah, that does sound familiar.'

Suddenly, he jumped up and grabbed the large folder

that held the original witness statements. Flicking through the pages of statements, he exclaimed, 'Yes!'

He removed the statement from the folder, passed it to Danny and said, 'Scott Taplow was one of the security guards involved in the recovery of Jurgen Hauptmann's Porsche when it was taken to the Beeston laboratories after Hauptmann was abducted. He didn't get in the car, but he ignored his boss's specific order not to touch anything.'

'He's a security guard?'

Rob said, 'Yeah. But Taplow's a shaven-headed idiot who can barely string a coherent sentence together. I can't see him ever graduating from anywhere, let alone Cambridge, with a doctorate to his name.'

'Find the number for the head of security,' Danny said. 'We need to talk a bit more to Taplow.'

As Rob scanned the reports to find the number for Alan Villiers, Sharon Whittle walked in holding the coroner's file.

She immediately handed the folder to Danny, who began urgently flicking through the pages.

He held a sheet of paper up to Rob and said, 'It's here. The post-mortem that determined Rebecca Haller had taken her own life was conducted by Seamus Carter.'

'Christ,' Rob said, a look of horror on his face. 'If that's the case, he could be in danger. Every one of these murder victims, these people who have been abducted and are missing, have some connection with Rebecca Haller.'

'Not all. McAvoy had no connection to Haller,' Sharon Whittle said. 'Has something happened to this pathologist?'

'He failed to return home after work last night. I'll tell you the full circumstances shortly. I need to make this call.'

Danny picked up the phone.

It was answered on the second ring. 'Alan Villiers.'

Danny said, 'Mr Villiers, it's Chief Inspector Flint from the Major Crime Investigation Unit. I'm pleased you're in work early today, as we're going to need to talk with one of your security personnel, Scott Taplow, urgently.'

'Not possible, Detective. Scott's taken a fortnight off. He flew out to Benidorm yesterday. That's one of the reasons I'm here so early. I couldn't arrange cover for him today.'

'Any idea which airport?'

There was a brief silence before Villiers said, 'I can't be sure, but he said something about not having to drive far to the airport. I'm sure he said it was either East Midlands or Birmingham.'

'I take it you'll be in the office all morning?'

'Yes. I'll be here. I know Scott fucked up with the Porsche, and he's not the sharpest knife in the drawer, but he's a good lad and a diligent worker. Why do you need to talk to him?'

'What do you know about his history prior to him joining your staff?'

'He came with impeccable references and presented very well at his interview. He had no criminal record and was physically very strong. He was the ideal candidate.'

'Did you check his references?'

Villiers hesitated, and his reply, when it came, sounded sheepish. 'I made a cursory phone call, and there were no issues.'

'Were you satisfied that his references were genuine?'

'Yes, there was no reason to think otherwise, and he's been a model employee ever since he started here. He's never taken a day off sick, and his timekeeping is good.'

'Where's his home address?'

'Just a second. I'll grab his personnel file.'

There was a brief delay, and then Villiers said, 'He lives at forty-three Bainton Grove, Clifton.'

'Does he have any family or friends?'

'There's no family listed. Scott's a loner. He doesn't socialise with any of the other guys. He's a gym fanatic, but that's it for hobbies, as far as I'm aware.'

'Girlfriend?'

'Not that I know of.'

'How does he travel to work every day, if he lives at Clifton?'

'He's got a motor. He drives this clapped-out van.'

'Do you have the number?'

'Just a second. Here it is. The van's a white Ford Escort, registration C552 JTF.'

'When's he due back into work?'

'His first day back will be the seventeenth of this month.'

There was a long pause, and then Villiers said, 'Is he in any trouble?'

'I don't know. Thanks for your help, Mr Villiers.'

Danny replaced the phone, and as the office was getting busy with detectives arriving to start their shifts, he said, 'Let's take this in my office.'

Seeing Jag arrive, he said, 'Jag, join us in the office, please.'

Jag took his coat off and followed Danny, Rob, Sara and Sharon into the office.

Danny looked at Sharon and said, 'Is it feasible that the security guard at Future Visions is the same Scott Taplow who graduated from Cambridge University?'

'I take it you now suspect that Scott Taplow is in fact Sebastien Haller?'

'I don't know. Before I do anything else, I need to establish that.'

He turned to Sara and said, 'You've made all the enquiries at Cambridge thus far. I want you to go back to the university this morning and find out what you can about Scott Taplow. I want photographs and any background information you can glean. Ask if they've had any contact with him since he left the university. Any acquaintances he made while he was there?'

He looked at Rob. 'You've seen Scott Taplow recently, so go with Sara. Once you've seen a photograph, if you think the Taplow who graduated is the same man who's now a security guard, I want to know immediately.'

The two detective inspectors nodded. Sara said, 'We'll leave straightaway, boss. It's a two-and-a-half-hour journey at this time of day.'

'Okay. Let me know as soon as you've got something.'

As they left, Danny said to Jag, 'Forget about everything you had planned for today, Jag. I need you to do two things as a matter of urgency. Firstly, check the local airports for all flights to Alicante that left over the last two days, then consult with Special Branch officers at the airport and check the manifests for each of those flights. I need to know if Scott Taplow was listed on any flights to airports serving Benidorm.'

He paused, then said, 'Once you've done that, I want you and Glen Lorimar to start preparing an operational order to search forty-three Bainton Grove, Clifton. I'll need you to get a search warrant from the court.'

'Okay, boss,' Jag said as he stood to leave.

'Keep me informed of progress throughout the day.'

Danny was left alone in the office with Sharon Whittle,

who looked deep in thought. 'Do you think this is possible, Sharon?'

'If this man is as fixated on avenging the death of his mother and is as intelligent as you think he is, I'd say it's not only possible but extremely likely.'

'How so?'

'This killer is such a methodical and meticulous planner. I believe it's possible he's been obsessing over and planning this from the day he was informed of his mother's tragic death. Can you think of a better way for him to get close to the people he blamed for her death than to work among them?'

She sat back in her chair as though warming to her theme. 'Not only does he apply to work at the same location as his mother worked, but he's smart enough to work in a capacity that he knows will draw no comparison to his scientist mother. As a security guard, he would cause no suspicion nor offer any threat to the scientists who worked there.'

'But why go to Cambridge and study chemistry?'

'Because he believes he's clever enough to get away with these killings and then resume a life of science somewhere else. He never intended this to be his life's work. He's not just desperate for revenge, he also wants a life afterwards. He's obviously a critical planner and master of the long game. Studying chemistry at that level would also afford him the requisite skills he would need to kill his victims in the way he does. Always remember that it's much easier for an intelligent person to portray themselves as stupid than the other way round.'

'But why not just get a job as a scientist? If he's using a different name anyway?'

'Don't forget that by getting a job on the security team,

he would have ready access to all the personal information of his targets.'

'I can see that.'

'It all fits, Danny. I've always believed the key to these murders lay at Future Visions Pharmaceutical. I guarantee that Taplow would have had a completely different appearance at Cambridge from how he looks now. He may even have thought about joining the company as a scientist, but once he knew that Simon Archer had applied to the company, he would have had to rethink things.'

Danny nodded. 'Let's see what the enquiries at Cambridge reveal.'

79

10.00 a.m., 4 August 1991
University of Cambridge, Trinity Lane, Cambridge

I t had been a long and tiring drive to Cambridge. Traffic had been busy, and progress had been slow.

Sara Lacey had requested to speak with Professor Dierdre Bateson again, as she had found her extremely helpful previously.

A receptionist walked with the two detectives through the halls until they stood outside Professor Bateson's office. The receptionist knocked twice and said, 'I'll leave you to it,' before walking back down the long corridor. The oak panelled door opened from within.

Professor Bateson invited the two detectives inside and said, 'Hello, Detective. I understand you may need my help again?'

As they stepped inside, Sara glanced towards Rob

Buxton, standing beside her, and said, 'This is my colleague, Detective Inspector Buxton, from the Major Crime Investigation Unit.'

With the introduction out of the way, Sara said, 'Yes, I think we do. Our enquiries have now revealed that it's possible there was another student who achieved his doctorate in chemistry at the same time as Archer, who could also have a connection to the crimes we're currently investigating. His name is Scott Taplow.'

Professor Bateson sat down behind her grand walnut desk and gestured for the detectives to also take a seat. 'I remember Mr Taplow very well indeed.'

'What made him stand out?'

'In a postgraduate class full of brilliant minds, Scott Taplow was exceptional, close to genius. If I had to pick any student to make a major contribution to science in their lifetime, it would be him.'

'He was that good?'

'He was simply outstanding. He had a natural flare for chemistry and was totally driven in everything he did; his work ethic was second to none. Can I ask why you suspect such a brilliant man is involved in serious crime?'

Rob ignored her question. 'What can you tell us about Scott Taplow, the person? Did he have any family?'

Clearly feeling slightly put out that her gentle question had been so blatantly ignored, Professor Bateson said, 'That's personal information, Detective, and unless you can give me a good reason to, I won't be divulging anything of that nature.'

Undeterred, Rob pressed on. 'We strongly suspect that Scott Taplow is the son of a scientist named Rebecca Haller, and that his real name is Sebastien Haller. You need to understand the seriousness of this situation. We also strongly suspect that Sebastien Haller is now exacting murderous revenge against the people he believes are responsible for his mother's death.'

Rob paused and maintained eye contact with the professor, allowing his words to sit a moment before continuing, 'We need your co-operation, desperately. I am not exaggerating when I tell you this could be a matter of life and death. We already have three murder victims, and there are currently three other people who are missing, believed to have been abducted by this man.'

Dierdre Bateson held up both hands in a gesture of appeasement. 'Detective, I think I understand the gravity of the situation.'

She reached across her desk to a pile of folders and started to flick through them. Eventually she took out one file and said, 'When I got your message that you wanted to see me again, I accessed all the files relating to the students of that chemistry year. Everything we have for Scott Taplow is in this folder. What I can tell you from first-hand knowledge is this, Scott listed no next of kin when he joined the university. He gave his home address as being in Buxton, Derbyshire. You are welcome to take this file and peruse it at your leisure.'

'Thank you,' Sara said, then asked, 'Are there any photographs of Taplow?'

'There are two in the folder. One is his graduation photograph, and the other is a photograph that appeared in the university paper. It shows him working out in the gym. I remember it caused quite a stir at the time because Taplow, being such a private person, was extremely angry that it had been used in the paper without his permission.'

Sara picked up the file and said, 'Thank you. If this all comes to nothing, I'll return the file personally.'

Rob said, 'Have you heard from Taplow since he graduated?'

Professor Bateson shook her head. 'Not a word. But that's not unusual for someone as private as he was. Equally, it's not unusual for some students to remain in touch. But someone like Scott, we would only tend to hear about them when they've achieved some breakthrough in science or their other chosen fields. On the teaching side, we don't foster relationships with past scholars, as we very much concentrate on the students of today. Looking to the future, if you will.'

As the detectives stood to leave, Rob said, 'Thank you for your time and your help this morning. It's appreciated.'

'No problem, Detective. I hope you are wrong about this. I was always optimistic for Mr Taplow. I thought he would achieve greatness within his lifetime.'

As soon as they had left the office, Sara opened the file and removed the two photographs. She handed the graduation photo to Rob. Both images showed a tall, well-built young man, with long dark hair and a full beard.

Rob looked at Sara and said, 'I can see why even the foster parents confused Simon Archer with Haller; they're so alike.'

Sara nodded and said, 'But he looks nothing like Scott Taplow. You said he was a shaven-headed brute.'

Rob stared hard at the image. 'Don't be fooled. If you remove all that hair and the beard, that's Taplow. I'd stake my police pension on it.'

'In that case,' Sara said, 'we need to find a phone.'

80

10.30 a.m., 4 August 1991
MCIU Offices, Mansfield, Nottinghamshire

Danny rubbed his eyes and took another long drink of black coffee. He was feeling exhausted but determined to try to locate his friend.

The phone on his desk started to ring; he snatched it off the cradle and said sharply, 'Flint.'

Sue said, 'Hello, Danny. Any news?'

Realising it was his wife on the phone, Danny tempered his voice. 'Not really. We've an idea what may have happened, but nothing definite yet, and we're no nearer locating him. How's Gemma?'

'She's asleep in the spare room. I gave her something to help her rest; she was totally worn out. How are you doing, Danny?'

'I'm okay. There's so much to do here. I've got to keep going. I'll rest later, sweetheart.'

'Okay, but please be careful.'

'I will be. Don't worry about me. I'm fine.'

'See you soon. Love you.'

'Love you too.'

Danny put the phone down and stretched his back, lifting his arms up and over his head.

There was a knock on the door, and Andy Wills walked in. 'Have you got a minute, boss?'

'Of course, grab a seat.'

'It's looking like Archer wasn't acting suspiciously last night when he gave us the slip. Enquiries at the gym this morning revealed that Archer had badly sprained his left wrist, lifting a dumbbell, and felt unable to drive to the hospital. It was staff at the gym who called the taxi. He's also called them this morning to arrange for someone to drop his van off at home for him, as the doctor has advised him not to drive for two weeks.'

'Okay. What about the hospital? Why couldn't you find him?'

'It turns out he was seen immediately at A&E and taken directly to the X-ray department. He must have been inside having the X-ray done when we checked, because we didn't see him. From there he was taken to minor injuries, where his left wrist was heavily strapped. Enquiries with the taxi firm who took him to the hospital revealed that the same firm also picked him up from the hospital about an hour later and took him to his home address. I've no idea how we missed the taxi picking him up. I'm sorry, boss.'

'I'm sure you'll thrash out all the shortcomings over a debrief. There will be plenty more losses for your unit.'

Danny sighed as he rested his chin on his hands. 'It's the nature of surveillance work.'

Andy nodded. 'Do you want us to maintain the observations?'

'There's no real need to now, Andy. I'm satisfied that he's not our killer. It's up to you. If it's a good exercise for your team, then I don't mind.'

'Okay. Thanks, boss. I'll let the unit run with him for a couple of days and then debrief it all. They need the live exercise to sharpen their skill set.'

No sooner had Andy left than the phone started to ring again. Once again he snatched the receiver up and said, 'Flint.'

'We're about to leave Cambridge,' Rob Buxton told him. 'We've got a photograph, and I'm satisfied that the Scott Taplow who graduated is the same Scott Taplow who is now a security guard at Future Visions.'

'Did the university give you any background information on Taplow?'

'The information is scant. The university had no next of kin listed, and he gave his home address as Buxton. I've already made a call to Derbyshire control room and made a request for officers to check that address and establish if Scott Taplow is known there.'

'Good work, Rob. Let me know as soon as you get a reply from Derbyshire.'

'I've asked them to contact the MCIU office with any updates, as we will be a while travelling back.'

'Good thinking. See you back here.'

Danny put the phone down and walked into the briefing room, where he saw Jag and Glen on the phones.

He waited for Jag to put the phone down and said, 'How are you getting on with the airports and Special Branch?'

'That was the last call. We've now had Special Branch check all flights to Alicante from East Midlands, Birmingham, Manchester and Newcastle over the last two days. There's no record of Scott Taplow on any flight manifest. Special Branch have also been in contact with the Spanish police and conducted a reverse check with their passport control. There's no record of Scott Taplow arriving at either Alicante or Murcia airport over the last two days. They've also checked the passport records for Alicante port and Santander port. It's safe to say that wherever Taplow is, he isn't holidaying on the Spanish costas, and he certainly isn't in Benidorm.'

'Good work, Jag. Brilliant. I've just heard back from Rob, and he's satisfied that Scott Taplow, the security guard, was also a graduate from Cambridge University. I want you and Glen to concentrate on preparing the operational order to search his home address at Clifton. I'll make a call to Chief Inspector Chambers at the Special Operations Unit to join us for planning the operation; it should be an armed raid, bearing in mind what happened to Sergeant Stringer.'

'Okay, boss. I'll go to court and organise the search warrant.'

81

10.30 a.m., 4 August 1991
Carburton Forge Dam, Limetree Avenue, Welbeck, Notts

P C Alison Oliver had been on patrol all morning. She had been to Worksop police station for her meal break and was now driving back onto her area. She covered the picturesque rural mobile beat of Welbeck, Norton, Carburton and Cuckney villages.

It was a quiet rural area, and reported crime was low. There were the occasional thefts of plant and equipment from farms, the odd domestic dispute and low-key pub fight to deal with on summer nights, when the beer was in and the wit was out.

She had patrolled this area for the last three years and loved her job. Over that time, she had come to know the locals and had established a great rapport with many of them.

As she drove slowly along the A616 towards Cuckney, she saw a tractor approaching from the opposite direction. The lights on the tractor suddenly flashed, and Alison slowed the police car as she approached.

As she got closer, she could see it was being driven by Reg Knowles, the owner of Redgates Farm in Norton.

He was waving towards her, so Alison indicated, pulled onto the grass verge and stopped opposite the tractor.

She wound her window down as Reg got down from the tractor cab and crossed the road.

'Morning, Ali. There's something up by Carburton Forge Dam you should probably have a look at.'

'Righto, Reg. What is it?'

'Looks like a burned-out car to me, lass. I reckon it's probably a Volvo, but I can't be sure. Have you had any reported stolen?'

'No, we haven't, not this morning. Thanks, Reg, I'll go and check it out. Did you see anybody with it?'

'There's nobody about, lass. It was still smouldering though, so I don't reckon it's been there long.'

As she drove slowly away from the verge, she shouted over to the farmer, 'Thanks, Reg. I'll let you know what it was all about next time I see you.'

The old farmer raised his hand and shouted, 'Okay. Be careful, lass.'

Alison knew the location of the forge dam on Carburton Lake, but unless you were local to the area, you would have no idea it existed. It was a well-hidden and mostly unknown spot.

She pulled off the main road and onto the dirt track that led to the forge dam. The metal gate was still closed but not locked. She stopped the car, opened the gate and drove through. A hundred yards down the lane, she finally saw the vehicle.

It had been driven off the lane and into a ditch before being set ablaze. It was completely burned out and was indeed still smouldering. The hawthorn bushes that bordered the ditch had been scorched by the intense heat.

Getting out of the patrol car, she approached the vehicle, and her nose wrinkled in disgust at the acrid fumes being given off. She reluctantly peered inside and was relieved to see no sign of any burned bodies. Having established that, her attention turned to trying to find an identifying feature for the vehicle.

Both the registration plates had melted in the fire and were of little use. She took the tyre iron from the boot of the patrol car, prised open the front passenger door and wiped the black soot from the door sill. Underneath the grime she found the stainless-steel VIN plate. She spat on her leather gloves and rubbed the soot from the plate. She was pleased to see the engine number was still visible. She made a note of it before walking back to her car.

She sat with the car door open as she spoke into the radio. 'Whisky Romeo Three Five to control. Over.'

The reply was instantaneous. 'Whisky Romeo Three Five, go ahead. Over.'

'I'm at the forge dam at Carburton Lake with a burned-out vehicle. It looks like a Volvo, but the only identifying feature I can find is an engine number from the VIN plate. Can you check it on the PNC for me? Over.'

'Whisky Romeo Three Five, pass the details. Over.'

She relayed them and waited.

After a short delay, the radio crackled back into life. 'Whisky Romeo Three Five. Over.'

'Go ahead, control. Over.'

'Vehicle is a dark blue Volvo, estate. Registered keeper is Seamus Carter. Home address is at Rolleston. There are no reports of it being a stolen vehicle. Over.'

There was a pause, and then the radio operator added, 'Whisky Romeo Three Five, there is an interest report on the vehicle that was placed on the PNC this morning by the Major Crime Investigation Unit. Over.'

'To control. Like I said, this vehicle is completely burned out. Can you contact the MCIU while I'm here with it and ask what their interest is, please? Over.'

'Stand by. Over.'

Her interest piqued by the PNC report, she got out of the police car and had another look around the vehicle. She tried the boot but couldn't open it, as the heat had buckled the metal. She peered inside the shell, trying to see into the boot from the rear seating area. There was a metal plate that blocked her view.

She was about to try to force the boot when she heard the radio and snatched it up: 'Go ahead. Over.'

'From control. You are to remain with the vehicle. You will be joined by detectives from the MCIU and scenes of crime staff as soon as possible. Don't touch the vehicle any more than you already have. Over.'

'Received. Over.'

She walked back to the patrol car, threw the tyre iron back in the boot and wondered how long it would take the detectives to arrive and deal with the vehicle. 'Why,' she muttered to herself, 'are the MCIU so interested in a bloke called Seamus Carter from Rolleston?'

82

6.00 p.m., 4 August 1991
43 Bainton Grove, Clifton, Nottinghamshire

The planning for the raid on Scott Taplow's home address had become even more urgent now that the wreckage of Seamus Carter's Volvo had been found near Carburton Lake.

Danny was even more convinced that his good friend was in a life-threatening situation.

The danger of the upcoming raid, which was to be conducted by armed officers from the Special Operations Unit, had been highlighted when it was discovered Scott Taplow was the holder of a current shotgun licence, and that there were two shotguns listed at his home address.

Every officer on the SOU was fully aware of the callous way in which their unarmed colleague Sergeant Gary

Stringer had been mercilessly gunned down by the person suspected of carrying out the recent spate of acid murders.

Danny now felt helpless as he waited in the car three hundred yards away from the target address. He was sitting next to Rob Buxton on the back seat, immediately behind Chief Inspector Chambers, the officer in command of the Special Operations Unit.

His feelings of anxiety weren't helped by the ambulance, containing two paramedics, parked immediately behind their vehicle.

Chambers checked his watch and gave his men the thumbs-up as he saw the ten armed officers being led by Sergeant Graham Turner filing down the road towards the neat semi-detached house, which was Taplow's home address.

The front of the property was easily accessible, as the front garden had been laid to gravel to form a parking area. Even though there had been no sightings of Taplow at the address, the time constraint on the safety of Seamus Carter – who they were assuming had been abducted – meant there was no choice but to raid the property and hope Taplow was inside.

The front door of the property, and every window, had white uPVC frames. Danny noted that that one of the SOU officers carried the hydraulic equipment used to silently open uPVC-framed doors.

The element of surprise was the only advantage these men would have as they entered the property to search for a potentially armed and dangerous man.

Danny could feel his heart racing as he heard the radio crackle into life: 'Sergeant Turner to control. In position and about to make entry. Request radio silence from now. Over.'

The control room acknowledged the sergeant's request by signalling two clicks on their transmitter.

Seconds later, in the distance, Danny saw the black-clad officers, their weapons raised, stealthily making their final approach towards the property.

There were no shouts as they entered; everything was done in complete silence.

A tense five-minute wait ensued before Danny heard Sergeant Turner's calm voice: 'Target address cleared. No sign of suspect. It's safe to move forward now. Over.'

The three senior officers stepped out of their vehicle and made their way down Bainton Grove to Taplow's home. Sergeant Turner was waiting for them at the front door.

The sergeant spoke to his senior officer. 'There's no sign of Taplow, sir. The place doesn't look like it's been lived in for a while. There's no clothes and no personal possessions inside. There's a couple of old pieces of furniture, but no food in the kitchen. I think our bird has flown the nest quite a while ago.'

Danny asked, 'No sign of any weapons or a gun cabinet?'

The big sergeant shook his head. 'My lads are up in the loft now, ripping up the insulation, but they haven't found anything yet.'

Danny cursed under his breath and turned to Rob. 'Let's get our detectives up here and start knocking on the neighbours' doors.'

Rob glanced around. He could see that the presence of the armed officers was already arousing interest from other residents. He spoke into his radio and summoned the detectives waiting on standby at the rendezvous point to come forward immediately.

Danny said, 'Make sure the local officers maintain the

roadblocks at either end of this road for the time being, Rob. We haven't got time for a crowd to start gathering and impede our work.'

'I'm on it, boss.'

Danny turned to Chief Inspector Chambers, who was still in conversation with Sergeant Turner, and said, 'Thanks for doing such a professional job once again.'

Chambers nodded and said, 'I know that speed is a major factor in this inquiry, and I understand how quickly you need this search completed, but we always have to err on the side of safety.'

'Absolutely. I totally understand that these things can never be rushed.'

Danny saw Rob briefing the first MCIU detectives as they arrived at the scene. He walked over and said, 'As soon as the SOU have completed their physical search inside, I want scenes of crime to go over the house with a fine-tooth comb. You never know, there may be something inside that gives us an indication as to where Taplow is now. We need to find something and quickly. The clock's ticking for Seamus and the other missing people, I'm sure of it.'

83

8.00 p.m., 4 August 1991
Woodland near Welbeck, Nottinghamshire

The big man grunted behind the gas mask as he
trudged down the long tunnel. He was carrying a
plastic bag that contained three bottles of water
and three packets of biscuits.

He was reluctant to, but he needed to feed and water his
captives, as he had things to do before he could deal with
them properly. He was collecting his van from the garage at
Worksop tomorrow. The vehicle had been off the road after
the brakes almost failed. The brakes had now been repaired,
and it would be available to pick up tomorrow afternoon.
The van was vital. There was no point in dealing with the
captives until he had the means to take them to the staging
areas he had chosen for them.

He was disturbed by the number of times the police kept

coming back to the labs at Beeston, so had taken the decision that it was now time to leave the dull security job and bring his move abroad forward.

He already had the air tickets booked for his new life working for Chugai Pharmaceutical Company, based in Tokyo.

He had applied for a position within that company, as a research scientist, three months ago. He had used the name Scott Taplow to apply but intended to revert his name back to Sebastien Haller after he had been in post for six months. He needed to keep using the alias for the time being, as all his documents and qualifications from Cambridge were in that name. There would be plenty of time for him to reclaim his true identity once he was settled and living a new life in Japan.

The prestigious Japanese pharmaceutical giant had been excited by the prospect of such a brilliant Cambridge scholar joining their ranks and had barely hesitated to offer him a post.

It had been agreed with the Chugai directors that he should start work with them at the end of August.

But now he needed to bring the deaths of the wrongdoers forward, so he intended to arrive in Japan a lot earlier.

As soon as he had his vehicle back, he could complete his long-awaited revenge. He anticipated it would take him five days to despatch and dump the three captives he already had. The sixth name on his list would be granted a temporary reprieve, as he had no time left to deal with her.

He would visit her at a much later date.

He smiled at the prospect of a new life following the career he loved. Chemistry had always been his passion, and he intended to dedicate every discovery he made to his dead mother, so her name would live on for ever.

However, his mood darkened instantly as he saw the row of wire cages coming into view. He had already sacrificed so much time and taken such drastic steps to get even with the scum he now held in those cages. They had all either directly contributed to her death or to its cover-up afterwards.

He remained silent behind the mask as he placed a bottle of water and a packet of biscuits next to the cages that contained his captives.

The first two occupants cowered as far back as they could, desperate to get as far away as possible from his monstrous appearance. The third captive, the giant with the beard, began to rattle the cage violently, shouting as he did so, 'Let me out of here, you crazy bastard!'

The big man kicked the wire cage and said, 'Be quiet, Carter. You're in no position to dictate anything to me. Be patient, and you'll be out of that cage soon enough.'

As Carter raged, his broad Irish accent became even stronger. 'I will. And on that day there's going to be a reckoning between you and me, boyo. I'm just itching for you to undo that lock. Don't expect me to go gently into the night. I know what your murderous intentions are, you maniac, and I'll fight you with every fibre of my being, so you'd better get ready.'

The man with the mask kicked the wire mesh again and stamped on the packet of biscuits in front of the cage, grinding them into the dirt floor before kicking the bottle of water back down the tunnel.

He snarled, 'Keep gobbing off, big man, and you'll be the first to leave.'

Unbowed, Carter growled back, 'I'm ready when you are.'

The man turned away from the cage and stomped back along the tunnel.

Carter raged on behind him: 'You're going to have to open this door some time, boyo.'

The big man roared with laughter behind his mask and disappeared into the darkness.

84

9.00 p.m., 4 August 1991
Woodland near Welbeck, Nottinghamshire

Seamus could hear the woman in the cage next to his sobbing.

He said softly, 'Are you okay?'

Between sobs she said in a faltering voice, 'I don't understand any of this. Who is that monster?'

'I don't know.'

'But you said you knew what his murderous intentions were. What did you mean?'

Seamus could hear the fear in the woman's voice and could tell she was barely holding herself together, so to try to ease some of those fears, he said, 'I didn't mean anything. I was just trying to get under his skin a bit.'

'Why would you do that? Can't you see he's crazy?'

Seamus wasn't going to argue with her on that point.

Then a man's voice said, 'I'm Dr Greg Thornhill. Who are you?'

'Seamus Carter.'

'What do you do, Seamus?'

'I'm a pathologist; why?'

'I'm just trying to see if we're in any way connected. He knows all our names, and it doesn't sound to me as though this madman has chosen us at random. I believe we've been carefully selected for some reason. Like this lady, I don't understand any of it. Why are we here? What have we done to deserve this?'

Seamus replied, 'I don't think any of us will ever understand the mind of this person, whoever he is.'

The woman said, 'Why does he wear that awful mask?'

Seamus said, 'To scare us, I think.'

'I don't know if it's just that,' Greg said. 'My throat's feeling sorer every hour I'm down here. I'd like to know what's causing that awful stench of rotten eggs.'

Seamus knew the answer to the doctor's question, but thought better of informing him that the smell was probably caused by residue fumes from an exposure of sulphuric acid in the tunnels.

Instead, he brushed the question off, saying, 'I think the air's so still down here that it's almost dead. The oxygen levels feel extremely low. I must admit I'm feeling slightly light-headed myself, and being cramped up in this cage isn't helping my breathing.'

Greg said, 'Did you mean it?'

'Mean what?'

'Are you going to fight when he opens the cage?'

You'd better believe I'm going to fight, he thought. But what he said was, 'Time will tell. If the opportunity arises, I won't be going quietly along with whatever he's got planned for me, that's for sure.'

The woman said, 'He drugged me to get me down here, so you may not have that opportunity.'

Seamus sat in the darkness contemplating his desperate situation and thinking about recent cases he'd worked on where there had been an element of controversy. His head was spinning with unanswered questions.

Have I been missed yet?

Why has this madman brought me here?

Who is he?

Do I have any chance of escape?

Is anybody looking for me?

The last thought sent an icy chill screeching through his body.

Am I going to die down here in this tunnel?

85

9.00 p.m., 4 August 1991
MCIU Offices, Mansfield, Nottinghamshire

The MCIU briefing room was full to bursting with detectives and armed officers from the Special Operations Unit. They were gathered there to debrief the armed raid and subsequent search of the property at Clifton, plus the enquiries made with Scott Taplow's neighbours.

Standing quietly at the back of the room was Professor Sharon Whittle.

Danny was sitting at the front of the room, flanked by Chief Inspector Chambers and Rob Buxton.

Danny brought the room to order and sought out Sergeant Turner, the man who had led the raid. 'Graham, let's start with you. Overall impression of the raid, please?'

'The raid itself went very smoothly. Obviously, we'll be holding our own operational debrief about the entry and other matters that need addressing, but the main points for this debrief are that access was gained silently and effectively. Each room was searched quickly and methodically. The entire property was cleared in less than two minutes. Mainly because of the lack of furniture inside.'

He paused and then continued, 'My overall impression was that the property hasn't been lived in for quite a while. There was plenty of unopened junk mail by the front door, which was all addressed to Scott Taplow, so he has lived there in the recent past.'

'Any sign of where he may have relocated to?'

'Sorry, sir. No.'

Now Danny looked for Jag, who had supervised the house-to-house enquiries conducted with the neighbours, and said, 'Is that impression borne out by your work today, Jag?'

Jag nodded. 'Yes, boss. The consensus we found was that Taplow moved out of the address at the beginning of June. He arrived one day, started filling his van with his stuff and hasn't been seen since.'

'Were any of the neighbours on friendly terms with him?'

Jag's answer was an emphatic, 'No.' Then he continued: 'He wasn't well liked by anybody we spoke to. Various people differently described him as being a weirdo, a nut job and an arrogant shit. None of it was very flattering. The neighbours tended to avoid him because they felt intimidated by his moody demeanour and sheer size. Nobody on that street was sorry to see him leave, and nobody we've spoken to has any idea where he may have moved to.'

'Good work,' said Danny. 'Was anything found inside the house?'

Sergeant Turner answered, 'Our search didn't reveal anything useful, sir. The scenes of crime team are still there doing a full forensic sweep. I spoke to Tim Donnelly before we left to see if he needed any of my staff to remain behind to watch their backs on the estate. He declined our offer, as the local cops were already at the property, speaking to the locals who had gathered outside. He told me he wouldn't be finished examining the inside of the house until the early hours of the morning, sir.'

'Thanks, Graham. Can you ensure any statements we need from your officers are submitted before you go off duty, please.'

'No problem, sir.'

Danny addressed the room. 'I want to thank each of you for the professional job you've done today, both in preparation for the raid and the way it was conducted. To all MCIU staff, finish what you're doing, go home and get some rest. We're all going to have some long days until we find that van. I want you back on duty tomorrow morning at eight o'clock. Thanks.'

As the room cleared, Danny said to Jim Chambers, 'I need to run something by you before you go.'

Chambers nodded, and the two men walked towards Danny's office.

Danny beckoned to Sharon Whittle and called her over, too.

Danny sat down wearily and introduced Sharon Whittle to Jim Chambers before saying, 'I don't know about you, Sharon, but I think time's running out.'

The professor nodded. 'I totally agree. By abducting all

three people at once, he has escalated his behaviour. I believe he can now see his end goal in sight.'

'His end goal being the deaths of those three missing people.'

She gave a grim nod. 'I believe so.'

Danny looked at Jim Chambers. 'Our only viable lead is the white Ford Escort van owned by Taplow. I've circulated it on the PNC and put a warning marker on the circulation that if the vehicle is seen, it's to be observed only, as the driver may be armed and dangerous.'

Chambers said, 'I know what you're going to ask me. You want an armed team on standby, don't you?'

'The second we locate that vehicle, and we will find it, I'm going to need the capability to approach it and deal with the occupant as soon as possible. That means an armed response team ready to engage at a moment's notice. When we find that van, we'll find Taplow. He needs the van to move the bodies once he's murdered them. The van is our only hope of getting to those three missing people before he kills them. I'm dreading another phone call informing me that another body's been found.'

Chambers was deep in thought. Eventually he said, 'I can put two full sections of the SOU at your disposal on a twenty-four-hour standby for the next two days. It will mean the men pulling twelve-hour shifts, but as they will be on standby for much of that time, it won't be too arduous a duty. I'd like you to have that capability longer, but there's a royal visit planned for sixth August, which necessitates at least three sections. My guess is by that time, we'll have either found the van and Taplow, or we'll have three more bodies.'

Sharon Whittle said, 'I believe you're absolutely right,

Chief Inspector. You need to locate that van within the next twenty-four to forty-eight hours, or you'll start getting those calls telling you another body's been found.'

86

11.30 p.m., 4 August 1991
Mansfield, Nottinghamshire

Danny quietly closed the front door and wearily trudged up the stairs. He felt exhausted. He hadn't slept for over twenty-four hours and was barely awake as he undressed and climbed into bed.

Sue stirred and said, 'Any news?'

As Danny's head hit the pillow, he said, 'Nothing positive. I know who's got Seamus, but we can't locate him.'

'Why would anybody want to harm Seamus? It doesn't make any sense.'

'It's a long story. I understand this madman's motives a little better now, thanks mainly to Professor Whittle. I struggle to work out what makes these monsters tick. They don't think like you or me. They're wired different.' He yawned. 'But I don't even think I want to understand them anymore.'

'Do you think Seamus will be okay?'

'I honestly don't know. How's Gemma?'

'I've made up the spare room for her. I don't want her being alone right now; the poor woman's at her wits' end.'

Danny turned over onto his side, closed his eyes and said wearily, 'I'm sorry, Sue. I need to sleep now. We'll talk more in the morning.'

'Of course, get some rest, sweetheart.'

'Wake me at seven o'clock,' Danny mumbled. 'I need to be back in the office at eight.'

87

11.30 a.m., 5 August 1991
MCIU Offices, Mansfield, Nottinghamshire

Mark Slater had driven to the MCIU offices to establish what was being done to trace the whereabouts of Scott Taplow after the raid on his home address the evening before.

Danny had been in conversation with Rob, Sara and Sharon Whittle when Slater walked in. He cut straight to the chase. 'What have you organised to locate Taplow's vehicle?'

'It's been the main subject of every briefing for officers parading on duty force wide, since the raid in Clifton. The control room are putting out a reminder message of the observation request over the air every thirty minutes. We're doing everything we can to make the urgency of the situation known to every officer on patrol.'

'How long do you think you've got?' Slater looked

worried. 'Are you running out of time? Hasn't there always been a considerable time gap between the victims being abducted and their bodies being discovered?'

Sharon Whittle said, 'May I say something, Chief Super-intendent?'

Slater responded, 'Of course.'

'I've spoken to DCI Flint about this already. I see the abduction of the three potential victims so close together as indicative of a significant escalation in this offender's behaviour. For me, it demonstrates that he's gone from being extremely ordered and considered in everything he does to being a bit more reactive. It's as though something has spooked him and caused him to speed up his plans. It also demonstrates that wherever he's holding these three people is extremely well hidden, and he feels secure in the knowl-edge that he's unlikely to be disturbed by a member of the public.'

She tapped her finger on the photograph of the white Ford Escort van, taken from the security camera footage at Addison's factory, which was displayed on Danny's office wall. 'Your men need to locate this vehicle very soon,' she said, 'or you'll be finding more bodies.'

She paused to let that comment sink in before continu-ing, 'The only possibility of redemption you have is that the amount of time it takes this killer to carry out his chosen method of murder may buy you a little more time. I pray you can locate the vehicle before his next victim is already dead and inside it.'

Slater nodded grimly. 'Is it time we got the public involved, Danny?'

'That's what we've just been discussing, sir. I'm loath to do it yet, as we know Taplow is armed and that he has no compunction about using that weapon on anybody who gets in his way. The last thing we need is for a public-spirited citizen to spot the vehicle and then get themselves killed.'

'I hear what you're saying, Danny, but you may not have any choice. We both know the quickest way to find that vehicle is to make it known to every person out there that we need to locate it as a matter of urgency. You can, of course, stipulate that if it's seen, members of the public are not to approach it under any circumstances.'

'You're right.' Danny nodded. 'Let's get that organised, Rob. I want it on every radio channel and on the local lunchtime news.'

Rob stood to leave the office and said, 'Yes, sir. I'll talk to the press liaison officer.'

Slater looked at Danny and said, 'I'm going to stay here for the time being, Danny. I need to know what's happening.'

88

6.40 p.m., 5 August 1991
4 Valley Road, Worksop, Nottinghamshire

Mick Daynes had spent a long day at the garage he owned and ran as a sole trader. It was a backstreet business and was demanding work with long days, but it provided a good living for his wife and two young children.

He felt full after eating the steak and kidney pie and chips his wife had prepared. As he sat down in his favourite armchair to watch the evening news, he pulled the ring tab on a cold can of lager.

He took a long, welcome swig as the local news started. The first story was an appeal by the police for any sightings of a white Ford Escort van, registration number C552 JTF.

He put his can down and sat forward, staring at the grainy image of the white van on the TV. He shouted,

'Tracey, can you bring me the appointment book through, love?'

His wife shouted down the stairs, 'You'll have to get it yourself. I'm just getting the kids out of the bath.'

He walked into the hallway and grabbed the large black book that was next to the phone.

Being self-employed, Mick needed to be able to book any repairs in at any time, day or night. The appointment book never left his side. It was the lifeblood of his business.

As he flicked through its pages, his wife came downstairs, followed by his two young sons. 'Is there a problem with a booking, love?'

He said, 'You know that gobby sod I was telling you about when I got home?'

'The one who made you late?'

'Yeah, the guy who wanted the brakes done on his van in a major hurry. I'm sure I've just heard on the news that the cops are looking for that van.'

He flicked through the pages frantically now until he found the page for that day's date. 'It flipping well was that van, Tracey. I need to phone the cops.'

He quickly dialled the number for the local police station and said, 'Yeah, that white Ford Escort van you're looking for. Well, I've been doing repairs on it most of today at my garage.'

The officer asked, 'Can you give me your name and address, please?'

'Yeah. Mick Daynes, four Valley Road, Worksop. My garage is in Gateford.'

'What repairs did it need?'

'The brakes needed doing.'

'Is the van still at your garage, Mr Daynes?'

'No. He collected it around five thirty this evening.'

'Can you describe the person the van belongs to?'

'Yeah, he was a big nasty sod. Looked like that bloke in the film that's just been on at the flicks, *Terminator*.'

'Did he give you a name when the vehicle was booked in?'

He scanned the page and said, 'Yeah. He said his name was Scott Taplow.'

'Have you got an address?'

'No. I just got his name and the van registration number. Sorry.'

'Don't worry. Thanks for the call. Two detectives will be with you within the next hour. I take it you're not going out this evening?'

'No. I'll be at home.'

He hung up the phone, his face pale.

'What did they say?' his wife said.

'Two detectives are coming tonight. They'll be here to talk to me in the next hour or so. We'd better have a quick tidy, love. The kids' toys are still all over the place.'

89

9.00 p.m., 5 August 1991
MCIU Offices, Mansfield, Nottinghamshire

Sara Lacey and Jag Singh walked into Danny's office; they'd just returned from interviewing Mick Daynes at Worksop.

Rob Buxton and Sharon Whittle were already there, talking to Danny.

'Well?' Danny said. 'Does it sound like Taplow?'

Sara replied, 'The description certainly fits Scott Taplow, and Daynes was adamant he's got the right registration number of the van.'

Jag added, 'It's definitely a white Ford Escort van as well.'

Danny asked, 'How did he describe the owner?'

Sara said, 'He gave a very good description. A big muscular man, over six feet tall with a shaven head. Dressed in a navy blue sweatshirt and jeans.'

'Did he say anything that would give us an idea where he's currently living?'

'The only thing Daynes said that might help us was that the guy had moaned about having to catch a bus and that it had taken him half an hour to get to the garage.'

Rob immediately stood up and left the office. He returned moments later with a large map of the north of the county. He pinpointed the address of the Daynes's garage at Worksop, then studied the map.

He said, 'Thirty minutes in a car could take him as far north as Sheffield or as far south as Mansfield Woodhouse. A bus journey would be slower, so it may bring the area in a little. I'll get onto the bus companies and find out what the routes into Worksop are.'

'Leave the map, Rob.'

Rob pinned the map to the whiteboard behind Danny's desk and left the office.

Danny stared at the map, studying it. He took a handful of brightly coloured drawing pins and placed one on the map, saying, 'Okay. Let's plot this killer's significant acts on here. Starting with the deposition site for Terrence McAvoy, Worksop golf course.'

Sara said, 'There was one act prior to that one. McAvoy's abduction.'

Danny nodded in acknowledgement and placed another pin above the first. 'We know McAvoy was abducted from a Sheffield industrial estate, which would be here.'

Sharon Whittle joined the three detectives now. She stared at the map as she said, 'Try to put the pins down in the order they happened. Next was the murder of Sergeant Stringer. Where would that be on this map?'

Sara picked up another pin and placed it on the village of Shireoaks. 'Sergeant Stringer was shot here.'

Jag pointed to the map and said, 'Then came the abduction of Sir Anthony Pemberton at Oxton golf course.'

Danny placed a pin on the village of Oxton and placed another one below the map, saying, 'This one is to indicate the laboratory at Beeston where Hauptmann was abducted.'

Jag said, 'The Manor School at Mansfield Woodhouse was the deposition site for Sir Anthony.'

Danny placed another pin on the map and said, 'And this one is the deposition site for Jurgen Hauptmann, the Carrs at Warsop.'

Danny took a pace back and said, 'There's a definite pattern here. Everything, with a couple of exceptions, is located within the same area.' Now he leaned forward and located another point on the map and said, 'This is where Carter's Volvo was found at Carburton, so although he was abducted from the Queen's Medical Centre in Nottingham, there's still a connection to this particular area around Worksop.'

'Don't forget about Miriam Jackson and Greg Thornhill,' Sara said. 'She was also abducted from Nottingham, but he was abducted from his home address at Kirklington, which is quite a way from Worksop.'

Danny nodded, made a circular motion with his hand around the brightly coloured pins and said, 'Taplow's got to be in this area somewhere, I'm sure of it.'

Sharon Whittle pointed at the map and said, 'There's miles and miles of remote woodland shown on this map. Is there anything there that could be used for his base? He needs that remote location to kill his victims in the way he does. He needs to feel secure in the knowledge that he isn't going to be disturbed, partly because of the length of time it takes to kill his victims – and also because of the horrific way he does it.'

The three detectives stared hard at the map, and then Sara said, 'Is that part of the Welbeck Abbey estate?'

'Yes, why?' Danny said.

'It was something Sebastien Haller's foster parents, Stuart and Janice Wainwright, told me. They said that when Sebastien was a pupil at Welbeck College, he was constantly in trouble for playing in some tunnel that runs below the estate. Is that tunnel still there?'

Rob Buxton walked back into the office in time to hear Sara's remark. 'It's more than one tunnel, Sara,' he said, 'and they're still there, all right. Most of them are in an extremely dilapidated, dangerous state now, but they still exist.'

Sara said, 'Do many people know of their existence?'

Rob shook his head. 'Few do. The only reason I know about them is because I dealt with a cannabis grow that had been set up in one of them, when I was a detective at Worksop.'

'I've lived around here all of my life,' Danny chipped in, 'and I didn't know about them.'

Sharon spoke directly to Rob now. 'You've heard me describe the kind of remote location this killer would need to conduct these acid murders. Would the tunnels suit his needs?'

Rob thought for a moment or two. 'They would be perfect. It's been a lot of years since I was down them, but if my memory serves me right, they stretch for miles, and there are numerous entrances, some of which are now overgrown and hidden.'

Danny stared hard at the map and said, 'I don't like to

become fixated on one idea, but would it be possible to carry out a methodical search of those tunnels?'

'It's possible,' Rob said, but it would be dangerous and could take days. Do we really have the time to embark on a search like that?'

Danny sat down, deep in thought. 'It's too late to do much tonight, but at first light tomorrow, I want Worksop and the surrounding area, including the Welbeck estate, flooded with as many police patrols as we can muster. We now know that Taplow, sorry, Haller is in possession of the van again, and if he's operating around Worksop, our best bet to locate the van will be to get as many police officers into that area as possible. I want everybody back on duty at six o'clock and patrolling that area. I'll talk to the control room and ensure that any traffic patrol and dog section officers who come on duty tomorrow are directed to that area. If that van is there, we're going to find it.'

Rob said, 'What about getting the SOU firearms team on standby at Worksop police station? They would be closer and be able to respond more quickly if we do locate Haller's vehicle in that area.'

'Good thinking. I'll get onto the SOU and set that in motion.' He reached for his jacket and said, 'Rob, Sara, Jag, I want you to phone round and get all our staff back on duty at six o'clock in the morning. Once you've done that, go home and get some rest.'

Sharon said, 'Could you drop me at the guest house on your way home, Danny?'

'Of course,' Danny said; then, as they walked out of the building, he asked, 'Do you think I'm doing the right thing?'

'There's merit in your thinking. This killer needs a place just like those tunnels in remote woodland. My worry is that if we concentrate just on that single area, the killer could slip through the net. The problem is you won't know if that's what's happened until the next dead body turns up.'

'That's my biggest fear, but I don't see any other option. We all know that time's running out for those three people.'

As Danny slowed the car to a stop outside the guest house, Sharon said, 'You've got to stay proactive, Danny. Waiting for something to happen isn't an option. Let's hope you're right and that Sebastien Haller is indeed somewhere around those tunnels.'

As the forensic psychologist got out of the car, Danny said, 'It seems strange hearing you use the name Sebastien Haller. There have been so many other names thrown up in this investigation, Simon Archer, Steven Archer, Scott Taplow as well as Haller. It's almost easy to forget that the man we're looking for is Sebastien Haller.'

'In my mind it's always been Haller,' Sharon said. 'Could you pick me up on your way in tomorrow morning, Danny? I'd like to be there from the outset; despite my reservations, I've a good feeling about this.'

'Of course. I just wish I could share that good feeling. I've an overwhelming icy dread about what tomorrow might bring.'

90

6.30 a.m., 6 August 1991
Woodland near Welbeck, Nottinghamshire

Sebastien Haller hadn't collected his van from the garage at Worksop until quite late in the afternoon the day before. He had been expecting to pick up the vehicle in the morning, first thing, and had been livid at the delay. By the time he'd gone to pay the bill and collect the vehicle, his mood was foul.

The owner of the garage had tried patiently to explain that the delay had been caused by the scarcity of the brake pads required, and that it had taken him most of the day to source them. He had assured the angry Haller that the repairs on the vehicle had been completed as quickly as they could be.

The reason for Haller's bad temper was simple. It had nothing to do with the brake pads and everything to do with yet another delay to his plans. Still seething, he paid the bill and drove away from the garage at speed.

He was now sitting in his van, which was parked up in the forest, about one hundred yards from the entrance to the tunnel he had chosen.

His temper had subsided, and he allowed a smile to form as he thought about the mouthy Irish pathologist, Seamus Carter, who had angered him so much the day before with his pathetic ranting.

He was a little concerned about the threats the big man had made about not going gently into the night, and he realised that his comment about knowing what lay in store for him meant he must have worked on the other deaths.

He trusted his own brute strength would prevail in any struggle with the pathologist, but he couldn't afford to waste time fighting, so he had a plan to deal with the Irishman.

He got out of the van and stretched his bulk before opening the back doors. He reached inside and grabbed the gas mask, torch, loaded syringe, double-barrelled shotgun and a handful of cartridges from a box. He clipped the gas mask to the belt of his overalls and began to feed two cartridges into the barrels of the twelve-bore shotgun. He stuffed a couple of loose rounds of ammunition into the pocket of his wax jacket, leaving the box containing the rest in the rear of the van.

Without locking the vehicle, he began to make his way through the dense woodland until he reached the entrance to the tunnel.

He slipped the sheet of corrugated iron away from the overgrown entrance and stepped inside. He didn't replace the metal sheet and used the scant light filtering in from outside to prepare his equipment. He carefully placed the shotgun on the floor before slipping on the gas mask. The fumes weren't too bad near the entrance, but he knew the further into the tunnel he went, the worse the air quality would become.

He felt inside his jacket pocket for the powerful torch and the syringe he would need later. He held the torch in his right hand and picked the shotgun up with his left.

It was time to set the final act in motion.

He began to walk slowly along the tunnel, being careful where he placed his feet. He couldn't afford any slip-ups now, and he was conscious that there was new debris on the floor of the tunnel every time he came down here. This particular tunnel was in a very poor state of repair, and crumbling bricks regularly fell from the roof.

After ten minutes, making careful progress, the beam from his torch picked out the row of wire cages ahead.

He placed the torch on the tunnel floor, illuminating the space, and levelled the loaded shotgun at Seamus Carter's head before saying, 'I'm going to unlock your cage. If you try anything, I'll shoot you where you sit. Do you understand?'

The pathologist stared hard at his captor and nodded. 'Like I thought, you're nothing but a coward. A coward who needs to hide behind a gun.'

Haller ignored the insult and simply said, 'Get out.'

As Carter extracted himself from the cramped cage, Haller saw the man's legs wobble. It was obvious that the time spent in the cramped space and the poor air quality had taken a toll.

Still not prepared to take any chances, he maintained his distance and kept the shotgun pointing directly at Carter's head as he said, 'Move.' He shone the torch along the tunnel and hissed menacingly, 'I said move!'

Carter took a couple of faltering steps before steadying himself against the wall of the tunnel and saying, 'You won't get away with this. Why don't you stop all this madness now, while you still can.'

Haller jabbed the barrels of the shotgun into the big Irishman's back and said, 'No more talking, Carter. Just walk.'

The two men moved in silence along the tunnel until Haller said, 'Stop. Get on your knees and place both hands against the wall.'

As Carter complied, Haller slipped the torch under his armpit. He took the full syringe from his pocket, stepped forward and plunged the needle into the pathologist's neck.

Carter flinched, grunted once and then collapsed sideways.

Haller leaned forward and felt for the pulse in his captive's neck. It was still there, but extremely shallow. He reached around and flicked the man's eyelids. When there was no response, he knew his victim was fully unconscious and safe to move.

He propped the shotgun against the wall of the tunnel and opened the dilapidated wooden door that led into the killing room. He dragged the unconscious Carter into the room, lifted him from the floor and into the heavy chair. It took all his strength to manoeuvre the dead weight of the big man into position. He allowed himself a grim smile of satisfaction as he strapped the pathologist into the chair, and as he secured the man's head, he growled beneath his mask, 'Not so mouthy now, are you, Carter?'

Having strapped his victim into the chair, he began topping up the levels of acid, which were contained in the pump mechanism located behind the chair. He was careful not to leave the lids off the various acid containers any longer than he needed to. He knew that the more toxic fumes there were in the air, the longer it would take Carter to regain consciousness.

He needed the Irishman to be fully awake when the first droplet of acid fell. He wanted him to experience the full agony and horror of his mother's death, the death that he had so unfeelingly written off as suicide. He would wait and witness that awful moment of recognition as the lethal acid fell, and his victim experienced the first searing bolt of pain, which would signal the beginning of this man's lingering, painful death.

91

7.15 a.m., 6 August 1991
Woodland near Welbeck, Nottinghamshire

PC Roger Barker was an experienced police dog handler and was on an early shift, covering the north of the county. In the back of his van was his trusted partner, a German shepherd he had named Zoltan.

They had been working as a team for the last three years, and PC Barker had complete trust in his dog. Zoltan was an excellent tracker, as well as fearless with a strong bite instinct.

At over six feet tall and weighing a good eighteen stone, PC Barker was himself a force of nature. The two together made a formidable team.

Roger had been surprised at the specific orders every officer had been given at that morning's briefing at headquarters. All dog patrols, including those meant to be covering the city, had been despatched to the north of the county with instructions to patrol the vast area between Nottinghamshire's border with South Yorkshire right down to the market town of Mansfield. Their instruction had been simple. They were to try to locate a white Ford Escort van, registration C552 JTF.

The orders given at the briefing had been unequivocal and brief. If the van was located, it was to be a watching brief only. The suspect vehicle wasn't to be approached, as the driver was suspected of gunning down Sergeant Gary Stringer at Shireoaks, just a few short weeks earlier. The same man was also suspected of being responsible for the recent acid murders that had occurred within the county. A section of ten armed officers were waiting on standby at Worksop police station, ready to engage the threat once the vehicle had been found.

Roger had been on patrol for over an hour and had seen plenty of white vans fitting the description, but none that carried the correct registration number.

As he stopped at the junction near to Cuckney cross-roads, he looked over his shoulder at Zoltan. The dog immediately pricked up his ears, waiting for his master to speak. Roger said, 'Are you ready to stretch your legs for five minutes, buddy?'

The dog answered with a single bark. The booming sound of that deep bark filled the confined space of the van, and Roger said, 'Five minutes and you can have a run in the woods.'

After driving north along the main A60 towards Worksop, Roger steered the dog van into the dense woodland that bordered the Welbeck Abbey estate. He was aware of a secluded track that led deep into the woods at this location.

It was the perfect place to allow Zoltan to stretch his legs and get a drink of cool water. He knew his dog always worked better when he got plenty of exercise during a shift. Some days that just wasn't possible, as the control room despatched them from job to job.

He stopped the van, got out and arched his back before walking to the rear of the van. Opening the doors, he immediately made a fuss of Zoltan and allowed him to jump out, saying, 'Stay close, buddy.'

The dog made no attempt to run off into the woods; instead it trotted about three yards away and defecated into a patch of ferns.

Now, as Roger poured some cool water from a large container into a metal dog bowl, he smiled and said, 'Good lad, Zolts.'

Looking pleased with himself, the dog bounded back to his handler and began drinking thirstily, slopping the water everywhere as he did so.

Roger leaned on the side of his van and looked out at the beautiful dense woodland. As he did so, a glint of early morning sunlight reflecting off something shiny caught his eye.

He waited for Zoltan to finish drinking before he slipped the short lead on him and said, 'Let's check that out, buddy.'

With Zoltan walking obediently to heel, Roger strode into the woods. Thirty yards into the trees he saw what had caused the glinting. It was the dappled rays of the low morning sun that had bounced off the windscreen of a vehicle.

Roger immediately checked his dog and squatted down behind a clump of nearby brambles. Peering over the top, he could now see that the registration number on the white Ford Escort van was C552 JTF.

There was nobody with the vehicle, and as he quickly glanced around the surrounding woodland, he could see nobody loitering in the trees.

He turned to Zoltan and whispered, 'Bingo. Come on, buddy.'

Stealthily, he made his way back to his vehicle, and after one last look at the surrounding woodland, he started the engine and reversed back down the track. Fifty yards further back, he reversed the van behind thick shrubs. From his new position he could still see the exact location where the target vehicle was parked.

He knew that if the suspect returned to the van, there was only one way the vehicle could be driven out of the woods. He would need to pass his location. If that happened, then he knew he would have a decision to make, but in the meantime he concentrated on following the strict instructions given at the morning's briefing. He picked up the radio handset and said, 'Oscar Victor Five Three to control. Over.'

The radio was answered immediately. 'Oscar Victor Five Three, go ahead. Over.'

'From Oscar Victor Five Three, I am in woodland adjacent to the Welbeck Abbey estate. About two miles north of Cuckney crossroads, there is a dirt track a couple of hundred yards beyond the entrance to Lady Margaret Hall. Over.'

'Oscar Victor Five Three, we have logged your position; pass your message. Over.'

'From Oscar Victor Five Three. I have located target vehicle, white Ford Escort van registered number Charlie Five Five Two Juliet Tango Foxtrot. It's parked deep in the woods and is currently unattended. Over.'

The control room inspector took over. 'Oscar Victor Five Three, do you still have the vehicle in sight? Over.'

'Affirmative. I have retreated and am now a good fifty yards away, hidden in dense undergrowth, but I have the vehicle in sight. Over.'

'Oscar Victor Five Three, maintain your position. The firearms response team is already travelling to your location. Their ETA is approximately fifteen minutes. Under no circumstances are you to try to stop the target vehicle should it move off. Over.'

'From Oscar Victor Five Three, understood. Over.'

'From Control to Oscar Victor Five Three, you now have priority on the radio. Any movement, we need to know immediately. Over.'

'Understood, Five Three over.'

Roger turned to face Zoltan, who was staring eagerly back at him. The intelligent dog knew when he was working and was keenly awaiting his next instruction.

Roger smiled at Zoltan before turning to watch the woods. He wound the driver's door window down so he would get an early heads-up if the target vehicle was started; then he settled back to wait for the firearms team to arrive.

Right now, the woods were a picture of tranquillity. The only sounds came from the birdsong that filled the air, and the whispering of leaves as the slightest of breezes ruffled the laden branches above his head.

PC Barker had already made his mind up that he wasn't going to sit idly by and allow the target vehicle to be driven away by the man who had callously gunned down his unarmed colleague.

92

7.30 a.m., 6 August 1991
MCIU Offices, Mansfield, Nottinghamshire

Danny was feeling the pressure as he stared at the clock on the briefing room wall. He was transfixed by the second hand as it slipped relentlessly round the clock face. He knew that every minute that passed could signal the grisly death of one of the three abducted people. One of whom was a close friend.

The strident sound of the telephone ringing snatched him back from his dark thoughts. He picked the handset up on the third ring and snapped, 'Flint.'

'Sir, this is Inspector Handley in the control room. Your target vehicle has been sighted just north of Cuckney crossroads. It's unattended and parked in woodland near the Welbeck estates.'

Danny immediately waved to Rob, Sara and Sharon to

get their attention before saying, 'Who's with the vehicle now?'

'A dog handler, PC Barker. He's got the van under observation, but nobody's with it at the moment.'

'Have you got armed officers travelling to his location?'

'Yes, sir. They're estimating ten minutes before they are on scene. Sergeant Turner has suggested using Lady Margaret Hall as the rendezvous point.'

Danny stared at the large map pinned to the whiteboard and located the hall. 'How far is the hall from PC Barker's current location?'

'Three hundred yards at the most.'

'I want armed officers with him as soon as they arrive. I don't want an unarmed officer facing that threat any longer than he needs to,' Danny instructed. 'Is that understood?'

'Yes, sir. I'll get back onto Sergeant Turner and advise him accordingly.'

'Thank you. Can you co-ordinate an outer cordon, with other uniform officers in the area?'

'Already in hand, sir. I've got roadblocks established half a mile in every direction from the target vehicle's location.'

'Good work. Can you show myself, DI Buxton and DI Lacey as all travelling to the rendezvous point? Our vehicles are fitted with VHF radios, so we'll be monitoring your signals once we're en route.'

'Will do, sir. For your information, Sergeant Turner has just responded to your request. As soon as he arrives on scene, he will initially deploy four armed officers to put a containment on the target vehicle.'

'Good. Have PC Barker resume to the rendezvous point as soon as that containment's in position.'

'Yes, sir.'

'And I want two ambulances on standby at the rendezvous. Quick as you can. I don't want the shit to hit the fan and those officers to have no medical support on scene.'

'That's also in hand, sir. It was a stipulation on the operational order submitted by Chief Inspector Chambers.'

'Of course it was, sorry. Excellent work, Inspector.'

Danny terminated the call and looked up to see the expectant faces of his two DIs and Sharon Whittle staring at him.

'They've found the van,' he exclaimed. 'At Welbeck estates, in the woods.'

'The tunnels?'

Danny raised his eyebrows. 'Possibly. It fits. Get onto the Welbeck estate manager and ask him to meet us at the Lady Margaret Hall. We're using that location as the rendezvous point for the armed operation. The estate manager might be able to shed some light on where the nearest tunnels are in relation to where the target vehicle's been sighted.'

'I'm on it, boss.'

Danny looked at Sara. 'Grab some car keys – cars fitted with VHF radios. We'll need to monitor the control room as we travel to Welbeck.'

Sharon said, 'Should I stay here?'

'There's no reason you shouldn't come to the rendezvous point. You'll be safe there. It's your choice.'

'I'll grab my coat.'

93

Lady Margaret Hall, Welbeck, Nottinghamshire

The car park at Lady Margaret Hall was already busy with emergency service vehicles. The two plain white Ford Transit vans, used by the Special Operations Unit, were parked next to the two ambulances, and there were several MCIU vehicles that had converged on the rendezvous point.

As Danny got out of his car, he saw PC Barker's police dog patrol van in the corner of the car park.

The officer was standing at the rear of his van as Danny walked over. As he did so, PC Barker said, 'Don't come any closer, sir. My dog's having a wander at the back of the van. Let me put him away before you get any nearer. He doesn't like strangers being between me and him when he's in work mode.'

Danny said, 'No problem.'

As soon as the burly dog handler had secured Zoltan in the rear of the van, he said, 'It's okay to approach now. Better safe than sorry.'

Danny said, 'I'm Chief Inspector Flint, from the MCIU. Are you PC Barker?'

'Yes, sir.'

'Good work finding the van this morning. What made you look in the woods?'

'Pure chance, sir. My dog needed to be let out of the van, so I drove into the woods to let him out for a few minutes. I happened to see something shining in the trees, and when I went to check it out, there was the van.'

'And you haven't seen anybody else in those woods?'

'No, sir. But I get the feeling he's in there somewhere, if you know what I mean. The van isn't abandoned. He's around, all right.'

'How well do you know these woods?'

'Not that well. That track is somewhere I bring Zoltan when I'm working north of the county. I haven't been on patrol up here much lately. I've spent the last few months patrolling Nottingham city centre and the conurbation area.'

'Do you know anything about the tunnels that run under the estate?'

'I've heard the rumours, but I've never been down them myself.'

Now Danny heard Rob Buxton shout his name, and he turned to see his DI talking to a tall, slim man, who was wearing a Barbour coat and a flat cap; they were both standing next to a dark green Land Rover.

Danny acknowledged Rob's shout, then turned to face

PC Barker. 'Don't go anywhere. We may need you and Zoltan for some tracking work later.'

'I've only popped out to give Zoltan a stretch. I'll be going back inside now to carry on briefing with Sergeant Turner. Zoltan's a trained tactical firearms dog and one of the best trackers on the section, sir.'

As the two men crossed the car park and approached Rob, the DI said, 'Sir, this is Spencer Marley. He's the manager of the Welbeck estate. He's brought maps of the estate that show most of the tunnels.'

Danny extended his hand and said, 'DCI Flint. Pleased to meet you, Mr Marley. Let's take the maps inside, shall we.'

Inside the hall, Danny found Sergeant Turner, PC Barker and the remaining SOU officers doing equipment checks and preparing their plans of operation, should the suspect be sighted.

Danny introduced the estate manager and said, 'Mr Marley has maps that may be useful for your planning, Graham.'

The maps were spread out on a large table, and Spencer Marley pointed to a track and said, 'From what Inspector Buxton told me on the phone, I believe the van you're interested in has been sighted here.'

PC Barker nodded and said, 'That's where it is all right.'

Graham Turner said, 'The containment officers have seen no sign of anybody in the area around the van, not since they went in. I've heard a lot about tunnels under this place; are there any entrances near to that track?'

Marley studied the map. 'I believe the nearest one would be in this vicinity.' He drew a circle with his finger, which outlined approximately one hundred yards from the target vehicle's location.

'You don't know for sure?'

'The tunnels that run beneath this end of the estate are all in dreadful condition and as such are unsafe. None of my staff have been down them for years. I recall there being a long spine tunnel that does have an entrance in this vicinity. There are several large store rooms off that spine tunnel. The tunnel was in such a shocking state the last time we went in, I had the entrance sealed up to prevent anybody going inside.'

'When was that?'

'Over a year ago. I had it sealed with corrugated iron. The last thing the estate needed was somebody to have an accident inside the tunnel.'

'How big is that spine tunnel?'

'Lengthwise it runs for at least half a mile. It's dimensions are huge. It was built to enable a horse and carriage to be driven along it. To really understand the scale of these tunnels, you need to understand why they were built. The fifth Duke of Portland was a recluse, the Howard Hughes of his generation. He was also an engineering genius, way ahead of his time when it came to construction. He built the tunnels so he could travel around the estate without being seen. Like I say, some of them were big enough to accommodate a horse and carriage.'

'What were the store rooms used for?'

'Various uses. Some were tack rooms for the horses' equipment. Others were used for the storage of other items used on the estate.'

'And what size are they?'

'I would estimate anything between twelve and twenty feet square.'

'Quite substantial, then?'

'Yes. Everything underground was built to a grand scale.'

'Any other exits from that spine tunnel?'

'It runs through to the underground ballroom. There are several exits from the ballroom to the main house, and those are still in use today. If my memory serves me right, there are exits from a couple of those store rooms into the surrounding woodland. I ordered them to be bolted from the inside to prevent access from outside, before sealing the tunnel entrance.

Graham Turner looked incredulous. 'Did you say there's an underground ballroom?'

'Like I said, everything is on a grand scale. It's a subterranean labyrinth down there.'

'If we take you into the woods, could you point out the entrance you're referring to? The one that you had closed off.'

Marley was thoughtful for a minute, then turned to face Danny and said, 'I could point out the entrance to you, no problem. But is it safe for me to be in those woods?'

Danny said, 'It must be your choice, Mr Marley. You'll be accompanied by armed officers, and we would provide you with body armour, but there would be an element of risk, as we haven't located the suspect yet. I believe he's using the tunnels, and I think he'd want to leave his vehicle as close as possible to the entrance he's using. If it reassures you, I'll come into the woods with you.'

Marley nodded thoughtfully. 'Okay. I'll do it.'

Graham Turner shook his hand. 'Good man. Let me get you both kitted out.'

As Danny started to put on the body armour, Rob said,

'Are you sure you want to do this, boss? Don't you think it's a bit soon after what happened in Durham?'

Danny secured the last of the Velcro straps and looked straight at Rob. 'I'll be fine.'

94

8.15 a.m., 6 August 1991
Woodland near Welbeck, Nottinghamshire

Danny and Spencer Marley stayed close to Sergeant Turner as they moved through the woods towards the containment officers watching the van.

The SOU sergeant suddenly stopped and squatted down, signalling for Danny and Marley to do the same. He crawled forward to where the first containment officers were hidden in the dense undergrowth.

PC Tom Naylor was peering through the scope of his rifle at the van, and his observer, PC Matt Jarvis, was looking through binoculars, scanning the area surrounding the target vehicle.

Graham said, 'Any movement?'

Matt said, 'Not a thing, Sarge.'

'I've a civilian and DCI Flint with me. We need to go forward to locate an entrance to the tunnels that's believed to be nearby. Matt, I want you to accompany us as we go forward.'

'No problem. Let me contact the other containment team before we approach. They are watching from the far side. We've set up so we have an arc of fire without any crossfire issues. It gives us the best options to view all the approaches to the van.'

'Okay, good. Let me know when we can move forward.'

Graham crawled back to where Danny and Marley were waiting while Matt contacted Bravo team on the other side of the van.

After a couple of minutes, Matt made his way back to Graham and said, 'It's okay to move forward now.'

Graham said to Danny, 'Did you want to remain here with PC Naylor, boss? There's no need for us all to go forward.'

Danny glanced at Marley, who now had a look of abject terror on his face. He said, 'There's no problem, Graham. I want to see this tunnel entrance for myself.'

'Okay, sir. Stay close, both of you, and do whatever I tell you to do without question. Understood?'

Danny and Marley nodded.

After five minutes of slow progress through the thick woodland, Marley whispered, 'It should be around here somewhere.'

Matt crawled forward on his own before returning and saying, 'It's just up ahead. There's a length of tin propped against a brick wall, and I can see the entrance to the tunnel behind it.'

Marley said, 'The corrugated iron was screwed in place when we left it. Someone must have taken it down.'

'The vegetation around the entrance has been trodden down a lot,' Matt said. 'Somebody's been going in and out of there a lot recently.'

Graham said, 'Any sign of movement?'

'Nothing. There was no noise from inside the tunnel either.'

'Okay. We know where it is now. Let's get back.'

As the four men made their way back through the woodland to Tom Naylor's position, Danny said, 'Has anybody actually checked the van?'

Matt replied, 'Yes, sir. The first thing we did was check the rear of the van to make sure no one was hiding inside. The van has been left unlocked. We peeked in the back to make sure nobody was inside and then set up the containment arc.'

'I'd like to see inside the van before we leave.'

Matt looked at Graham for guidance. The SOU sergeant said, 'Okay. But let's make it quick. I don't like all this movement around the van.' He paused and then continued, 'Matt, you take the chief inspector to the van. I'll cover you from here. Mr Marley, you wait here with me. Okay, move.'

Danny followed Matt. The van's back door was opened quietly, and Danny peered inside. The first thing he saw were two sharpened wooden stakes. Next to the stakes was a length of rope and a bag full of black plastic cable ties. Most alarming of all, he saw a half-empty box of twelve-bore shotgun cartridges.

He turned to Matt and said, 'Didn't you notice any of that stuff before?'

'We were looking for a man, nothing else, sir.'

Once they were out of the woods and driving back to Lady Margaret Hall, Danny said, 'Graham, there was a half-empty box of shotgun cartridges inside the van. Do you think that means our suspect is armed?'

'No point in having ammunition without the weapon to fire it from, boss. I must assume he's armed. A twelve-bore shotgun is a lethal weapon anyway; in a confined space like those tunnels, its effect would be devastating.'

Suddenly Spencer Marley blurted out, 'I think I've seen that van before on the estate.'

Danny turned to face him and said, 'What?'

'Ever since I saw it in the woods just now, I've been thinking where I'd seen it before.'

'Where do you think you've seen it?'

'I've recently let one of the stone lodges to a man on a short-term let, and I'm sure that's his van. When I spoke to your inspector earlier, the fact he was talking about a white van didn't register. It was only when we walked by it just now that I realised.'

'Are you sure?'

'The more I think about it, the more certain I become. I remember the man well because of his name.'

'How come?'

'It was his surname that was unusual. I'd never heard the name Taplow before.'

'What did he look like?'

'He's a big man, looks very strong. Soft spoken, but quite brutish. His head is shaved, so he looks quite menacing. But whenever I've spoken to him, he's always been extremely polite and well mannered. I suppose appearances can be deceptive.'

'Did he say why he needed to rent the cottage?'

'He told me the lease had expired on his previous accommodation, and the landlord had already lined up new tenants to move in. The job he was due to start overseas had been delayed for three months, so he found himself needing to rent at short notice.'

'Did you see any references?'

'Because it was only for three months, and as he paid cash up front for the entire time, I didn't bother. And since he moved in, he's been absolutely no problem. He's a model tenant.'

'Where on the estate is this lodge?'

'It's on the other side of the A60, towards the village of Holbeck Woodhouse. About half a mile from here.'

'I need you to show me on the map as soon as we get inside the hall.'

As the van was driven into the car park, Danny saw Chief Inspector Chambers standing next to another officer wearing a black beret.

He said, 'Who's the man with your boss, Graham?'

'That's the new firearms tactical advisor, Sergeant Colin Ripley. The boss has obviously decided that sometime today we'll be taking positive action and going into those tunnels.'

Having heard the way the sergeant had described the devastating effects of a shotgun used in confined spaces, Danny marvelled at the quiet, understated courage of the sergeant's last remark.

He stayed silent, but his own thoughts already mirroring what the burly sergeant had said. He knew the length of time the suspect had been out of sight meant that if he was in those tunnels, he could already be administering a lethal dose of acid to his next victim.

The other thing worrying Danny was the information

he'd just learned from Marley: Sebastien Haller was intending to move overseas in the very near future.

He knew the SOU had a doctrine when it came to armed operations. They trained never to advance towards a loaded gun, preferring to wait the situation out. The long game was infinitely safer and produced better results. The only change to that rule was when hostages were involved. In that case the overarching responsibility became the preservation of life.

For Danny, they were in a hostage situation right now.

For this maniac's three abducted victims, time was running out.

And waiting for the killer to emerge from the tunnel carrying another corpse was not an option.

95

8.30 a.m., 6 August 1991
Lady Margaret Hall, Welbeck, Nottinghamshire

D anny stood next to Spencer Marley, Graham
Turner and the tactical firearms advisor, Sergeant
Ripley. All four men were staring at a map of the
Welbeck estate.

Danny asked, 'Is Chief Inspector Chambers not joining
us?'

Graham Turner said, 'There's a royal visit today, sir. The
rest of the unit is committed doing the search and seal of the
new radiography wing of the Queen's Medical Centre. It's
being officially opened this afternoon. Chief Inspector
Chambers has had to leave to supervise that. He's happy for
any tactical decisions to be made by Sergeant Ripley.'

Danny looked at Ripley. 'My thoughts are that we search
the lodge first. I'm acutely aware of the dangers posed to

these men if the tunnels are searched, so I think we should clear the lodge first.'

Ripley looked thoughtful. 'I agree. It would be infinitely better if the suspect is contained in that lodge rather than the tunnels. The problem you have is that the number of armed staff here are limited. All the other sections of the SOU are currently committed with the royal visit. In my opinion, it would be unsafe to leave the four containment officers without any backup close to their location.'

Graham Turner said, 'How big are those lodges?'

Marley responded, 'They're very small. Downstairs consists of just a small lounge and a kitchen diner. Upstairs there are two small bedrooms and a bathroom.'

Graham looked at Ripley and said, 'I'd be happy to enter and clear a building of that size with four officers and a dog handler. That way we could leave the rest of my team to act as backup to the containment team already watching the van. That would make seven officers available to confront the suspect should he approach the van.'

Ripley said, 'It's a risky option, Graham.'

'We need to factor in the amount of time the suspect has been away from the van,' Danny said. 'If he's already in the tunnels, it could mean that one – or more – of the hostages is in mortal danger. We know it takes a long time for the victims to die from the method used by this killer, and I genuinely think time could be running out for at least one, if not all of them.'

'Okay,' Ripley said crisply. 'We'll need a trained tactical firearms dog and handler here.'

PC Barker said, 'We haven't met, Sarge. PC Barker. I'm here with my dog, Zoltan, and we've both worked alongside Sergeant Turner and his firearms team before.'

Ripley looked at Turner, who gave the tactical advisor an almost imperceptible nod, before saying, 'I say we do it. It's what we train for, and we know the risks.'

Ripley nodded. 'Okay. We clear the lodge first and make sure the suspect isn't there. As soon as your men have cleared that building, I want everyone, including PC Barker and Zoltan, to the tunnel entrance. To delay any further could cost the lives of any hostages who are down there, so we're going to make a cautious tactical entry into the tunnels.'

Graham said, 'I'll get the lads ready and get PC Barker briefed on the building entry. We'll be good to go to the lodge in fifteen minutes.'

Danny called Sara and Jag over and said, 'Are scenes of crime here yet?'

Jag said, 'Yes, boss.'

'Okay. Special ops are going to raid the lodge and clear that before moving into the tunnels. I want you two to go with scenes of crime, and as soon as the armed officers have cleared the lodge, I want it searched for evidence that Scott Taplow has been living there.'

'Yes, sir,' Sara said. 'What if Taplow's at the lodge?'

'If he's there, SOU will make the arrest. It will still need searching once that's done. Personally, I don't expect him to be there. I think he's already in the tunnels, doing his worst. That's why we need to get cracking. Let's go.'

96

8.45 a.m., 6 August 1991
Holbeck Woodhouse, Nottinghamshire

Sergeant Graham Turner was a man who had a reputation for always leading from the front, and the men on his section of the SOU held him in the highest regard. He was now at the head of a row of four officers all making their way towards the small stone lodge, in woodland near to the village of Holbeck Woodhouse.

When they reached the wooden door of the lodge, he raised his hand to halt their progress before waving PC Barker to approach with Zoltan.

He reached up, tried the black door handle and smiled when he realised the door was unlocked. He turned to PC Barker and said, 'We're in business; the door's open. As soon as you're ready, Rog, I'll open it enough for the dog to get inside.'

PC Barker nodded as he held an eager Zoltan by his shoulders. As the door opened silently, he whispered, 'Seek him,' and released the pressure on his shoulders. This was the dog's signal to start work, and he flew inside the building.

PC Barker followed. The SOU officer designated as the dog handler's personal protection officer, PC Steve Kemp, followed him in. The other armed officers filed inside behind them.

The armed officers had to trust the police dog to indicate if the suspect was hiding inside.

There were no closed doors downstairs, and no indication from Zoltan that anybody was in the lodge.

As the armed officers visually cleared the downstairs rooms, PC Barker grabbed Zoltan and held him again at the foot of the narrow stairs. He gave the same whispered order, 'Seek him,' before guiding the dog up the stairs. He could hear the dog's claws on the wooden floors as he ran from room to room upstairs. After a minute the dog trotted back down the stairs. He hadn't made a sound.

PC Barker turned to Graham Turner and said, 'It's clear, Sarge.'

Trusting in the handler and his dog, Turner nodded and made his way carefully up the stairs, his Heckler and Koch MP5 levelled in front of him, ready to engage any threat. The rooms were small, with very little furniture, but they still had to be visually cleared by the armed officers. It took another ten minutes for all the beds and wardrobes to be checked to confirm what the police dog had already indicated.

The lodge was empty.

The armed officers and PC Barker stepped outside, and

Turner said, 'There are still a couple of outbuildings we need to clear, Rog.'

PC Barker placed Zoltan on a tracking lead and cast him out to the two outbuildings. Once again, it took the dog and his handler just a matter of minutes to clear the two stone buildings.

PC Barker turned and gave a thumbs-up to the SOU sergeant. 'There's nobody in them, Sarge.'

Turner nodded and moved forward to visually clear them for himself before speaking on his radio. 'Sergeant Turner to DCI Flint. Over.'

Danny answered immediately. 'Go ahead.'

'The lodge has been cleared. There's no sign of the suspect at this location. It's safe for scenes of crime and your staff to enter the building now. We're redeploying to the tunnel entrance, to join the rest of the section. Over.'

As the scenes of crime vans, followed by two CID cars, pulled into the lane where the lodge was situated, PC Barker and the SOU van pulled out.

Sara and Jag approached the scenes of crime van, and Sara spoke to Tim Donnelly. 'We'll do a quick visual check of the lodge before your team move in to do a full forensic search.'

'Okay. You know the drill: be careful where you tread, and make sure you've got protective clothing on before you go inside.'

Sara smiled. 'Thanks for the reminder, Tim.'

The scenes of crime supervisor grinned back and said, 'Can never be too careful, ma'am.'

She turned to Jag. 'Have a quick look in the outbuildings before you come in.'

Jag nodded and made his way over to the two buildings before returning minutes later.

Sara said, 'Anything?'

'There's a Suzuki 250cc motorbike, but that's it.'

'Is it a runner?'

'Looks new, so I would think it's working. I'll check it on PNC.'

As Sara began a visual check inside the property, Jag made his way back to the car and checked the motorcycle.

Having passed the registration number to the control room, he waited for their reply. It took less than a minute. 'Control room to DC Singh. Over.'

'Go ahead. Over.'

'Your vehicle check comes back as a black Suzuki 250cc motorcycle. Registered keeper's shown as Scott Taplow; the address is Bainton Grove on the Clifton estate. Over.'

'Received. Over.'

Jag made his way back to the lodge and said, 'The bike's registered to Taplow. I think that's enough to confirm he's living here. Have you found anything?'

'Nothing startling. I say we let scenes of crime in to do their full forensic search now.'

97

9.15 a.m., 6 August 1991
Woodland near Welbeck, Nottinghamshire

S eamus Carter slowly stirred. He felt groggy and disorientated as the effects of the drug he had been injected with wore off. As his eyes started to focus in the dim light, he could just make out a large figure standing in the corner. He tried to move and realised he was now strapped to a heavy chair and had been totally immobilised. He couldn't even turn his head to try to see his surroundings better.

The wood of the chair was covered in a hard plastic-type material. Carter grimly registered that the substance he was sitting on was Teflon. One of the only substances resistant to the effects of acid. He shuddered as he realised he was now in the room where the acid was located.

The menacing figure in the corner stepped forward and

growled, 'So he finally awakes. Where was all that fight you spoke about, Carter? You're the same as the others, weak and ineffectual.'

Carter could see the man was wearing a gas mask and holding a shotgun. His voice croaked as he tried to speak, the effects of the acid fumes already taking a toll. 'It's not too late to stop this madness. I've never harmed a soul. I'm a pathologist, for Christ's sake.'

'I know exactly who you are and what you do. I've seen how you bend to the will of corporate giants.'

'What are you talking about?'

'How you yielded to the pressure from Sir Anthony Pemberton and Jurgen Hauptmann to reach the suicide verdict you did, so there were no repercussions for Future Visions Pharmaceuticals for my mother's murder.'

'What murder?'

'Rebecca Haller. Do you remember her name?'

Carter tried to recall the woman's name but couldn't.

'You see. You don't even know her name. Well, her name will be the last you hear on this earth. You covered her murder up by recording a finding of suicide at the post-mortem you carried out. The fact she had been driven to drink that acid by two unscrupulous men meant nothing to you. She meant nothing to you. My precious mother meant nothing to you, and now you'll pay the same price she did.'

The figure stepped forward and flicked two switches immediately behind Carter. Instantly, a generator sparked into life, and Carter could hear pump machinery whirring behind him.

Carter knew exactly what the machine was and shuddered. In a last-ditch attempt to prevent a prolonged and painful death, he gritted his teeth and said, 'Why don't you be a man and use the shotgun? If you want me dead that much, just pull the trigger, you arsehole.'

The figure lowered the shotgun, pointed it directly in the pathologist's face and began laughing, behind the gas mask.

'I've waited so long to see you and the others die, but death alone isn't enough. I need you to suffer in the same way my mother suffered. I want your last moments to be agonising and full of pain. The full price must be paid, Irishman.'

Then he paused before adding, 'When that first drop of acid falls on you, I want you to remember the name of Rebecca Haller.'

The figure stepped back and stared intently.

The first drop of acid fell from the machine.

Carter felt the droplet, and for the first couple of seconds nothing happened. Then, as the caustic liquid slipped through his thick hair, he felt tremendous, searing pain as it attacked every nerve ending in the flesh of his scalp. He frantically began struggling against the ties that bound him, desperately trying to free himself. He strained every sinew to rock the chair and tip it over. But it was just too heavy, and he couldn't move it.

Breathing heavily from his exertions, he stopped struggling, momentarily resigned to his hideous fate, but knowing in his heart that when the next drop of acid fell, he would struggle even harder for survival.

98

9.20 a.m., 6 August 1991
Woodland near Welbeck, Nottinghamshire

Graham Turner led the final briefing of his men before they made the perilous entry into the tunnels. Each man knew the risks and the danger they faced. A shotgun being fired at them in such an enclosed environment was a dreadful proposition.

Turner said to PC Barker, 'The estate manager has indicated that there may be exits out to the woodland from this tunnel, so we may need your skills to track the suspect if he tries to escape. There are bound to be fumes, toxic ones, down there. Are you happy for your dog to work in that environment?'

'I'm not happy about it, but we'll be going with you. If the dog starts to suffer, I'll withdraw. The only guide I have is that the CS gas we use in training has never affected him.

Only a vet would know for sure if it's safe, and there isn't one here, so we press on.'

Sergeant Ripley added, 'Good man. I want you and your dog at the front of the column. I want you to move forward in short distances. Stick to your line of sight. You'll always have PC Kemp with you as your protection man, and the rest of the section, led by Sgt Turner, will be close behind you. You move as per your training, okay?'

'I'm good with that, Sarge. The only problem may be if the dog starts showing signs of distress because of the fumes. If that happens, he won't be effective, and I'll have to withdraw him.'

Sergeant Ripley nodded, then addressed the rest of the men. 'Remember your training, move quickly but safely. Support each other and watch your distances and arcs of fire in that enclosed space.'

The men made one final check of their weapons before putting on respirators and moving forward to the tunnel entrance.

Once inside, they lined up against each side of the tunnel wall and squatted low, allowing their eyes to adjust to the dim light.

Sergeant Turner checked the position of every man before giving the signal to move forward.

As PC Barker cast Zoltan out to the first checkpoint, the silent, still air was shattered by a haunting scream that reverberated down the tunnel. Each man instinctively dropped lower and waited.

It was a blood-chilling scream and one the men in that tunnel would never forget.

Turner turned to face his men and said urgently, 'We need to move, come on.'

They all heard two more blood-curdling screams of agony before PC Barker reached the row of wire cages, which were now illuminated by the headlamp he wore.

He said, 'Down!'

Instantly his dog stopped in its tracks and waited for the next command.

Roger turned to Graham Turner and said, 'There's a row of cages ahead and movement.'

Turner said, 'Can you send the dog forward to the cages?'

'No problem. Stand by.'

He whispered to Zoltan, 'Seek on.'

The dog moved forward and barked once.

Roger called the dog back and said, 'There's something ahead, but it's not a threat, or he would have indicated more. I'll check it out.'

Roger and Steve Kemp moved forward, the SOU officer training his weapon into the darkness of the tunnel, ready to engage any threat.

As they got closer, they became aware of people squatting inside the first two cages. There was nothing but darkness beyond them, as the tunnel stretched away into the distance.

Realising the cages were secured by padlocks, Roger called for one of the support team to bring forward bolt croppers.

Graham Turner moved forward to join Roger, and after setting up two men to train their weapons into the darkness of the tunnel, he said, 'Get the locks off and get these people out of here.'

As the first padlock snapped, a woman almost fell out of the cage. She was sobbing and breathless.

Turner said, 'Who's been screaming?'

The man in pyjama bottoms released from the second cage said, 'It's the pathologist. Big guy with a beard. That maniac took him away some time ago.'

'How many screams have you heard?'

Just as the question was asked, yet another horrifying, haunting cry filled the tunnel.

The released man flinched and said, 'Four or five.'

'Have you seen the man who's doing this since he took the pathologist away?'

The man shook his head. 'No. He's still down that way,' he said as he indicated the darkness of the tunnel. 'He's got a shotgun,' he added.

Turner spoke rapidly into his radio. 'Sergeant Turner to DCI Flint. Over.'

To his dismay, the only response was heavy static. He cursed. 'I want two men to escort these people out of here.'

As two men stepped forward, Turner said, 'The radio signals down here are crap, so make sure you tell DCI Flint and Sergeant Ripley that we're in pursuit of the offender in the tunnel. He may be making his way towards a secondary exit, and he's armed with a shotgun. Depending on where the second exit is located, Flint may need to withdraw the personnel from the lodge as soon as possible. If the offender is intending to make his way back there, they could be in danger.'

The two men nodded and assisted the two hostages to their feet, ready to help them out of the tunnel.

Turner faced the remainder of his men and PC Barker before saying, 'The rest of you, on me. We're going to need to move faster. That doesn't mean I want unnecessary risks being taken. Remember your training and stay alert. Now, let's find the last hostage.'

99

9.35 a.m., 6 August 1991
Woodland near Welbeck, Nottinghamshire

Sebastien Haller hadn't heard anything untoward in the tunnel as he left the killing room. As soon as he had heard Carter's first scream and saw his reaction to the acid, he allowed himself a grim smile of satisfaction. He knew it was now only a matter of time before the pathologist succumbed to his ghastly injuries and died a horrific death.

He would return shortly, but first he needed to check on the other captives. It wouldn't take long, and there would be plenty of time to return and witness the suffering of Seamus Carter.

He picked up the shotgun and started to make his way back along the tunnel towards the exit. It would be hours before Carter died, and he needed to get this clammy respirator off his face. He had cold water in his van. He was desperate to quench his thirst and rinse the metallic taste of the respirator filter from his mouth.

As he got closer to the cages, he heard movement and saw light from torches bouncing off the tunnel walls. He then heard a single, deep bark from what sounded like a large dog. Some instinct told him it was the police in the tunnel. He could see from the number of torches bouncing off the walls and the ceiling that at least several people were in the tunnel.

He cursed before turning and making his way back along the tunnel, towards the killing room. He heard Carter groaning loudly as he moved past. His expansive knowledge of the tunnel system meant he knew there was a secondary exit from this tunnel. It was in another of the store rooms some fifty yards further along.

He passed three doors before finding the correct one. He made his way across the rubbish-strewn floor to the heavy wooden door that led to the outside world. The door had been bolted from the inside.

With a lot of effort, he managed to slide the two rusting bolts back before stepping out into the woodland. There was a steep rise in the ground that led from the overgrown door out to the forest floor above. After the gloom of the tunnel, the bright morning sunshine initially dazzled him, and he squinted as he ripped off his respirator.

Once his eyes had adjusted to the light, he checked his shotgun was still loaded and climbed to the top of the rise, where he waited behind a fallen tree. He knew the police would be right behind him after discovering the caged captives, and the presence of the dog meant he couldn't outrun them. He needed to slow them down before he made his way back to the lodge.

Now that he was cut off from the van, he needed to use his secondary mode of transport. He silently congratulated himself for having the foresight to stash the Suzuki in one of the lodge's outhouses. All he would need from the lodge was the motorcycle keys, passport and air ticket.

As he settled down to ambush the police, he wondered how they had managed to find his lair so quickly. He cursed that he wouldn't be able to complete his revenge, but he realised it was now time to take heart from what he had achieved, and to start a new life.

Revenge could always come later.

100

9.35 a.m., 6 August 1991
Woodland near Welbeck, Nottinghamshire

Seamus Carter gritted his teeth and tried desperately to control his breathing. The pain in his head was unimaginably intense, and with each new droplet of acid that fell came another lightning bolt of pain searing through his entire body.

He had thrashed his arms, legs and head against his bindings, but he couldn't move even half an inch.

And so he had sat in the darkness, panting and waiting for the next droplet to fall. Each one caused a brand-new burning sensation that felt like it was searing a fiery path right through his skull.

Each bolt of pain made him gasp and suck in the foul, fume-laden air that surrounded him. The toxic fumes from the exposed acid were starting to burn his throat and windpipe.

Having carried out the post-mortem examinations of this madman's previous victims, Carter knew exactly what was coming. He could feel sweat pouring down his face. Some of those rivulets of sweat carried residue from the acid, which in turn bit into the flesh of his face. He blinked hard, desperately trying to protect his eyes.

He braced himself, waiting for the next droplet to fall, before closing his eyes and saying a silent prayer.

Seamus Carter knew he was about to die.

101

As Graham Turner and his men progressed along the tunnel towards the sound of the agonised screams, he constantly urged his men to make progress. 'Sounds like he isn't far ahead of us now. Come on, let's do this properly, but do it faster. We need to get that poor sod out of there before it's too late.'

Each time PC Barker and his dog located a door, the dog would be put into the room to clear it. That room then had to be physically checked by armed officers before they could move forward. It was a time-consuming process but one that had to be done. Three store rooms had been checked before they reached what they knew was the killing room. It had taken the team twenty minutes to reach the door where the screams were emanating from.

Roger faced Steve Kemp and said, 'Open the door, and I'll see if I can get a visual before I send the dog in.'

Steve nodded and twisted the handle. This room was smaller than the others and was illuminated by a single red light from a humming generator.

Roger held the dog and quickly looked inside the dim room. He could see a large man strapped into a chair of some kind, but there was no other movement, and although Zoltan indicated the presence of the man in the chair, Roger could see no other discernible movement.

Sergeant Turner approached, 'What have we got?'

Roger said, 'The hostage is inside. The room still needs clearing properly, but it looks clear.'

Graham looked at his armed team and said, 'Right. Be in no doubt that this lunatic may be hiding in this room, watching his handiwork, so take the utmost care. I'll make first entry. Naylor, you're in second. Let's clear the corners fast. The rest of you, cover the door.'

The heavy wooden door was already slightly ajar, and Tom Naylor now reached for the handle, ready to open it wide to allow his sergeant access into the fume-filled room. Both men were sweating heavily, and the view through their respirators was compromised, limiting their visibility.

They made a final check of their weapons, checking the safeties were off. With that done, Graham Turner silently counted down using his fingers to signal three, two, one.

Tom yanked open the door, and Graham instantly moved into the room, squatting low and moving to his right as he cleared the corners. Tom immediately moved in behind him, concentrating his weapon on the heavy wooden chair, ensuring nobody was hiding behind it.

As soon as Turner was confident the suspect wasn't in

the room, he stood up and switched off the generator, stopping the machine.

Seamus Carter was slumped in the chair. His neck was bent at a grotesque angle, as his head was still securely fastened to the chair. Tom grabbed his boot knife and began slicing through the bindings that secured the burly pathologist.

As soon as the last of the bindings was cut, Tom, assisted by other officers, dragged Carter from the killing room and back out into the tunnel.

As Turner stepped back out into the tunnel, he said, 'Is he alive?'

Tom nodded. 'There's a strong pulse, Sarge, but his breathing's very shallow.'

'Good. Get some water on his head. Wash that shit off, but do it back over so it doesn't run down his face.'

The SOU officers laid Carter on the floor and began drenching the top of his head with water from their bottles, being careful to protect the Irishman's face and eyes.

As the cold water hit his head, the pathologist stirred a little, but was still almost comatose from shock and pain.

Turner barked orders. 'I want two men to get him out of here as quick as you can. Carry him if you must; he desperately needs urgent medical attention. The rest of you, let's continue to move forward. We've still got a job to do.'

102

9.55 a.m., 6 August 1991
Woodland near Welbeck, Nottinghamshire

As the SOU team made their way slowly along the tunnel, PC Barker suddenly squatted down and raised a fist, halting progress.

Sergeant Turner moved forward and said, 'What is it, Rog?'

'There's light ahead, Sarge. I can see daylight.'

Graham peered through the gloom and could see faint light emanating through an open door that led off the tunnel.

He cursed under his breath and said, 'Looks like our man's back outside. It's time for you and your dog to start tracking through the woods. Is the dog okay?'

Roger nodded. 'He's fine. He's done a bit of sneezing, but he seems good to go.'

After making their way into the storeroom, Turner and the team could now see the door that led to the woodland beyond.

Roger said, 'I'll move forward with Zoltan and see if we can get a visual.'

Graham said, 'Okay. Be careful,' before turning to Steve Kemp and saying, 'See if you can give him some cover with the short ballistic shield.'

PC Kemp nodded and took the heavy shield from one of his colleagues.

Now Turner spoke into his radio. 'Sergeant Turner to DCI Flint and Sergeant Ripley. Over.'

The burly sergeant breathed a sigh of relief when he heard the response: 'DCI Flint. Go ahead, Graham. Over.'

'To DCI Flint, all the hostages have now been released and are being brought out to your location. Seamus Carter is seriously injured and needs urgent medical attention. Over.'

'Received.'

'We're now about one hundred and fifty yards from your location, moving south, and there's another exit from the tunnel back out into the woods. Over.'

Danny said, 'From DCI Flint to Sergeant Turner, have you had any contact with the suspect? Over.'

'No, sir. One of the hostages confirmed that the man who has been holding them is armed with a shotgun, so our progress has had to be slow. We're going to see if the dog can pick up a track, as it looks like the offender is now back out in the woods. Over.'

'Received. Be careful, Graham. Good work getting the hostages out. Over.'

103

9.55 a.m., 6 August 1991
Lady Margaret Hall, Welbeck, Nottinghamshire

Spencer Marley was standing next to Danny as the radio message came through. He pointed down at the map of the tunnels and said, 'That secondary entrance is located here, which means if your suspect has managed to force the external door my staff secured, theoretically he could be heading back towards the lodge he's rented, which is here, about half a mile away.'

Marley again pointed at the map, indicating the lodge at Holbeck Woodhouse.

The gravity of the information wasn't lost on Danny. He picked up the radio and said, 'DCI Flint to DI Lacey. Over.'

'Go ahead, sir. Over.'

'Sara, it looks like Haller could be making his way back

towards your location. It's been confirmed that he's armed with a shotgun. I want everyone out of the lodge and back to the rendezvous point immediately. Over.'

'Received. I'll message again when we've withdrawn. Over.'

104

9.55 a.m., 6 August 1991
Woodland near Welbeck, Nottinghamshire

P C Barker inched his way through the door and out into the daylight. He paused to allow his eyes to adjust to the bright sunshine before scanning his surroundings.

From the doorway, the ground immediately in front of him led up a steep incline that was covered in ferns and brambles. It was as though the surrounding woodland had been scooped out to accommodate the door into the tunnel.

He could see that some of the foliage on the incline had been trampled, but he couldn't see or hear anything moving beyond the ridge in front of him.

He gripped the tracking lead tightly in his right hand before whispering to his dog, 'Seek him.'

As Zoltan moved out of the doorway, he immediately

shifted to the right, away from the flattened brambles and ferns.

The experienced dog handler glanced upwards at the trees and could see that the breeze was blowing left to right. He knew that could be blowing any air scent given off by the offender to the right of his actual path.

As he tried to inch out a little further to keep a visual on his dog, Steve Kemp crawled alongside him, covering the dog handler's head with the ballistic shield.

The dog didn't appear to have located any track, so Roger called him back.

As the dog returned and the two men were about to retreat inside the storeroom, the peaceful quiet of the forest was shattered by the roar of a shotgun.

The bulk of the twelve-bore pellets hit Kemp on his left side. The force of the blast from such close range knocked him sideways, into Roger and the police dog. Both men and the dog ended up in a heap on the floor of the storeroom.

Eager hands gripped Kemp and dragged him further into the safety of the room. Graham Turner instantly reached for his radio. 'From Sergeant Turner. Shots fired at the entrance to the tunnel. I've an officer down. Over.'

Danny grabbed the radio. 'What injuries? Over.'

'Steve Kemp's been hit in the side. It looks like his body armour has taken the brunt of the pellets, but his left shoulder has also been hit, and he's losing blood. I need to get him out of here asap. Over.'

'Received. I'll delay the ambulance leaving with Seamus Carter until Kemp's evacuated. The paramedics can treat him here for his acid burns. Over.'

'Thank you, sir. I'll be sending two men out with Kemp,

so that will leave me and four plus PC Barker and the dog. Over.'

Sergeant Ripley, the tactical advisor, picked up the radio. 'From Sergeant Ripley, received that. The hostages are safe now. I don't want you putting your men at any further risk. Remain at your current position. Do not proceed towards a loaded gun. Over.'

Graham replied, 'Received that. Over.'

The experienced sergeant calmly organised first aid for his wounded officer and allocated two officers to assist in his evacuation, before turning to PC Barker. 'What do you think, Rog; could your dog get to him before he fires again?'

PC Barker looked down at his dog, which stared back at him, and said, 'It's possible. This could just be a delaying tactic to make us wait it out. We've already waited five minutes since that shot. We're losing precious time. He's not going to want a stand-off with the police, is he? I reckon he's either trying to get back to that lodge for the motorcycle in the outhouse or doubling back to his van. Either way, I don't see him hanging around outside this door.'

Graham Turner grinned. 'My thoughts exactly.'

'What about Sergeant Ripley's order to wait it out?'

'I'm Raid One, and it's down to me to make the decisions on the ground. I'll move up and be your protection officer. Let's do this.'

105

Holbeck Woodhouse, Nottinghamshire

The heavy rumble of the diesel engine growled as the scenes of crime van was driven away from the stone lodge, leaving DI Lacey and DS Singh standing next to their respective cars.

'That's everybody out,' Sara said. 'Come on, Jag. Let's go.'

They both started their cars and began driving away from the lodge. As Sara pulled onto the lane first, Jag suddenly stopped his car, got out and sprinted back to the lodge.

He raced inside and grabbed a heavy-bladed knife from the kitchen.

Making his way towards the outhouse, he kept his eyes focused on the surrounding woodland.

Just as he reached the door to the outhouse, he heard the

unmistakeable sound of a dog barking. It didn't sound that far away.

He muttered, 'This shit's getting real,' before ducking into the outhouse containing the Suzuki.

Using the knife he had grabbed from the kitchen, he sliced both the bike's tyres until they each had a five-inch slit in them. He allowed himself a grim smile as he looked down at the motorcycle that was now sitting on the rims of its deflated tyres.

He slipped the knife in his jacket, bolted from the outhouse and raced to his car. He turned the ignition and cursed as the engine spluttered. With a sense of rising panic, he tried again, and this time the engine fired into life, and he drove away at speed.

106

Having shot the police officer at the exit door of the tunnel, Haller knew he had bought himself some time. But as he battled through the dense woods back towards the lodge, he cursed under his breath. He had waited too long at the entrance to delay the police. They had taken what had seemed an age to emerge from the storeroom, and as the time ticked by, he'd realised he could have made it back to the lodge ahead of them, without waiting to slow them down.

The longer he had waited, the more quickly that option diminished until it had become no option at all.

He now found himself racing towards the lodge. He could hear the police dog barking and knew it was close – and getting closer.

He had slowed his pace as he approached the A60 and cursed again as he was forced to wait for two cars to pass before crossing. If the police had located him in the tunnels, he realised, it was possible they knew where he had been living as well.

As he reached the lodge, he carefully skirted the perimeter to see if anyone was lying in wait.

The sound of the dog barking in the woods not too far behind him focused his mind and made his decision for him. He knew time was running out if he wanted to make good his escape.

All he needed was the keys for the Suzuki, his passport and the air tickets.

He reloaded the shotgun, and throwing caution to the wind, he made his way into the lodge, holding the weapon at his shoulder, ready to fire if he was challenged.

He snatched the Suzuki keys from the sideboard drawer and the passport and the ticket from the inside cover of a science reference book on the bookcase. All he needed now was to focus on getting away.

Still holding the shotgun in the aim position, he made his way to the outhouse. He propped the shotgun against the wall, wedged open the door, sat astride the powerful Suzuki and kickstarted it into life.

The engine fired up straight away, and he carefully rode out of the outhouse. As soon as he was outside, he opened the throttle. Only then did he realise that both tyres were flat. '*Shit!*'

He was getting off the machine to retrieve the shotgun when he was startled by a cry of, 'Pass auf!'

He turned just in time to see a black and tan missile racing towards him. He made a grab for the shotgun but couldn't move fast enough, and before he knew what was happening, the missile launched itself and locked its teeth around his arm just above the elbow. The force of the attack knocked Haller from the bike, and both dog and man ended up on the floor. It took all of Haller's considerable strength to hold the dog, but there was no way he could loosen the grip of its jaws from his arm.

He yelled as the pain from the bite intensified when the animal shook its powerful head. It was then that he saw a police officer emerge from the woods, followed immediately by a man dressed all in black. That man was pointing a semi-automatic weapon at his head.

The police officer shouted, 'Down!'

The dog instantly released its grip, and Haller instinctively rolled sideways to be further away from those vice-like jaws. He could feel warm blood on the sleeve of his shirt.

He started to shift carefully towards the outhouse to grab the shotgun when the black-clad officer yelled, 'Remain still! If you move again, I will shoot you.'

Haller froze. The tone of the armed officer's voice left no doubt in his mind that, if he moved again, this man would shoot him.

That same officer now took a pace forward and pointed his weapon directly at Haller's head. 'Turn over! Do it now!'

Haller didn't move a muscle, and the voice commanded again. 'I said face down and put your arms out to the sides. Do it now!'

Haller could see the police dog straining to get back at him; it looked like it was only the handler's strong grip that was preventing the beast from hurtling at him again.

And so, this time, Haller did exactly as he was instructed, fully compliant. As he put his arms out to the sides, he felt powerful hands gripping his arms as his wrists were secured with handcuffs.

He winced as he was hauled to his feet, the pain from the dog bite now intensifying.

The police officer who had so far done all the talking said, 'Sebastien Haller, I'm arresting you on suspicion of murder.'

Haller said nothing but maintained a steely eye contact with the armed officer.

107

10.25 a.m., 6 August 1991
Holbeck Woodhouse, Nottinghamshire

Sebastien Haller had been searched and conveyed to Mansfield police station under armed escort, and everyone had now converged on the small lodge house at Holbeck Woodhouse.

Scenes of crime personnel under the supervision of Tim Donnelly were crawling all over the lodge.

Armed officers were standing in a huddle next to PC Barker. They were in good spirits and having an animated discussion about the successful apprehension of Haller.

Graham Turner said, 'I don't know how you do that all the time. It was all I could do to keep up with you and the dog. I think I've left half my face on the brambles in those woods.'

Roger Barker made a fuss of Zoltan and said, 'When he's on it, I just need to let him go. It's all I can do to keep a grip on that tracking line.'

'I was pleased when we got to the A60, and you had to slow him down for a minute.'

'I knew we were close. The wind direction was definitely in our favour. Zolts had his head down and his tail up, a sure sign we were closing in. I was just glad there was no traffic, so we could get straight across.'

'What happened when you got to the lodge?'

'As we emerged from the treeline, I could see the offender astride a motorcycle. I knew that Zolts had line of sight, so I yelled, "Pass auf!" and let go of the tracking lead. My boy nailed him and knocked him off the motorcycle.'

Turner grinned. 'That was all I saw as I came out of the woods: Haller rolling on the ground with your dog gripping him. It was a wonderful sight to behold.'

The mood among the men changed as Sergeant Ripley approached the group. He had a face like thunder.

He spoke directly to Graham Turner. 'What part of "do not pursue" did you not understand, Sergeant?'

Graham was calm with his response. 'I understood your recommendation, but that's all it was, a recommendation. I'm the person responsible for taking action on the ground. After talking to the dog handler, I made the decision that it would be safe to proceed with caution. I stand by that decision.'

'You put your men's lives and your own life in grave danger with your reckless actions.'

'Nothing I did was reckless,' Graham asserted. 'The proof is in the result. It was obvious that Haller wasn't going to wait at the entrance of the tunnel for a gunfight. He was too hell-bent on trying to flee the scene. The only reason he fired that shot was to either delay us or stop us altogether. There are risks every time we carry out an armed operation. My men and I know those risks and are prepared to face them. Now I suggest you save anything else you've got to say until the debrief proper at headquarters. This is neither the time nor place.'

'Don't worry, Sergeant. I'll be making my thoughts known to your senior officers.'

And with that, the tactical advisor stormed off.

Danny and Sara approached the group of officers, and Danny asked, 'What was all that about, Graham?'

'Nothing,' the gruff SOU sergeant replied. 'Just a difference of opinion on tactics. It will get thrashed out at our debrief. It's his first live job, and I don't think he quite understands the dynamic yet.'

'For what it's worth,' Danny said, 'I think it was courageous work by you and your men, and I'll be passing on my thanks to Jim Chambers.'

Turner replied, 'It was Roger and Zoltan who need to take most of the credit, boss. They kept us hard on the heels of Haller as he made his way back here, and then nailed him to make the arrest.'

'Well done, good job,' Danny said.

As if in reply, Zoltan growled as Danny's hand extended towards his handler, and Roger hissed, 'Down.'

As the dog settled at his feet, Roger accepted the handshake and said, 'Thank you, sir. As always, it was a team effort.'

Graham Turner asked, 'How are the injured men doing?'

'Steve Kemp's conscious but in a lot of pain. The paramedics have stemmed the bleeding, and he's now on his way to the hospital. It looks like his body armour took the brunt of the blast; six inches higher and it would have been a different outcome.'

'Thank God for that,' Graham said. 'Which hospital have they taken him to? I need to get there and check on him, boss.'

'He's gone to Bassetlaw. You can travel up with Sara; she'll be leaving shortly to check on the condition of Seamus Carter and the other hostages.'

Turner looked towards Sara. 'How is Carter?'

'Being treated for the burns and still very much in a state of shock, but he'll be okay.'

'That's good to know. I'll get my guys organised first if that's okay with you, ma'am.'

Sara said, 'I'll be ready when you are.'

Graham glanced towards the Suzuki motorcycle and said, 'When I heard that thing start up, I thought we were going to lose Haller. It's a miracle it had a couple of flats.'

Danny smiled and pointed at Jag Singh, who was taking possession of Haller's shotgun from the outhouse. 'You've got DS Singh to thank for that. He stayed and slashed the tyres before leaving the lodge, even though he knew Haller was on his way back here.'

Graham walked over to Jag, offered his hand and said, 'Great work, Detective. Without your quick thinking, Haller would have been in the wind.'

Jag grinned and accepted the handshake. 'It seemed like the obvious thing to do. He was clearly making his way back here for a reason.'

'Maybe so, but you knew he'd already shot one of my men, so it took guts to stay behind like that.' Now it was Turner who grinned before continuing, 'Now, do you want me to clear that shotgun properly before you bag it up?'

Jag gave a nervous laugh. 'Good point, Sarge. Thanks.'

108

10.40 a.m., 6 August 1991
Woodland near Welbeck, Nottinghamshire

Back at the tunnel entrance, scenes of crime personnel wearing full chemical hazard protection suits and breathing apparatus made their way into the tunnel. They had the dangerous, unpleasant task of searching the tunnels and recovering any hazardous material being stored there.

Graham Turner had briefed them about what they could expect to find in both the tunnels and the killing room. He had seen barrels of chemicals and knew that the hideous killing machine was still fully laden with the acid that Haller had loaded it with to murder Seamus Carter.

Everything would need to be photographed in situ before it was dismantled and recovered.

Using dragon light torches, the scenes of crime technicians illuminated the tunnel and found the row of wire cages first. They methodically photographed and listed every item that Haller had used before removing it from the tunnel.

It would take hours of painstaking work in the killing room itself to safely retrieve the evidence of Haller's crimes.

109

1.30 p.m., 6 August 1991
MCIU Offices, Mansfield, Nottinghamshire

The briefing room at the MCIU offices was packed and noisy as detectives spoke in excited tones to the Special Operations Unit officers. There was a real sense of elation that the man who had murdered their colleague – and three others – had finally been stopped before he could commit any further crimes.

Danny sat at the front, flanked by his two detective inspectors. He raised both hands to silence the room before saying, 'I know we're all relieved that the hunt for this maniac is over; however, we still have plenty of hard work to do if we want to ensure that Haller is convicted and taken off the streets permanently.'

He turned to face Sara Lacey. 'I'd like to start the debrief with your update from Bassetlaw Hospital on the condition of PC Kemp and the hostages.'

Sara said, 'PC Kemp has undergone emergency surgery to have several shotgun pellets removed from his shoulder. There was some concern earlier when they realised one of the pellets had embedded itself in Kemp's neck. It was millimetres from the jugular vein, so it became an extremely delicate operation to remove it.'

Danny let out a low whistle. 'Bloody hell, that was close. Sounds like he's had a very narrow escape.'

Sara nodded, her expression serious. 'PC Kemp has come through the operation, and although still sedated, he's now being cared for on the ICU. His condition isn't life threatening, and the doctors expect him to make a full recovery, without any loss of use to his arm or shoulder.'

She paused. 'Seamus Carter has been treated for serious acid burns to the crown of his head and minor burns to his scalp and face. There could be some scarring, but his condition isn't life threatening. He's being kept in hospital for observations, as the doctors are concerned there may be some damage to his lungs from breathing in the toxic fumes created by the acid. It's too early to tell if this could lead to a permanent disability.'

Danny said, 'Any idea how long he's likely to spend in hospital?'

'The doctor wants to keep him in for the next week, at least.'

'Okay. What about Miriam Jackson and Greg Thornhill?'

'They have both been treated for shock but are otherwise uninjured. Their lung function is good, and they are both expected to make a full physical recovery. The mental trauma may take longer to get over. Our detectives are with them right now, obtaining their witness statements.'

'Thank you.' Danny now searched the sea of faces until he saw the scenes of crime supervisor, Tim Donnelly. 'Tim, what have we got from the lodge?'

'As well as the air tickets and passport recovered when Haller was searched following his arrest at the lodge, we have recovered the shotgun Haller used to shoot PC Kemp; a further shotgun has also been recovered, along with a quantity of ammunition for both weapons. There's a lot of documentary evidence that highlights how Haller has used various names to plan and carry out these attacks. We have found documents in the names of Archer and Taplow, as well as his real name, Haller. We've also recovered a list of names of the victims.'

'Are there any names on the list we didn't know about?'

'Yes. There was one: DC Marie Petch. She was the detective who made the initial enquiries into Rebecca Haller's suicide and prepared the file for the coroner.'

Danny turned to Rob. 'Have we carried out a welfare check on DC Petch?'

Rob nodded. 'Yes, boss. She's fine and is about to start an afternoon shift at Beeston CID.'

Danny looked back at Tim. 'What about Haller's vehicles?'

'The Ford Escort van and the Suzuki motorcycle have both been taken to headquarters by the vehicle examiners to undergo a full forensic examination.'

'Have you completed your forensics at the lodge?'

'There's at least another couple of hours' work before I'll be happy to sign it off.'

'What about the search of the tunnels?'

'Everything in the tunnel has been photographed. And guided by PC Barker, I've also had photographs taken of the route Haller took through the forest as he made his way back towards the lodge. It shows how much forward planning he's carried out.'

'Good work. Anything important recovered from the tunnels yet?'

'We've safely recovered barrels of sulphuric acid, the labels of which identify them as being identical to those stolen from Addison's factory during the burglary when PC Stringer was murdered. There are also other barrels of chemicals that carry Future Visions Pharmaceutical labels.'

'How long before you've finished there?'

'I can't say, boss. The biggest problem will be the safe dismantling of the machine Haller built to administer the acid to his victims. That's going to be an extremely painstaking process, and the people doing it are having to wear full protection and respirators. It's going to be a while yet.'

'Okay. Safety first, there's no rush.'

Danny now addressed the room. 'Today has been a good day. Let's not mess up all that good work by not doing the basics right. Anybody who needs to submit a statement, ensure it's completed before you go off duty.' Then Danny looked at Graham Turner. 'Can you ensure your team have all completed their statements before leaving the station, please?'

'Of course, boss. No problem.'

'My thanks to you and your team for their efforts today, and please keep me informed of PC Kemp's recovery.'

'Will do, sir.'

'Have we got PC Barker's statement?'

'He left it with me, boss. He needed to get Zoltan back to headquarters for some food and drink.'

'Well, let's hope he gets a big fat juicy bone for his work today.'

'I think Zoltan's probably full after munching on Haller's arm, sir.'

As the room erupted with laughter and applause, Danny turned to Rob and said, 'I want to see you, Glen Lorimar and Professor Whittle in my office. We need to start planning the interview with Haller.'

With the debrief over, the noise level in the room slowly began to increase as Danny made his way back to his office, followed by Rob, Glen and Sharon Whittle.

Danny waited for everyone to sit down before closing the door. 'Rob, Glen, I want you to carry out the interviews with Haller. I'll observe, along with Professor Whittle.'

Rob said, 'He's asked for a solicitor, so I don't know if he'll be saying much to us.'

Danny looked at Sharon and said, 'Any thoughts on a strategy?'

She looked thoughtful and then said, 'I've a sneaky feeling Haller is going to want to talk to you. I believe he wants the world to know exactly why he's committed these murders. I expect him to be highly intelligent and articulate when you interview him. He'll be totally different from the thuggish demeanour he portrayed when acting as the security guard. He'll be fully aware that you already have a mountain of evidence from the lodge and the tunnels, so there's not much point in him going "no comment".'

'That will be unusual,' Glen said. 'Why do you think that?'

'Several reasons. Mainly, his method of killing, the elaborate staging of the victims in public places so they would be found quickly. These actions point towards a person who wants the world to know, and more importantly understand, why these people have died at his hand.' She took a deep breath. 'I believe these killings have always been about the death of his mother, so I suggest you start the interview with questions relating to her. Try to establish what his childhood was like and how the loss of his mother impacted on his life. I think he won't be able to resist answering those questions, and once he starts, he won't be able to stop.'

'Thank you,' Danny said. 'That's really useful. Rob, when will Haller be ready for interview?'

'I spoke to the custody sergeant before the debrief. Haller's been seen by the police surgeon about the injury from the dog bite, and he's been deemed fit for interview. He's expecting his solicitor any time now. He's going to contact me as soon as the solicitor arrives so we can give disclosure. Then I anticipate there being a lengthy wait while the solicitor's in private consultation with Haller. I think it will be at least another couple of hours or so.'

'Okay. Utilise that time well. I want you to sit down with Sharon and go through your various responses to whatever approach Haller decides to take. If he talks, great. But if he doesn't, I want you to go through everything methodically. That couple of hours will go quickly, and there's a hell of a lot to consider, so get cracking.'

110

4.00 p.m., 6 August 1991
Mansfield Police Station, Mansfield, Nottinghamshire

Sebastien Haller had cut a menacing figure, dressed in a white paper forensic suit. He rested his big forearms on the table and stared intently at the two detectives as they had entered the room. He had refused his solicitor's advice not to answer any questions and had spoken freely to the detectives questioning him, just as Professor Whittle had predicted he would.

Glen Lorimar had questioned Haller at some length about his childhood before reaching the point when his mother's life had been turned upside down by being sacked from Future Visions.

He asked, 'Exactly what changed?'

For the first time, Haller looked down at the desk in front

of him, swallowed hard and answered with a single word, 'Everything.'

'Can you be a little more specific?'

'In that one instant, my mother not only lost her job, but she also lost her career, which she loved passionately, plus the respect of her scientific peers and subsequently her home and child. When social services placed me into care, it was the final straw for her.'

'How much did you understand of what was happening at that time?'

'All of it,' Haller said. 'I was a bright child, and I completely understood what had been done to her. As soon as Hauptmann lied about that scientific breakthrough, her fate was sealed.'

'Why are you so sure Hauptmann lied and that it wasn't his work that made the breakthrough?'

Haller looked up and glared at Glen, his anger barely contained. He virtually spat his reply. 'I have all my mother's work journals locked in a safety deposit box. They are a daily record of her research, and she kept them religiously. Her notes were meticulous in their detail, and she kept copies with her at all times. Everything is there in black and white: the steps she took every day for months to finally make that breakthrough. Hauptmann stole her work and the journals she kept at work, as I had been rushed into hospital with a burst appendix. Hauptmann used her absence as she cared for me to steal her notes and claim them as his own, unaware that she kept duplicate copies at home. He callously took advantage of her love and care for me to take the credit for her genius.

'The man was a thief and a fraud. I needed to show the world exactly what he had done.'

'Exactly how did you expect to achieve that?' Glen asked.

'After I had exacted full revenge for their crimes, I was going to publish my mother's work journals so the world could see for themselves and judge exactly who the charlatans were.'

Glen leaned back in his chair and said, 'I understand your loathing of Hauptmann, but how do his actions justify you taking the lives of other people?'

'They were all complicit in my mother's death.'

'Let's talk about Sir Anthony Pemberton. In what way was he complicit?'

'He defended Hauptmann's lies, and he fired my mother. He was just as responsible for her death as that fraud Hauptmann.'

'Were you aware that it was Sir Anthony who continued to pay the private school fees for your education,' Glen said, 'after your mother lost her job at Future Visions?'

'I knew. My housemaster at Welbeck informed me that Sir Anthony was paying the fees. As far as I'm concerned, it was conscience money. Blood money, if you like. He realised he'd made a grave mistake by crediting Hauptman but was too much of a coward to stand up and say as much, as he didn't want to discredit the precious company name.'

'At what point did you decide on this course of action?'

'In my last year at Welbeck College,' Heller said, his voice matter of fact. 'I sat and read my mother's journals, and for the first time I properly understood the work she had undertaken. It was then I knew for sure that the scientific breakthrough she had made had been stolen from her. I started to plan from that moment. I used to sit for hours in those dark tunnels underneath the Welbeck estate, carefully planning my future.'

'And how did you see that future?'

'Like my mother, I was in love with the study of chemistry. That was where I saw my future. But the here and now was dominated by the need to avenge my mother's savage and needless death. While I was studying at Cambridge, I had the perfect opportunity to research her death and to start drawing up my list of the people responsible. The more research I did, the more people I found culpable.'

'And once you had that list, what was your intention?'

'To kill them all in the same painful way my mother had met her death.'

Glen took a deep breath and rested his hands flat on the table in front of him. 'I'm going to go through that list of names with you. I want you to tell me why you established that individual as being in some way responsible for your mother's death.'

Haller nodded. 'I'll be glad to, Detective. I want people to understand that I'm not some kind of monster. I believe in justice, that's all. Those people all deserved to die.'

'Sir Anthony Pemberton.'

'We've already spoken about him. I've made my feelings clear on the reasons he had to die. Next.'

'Did you kill him?'

'Yes.'

'Jurgen Hauptmann.'

'Again, I've already told you, so I'm not wasting any more time on that fool. Next.'

'Did you kill him?'

'Yes, with a certain relish.'

'The social worker, Miriam Jackson.'

'That woman was responsible for placing me in care. Removing the last element of love from my mother's life. I believe her actions were the final straw for my mother. She had to die.'

'How did you abduct her?'

'I waited for her outside her workplace.'

'Was it your intention to kill her?'

Haller said matter-of-factly, 'Yes. She was going to die for what she did.'

'The hospital consultant, Greg Thornhill. What did he do?'

'He refused my mother medical care when she was at her lowest ebb. If he had helped her when she asked for it, things may have turned out differently.'

'How did you abduct him?'

'I broke into his home and snatched him from his bed as he slept.'

'What fate did you intend for him?'

'The same as the others. I was going to kill him. I wanted to do them in a certain order, but the Irishman kept gobbing off at me after I snatched him from the hospital, so I decided to strap him to the machine first.'

'That's the pathologist, Seamus Carter?'

'Yes. The man who took any blame away from the others by writing in his report that my mother had committed suicide.'

'Your mother drank drain cleaner. That's what killed her. It was suicide.'

'That is what killed her, you're right, Detective. His report, like the report prepared for the coroner by the police, never thought to question why she did what she did. I'm setting out to you now all those reasons and all the people responsible.'

'When we found Seamus Carter in the tunnel, he was

already strapped to your machine,' Glen said. 'Exactly what did that machine do?'

'After I immobilised him in the chair, the machine was programmed to allow a drop of acid to fall onto the top of his head every four minutes. Each droplet contained five millilitres of acid. After many hours, enough acid would have landed on his head to eat through the bone of the skull and start attacking his brain.'

'And when the brain was hit by the acid?'

'Death would follow quite quickly. The acid has a devastating effect on the soft tissue of the brain.'

'Why that method?'

Haller almost smiled. 'It needed to reflect the pain and suffering those people put my mother through.'

'Did you use this method for all the murders?'

'Yes. It worked perfectly.'

'Why did you use the tunnels under Welbeck?'

'I told you earlier. I spent hours in those tunnels when I was a boarder at Welbeck College. I knew they were derelict and that nobody went down them anymore. They were perfect for my plan.'

'You mentioned a police report earlier, the one prepared for the coroner's inquest. The final name on your list was DC Marie Petch, the officer who prepared that report. Had you any plans to abduct her?'

'Yes.' Haller looked straight at Glen as he spoke. 'She would have been the final one, but I had to abandon my plans for her, as I knew you were starting to get close. I thought it was only a matter of time before you realised that Scott Taplow was me, Rebecca Haller's son.'

'Thank you for explaining all that, Sebastien,' Rob

Buxton said. 'I have a couple of further questions. The first person who died by this method was a man named Terrence McAvoy. Can you tell me about him?'

'Is that the homeless man? Was that his name?'

'Yes, it was. We could find nothing to connect him with your mother's death, so why did you take him and subsequently kill him?'

'Simple. I needed to test the machine, then test how easy it would be to convey the body to where I planned to leave them, then finally to test the staging method.'

'So there was nothing to connect him to your mother?'

'No. He was the final experiment. I'm a man of science. Things need to be tested again and again to get things right.'

'An experiment?'

Haller nodded. 'Yes. That's all he was.'

'Don't you think that sounds callous?'

Haller looked thoughtful at the detective's suggestion. 'To the layperson it probably does seem that way,' he said after a pause. 'It was a necessary evil. I learned a lot of lessons from his death.'

'Such as?'

'The acid I was using wasn't right. It took way too long for him to die.'

Rob nodded. 'And where did you find McAvoy?'

'I picked him up from an industrial estate somewhere in Sheffield.'

'How?'

'I fed him, and his scrawny little dog, corned beef sandwiches and gave him a drugged hot drink. It was all very easy.'

'Did you kill him?'

'Yes, eventually.'

'All your victims were elaborately staged and left in very public places where they were sure to be found quickly. Why did you do that?'

'Because I wanted maximum exposure from the media so that when I later published my mother's journals, the maximum number of people would understand why my victims had died that way.'

'How did you plan to publish your mother's work journals revealing Hauptmann's deceit and not therefore be implicated in his murder?'

'I didn't need to take any personal credit. There are plenty of reputable magazines who would be only too pleased to publish such a story without revealing the source of their information. Don't worry, Detective, I've thought this through. I've had years where I thought about nothing else.'

'You mentioned that McAvoy's death made you realise the acid wasn't right. How did you rectify that?'

'I stole sulphuric acid from a factory at Shireoaks. I know what you're going to ask me, Detective. You want to know about the death of your colleague.'

'You're right.' Rob nodded. 'I do.'

'That's the one death that was unnecessary and that I regret. He literally was in the wrong place at the wrong time and caught me as I was loading my van up. I panicked when he identified himself as a police officer. He had seen my face and my van's registration plate. I had no choice but to shoot him. I hadn't even started then, so I couldn't let him stop me. I'm sorry for his death and wish I'd left five minutes earlier; then it never would have happened.'

'What did he say to you when he saw you?'

'He knew he'd disturbed me stealing, and even when he saw the gun, he wasn't going to back down. He never tried to run; he just walked towards me.'

'Was it your intention to kill him?'

'Yes, it was. I didn't want him to stop me.'

'You also fired that shotgun at police officers who were searching for you today. One of those officers was seriously injured. Why did you do that?'

'I didn't realise I'd hit either of the officers. I was aiming for the police dog. I just wanted to slow them down so I had time to get to my motorcycle. I didn't mean to shoot him.'

'You had air tickets for Japan and a passport in your pocket when you were arrested. Why?'

'My intention, before that bloody dog intervened, was to get away on the motorbike. Ride down to London, catch the flight from Heathrow and start a new life in Japan, as a research scientist.'

'What about the people on your list?'

'If you hadn't stopped me, the people in the tunnels would have all died; then I would have returned in a couple of years to deal with DC Petch.'

'Explain what you mean by deal with her?'

'I didn't want her to escape the natural order of justice simply because I ran out of time. I would have killed her in a similar way to the others.'

'Do you have any remorse over what you've done?'

'Why would I? I haven't seen any remorse from these people over the death of my mother. I've said all I'm going to say.' Haller leaned back in his chair. 'I've got nothing else to add, so I won't be answering any further questions.'

Rob Buxton continued with his questioning, but Haller

never responded in any way. Not even with a 'no comment' statement. He just stared at the wall and took the occasional sip of water from the paper cup in front of him. From that point on, he never acknowledged the presence of anyone else in the room.

111

2.00 p.m., 14 August 1991
Rolleston, Nottinghamshire

The invitation had come as a surprise to Danny, as it had only been two days since Seamus Carter had been allowed home from hospital. The pathologist and his fiancée, Gemma, had invited Danny and Sue to the quaint stone-built cottage they shared in the pretty village of Rolleston for drinks and a catch-up.

Sue had quickly arranged for a babysitter to take care of their daughter, Hayley, as she felt it might be a bit much for the recovering Seamus to have a boisterous toddler running around the place.

The weather was beautiful, and the four of them sat outside in the back garden. Rolleston was a peaceful place, and the only sounds to be heard were the singing of the birds and a hand-pushed lawn mower being used somewhere in the village.

Seamus bore the physical signs of his recent ordeal. The hospital had shaved his head and his beard to aid the healing process and to prevent infection of the burns. The top of his head had completely scabbed over and was healing well. There were still vivid red lines visible on his face where the acid had dribbled down from his scalp. Reclined on the lounger Gemma had set up for him, he looked tired.

A pitcher of iced Pimm's and lemonade sat on the table in front of the two women, while the men both held cold glasses of non-alcoholic shandy.

As Danny took a sip of the soft drink, he said, 'I take it you're still on medication, Seamus.'

Seamus grinned and said, 'Still on strong painkillers and antibiotics. I could murder a beer, but I'd better stick to doctors' orders. I've got a Guinness in the fridge if you want one.'

Danny shook his head. 'I'm fine with this; it's refreshing on a hot day.'

The conversation had mainly been small talk since Danny and Sue arrived, but Danny noticed an almost imperceptible nod Seamus gave to Gemma just before she stood up and said, 'Sue, can I show you the orchard at the bottom of the garden? I'm delighted with how everything has grown. We've had a bumper crop of apples, pears and plums. You're more than welcome to take some home with you later.'

Sue had always held a keen interest in gardening. 'I'd love to,' she said. 'I didn't realise you were a gardener.'

With a little chuckle, Gemma said, 'I lived in Kent for almost ten years; we're all gardeners there.'

As soon as the two women were out of earshot, Seamus said, 'I need to know what this was all about, Danny. What did Haller say?'

Danny took another sip before saying, 'He made full admissions but has since indicated to his legal team that he intends to enter a plea of not guilty at Crown Court.'

'What's the point of that?'

'I'm limited as to what I can tell you, my friend, because you'll be asked to give evidence at his trial. Personally, I think he wants the full media circus to focus on his crimes. He has this notion that once he's explained his reasons for his actions, people will understand him.'

'Do you understand?'

Danny shook his head. 'I've listened to the tapes of the interviews several times, and each time they seem more chilling. He displays absolutely no empathy or appreciation of the suffering he put you and the others through.'

'A classic psychopath.'

'Maybe. That's certainly Professor Whittle's take on things. I gave up a long time ago trying to ascribe any rhyme or reason to the crimes these people commit. The main thing is you survived the ordeal, and you can move on with your life.'

'Unlike those other poor souls.'

Danny remained silent, as he knew Seamus wanted to say more.

Eventually the big Irishman said, 'I've hardly slept since this happened, Danny. I'm exhausted.'

'That's a very natural reaction to what was such a deeply traumatic event. I had the same lack of sleep after Durham. Sue put me in touch with a friend of hers, a psychologist. Dr Freda Maher specialises in dealing with people suffering post-traumatic stress disorder. I was sceptical at first and thought I'd be able to work myself out of the depression I was feeling, but I couldn't.'

Seamus sounded surprised. 'You've had therapy?'

'Yes, I have.'

'Did it help?'

'Massively. If you're suffering, you really should get some help, Seamus. It's the best thing I did. I don't know if I would have got over the trauma of what happened in Durham without it.'

'Does your job know?'

Danny shook his head. 'You're the first person I've told. I don't see that it's anybody else's business.'

Seamus looked thoughtful for a long moment. 'Thanks for sharing that, Danny. Could you let me have Dr Maher's contact details?'

'Of course. I don't think you'll regret talking to her.'

Seamus drained the rest of his soft drink. 'Here come the ladies.'

As Gemma returned to the cottage to get a bag for the fruit, Sue said, 'Those trees are laden with fruit. What are you going to do with it all?'

'Jam?' Seamus said with a laugh. 'I've never bothered with the garden much before, but Gemma's all over it. I never had the time; it was always work, work, work. I realise now what a wonderful space it is and so peaceful.'

'The perfect place to convalesce.'

'Certainly is. Especially when the weather's as glorious as today.'

'I never realised you were such a handsome man,' Sue said with a smile. 'Hiding your face with all that beard. You look ten years younger.'

Gemma returned with a plastic bag so Danny and Sue could take some fruit. 'Don't go telling him that. I love his beard. I can't wait for it to grow back.'

Danny said, 'What have the doctors said? How long have they given you off work?'

'I'm going to be off work for at least another two months,' Seamus replied. 'They're pleased with how things are healing, and they say the red marks on my face will gradually diminish. I've got to stay out of direct sunlight; that's why the sun shade is up today.'

'What about your breathing?'

'I do have some reduced lung capacity, which is the reason the doctors have given me two months to recover. They are hopeful that will improve with time. I do get tired quickly now, and part of that is due to a diminished oxygen intake.'

Gemma said, 'He's just got to take things easy and try to rest more. Hopefully start to get more sleep at night.'

Danny said nothing but thought to himself, *Speaking with Dr Maher will do that, my friend.*

Sue said, 'You do look tired, Seamus. It's good to see you, but we're not going to stay much longer.'

Gemma said, 'Come on, Sue, let's collect some fruit before you leave.'

Danny waited for the two women to head down into the garden before taking a pen and notepad from his jacket pocket. He scribbled down the contact details for Dr Freda Maher and said, 'Just tell her you were recommended to call her after talking to me. She'll really help you, I'm sure of it.'

'I appreciate you confiding in me like this,' Seamus said sincerely. 'I knew I needed some help; I just didn't know where to get it.'

He paused, and Danny could see tears welling in the big man's eyes.

When Seamus finally spoke again, his voice cracked with emotion. 'Thanks for coming over today. You know, I honestly thought I was a dead man. Thank you for getting me out of that tunnel alive.'

EPILOGUE

10.50 a.m., 16 August 1991
Choppington, Northumberland

The weather had a distinctly autumnal feel. Dark clouds scudded menacingly overhead, and the blustery wind swirled around the graveyard of the church of St Paul the Apostle at the tiny village of Choppington in Northumberland.

Danny was pleased he had decided to wear his thick Crombie coat over his dark suit for the funeral of Sergeant Gary Stringer. The cold wind seemed to be blowing in directly from the North Sea.

He was standing on the path next to the graveyard alongside DC Lisa Bettridge, who shivered as another gust of wind blew through them both.

She glanced towards the small stone church as the single bell in the open tower continued its mournful tolling.

Danny whispered, 'They're here.'

She turned and could see Gary Stringer's parents getting out of the first of the two black funeral cars. His mother and father waited patiently just outside the churchyard while the undertakers took the coffin from the back of the car.

As the coffin was carried past the two detectives, they both bowed their heads in respect.

There were around twenty family and friends, and they waited for them to all enter the church before filing in and sitting at the back.

Gary Stringer's parents, Frank and Pam, hadn't wanted a full police honours funeral, but they did want to acknowledge the help and dedication shown by his colleagues in the force. Pam had sent personal invitations to Danny, as the detective leading the hunt for her son's killer, and to Lisa, who had spent the most time with the family throughout the whole dreadful tragedy.

It was a very intimate service that concentrated on Gary's childhood and how he was as a young man. The reverend only mentioned the police force once, at the very end of the eulogy. He told the small congregation of mourners that Gary had died doing the job he loved and that it had always been his passion to try to protect others from harm. That was the true measure of him as a man.

There were no hymns, and the service only lasted twenty minutes before the pall-bearers carried the mahogany coffin back outside to the graveyard – and to the freshly dug grave, near one of the stone walls that bordered the cemetery.

As the reverend spoke the words of the interment service, Danny's mind wandered to Haller's chilling comment when he was questioned about Sergeant Stringer's murder:

He was in the wrong place at the wrong time and caught me as I was loading my van up. I panicked when he identified himself as a police officer. He'd seen my face and my van's registration plate. I had no choice but to shoot him.

As the service ended, Frank and Pam Stringer walked slowly to the stone path and waited for the other mourners. Both appeared stoic and very much in control of their personal emotions as they thanked every person individually for attending.

Danny and Lisa were the last two in the line of mourners.

As Pam saw Lisa, she suddenly threw her arms around the detective and whispered, 'Thank you so much for coming, Lisa. You've been such a wonderful help, getting us both through this nightmare. We really appreciate how you kept us informed of everything that was happening. Every new development we heard from you first and not the TV or newspapers. That meant so much to us.'

Danny could see the emotion on both women's faces and swallowed hard.

Frank Stringer held out his hand to Danny and said, 'Thank you for coming, Detective. When we first met, you gave me your word that you and your team would not stop working until you found, and brought to justice, our Gary's killer. As soon as I shook your hand back then, I knew you were a man of your word. Thank you for doing exactly what you promised, Mr Flint.'

WE HOPE YOU ENJOYED THIS BOOK

If you could spend a moment to write an honest review on Amazon, no matter how short, we would be extremely grateful. They really do help readers discover new authors.

ALSO BY TREVOR NEGUS

EVIL IN MIND

(Book 1 in the DCI Flint series)

DEAD AND GONE

(Book 2 in the DCI Flint series)

A COLD GRAVE

(Book 3 in the DCI Flint series)

TAKEN TO DIE

(Book 4 in the DCI Flint series)

KILL FOR YOU

(Book 5 in the DCI Flint series)

ONE DEADLY LIE

(Book 6 in the DCI Flint series)

A SWEET REVENGE

(Book 7 in the DCI Flint series)

THE DEVIL'S BREATH

(Book 8 in the DCI Flint series)

I AM NUMBER FOUR

(Book 9 in the DCI Flint series)

TIED IN DEATH

(Book 10 in the DCI Flint series)

A FATAL OBSESSION

(Book 11 in the DCI Flint series)

THE FIRST CUT

(Book 12 in the DCI Flint series)

A DARK PLACE

(Book 13 in the DCI Flint series)

∾

DCI DANNY FLINT BOX SET (Books 1 - 4)

Made in the USA
Columbia, SC
13 November 2024